CALL

MARTIN VAN ES

ME

ANDREW CROFTS

JOE

Red Door

Published by RedDoor
www.reddoorpress.co.uk

ISBN 978-1-913062-35-4

A CIP catalogue record for this book is available from the British Library

Cover design: Rawshock Design

Typesetting: Jen Parker, Fuzzy Flamingo

Print and production handled by Nørhaven, Denmark

For Sis, who I love so much

"Be the change that you wish to see in the world"

Mahatma Gandhi

ONE

At the moment when the sun went down, Sophie was staring fixedly out of the window, only half listening to the headmaster's voice.

Job etiquette required that she should have been looking him in the eye and listening to him as he reminded her yet again of her responsibilities, both to the school and to the parents who entrusted the care of their children to her, but she had heard what he had to say so often she was worried she would end up laughing if she caught his eye.

"We have a sacred duty to safeguard these children," he was saying, "not just protecting them from physical harm, but from anything that might jeopardise their mental and emotional development as well."

Wanting to continue to show him the respect that his position and reputation deserved, she remained politely quiet, refusing to be drawn into an open argument which might give him an opportunity to sack her. Rather than answering back to the patronising way in which he was now addressing her about her "duties" and "moral responsibilities", she had been staring out of the window at her class as they played their various sports among the children from other year groups.

It was a particularly idyllic day and she was cross with him for spoiling her previously benign mood by summoning her to his office to tell her yet again that she was too friendly with the pupils. It had been a long struggle to get to this comfortable point in her life and she did not intend to let anyone take it away from her.

The sun had bathed the school grounds in a warm golden light as the boys spread out across the vivid green of the cricket pitches at what looked from above like a leisurely pace, and the girls filled the crowded netball courts with swirling bursts of activity. Even the security personnel seemed to have relaxed in their various posts around the edges of the premises, their faces inscrutable and their eyes invisible behind their dark glasses. Lulled by the warmth, they had momentarily become spectators to the scene like her, rather than the guardians of its safety, which was what they had been employed to do. It had been a while since there had been any sort of real threat to the school's security and no one could realistically be expected to stay on high alert indefinitely, however much military-style training they might have received when first recruited.

"You need to maintain a distance," the headmaster was droning on, "they are your pupils, your charges; they are not your friends…"

The relative tranquillity of the cricket field was a sharp contrast to the excited shouts and cheers of the girls as goals were scored on the netball courts. Sophie felt a fierce sense of pride flicker inside her as she watched. She didn't care what the headmaster said; the children did feel like her friends. She had certainly grown to know them better than any class she had ever taught before, or any peer group she had ever been part of for that matter. They seemed to her to be an exceptional bunch of young people and she took credit for much of the progress they were making, both academically and emotionally.

Through the window she saw that Hugo had been sent to field at the furthest corner of the cricket pitch. He didn't seem to be concerned at being sidelined from the action going on around the wickets. He was gazing about him through his oversized Harry Potter glasses like he wasn't part of anything that was happening with the ball, his mind apparently a thousand miles away. Sophie hoped that the batsman wouldn't hit the ball in that direction while Hugo was staring dreamily up at the sky, partly because she knew the other boys were always looking for excuses to shout at the poor little chap, and partly because she feared that an unexpected blow from a hard cricket ball to the back of his head could easily prove fatal.

For a moment she feared she had gone blind, or perhaps been struck unconscious. Then she realised she was not in any pain and the exclamations from the headmaster told her that she wasn't alone in the sudden darkness.

"What's going on?" the headmaster shouted. "Sophie, are you there?"

"I'm here," Sophie said, unsure exactly where she was in the inky blackness. "What's happened?"

"Is it some sort of eclipse?" the headmaster asked. "Was there a warning? There was nothing on the radio this morning."

Outside the window she could hear the frightened screams of the children and the shouts of the now alert security guards and sports teachers as they tried to work out what had happened and what they should do about it. There had never been any sort of safety drill as to what to do in a situation like this. They all knew what to do if the school was attacked by a lone gunman or a suicide bomber or if a fire should break out, but no one had ever foreseen a need to work out a drill for the arrival of total darkness in the middle of a sunny afternoon.

Within a few moments the screams had transformed into nervous laughter as people realised they were unhurt and bumped into one another as they tried to feel their way to some place of safety.

"I've never seen an eclipse like this," Sophie replied.

The light snapped on in the room as the headmaster found

his way to the switch and outside the security lights started creating pools of light around the buildings which the children could make their way towards. Some of the guards had produced torches from their pockets and were moving around the children like sheep dogs, attempting to make sure that there were no stragglers, shouting instructions to one another, using military jargon they had never before had a chance to try out in a real situation.

The lights in the room flickered momentarily, threatening a return to darkness.

"There's probably been a huge surge in demand," the headmaster said.

Sophie was struck by how calm his voice had become. He certainly did have impressive leadership qualities when it came to a crisis. A lot of people said that the remarkable success of the school was in large part down to his personality and she had to admit that was probably true however annoying it was when he lectured her on her pastoral care techniques.

"We had better go to the children," he said. "Let's get them back into their classrooms until we know exactly what is going on. That way we can do a headcount."

By the time they reached the ground floor, most of the children were already crowding back inside the building which was now lit just as it would be on a winter's night. They were milling around in the communal areas, high and noisy on adrenaline, enjoying the interruption of normal school-day routines. The flickering of the electricity supply was becoming less pronounced as the power stations regained control of the supplies and demand became steadier.

"Everyone to their own classrooms," she and the headmaster shouted, adding to the noise levels, and other teachers followed their lead.

Sophie stepped out through one of the exits for a few

moments, to check that there was no one left behind. The excited babble of the voices thronging the corridors inside was masking the total stillness which had enveloped the world outside. There was not a breath of wind, and only the distant stars to break up the vast black emptiness beyond the school lights, seeming to stretch away from the Earth for ever.

"Is this the end of the world, Miss?" The small voice sounded more curious than scared.

"No, Hugo," she said, surprised by her own calmness. "I don't think so."

"What is it then?"

"I have no idea. I'm sure we will find out soon. Go to the classroom with the others for the moment while we work out what to do next."

"Get that child inside," a security guard barked, his voice sounding more frightened than Hugo's. Sophie noticed that he was brandishing a gun. "We're putting the whole premises on lockdown."

TWO

The television flickered silently in the background, the images taking up only a small part of Yung Zhang's attention. She had muted the interview with the Director of the International Monetary Fund, which she had only been half watching anyway as she dealt with more pressing issues on her phone, in order to take Simon's call from Hong Kong International Airport, where he was waiting for his flight to commence boarding.

As she talked she walked towards the window in order to stare at the panoramic view, while simultaneously performing perfectly balanced squats, stretching her spine upwards with the merciless self-discipline which had been instilled in her as a young ballerina.

She was acutely aware that these days she spent too many hours sitting in front of screens or in aeroplanes and so she had trained herself to be constantly exercising whenever she was taking calls. The habit had become such an intrinsic part of her life that she hardly even knew she was doing it any more. It had become as instinctive to her as breathing or blinking. Journalists who interviewed her often used analogies of "machine-like" efficiency when describing the way in which she performed every task – many of them simultaneously – but they would also comment on the exquisite elegance with which she made every physical move and the thoughtfulness with which she turned every phrase, whether she was talking in English or Mandarin.

Yung knew from direct experience, and from many years of intense research and development work, that it would not be long before her brain functions, however exceptional they might seem to other less informed people, would all soon be bettered by the developments being made in artificial intelligence. AI was her speciality and her skills in that area had made her both enormously rich and enormously endangered. Very few people in positions of power understood the potential of the projects she had been working on, and that made them fearful of her. She had discovered that when powerful people become fearful they tended to lash out. They would prefer to shut down whatever they didn't understand rather than trying to understand it.

She was well aware, therefore, that the only advantage she had over machines was her living, biological body. She knew that it was constantly deteriorating, albeit at an infinitesimally slow rate, and had a finite lifespan, which could easily be shortened if she did not take the greatest care of every muscle and organ through scientifically perfected exercise and nutrition regimes. She had been the first person to take CrossFit seriously in China and had woven its principles into every minute of her life. As a result there was not an inch of fat on her body and not a muscle that wasn't in perfect working order.

Whenever she was in the house she spent a lot of time in front of that window, allowing the vista to calm her soul and her emotions while her mind and body were otherwise occupied. She feared that whatever Simon was going to tell her was going to make her cry and she was determined to fight that instinct, wanting to rise above such a primitive urge to do something which she knew would make her seem vulnerable and would not help the situation. Staring hard at the view would help distract her from the pain in her heart.

It was this vista which had first drawn her and her husband, Liang, to the mountain location and made them decide to use it to create the ultimate twenty-first century house. There had been a building there before, but they had come with a vision for a new way of living, unlike anything that had ever been built in New Zealand before. Perhaps at the back of their minds they had guessed they would one day need to use it as an escape route from political pressures in China, but initially it had been more about escaping the everyday pressures of their working lives.

The original architect's plans were refined and improved on with every new invention and discovery made during the years that it took to build, resulting in one of the world's first fully intelligent houses, every element run by smart software to achieve maximum efficiency and maximum security from cyber attacks as well as from physical ones.

The focal point of this grand, man-made project, however, was still the natural view she was now squatting in front of, framed by a picture window the size of a swimming pool. The tree-covered mountains seemed to stretch to the sky, the blazing sun and small white clouds creating an ever-moving show of shadows all the way to the farthest horizon.

"Did you get to talk to anyone in Beijing?" she asked, dreading his answer, knowing the chances were it would be another dead end.

Simon was one of the few people she knew who she would ever trust with a mission this delicate and this dangerous. They had known each other a long time and he was by far the most skilful negotiator she had ever met, as well as being inscrutably honest and discreet. She was aware that she owed her current freedom and position in a large part to his legal skills and wise advice.

"I feel like I talked to everyone in the entire city," Simon replied. "Absolutely none of them wanted to talk to me, but they were all far too polite to actually say so."

"And did you find out anything? Did you find out where they have taken him?"

"Nothing. No one knows anything, or if they do they are definitely not going to tell me. As far as they are concerned Liang has not been arrested or detained, and they know nothing about his whereabouts. When I ask what they think could have happened to him they all just shrug and say things like, 'perhaps an accident?'"

Yung made an involuntary mewing sound, like someone had just trodden hard on a kitten, but regained control quickly. "Somebody must know something, Simon. If it was an accident it would have been reported to the police by now. They must have taken him somewhere."

"Listen," he said, "this is not something to talk about on the phone. They are always listening. Wait till I get to New Zealand."

That was the moment when the sun went out and the picture window turned black in front of her. Behind her the television coughed and spluttered before returning the picture, which was interrupted a few seconds later by a newsflash.

"Something just happened, Simon," she said. "It's gone completely black outside."

"Here too," Simon said. "What is it?"

"It's like someone switched the sun off," Yung said.

Her instinct was to be frightened, but her intellect told her that was a primitive reaction, not one that would occur to a well-programmed computer. She wanted to remain calm in order to take in exactly what was happening because it was incredibly interesting and she wanted to be able to recall every detail once it was over – unless the light never came back, in which case everything would be over pretty soon anyway.

Simon was still on the line and she could hear raised voices around him. It sounded like he was in the midst of some sort of panicked stampede. She could imagine him standing quietly amidst the milling crowds, calmly assessing the situation before making any decisions.

"It's kicking off here," Simon shouted. "People are trampling over one another to get out of the airport, but I don't know where the hell they think they're going to go. It looks pretty dark out there."

Yung could hear announcements over the airport public address system.

"What are they saying?"

"Telling everyone to stay where they are and not to panic," Simon said, "but no one's listening."

The line went dead and Yung was about to ring back when another call came in. At the same time as answering it she called out for the lights to come on and found the television channel changer, searching for the Weather Channel. The newly lit room emphasised the blackness of the picture window even more dramatically, reflecting the interior scene like it was a movie set with her at the centre, standing almost completely still as she took in what was going on and tried to work out what it all meant.

"What in God's name is happening over there?" Doctor Amelia's familiar, throaty voice boomed through Yung's earpiece.

"Where are you?"

"We're in Lagos, just getting ready to go to the airport. I was watching the news channel and they say the whole world has gone dark."

"It's totally black here at the moment." Yung turned up the volume on the television to be able to hear a little of what the presenters were saying.

"In the middle of the afternoon?"

"Yes. What does the sky look like in Africa?"

She could hear Amelia pulling back the curtains in her hotel room and the sound of someone praying in the background. "Oh my days! There's nothing. No moon, no clouds, nothing between us and the stars."

"I guess if there's no sun then there's nothing to light up the moon…" Yung could hear a note of panic in the normally cheerful voices of the television weather presenters as they tried to get through to astronomers and meteorologists via phone lines and shaky video links, their fingers pressed tightly to their earpieces and their eyes wide with the pressure required to be professional and keep the show on the road when all they really wanted to do was run home to their families. All of the experts they were getting through to were becoming extremely excited, talking about what might be happening to the weather, searching for explanations, expounding a range of mad theories.

"Do you think they will still be letting flights take off from the airport?" Amelia asked.

"I doubt they know what they're doing yet. Who knows if this situation is permanent or just a passing blip? Maybe it's a freak meteorological storm of some sort. I doubt that there is an air traffic control manual for an event this catastrophic. Who could possibly have predicted it?"

"Okay." Amelia was obviously thinking what to do. "Listen," she said after a few moments, "since the flight is booked, and the car is here to take us to the airport, we might as well go there as planned. Next week is too important for us to allow anything to get in the way. If there are any flights going out at all I will make sure I am on one of them."

"Your courage and optimism do you credit, Amelia," Yung said, "as always."

"Just getting the job done," Amelia laughed, "just getting it done."

Yung hung up as a text appeared from Lalit, who she guessed was in California. "Just woken up and there's no dawn! WTF?"

"Is there any precedent in recorded history?" the presenter on the Weather Channel was asking an agitated looking professor on a screen link. "Has the entire globe ever been plunged into total darkness before? Is this the sort of catastrophic event that finished off the dinosaurs?"

"As well as the loss of light, the lack of any movement in the air is deeply perplexing," the professor said, ignoring the question about dinosaurs. "I believe it is unprecedented, at least since records have been kept. It is too early to be able to guess what it might mean."

Across the bottom of the screen viewers were texting in questions.

"Is this the end of the world?"

"Is this the result of climate change?"

Although the experts had a variety of theories, none had any definite or credible answers for the frightened and worried viewers.

Yung texted back to Lalit. "Stick to the plan as agreed. If this is the end of the world we might as well go out fighting!"

"Yes, Boss," came the reply, with a selection of emojis, none of which she found amusing.

Calls and texts were now streaming in and she could also hear the ping of emails arriving on her laptop. She gave everyone the same answers. "Stick to the plan", "Get the first flight available", "Our work is more important now than ever".

At the same time as fielding people on the phone, Yung flicked over from the Weather Channel to a news channel where the disappearance of the sun and freak weather conditions were already the rolling topic of discussion. Reports were coming in from all over the world of major traffic pile-ups happening in the few seconds between the sudden fall of darkness and the ability of drivers to switch on their lights in time to avoid collisions. It seemed like the whole world was now being viewed from the fleets of helicopters being scrambled by news organisations in every country and sent up to report back to everyone left on the black Earth below.

Some of the callers to Yung's phone favoured waiting in whatever safe place they could find until it became clear what was going to happen next.

"I've got as far as Auckland," Ahmya, the world's foremost oceanologist told her. "I don't like the idea of going out onto the roads while there is so much chaos."

"Give it a few hours," Yung told her, "if nothing has changed hire a helicopter. Just get here."

She flicked on to another channel where a cross-section of religious experts were debating via video links the idea that the extinguishing of the sun was a sign from God that mankind must mend its ways or there would be terrible consequences. One was reminding the viewers of the descriptions of the Star of Bethlehem on the night that Jesus was born. Another pointed out that in the Book of Joshua, God stopped the sun and the moon during the battle between the Israelites and the Amorites. It seemed to Yung that even though the darkness had only been upon the world for less than ten minutes, people were already turning it to their advantage, claiming that it proved whatever theory they had been preaching before. All the doom-mongers who had been mocked for years for storing up tinned goods and bottled water in preparation for Armageddon now felt vindicated and were phoning in to shout their messages to the world. Their moment of triumph had finally arrived, their points had been proved and they were now certain they had been right all along.

Yung remained calm and businesslike, totally capable of the multi-tasking required, giving short, sharp answers to every question, ending conversations abruptly as soon as she had said whatever she wanted to say. All the time she was talking and listening to the calls and the television, she was thinking of her son and wondering if he was frightened and whether he might be trying to get through to her. She wished she could be with him to protect him and she felt guilty for being an inadequate parent. She wished Liang was with her because he would know what to do. Thinking of Liang and what he might be going through at that moment brought a familiar stab of pain to her heart, but there was still no time to cry.

THREE

The Director of National Intelligence was on his way into his bedroom from the bathroom in his home in Washington, knowing that he was scheduled to be rising early and would need to get his regular eight hours' sleep, when the phone rang. His wife, who was already in bed and reading a few pages of the Bible as she always liked to do before sleeping, gave a cluck of disapproval. She had told him repeatedly that, at close to eighty, he was too old to be doing such a high-pressure job, and receiving phone calls in the middle of the night – or even 10.30 at night – seemed to her to prove her point. This was not the sort of gentle retirement she had envisaged when stoically enduring all the years of her husband's steady ascent to the top of the political tree.

"Yes?" He answered the call quickly, as if simply curtailing the invasive ringing would remove the source of his wife's irritation. He listened to the voice reporting from the other end for a moment, aware that she was watching him over the top of her glasses and had not gone back to her reading, waiting to find out what could be so important as to disturb them in the privacy of their bedroom.

"What do you mean, the sun's gone out? It's the middle of the night." He walked to the window and pulled back the heavy silk curtains. It did seem unusually black outside, even for the nighttime. "The whole globe? So what are you saying, it's some sort of alien attack?"

His wife gave a snort of derision but threw her Bible aside as she climbed out of the bed to join him, barefooted, at the window.

"Aliens?" she mouthed the word at him, twirling her finger around the side of her head in a mime of insanity.

"Is it the Chinese?" he barked into the phone, ignoring her. "The Russians? Is it terrorists?... Have we heard from anyone else?... Anything from the Joint Special Collection Service?... Okay, call my driver, I'm on my way... No, don't call the president. Let's work out what the hell is going on before he starts declaring war on the Martians!"

He hung up and strode out of the bedroom towards the stairs.

"You're not dressed, dear!" his wife called after him.

"No time," he shouted back, stamping downstairs in his dressing gown and slippers. "Go back to bed."

She heard the slamming of doors and the purr of the official car pulling away outside. She returned to the window, stared into the darkness and murmured a quiet prayer.

* * * * *

The impact of the sudden darkness was obvious to everyone working inside the Chinese Ministry of State Security in Beijing. The Agency Head witnessed the event at the same time as all his workers. For a few moments he remained very still in his seat, his face expressionless, his brain going over all the possible causes, waiting to see what would happen next, wanting more evidence before drawing any hasty conclusions. The power to the lights and computers flickered but did not cut out. All the screens were still up and running and information continued to pour in. Slowly he stood up and walked out of his office onto the main floor. One or two people had stood up to look out of the window but quickly resumed their seats in front of their screens when they saw him emerge.

A team of neatly suited managers ran along behind all the screen workers, firing off questions and listening intently to the answers, trying to find explanations that would make sense when they attempted to relay them to their superiors. Three minutes later, they were lined up in front of their boss, giving oral reports on what they had found out so far, which was very little. The Agency Head was already on the phone to the President of China, who had been in his car at the moment the darkness struck and was now being driven at speed to a safe location. The Agency Head had to admit to his boss that they had no idea what was happening, which was not what the President wanted to hear and he made it clear that he expected to be properly briefed within ten minutes, or sooner if they had anything solid to report.

* * * * *

The Russian President was already up and working out in the gym when the call from China came through, moments before his own officials from the Ministry of State Security burst in to inform him that the sun had been extinguished. The Chinese-Russian translator sounded agitated as he relayed his President's words down the line.

"Is this something to do with the Americans or NATO?" the Russian President asked as he shrugged on a sweatshirt. "Is it a trick?"

His own officials looked nervous, unsure if he was addressing the questions to them or to the phone.

"Call the White House," the President shouted at them.

Two minutes later they informed him that the President of the United States had gone to bed and couldn't be disturbed. His eyes narrowed as if taking aim through the sights of a rifle.

"He won't take my call?"

No one in the room answered and a separate call came through to Moscow from the Intelligence Bureau of India, temporarily saving them from his wrath. The President answered immediately. He knew who would be calling. They were old friends from the days when he was a KGB officer and he had been seconded to train this man. They had drunk a great deal of vodka together over the years.

"The American President has gone to bed," he told the caller. "Is it a bomb?"

"No reports of an explosion. Just darkness."

The Russian President allowed himself a small smile. It seemed he had a few minutes' lead on his rivals, but what should he do to make maximum use of that time?

* * * * *

In Washington the Director of National Intelligence had arrived at the NSA offices, having been taking calls all the way through the seven-minute journey across town. His security detail flanked him as he flopped his way into the building in his elegant Turkish slippers, none of them registering any surprise at his night attire on their highly trained, stone cold faces.

He strode into the operations room where others were already gathering, all of them talking on phones or staring at screens.

"Sir," a young woman by the window called out to the Director. He glanced in her direction, raising an eyebrow to indicate his readiness to listen to her even though he was still talking to someone else on the phone and even though there were several other people in the room, all more senior than her, vying for his attention.

"The moon is back," she said, gesturing towards the sky outside. "The sun must have returned."

There was a rush of people towards the windows. Sure enough the moon had reappeared, reflecting the sun's light down onto their upturned faces.

"How long was the sun out?" the Director shouted to the room in general.

"Twelve minutes exactly," a voice replied after a few frantic seconds of research.

"And have there been any reports of alien activity anywhere?"

"A great many, sir," one of the aides standing closest to him replied, "but we have not yet been able to verify any of them. Should we inform the President now?"

"Christ, no," the Director responded. "Let him get a good night's sleep. Maybe by the morning we will have some sort of explanation to give him. We need to find out exactly what happened and whether it could happen again. We also need to have a plan of action for what we would do if the sun was extinguished permanently. How long would the world survive without it? Get answers!"

Everyone in the room dived back into their computers, none of them having the slightest idea where to start.

* * * * *

Alone in his cell, Liang Zhang could only follow world events from the snippets of conversation that he overheard his guards exchanging outside. It was hard for him to judge the passing of time with no window and no watch, but he was fairly sure that it had been longer than usual since his last interrogation, which suggested to him that something of greater importance had occurred and distracted the authorities from his case. He hoped that it had nothing to do with his family.

FOUR

The explosive reappearance of the sun made all the children in Sophie's classroom screw up their eyes as they refocused from staring out into the darkness from the window. A cheer rose up in the room and could be heard spreading through the rest of the school, followed by relieved laughter and applause, as if someone had fixed a fuse somewhere or a pilot had safely landed a plane in turbulence. Nothing seemed to have changed outside during the absence of light. The grounds looked strangely deserted in the bright afternoon light but otherwise untouched.

"Who's that weirdo?" one of the girls asked.

"Where?" Sophie came over and stood beside her.

"There," the girl pointed, "coming out of the bushes. He looks like some sort of tramp or something. Has he been sleeping rough out there all the time?"

Sophie could see him now but he looked far too clean to be a tramp. He almost seemed to glow. His long, black hair and beard positively shone with good health, as did his darkly tanned skin. Both contrasted dramatically with the simple white robe he was holding around himself.

"He's got no shoes," one of the boys pointed out. "He looks like Robinson Crusoe or something, like he's been shipwrecked on an island for years."

"He looks like a hermit to me," another joined in, "like he's been living in a cave up a mountain and he's only just come down to visit the modern world."

"Don't be ridiculous," Sophie laughed. "He probably just got lost in the dark. Maybe he's some sort of monk."

The man looked straight through the window, as if only just realising that he was being watched, and Sophie was struck by the kindness emanating from his dark brown eyes, and by the length of the lashes curling around them. He saw them all staring at him but rather than appearing embarrassed he simply smiled like it was the most normal thing in the world to be wandering alone around school grounds in such eccentric attire. He raised his hand in a friendly greeting before settling serenely down on an ornamental garden seat which had been donated to the school many years before by a grateful parent.

"How did he get past security, Miss?" one of the girls asked, eager to escalate the potential drama. "Shouldn't we go and get them? He looks like he might be a terrorist or something."

"He's got no backpack," one of the boys said, "so he's not a suicide bomber."

"Who knows what he's hiding under that blanket thing he's wearing," the girl protested.

"He hasn't got a gun either," another pointed out.

"He could be a serial killer," another suggested, "strangling girls with his bare hands."

"Why does it always have to be girls?" one of the girls asked. "Why do serial killers' victims always have to be girls? It's boys that need strangling most often."

"Don't be silly," Sophie said. "All of you sit down and get on with something. I'll go and see if I can help him work out where he is."

Several of them called after her in alarm as she left the classroom and walked away down the corridor, telling her she should get someone from security to go with her because that was the rule, but she took no notice. She knew they were technically right, of course, but she was curious to find out more about this strange figure and he hadn't looked dangerous to her. If she alerted security they would cart him off and she would never know where he had come from or why he was lurking outside her classroom.

"Hi," she said as she rounded the corner and found him still on the seat, his eyes closed as if enjoying the warmth of the returned sunshine. Her class were standing at the window, watching to see what would happen next and she sent them scattering back to their desks with a ferocious glare.

"Hi," he said, opening his eyes and rising politely from his seat to greet her with a respectful bow. "I hope you don't mind me resting here for a while."

"Of course not." She had no idea why she had said that, it just seemed like the right response to such a courteous request. Having those astonishing eyes look directly at her made her blush and flounder for words.

"So," he went on, sitting back down and draping his arm comfortably along the back of the seat, "how are you?"

"I'm sorry," she said, "but do I know you?"

He smiled and she was taken aback by how white and strong his teeth were. They were definitely not the teeth of a tramp or a shipwrecked castaway.

"I think," he said, "that if you look deep into your memory, you will find that you do."

It sort of made sense as he said it, but the moment she thought about it, it started to sound weird and she wondered if he was delusional. Maybe the kids were right and she should do something responsible about the situation and call for help. Perhaps he had escaped from a local institution and they were already looking for him.

"Are you here to see someone?" she asked in a voice which she hoped sounded authoritative and not just prim.

"Is it so impossible that I might be here to see you?"

She let out an embarrassing little giggle before regaining control of herself. Now he was just being flirtatious, which was a trait she normally despised in men, but not this time. For some reason she couldn't quite put her finger on, she liked it when he did it. Maybe it was because he was smiling so genuinely and because it didn't seem like he had any ulterior motives.

"I'm sorry to ask so many questions," she continued, "but do you work here?"

"My work is pretty much everywhere I go," he said, the warmth of his returning smile compensating for an evasiveness which would normally have incensed her.

"How did you get past security?" She sat down on the bench next to him, even though his arm was still stretched proprietarily along the back behind her.

"It was very dark. They couldn't be expected to watch every part of a place as big as this. They're only human after all." He grinned mischievously, as if he was sharing a private joke with her – a joke she didn't get.

"You came during that eclipse?"

"Is that what you think it was?"

"I have no idea what it was. Do you know what it was? It was very alarming."

"You don't have to be afraid of me."

"I didn't say I was," she laughed, "I don't think I was even talking about you, was I?"

"You're fun to talk to," he said. "Those children are lucky to have you as a teacher."

"Thank you. I wish you would tell that to my headmaster."

"I will if you like."

"No, really, I don't think you should do that, unless you want to get thrown off the premises instantly."

"That would be a shame. I would like to spend more time talking to you."

"They are very jumpy about security at the moment, ever since that shooting at the mosque."

He spread his hands wide. "You can see I don't have a gun. I come in peace."

"I'm still not sure what you are doing here, staring into my classroom."

"I believe it was me who was being stared at. I was just sitting here, resting."

"Well, I know it's a free world and all that, but I don't think you can stay here. This is a school and it is private property. Sooner or later someone is going to call security and you will be sent packing. They might even call the police and have you arrested. It would probably be better if you moved on voluntarily." Even as she was saying the words she was regretting them, wanting to keep him there a little longer, just so that she could stare at him. There were so many questions that she wanted him to answer and the fact that he was avoiding all of them just made her more curious.

"Do you want me to go?" he asked.

She didn't speak for a moment but he waited as if the silence between them was entirely normal.

"Where are you staying?" she asked eventually, evading the question.

"I've only just arrived."

"Arrived from where?"

"I'm not sure you would believe me if I told you."

"Do you have any luggage?"

"No" – he looked down at himself, gesturing towards the robe – "just what you see. Do you think I need some?"

"People usually have luggage when they arrive in a new place."

"I just wanted to sit and rest for a while. I'm quite tired."

Sophie heard the sound of a security guard's radio from the other side of the bushes. She looked back at the classroom windows and saw that the children were watching something that she couldn't see. One of the girls signalled to her that someone was coming. It looked like they were enjoying the drama of the situation.

"If security find you here they will call the police," she said, surprising herself with how adamantly she didn't want that to happen, didn't want anything to spoil the moment. "You need to hide."

"Hide?" He seemed amused by the idea.

"Listen" – she felt herself blushing as she spoke, shocked by her own forwardness with a stranger – "I have a staff apartment in that block over there. It's very small but you are welcome to rest there for a couple of hours while I finish my class, and then we'll work out what to do with you. Would that be helpful?"

"That is an act of great kindness," he smiled again and she felt her blush deepen even further. "Are you sure that you won't get into trouble?"

"The caretaker is a friend," she said, "he'll cover for me. We need to go quickly."

Without looking back at the classroom window she hurried him across to the staff block and opened the outside door with a code. Inside an old man was wrestling with a large rubbish bin, trying to get it out from under a staircase.

"George," Sophie said, "can you do me a favour?"

"Of course," the old man replied, looking suspiciously at the stranger. "What do you need?"

"This is a friend of mine. I need to get back to my class. Can you let him into my apartment and show him where everything is? He just needs to rest for the afternoon."

"Of course, not a problem."

25

"And maybe not mention that he is here to anyone else?" Sophie added. "He hasn't exactly been through all the security procedures."

"Don't you worry about any of that nonsense," George said. "I don't talk to any of them." He gestured contemptuously towards the area where the guards most often patrolled. "I know more about what's going on in this place than all of them put together, with their smart uniforms and guns and dark glasses. If they knew half of what I know…"

"Thanks George." Sophie pecked him on the cheek, making him chuckle.

She couldn't believe she was doing anything so spontaneous. She knew she was breaking at least six school rules, all of which were potentially sackable offences, but she didn't care. Helping this kind, strange, beautiful man seemed like the right thing to do. It felt good to trust a stranger for a change. She was fed up with being warned about men and strangers and all the other dangers that were supposed to be waiting in the outside world to ambush her. Maybe this guy really was just as amiable and harmless as he seemed. Why should she distrust him just because she didn't know anything about him?

"Help yourself to anything you fancy from the fridge," she called out to him as she walked away. "Not that there is much."

"You're very kind," he said. "Thank you."

She tried to work out where his accent was from. There didn't seem to be much point asking him since he didn't appear to want to give straight answers to any personal questions.

"See you both this evening," she said, and started running back to the classroom, feeling like a naughty schoolgirl herself and realising that she didn't even know what his name was.

"Did security catch him, Miss?" one of the boys asked as she arrived back at the classroom looking flushed and breathless.

"Is he your boyfriend, Miss?" one of the girls asked, making the others snigger.

"No, he is not my boyfriend," she said, "and none of you appear to have any books out."

"It's actually games time, Miss," one of the boys pointed out. "Can we go back outside now the sun has come back out?"

"We need to wait until we are sure it's safe."

"Why did the sun go out, Miss?" Hugo asked. "Lots of people on the internet are saying it was aliens."

The others all roared with laughter but Hugo seemed as unperturbed by mockery as usual.

"It would be great if it was," he added.

"I agree, Hugo," she said, "it would be great if it was, but the chances are slim and you are not supposed to be on the internet during school hours. You know that."

For the rest of the afternoon, Sophie found it hard to concentrate on work. Her mind was constantly wandering back to the stranger and imagining what he might be doing in the apartment. Would he have fallen asleep on her bed? Would he have used her shower? Would he have rifled through her clothes or her paperwork? Would he steal whatever he could carry and run away before she got there? From time to time she felt suddenly fearful that she might have been very unwise in allowing a stranger into her life so quickly, but then a sense of delicious anticipation would sweep over her at the thought of seeing him again and she would glance at the classroom clock, only to see that it had barely moved since the last time she looked.

FIVE

"Does anyone…" The Director of National Security raised his voice over the babble of noise and argument around the room and coming from the screens, waiting until he had all their attention before continuing. "Does anyone in the entire world know anything about what happened? Are there any plausible theories?"

The scientists shifted uncomfortably in their seats. All of them had spent their careers searching for logical, scientific explanations for all the miracles of life, from understanding the workings of the smallest quarks to developing theories about the origins of entire galaxies; it was exciting but unnerving to find themselves confronted with an entirely new puzzle which no one had foreseen and which had left no clues in its wake.

A Swiss scientist, who had been pulled away from his work at the Large Hadron Collider to attend this meeting in Washington via video link, cleared his throat. "It is possible that it was an imaginary event, a mass delusion of some sort which affected the entire population of the planet…"

"Good God!" the Director barked. "Are you trying to tell me that the entire world imagined the whole thing? That it was some sort of mass dream?"

"There have been recorded instances," the scientist continued cautiously, "where large crowds have been deceived into believing they have witnessed something which can't possibly have happened."

28

"Like a rabbit appearing from a magician's hat?" the Director asked.

"I wouldn't put it exactly like that, but there was the incident of Our Lady of Fatima in 1917 when an image of Mary appeared before a crowd of thousands. It was said to have been accompanied by a 'dancing sun'..." The scientist's words were drowned out by other voices wanting to dismiss his suggestion out of hand and putting forward their own views on this particular theory.

"Are you suggesting this was a gigantic magician's trick?" the Director boomed, making the others fall silent. "Or that the entire world got high on some invisible drug for twelve minutes and all imagined the same thing at the same time? Are you saying it was all a dream, like in some hokey TV drama?"

"All I am saying is that it is a possibility that it was a mass hallucination of some sort, but I have no evidence to support that theory yet," the scientist on the screen mumbled lamely. "At this stage we need to keep our minds open to all possibilities."

"Does anyone have anything better than that?" The Director addressed the whole assembly.

"To be honest," a voice with a deep southern accent spoke up from the back of the room, "there only seems to be one possibility."

"And what is that?" the Director asked.

"That it was an act of God. It lasted for exactly twelve minutes and twelve is a very important number in the Bible. It could be significant. We all know that there is a lot we don't know about, that there must be something 'bigger' behind creation that we haven't discovered yet, the thing some people like to label 'God'..."

Silence fell across the room as the finest scientific minds in the Western world took in the suggestion that all the research and experimentation of the previous centuries had been in vain and that they were no further on in their understanding of the universe than primitive tribesmen doing rain dances or making sacrifices to appease some all-powerful gods.

"Personally," the Director growled, "I think it is more likely it has something to do with the bloody Chinese. We need to find out how much they know. I doubt they will be suggesting it's the work of God or a magician. Do the Chinese even believe in a god?" No one answered and he sighed deeply before continuing. "So you guys are the geniuses. Explain to me what will happen if the sun goes out for any length of time."

The scientist sitting closest to him cleared his throat before speaking. "Everything on Earth, except some deep-sea worms, depends on the sun. Because it is about a hundred million miles from the Earth, which is around eight light minutes, nothing would happen for about eight minutes.

"Once the gravity well of the sun disappeared, however, the Earth would no longer move around the sun, but would follow a straight line. The Earth would continue to rotate on its axis, but there would be no seasons any more. We would just be staring at the same stars all the time.

"Other planets would disappear, Venus and Mercury after a few minutes, Mars within an hour, Neptune and Pluto within ten hours. The stars would remain visible, as well as the giant planets.

"Temperatures would drop rapidly, just as they do at night. Within a week the average temperature on Earth would be minus thirty degrees Celsius. Billions of people would die in tropical countries during that week. The ice sheets on Antarctica and the Arctic Ocean would expand rapidly. It would snow everywhere, first at the poles, and finally at the equator. After a few weeks, the sea would freeze everywhere.

"Power stations would soon give up and the remaining people and animals would die."

"Would anyone survive?" the Director asked in a subdued voice.

"Hiding in mines might be a temporary solution, because geothermal heat provides some relief. The best places to go would be volcanic hotspots like Iceland. But food and oxygen would soon run out, as would energy.

"Some seeds and trees would last for several more decades but once the temperature had fallen far below a hundred degrees, the CO_2, then the nitrogen and finally the oxygen would freeze."

As the scientist stopped talking, a terrible silence fell across the room.

* * * * *

"The Americans don't know anything," the intelligence officer informed his superior in Beijing. "We have listened to their chatter and they have no ideas beyond an attack by aliens."

The Ministry of State Security Chief allowed a smile to flicker across the corners of his normally austere, clenched line of a mouth.

"Do they believe everything that the Hollywood movies tell them? Are video games their answer to everything?"

No one in the room responded beyond the occasional nod of agreement.

"What about the Russians?" he continued.

"It is harder to know what they are thinking. They have been in touch with the Indians but they are not giving anything away."

"So, if none of us know what caused it, then it might happen again and we have no idea how to avoid that happening?"

"Yes, sir," several voices agreed.

"So we need a plan as to how we will survive on a planet with no light or warmth."

"Yes, sir."

"Find a way for me to talk to the Head of Russia's Foreign Intelligence Service, but make it clear I do not want to involve his president – and we do not need to trouble our president at this time either – not until we have a plan that we can put to him. He trusts us to do our best for our country. We must not disappoint him."

The heads of all the world's security services were talking to one another more than ever before, cautiously at first but with growing confidence as they all came to believe that no one else had any more information about the twelve minutes of darkness than they did. One thing that many of them were agreed on, though none of them were brave enough to speak the words out loud, was that they wanted to postpone directly involving their political leaders for as long as possible, knowing that those leaders would all be looking for ways to use the situation to further their own political agendas, jeopardising the possible security issues which they all foresaw could happen were the sun to disappear again, perhaps for ever.

A feeling of barely suppressed panic and imminent gloom hung over the whole international military and security community as they waited helplessly to see what would happen next and tried to think of things to say which might reassure the frightened politicians and public.

The Russian President, however, had no intention of waiting for his people to be able to furnish him with facts before looking for ways to benefit from the mysterious occurrence.

"Issue no denials," he instructed the men who ran his propaganda machine. "Let the rest of the world think that it might have been something to do with us. Suggest perhaps that we have computer hackers at work in St Petersburg who are clever enough to achieve such a feat. Then find out if there is any way we could do it, if we wanted to."

"Find a way to extinguish the sun?" someone bravely asked.

"If it can be done then we need to be the ones able to do it," he snapped.

SIX

After the final class ended on the day that the sun went out, Sophie was on the rota to go to the dining room to oversee supper for the boarders, delaying still further her chance to return to the man she had been thinking about ever since parting from him so hurriedly. The meal didn't go on for more than half an hour before the fastest eaters were clearing their plates away and peeling off to amuse themselves until bedtime. She had to wait for the last few stragglers but was far more lenient than usual in letting the fussier ones leave unwanted food on their plates, much to the indignation of the catering staff.

As soon as the last child had left the dining room she found herself running with undignified haste to get to her apartment. She forced herself to slow down and breathe deeply, not wanting to arrive red in the face and gasping for air. She was also keen not to alert any children who might be watching to her eagerness to see him again. They enjoyed teasing her at every opportunity, even when she didn't supply them with ammunition, and this would be a gift for them. Normally she didn't mind the jokes because they were usually centred around the various causes she was fanatical about like veganism and animal rights, and always seemed to be done with affection, but at that moment she was too unsure of her own thoughts and feelings to want to open them up to ridicule, however good natured it might be.

She arrived at the outside door of the block at the same time as one of her colleagues, which slowed her down because she had to endure an agonisingly long conversation about the episode of darkness before she could escape into the apartment. Her colleague obviously expected to be invited in to continue the conversation over coffee but found the door shut firmly in her face.

Inside the room the stranger welcomed her with the same smile she had been thinking about all afternoon and she noticed that he was reading one of her books, a treatise on re-wilding the planet. He was sitting on her couch, a pottery mug of water on the table beside him, decorated with a painting of a dolphin.

"You should have helped yourself to coffee or tea," she said, gesturing towards the modest kitchen area. Only now that she was looking at it anew through the eyes of a hostess did she realise just how modest and untidy it was. It occurred to her that the cramped bathroom would probably look even worse to a visitor and she cringed a little inside.

"I was fine with water," he said. "I thought it would be nice for us to eat together. It's not much fun eating alone, is it?"

"Oh," she laughed, pleased to think he planned to stay a while. "The children said that you looked like you have been living as a hermit up a mountain in a cave."

"Children see things very clearly sometimes, don't you think?"

"I certainly do."

Was he telling her that he had been living alone in a cave? Or was he teasing her? She was unsure how to respond. She knew she was breaking school rules by having someone from outside in her room without reporting it to the security staff, but she didn't care. She was pretty sure that if she went for permission they would take one look at him and demand to know everything about his past, to make sure that he was safe to have around children. It seemed like too undignified an ordeal to put such a dignified man through.

She wasn't sure why she felt so sure that she was entirely safe with him. Was it just because she found him so attractive? If so, then she was not behaving like a sensible teacher and custodian of children, especially as a number of them actually boarded at the school and were therefore the sole responsibility of the staff, twenty-four hours a day. The school specialised in taking international students, many of whom boarded full time because their parents were constantly travelling or lived far away. There were others who boarded at the school during the week and went home at weekends.

How many of the parents would be happy to know that a figure as eccentric as this was wandering around their children's school without knowing something about his past, or his intentions?

But she had met plenty of predatory men in her time, some of them the fathers of the children in her charge, and she got none of the same vibes from this man. She wanted to be able to trust her instincts. At that instant she felt so happy to be in his company that she could not even contemplate doing anything that might spoil the moment. If he was removed from the premises by security she might never see him again. The thought of going back to the routine of her life as it had been that morning, before he materialised outside the classroom window, was unbearable. In fact, if they had made him leave she was pretty sure she would feel compelled to go with him, even if it turned out that they were taking him back to a secure institution. It was weird because up to that moment she had been completely content with her life as it was. Why did the concept of returning to it now seem like such an unutterably dreary backward step?

"Are you hungry?" she asked, opening the fridge and peering inside at the sparse contents.

"Yes."

"I'm afraid I'm a vegan, so there's a limited choice on offer."

"Being a vegan is not a sin," he said.

"Some people seem to think it is."

He didn't say anything and when she turned back he was sitting forward on the edge of the couch, still holding the book and watching her with an amused look in his brown eyes which took her breath away all over again, making the blood rush back to her cheeks. The intensity with which he seemed to be examining her face made her feel certain that he found her attractive, which stained her blush even deeper. She never usually gave her appearance a second thought but as she turned away she glanced in the mirror on the far side of the room and realised that she was actually looking beautiful in her own, very natural way. It was like she was glowing. She felt ridiculously pleased with her own reflection and simultaneously irritated with herself for wasting time on such vanity.

"I'll just make us something, shall I?" she said.

"That would be very kind of you."

"Do you drink?" She held up a bottle of red vegan wine which had been sitting on the shelf ever since the beginning of term.

"Yes, if I am thirsty."

"Open that for us then." She handed him the bottle and a corkscrew and started unloading ingredients from the fridge onto the cramped work surface, deliberately avoiding looking in his direction until the blush had faded from her neck and cheeks and she could trust herself not to say anything gauche. She set to chopping vegetables. As he handed her a cup of wine their fingers brushed and she could have sworn she felt a crackle of electricity pass between them.

"I don't even know what your name is," she said as she went back to preparing the food. "Mine is Sophie."

"I know," he said. "It is a good name for you. It comes from Sophia, the Greek name. It means insight, intelligence and wisdom."

"Is that right?"

"Hagia Sophia, means Holy Wisdom. I believe it is from Sophie that we get the words sophistication and philosophy."

"A bit of an expert in languages are you then?"

He didn't reply.

"How do you know my name?"

He shrugged. "The caretaker must have said it."

"You still haven't told me your name."

"What would you like to call me?" he teased.

"I'll call you annoying if you keep playing games like this. Do you ever just give a straight answer to a straight question? Are you deliberately trying to create an air of mystery?"

He was standing so close she could feel the heat from his skin and was aware of the scent from his beard, a mixture of musk and jasmine. She wanted to turn to face him but forced herself to keep looking away, continuing to chop the vegetables even though they were already chopped small enough. He returned to the couch, leaving her feeling instantly bereft, and held up the book.

"This is very interesting," he said. "I assume you have read it."

"Of course. The whole planet is on the brink of total collapse," she said, always excited by the prospect of discussing the subjects that obsessed her, subjects like the imminent extinction of most of the world's species and the dangers of global warming. "The planet won't be habitable for much longer with the beating we're giving it. You don't look like you are leaving much of a carbon footprint. Do you have any possessions at all?"

"No," he laughed as if the very idea was ridiculous. "What possessions do you think I need?"

"Still answering questions with more questions – annoying!"

"Do you think there is an answer for every question?"

"There you go, doing it again!" she laughed as she dropped the vegetables into a pan of water. "Do you have any money?"

"No," he smiled at her fondly, "I don't have any money."

"Well, there you go. A straight answer. That wasn't so hard, was it?"

"No, that was an easy one."

"So, where were you planning on sleeping tonight?"

"I have no plans," he shrugged, apparently unconcerned by his homeless status.

"No money and no plans? Maybe the kids are right, maybe you are a tramp."

He laughed and she realised she had never felt so happy in the company of another person in her entire life.

"You are welcome to stay here if you like," she said, gesturing towards the couch. "I have a sleeping bag which has accompanied me to a fair few places over the years."

"Thank you. That's very generous of you."

She turned the television on. "Do you mind if we watch the news? I would like to find out more about what happened this afternoon."

The subject of the blackout was on every channel and they both watched as the cameras revealed the amount of damage that had occurred in those twelve minutes. The reactions from many world leaders appeared to annoy Sophie's guest.

"None of them seem to be telling the truth," he said. "They are all pretending that they know what happened and that they will make sure it never happens again. If they were wise leaders they would just admit that some things are beyond human understanding and that they are entirely helpless to do anything about it."

"Politicians believe they have to put people's minds at rest; make them feel that their futures are in safe hands."

"Like talking to small children?"

"Exactly."

"And do you think people believe them?"

"Not always," she laughed, "but more often than you would suppose possible, given the repeated evidence we get of their fallibility. We seem to want to give them the benefit of the doubt each time and then they end up disappointing us all over again, but we never seem to give up hoping."

"Why do you think they are so aggressive about everything?" he asked as two rival politicians tried to talk over one another and ignored the questions being put to them by the interviewer.

"They mistake aggression for strong leadership. It's a man thing."

"Oh, really?" He raised a quizzical eyebrow.

"No offence."

A knock on the door made her jump and a feeling of dread tightened in her stomach. Had somebody alerted security to the presence of a strange man in her room? Were they going to evict him from the premises? Would he allow her to go with him? Without saying a word she wiped her hands on a less than clean tea towel and opened the door, aware that he was watching every move she made.

"Please Miss, sorry to disturb you, Miss." A group of children, apparently led by Hugo, stood on the doorstep, all of them craning their necks to see round her into the room. "Can we come and talk to your friend?"

"How did you get in here?" she asked. "Why aren't you in your dormitory block?"

"The door was open downstairs and we wanted to make sure you were okay," Hugo said, blinking up at her through his glasses with magnified eyes.

"I'm fine, Hugo, thank you for your concern. But you guys are not allowed up here in the evening without permission from the headmaster, so skedaddle!"

"Oooh, Miss," they moaned.

"Let the children come to me," the stranger said, appearing behind her at the door, his body close to hers, exuding the same relaxing warmth. "What harm can it do?"

"Thank you, sir," Hugo said, leading the charge into the room, past their speechless teacher. They settled themselves expectantly on the floor and couch like a flock of noisy starlings coming to land in a tree.

SEVEN

Hakizimana had been in New Zealand several days, visiting the sights, and had already made it as far as the hotel in Christchurch where he had agreed to meet up with Tanzeel when the sun was extinguished.

The blackness chilled his soul, bringing back memories of the dark days and nights of the genocide in Rwanda, which he spent hiding in excrement in crudely dug village cess pits or beneath piles of corpses, many of them the raped and slaughtered bodies of people he had known and loved. Even at the worst moments of the hundred days which had defined his childhood and destroyed every other member of his family, the spark of hope had flickered on inside him. That ability to hope did not desert him during those twelve minutes of darkness when it looked as if the end of the world might finally have arrived.

"My name means 'It is God who saves'," he would tell the audiences who came to listen to him in universities and at peace conferences around the world, "and so it proved to be during those hundred days."

Yung and Liang had met Haki, as most preferred to call him, at the inaugural One Young World Conference in London ten years earlier. The couple had immediately warmed to him and with their backing he had set up a number of reconciliation centres around countries that had been scarred by ethnic cleansing campaigns and genocides. Haki was a strong believer in God and in the teachings of the Bible. They were the stories that his late mother had recounted to him and to his late brothers and sisters when they sat around the fire in the evenings.

He had never thought to question his beliefs until he met Yung and Liang and they explained why they did not feel the need for religion, and that the secular teachings of Confucius were enough for them, just as they had been enough for many generations in China before them. Their long conversations had given Haki much food for thought, but nothing they had said had ultimately rocked his own faith in the God his mother had told him about in all the stories.

When the sun went out that afternoon in New Zealand, Haki assumed it was the will of God and so sat quietly in his hotel room, staring out at the blackness. He simply waited, breathing slowly, switching off the parts of his brain which in others would have stimulated a sense of panic and the urge to flee. It was a skill he had mastered naturally by the age of eight and refined later through meditation and through his friendship with Tanzeel, a neuroscientist, spiritual leader and author.

At that moment Tanzeel himself was no more than a few metres away in another room in the same hotel, sitting cross-legged on his bed, also staring calmly into the blackness and nothingness, his mind entirely cleared of all thoughts, ready to accept whatever happened next with complete serenity.

Tanzeel, having written many best-selling books on meditation, consciousness and the power of the human mind, had been one of the elders at the One Young World conference in 2010 and had introduced Yung and Liang to Haki, his favourite disciple.

"As you know, when I was a young man I lived in Beirut," he had reminded the Zhangs, "at a time when the entire city was self-destructing, riven with civil war and hatred. I thought I had seen the worst that man could do to his fellow man, but young Haki has seen things and been to places that I do not think I would have been able to survive, and I believe he is a young man of considerable potential. There is something indestructible about him."

"You think we need to recruit him?" Yung had asked.

"I certainly do."

And so Haki had become the youngest member of their "club", as those who wanted to destroy them liked to refer to it.

The twelve minutes of darkness ended and both the men in the separate hotel rooms took deep breaths as they stood up and went closer to the windows to watch the light and warmth flood back across the city landscape. Tanzeel took out his phone and typed.

I have ordered a car for five o'clock. Care to join me?

Haki replied. *Thank you. That would be great. I will meet you downstairs.*

The Mercedes was waiting at the front of the hotel for them. The bustle of the lobby was continuing with little evidence that the black-out had ever happened apart from a greater number of conversations being struck up between strangers as they compared notes on what they had just witnessed. No one understood what had happened and everyone was talking about their own experience of the twelve minutes, but they still seemed to be doing their jobs and sticking to their schedules. Life was going on just as Haki had assumed it would.

"What happened, do you think?" he asked as they both slid into the back seat and the driver closed the doors with reassuringly solid thuds.

"It seems we were treated to a glimpse of the great nothingness that lies beyond consciousness," Tanzeel said with a smile. "It was an interesting experience, no?"

"Do you have everything you need?" the driver asked. "Is the temperature comfortable?"

"We are very comfortable, thank you," Tanzeel assured her and she turned her attention to the road outside, pulling smoothly and quietly away from the hotel, her eyes constantly flicking up to the rearview mirror.

"Treated to by whom?" Haki persisted. "By God?"

"Is that what you think?"

"At the moment I don't know what to think."

"It will certainly give us a lot to talk about this week," Tanzeel said.

"Have you been to Yung's house before?" Haki asked after a few minutes of comfortable silence.

"I came here while she and Liang were in the process of building it, when they were still spending most of their time in Beijing. It was an enormous project, taking many years. I am looking forward to seeing it now it is finished. I am told it is one of the most important new buildings in the world this century."

"Has anyone heard anything from Liang?"

"Not that I am aware of. It seems he has become one of the 'disappeared'."

Haki fell silent again; having family members disappear without explanation was a concept with which he was agonisingly familiar. He could imagine very clearly how much pain Yung and the rest of their family must be in. Both his parents had disappeared on the day that all his siblings were hacked to death and he had no idea where their bodies ended up. At least 800,000 people were cut down in those hundred days, creating far too many corpses for any survivors to ever hope to be able to find their lost loved ones.

The driver gave no indication that she could hear their

conversation, apparently fully immersed in the job of driving. Roads outside the city which were normally clear and free of all drama were dotted with evidence of accidents caused by the sudden onset of darkness a few hours before. There was a lorry which had veered off the road into a ditch and rolled onto its back like a huge animal surrendering its throat and vulnerable underbelly to an overwhelmingly more powerful opponent. Several cars had driven into trees and other obstacles, twisting their bonnets into angry snarls, but every accident victim they passed already seemed to have enough people helping them, so the Mercedes pressed quietly on towards their destination.

As they started their climb into the mountains, the roads became totally deserted apart from one small grey car which appeared to be travelling in their slipstream, never more than fifty metres behind. It seemed strange to the driver that whoever was behind the wheel should stay so close when there was so much space all around and no oncoming traffic to stop them from overtaking. She said nothing to her passengers but continued to glance regularly in her rearview mirror, prepared for the following driver to do something unpredictable, constantly aware of their presence. The stickers on the windscreen and its pristine condition suggested it was a rental car. She was confident that if necessary she would be able to pull away easily. She could make out that there was an elderly couple in the front seats, the man hunched uncomfortably over the wheel, his nose almost touching the windscreen. She decided not to inform her passengers until she was sure it was not just another innocent motorist who happened to be travelling along the otherwise deserted road in the same direction as them.

Snow-capped peaks were visible in the far distance and there were now no buildings to be seen in any direction. It felt like the two cars had left the overpopulated world of mankind far behind, the only sign of civilisation being the smooth tarmac flashing past beneath their wheels. They began to rise towards the snowline and as they came round the final bend the entire mountain range stretched out below them with no sign that the human race had ever existed. Then the road turned into the mountain itself, entering a short tunnel. The small car was still exactly the same distance behind them as it rounded the same corner. Now there was no way for it to turn back. It had no option other than to follow them into the tunnel.

"This is your destination," the driver said as they paused in the illuminated tunnel. They had reached a set of gates a few metres inside the man-made cave. The grey car pulled up behind, waiting like them.

Cameras swivelled above and around them and after a few seconds the gates slid back, revealing a steep ramp up and out onto a terrace, which had been cut into the side of the mountain. They had reached the end of the road. Above them towered Yung and Liang's steel and glass fortress.

Both cars came to a halt in front of a glass atrium. A man, who was dressed like a butler, although he looked more the shape of a bodybuilder, emerged from a side door and walked over to them. He was followed by two smaller men. They opened the doors of both cars and courteously helped the passengers out, relieving them of their luggage.

"Austin," Tanzeel greeted the tall man who was unravelling himself from the driving seat of the small grey car. "You drove yourself?"

The two men embraced and Austin introduced his wife, May, a small woman who wore her glasses permanently on the end of her nose, peering disapprovingly over them at the men who towered above her.

"We've taken the opportunity to spend a week touring around the South Island," Austin explained.

"In that?" Tanzeel pointed to the car. "With your long legs?"

"The English universities do not pay as well as your American ones," Austin laughed self-deprecatingly. In fact, he would always have chosen a modest car anyway. He and his wife had been brought up to live careful, unpretentious lives and no matter how distinguished he might have become in his profession he never felt comfortable with luxury or ostentation.

"And Austin's books don't sell to such a wide audience as yours," his wife added, without smiling. "He is not interested in being a bestseller." She seemed to be making a point.

Austin gave no indication of having heard his wife's sarcasm, moving on to pump Haki's hand enthusiastically. "Good to see you again," he said. "May, this is Haki, the young man from Rwanda I was telling you about."

"My husband is a big fan of yours," she said, shaking his hand.

"The professor is a great man," Haki said. "If I can achieve even a small part of what he has then I will die happy."

"Indeed," she burbled cheerfully. "I thought we were all going to die today when the light went out. What a scare we all had."

"What did you two make of that?" Austin asked as they all walked into the house, followed by the staff carrying their bags despite Austin protesting that he could carry his own. "I'd be very interested to know."

"Dear Austin always has to have answers to everything," his wife said with a mixture of exasperation and disdain. "He can't bear any sort of mystery."

The professor exchanged the smallest of glances with Tanzeel but said nothing. It had been a bone of contention in their marriage for close to forty years and he no longer saw any point in trying to explain the benefits of intellectual curiosity to someone who had long ago decided that deep thinking wasn't worth the effort and was, therefore, quite possibly a sign of bad manners.

"Miss Yung has suggested that I show you to your rooms," the butler informed the arrivals, "and then invites you to join her in the drawing room for drinks before dinner."

"Are we the first to arrive?" Austin asked.

"Not quite, Professor. Miss Minenhle is here."

"Oh, that woman," the professor's wife said. "Did you know she was going to be here, Austin?"

"Of course. We are all going to be here, hopefully. That's the point of the whole week."

"You didn't mention it."

"I told you 'everyone' was going to be here."

"You didn't tell me she was going to be here," May continued talking to the back of her husband's head as he gave his attention to the butler.

The butler cleared his throat with a discreet cough. "Before we go any further," he said, "I'm afraid I have to ask you to leave your phones and all other electronic devices with me. If you need access to them during your stay there is a room where the internet can be accessed, or phone calls can be taken outside. I hope that won't be an inconvenience."

"Are you suggesting," the professor's wife enquired archly, "that we are security risks?"

"Miss Yung is worried that all electronic devices are potential security risks," the butler replied without the slightest change in his tone.

"Of course." The professor stepped forward, proffering his phone in its battered leather case. "We completely understand. It'll do us good to be separated from the damn things for a while."

EIGHT

The children had filled her room to bursting point and were laughing and talking with a level of innocent joy Sophie had never witnessed before.

"What's your name?" Jess, a girl whose increasing tendency to flirt with older men had been a frequent subject of discussion in the staff room, asked the stranger.

"My name's Jesus," he replied, giving Sophie a sidelong glance as if to gauge her reaction to this news, a twinkle in his eye.

She raised a questioning eyebrow.

"At last," she said, "a straight answer to a straight question."

"Children deserve straight answers," he said, grinning.

She still wasn't sure if she believed him. Was he teasing the children or was that really his name and he had held back from telling her in case she laughed? He didn't seem to be a man who would mind if someone teased him about something so harmless.

"I doubt that," Hugo said, matter-of-factly, pushing his large glasses back up from where they had slid to on his small nose.

"He's just kidding, Hugo," the girl said. "Aren't you?"

"I'm not kidding," the stranger said, still grinning, "that's my name. Don't you like it?"

"I'm not going to call you that," Hugo said. "It sounds silly. What's your other name?"

"No other name," he said.

"The man with no name," Jess pouted. "Do you think it makes you interesting or something? Do you think it makes you a man of mystery?"

The stranger shrugged, as if it was up to them whether they believed him or not.

"We need to think of a name for him," a boy with the beginnings of a shadow moustache said. "Let's have a vote."

"Justin!" a voice shouted.

"Archie!" cried another.

"Thomas the Tank Engine," shouted a third and they all burst out laughing, throwing out more and more ridiculous names at the same time. Eventually, Sophie put her hand up to quieten them, afraid that neighbouring staff members would hear the commotion and come to investigate.

"Joe," Hugo said in a firm voice. "I'm going to call you Joe."

"Joe," the stranger rolled the name around his mouth thoughtfully, "like a shortened version of Joseph?"

"Yes," Hugo replied. "I suppose so."

"That's a name I would be very comfortable with." He turned to Sophie. "Do you think you could get used to calling me that?"

"Sure," she laughed. "What's in a name?"

"Quite a lot it would seem." He made a wry face.

As often happened when Hugo spoke up about something with his strangely high level of confidence, the other children all seemed to accept that Joe was a good name for their new friend. They also appeared to have grown bored of the name-choosing game and were ready to move on to bigger subjects.

"Where are you from?"

"How did you get here?"

"Why do you wear such weird clothes?"

"How long is it since you cut your hair?"

The questions were coming too thick and fast for Joe to be able to answer and he held up his hands as if to shield himself from so much curiosity.

"One at a time," Sophie shouted over them. "And not so loud unless you want the headmaster to find out you're all here."

"Did you have anything to do with blacking out the sun?" Hugo asked in the few seconds of silence that followed.

"Sure," Joe said. "Impressive, don't you think?"

"You are such a big fat liar," Jess laughed. "Are you some sort of wizard then? A sort of fit version of Gandalf?"

"Fit?" Joe laughed.

"Jess!" Sophie scolded.

The other girls hooted with laughter and set up a chant, accusing Jess of fancying him and making her blush, partly with pleasure at the attention and partly with embarrassment at having been called out for her brazenness.

"Do it again then," she said with a pout, half angry at being mocked but still wanting to keep the man's eyes on her. "Make it dark again. Make the moon go out."

"Now is not the time," he said. "I shouldn't really have done it at all. It was too much. People got hurt in accidents, which was definitely not my intention."

"So are you never going to do it again?" Hugo asked.

"Maybe I will. Let's see how things go."

He smiled across at Sophie, catching her staring at him as she tried to work out why he was saying such things, his steady gaze causing her to become flustered. Her obvious discomfort made some of the girls whisper and giggle, which annoyed Jess.

"So is he your boyfriend, Miss?" she asked with a hint of spite.

"Is he staying in here tonight?" another joined in.

"Don't be so rude," Sophie snapped, making both girls whisper and snigger even more.

Ever since she first saw him outside the classroom, Joe's face had seemed strangely familiar to her and now she remembered why. She'd had a dream a few weeks earlier in which a man looking exactly like this appeared to her, telling her that she was special and that God had a great plan for her. Despite the fact that she had always been an atheist, it was a pleasant dream, leaving her with a smile on her face when she woke up and a warm glow of excitement and expectation that something good was going to happen, a feeling she had never experienced before and which she couldn't explain.

Like most dreams it had become a faded memory within minutes of getting up and starting another busy day, but now it came back to her with a startling vividness. As she watched him interacting with the children she wondered if that dream had actually been a vision, telling her to expect this man and signalling that he was someone important who she needed to stay close to and listen to. Or was she in fact still dreaming? Was this what he had meant when she first talked to him and he told her that she would realise she knew him "if she looked deep into her memory"?

She dug her nails into the palm of her hand and it hurt. No, she was confident she was awake. So what exactly was going on?

She tried to concentrate on what she actually knew to be true. He had initially told the children his name was Jesus, so did that mean he was some sort of delusional nutter? Did he actually believe he was the Son of God and that was why he dressed that way? Or was he some sort of spiritual leader of whom she had never heard or, as the children had suggested, a hermit who had been hiding away in the mountains for years, meditating and preparing for whatever task he believed now lay ahead of him? If so, what would that task be? Why did she feel so overwhelmed by his physical presence?

A sharp knock on the door interrupted her thoughts and silenced the room. They all watched as Sophie opened it a crack, not wide enough to reveal Joe on the sofa. One of the senior tutors, who occupied the room above, was trying to peer in despite the fact that Sophie was obviously blocking her way.

"Is everything all right in there, Sophie?"

"Sure," she said, "we've just been doing some improvisations."

"It's past curfew time, you know," the tutor said, pointing to her watch, "they should all be in the dormitory block unless they have written permission from the headmaster."

"Oh my goodness," Sophie faked surprise, rather unconvincingly, making a few of the children giggle, "is that the time? The evening has gone so fast. Come on guys, all back to the dormitories."

The moment the last child had scurried out through the door she gave the tutor a friendly wave and closed it, just in case she tried to investigate further.

Joe smiled at her as she leaned on the door and breathed a theatrical sigh of relief.

"They love you," he said, "the children."

"One or two of the girls seemed pretty keen on you too," she said, raising an eyebrow.

"It's my cool style," he said, gesturing down at his robe and bare feet. "It's irresistible to women."

"Are you ready to eat now?"

"Absolutely."

As she walked past him to the kitchen area he caught her hand and gave it a squeeze, which could have been meant to be reassuring, or it could have denoted his gratitude for the meal and bed, or could have been merely affectionate. Again she was certain she felt a spark of electricity and instinctively jerked her hand away, immediately regretting such a foolish reaction. Did he now think she was some sort of prude? For a moment she wasn't sure if she would ever be able to breathe normally again and covered her confusion by busying herself with serving up the food.

"How come you didn't want to tell me your name was Jesus?" she asked over her shoulder.

"You saw the reaction it got from the children," he laughed. "It is a name which always elicits dramatic responses. Too many people have argued and fought about it over the centuries. It has too many connotations; some wonderful, of course, but many painful. It carries too much baggage with it. I like 'Joe' much better. Don't you? So call me Joe."

NINE

Although Hugo had been among the most outspoken of the children inside Sophie's apartment, he returned to his position as an outsider in the group as soon as they had left the staff block. All the other children formed into clusters of two, three or four, in order to gossip about the evening and marvel at their own audacity in turning up at a teacher's apartment uninvited. They all speculated on what might be happening now they were gone and the couple were in the room alone, some giggling foolishly and others feeling a little unsettled by their own imaginings. None of their chatter and gossip interested Hugo so he wasn't bothered that they didn't include him. He liked being alone with his thoughts anyway, having spent his first eight years as the only child in an adult household where everyone talked all the time about serious scientific, philosophical and political subjects regardless of whether he was in the room or not.

He walked alone to the dormitory, unnoticed by the others, which he preferred. Being invisible was better than being teased and it gave him the headspace that he wanted in order to process what he had just learned without having to pretend he thought the others were funny with their crude jokes and stupid innuendoes.

He changed into his pyjamas, folded his clothes far more neatly than anyone else, and brushed his teeth while the other boys lounged in groups on their beds, chattering excitedly about the events of a day that had without doubt been the most exciting of their young lives so far. He climbed into bed and took his glasses off, folding the arms and placing them carefully on his bedside table before lying on his back, barely disturbing the smoothness of the sheets and staring at the ceiling with none of the feelings of tiredness that would usually come over him at this stage of the school day.

The others gradually got ready for bed around him, all of them still talking, casually dropping their clothes on their chairs, unbothered if they slid to the floor, reluctant to quieten down even after the matron had come in to check they were in bed and to turn the lights out. As soon as she had withdrawn to her own quarters they went back to talking in the dark, none of them able to settle.

One voice after another dropped out of the conversation, until eventually silence fell over the whole room and the space soon filled with the rhythmic sounds of sleeping. Hugo, however, found himself still staring at the ceiling, his thoughts still churning and his imagination exploding like a firework display. After about an hour he slid out from under the sheets, slipped his phone from where he kept it hidden in his sponge bag, and headed silently for the bathroom.

He dialled his mother's number.

"Darling," she replied before it had even had a chance to ring, "are you okay?"

"Yes, definitely. Did you see the darkness?"

Yung rose from the chair where she had been sitting, listening to her guests arguing after dinner.

"Excuse me," she said to the room in general, "it's my son."

"Why is she allowed to keep her phone?" May enquired loudly before Yung was more than five paces away.

"It's her house," her husband replied, "and Yung is a technology expert. I'm sure she knows what she's doing."

Yung ignored them as she walked over to the window and stretched out her shoulder and back muscles. The others went back to their conversation without her. Fuelled by a large amount of wine, and now brandy, Minenhle was becoming aggressively evangelical about the urgency of impending climate change and May was sighing a great deal more loudly than was strictly polite.

"Yes, I saw it," Yung said. "Were you frightened?"

"No," Hugo replied, sounding partly puzzled and partly indignant at the suggestion. "I thought it was really interesting."

"It was certainly interesting," his mother agreed.

She could hear May's voice rising above the others. "But why does everyone have to be so boring about climate change? Going on and on. We know we have to do something, so let's just get on and do it and stop lecturing people all the time, making us all feel depressed that we can't do anything about it and guilty because we don't do anything about it."

The professor's voice did not carry so clearly across the room but it sounded like he was attempting to quieten his wife with diplomacy and having little luck. Yung had a very soft spot for the professor. He was an engineer by profession and had been instrumental in designing and building a number of futuristic eco-towns all over the world. They provided low cost, prefabricated housing, which had zero carbon footprints and were one hundred per cent run on renewable energy. If governments in developing countries were to whole heartedly adopt the methods which he had perfected they would be able to wipe out the problems of the fast-growing slums which surrounded every big city within ten years. It was a subject which came up frequently at their meetings but the professor was a shy man by nature and not the best promoter of his own dreams – a fact that annoyed his wife endlessly. May believed her husband should by now have been awarded at least a knighthood. Yung was convinced that his ideas had the potential to resolve the housing problems of the whole world.

"He just appeared outside the window of our classroom," Hugo was saying.

"Who did?" Yung asked, aware she had tuned out from listening to her son.

"This man. He's called Joe, well I call him Joe. He's so weird. He's dressed like he's a hermit who's been living for a hundred years in a forest..."

"And he got into the school grounds?"

"Yes, during the darkness, as if by magic. He looks like a wizard..."

"Did they catch him and escort him off the premises?"

"Who?"

"Security. They have security there, don't they?"

"No, because Miss Sophie invited him home to her room for his tea, and we all went round to see him, and that was when I decided to call him Joe, which he says is a name he likes. He's very interesting. He says that he caused the world to go dark but I think he was just teasing. I mean, how could he have done that anyway?"

"Listen, darling" – she interrupted his stream of consciousness, aware that once he got started he might never stop – "we need to talk about this weekend."

"Yes?" Hugo braced himself for disappointing news. So often when he was looking forward to seeing his mother she would have to cancel at the last minute.

"Well, I've got a lot of people staying in the house and we are going to be very busy and I won't have much time to spend with you. So I wondered if you wanted to bring a friend or two home so you have someone to play with. Is there anyone you would like to invite?"

"Not really," he said, and for a second Yung thought her heart would break.

"Can I ask Joe?"

"Who's Joe?"

"The man I was telling you about, the one who appeared. I knew you weren't listening."

"I am listening. Do you think he would want to come? Do we know anything about him?"

"I could ask Miss Sophie too. I think they like each other."

"Your teacher? You want to invite your teacher?"

"Yes," Hugo sounded puzzled again, "what's wrong with that? I like her. You met her at parents' evening. She's nice."

"Yes, of course, I'm sure she is. Okay, ask her to ring me tomorrow and we will make the arrangements. How come you are still awake anyway?"

"I was too excited to sleep."

"I'm not surprised," she laughed, "these are very exciting times, Hugo."

"I know. I'm really looking forward to the weekend now."

"Okay. Get Miss Sophie to call then. And go to bed now. I love you."

"I love you too."

"This sun thing is just a freak incident," Minehle was saying as Yung rejoined the group. "It's a side show. We cannot allow ourselves to be distracted from the main issue which is the long-term changes that are happening to the climate."

"I don't know how you can say that," May said, her words beginning to slur from the alcohol. "If the sun goes out again we'll all be gone within a few weeks. If you ask me it was an act of God. I mean exactly twelve minutes of darkness? Does that not seem like a sign of divine intervention to you?"

"I knew it was a mistake to invite guests for this week,"

Minenhle said as she drained her brandy glass. "We will just get side-tracked by superstitious nonsense from the things that are really important."

"There will be plenty of things to keep the guests occupied," Yung assured her.

"Excuse me for even thinking I could have an opinion," May said as she stood up unsteadily. "I'm going to bed, are you coming Austin?"

"I'll be there soon, my dear," the professor said, his voice as even as always, giving away nothing of what he was feeling.

TEN

Once the children's excited voices had finally faded into the distance and Sophie had returned to cooking the meal, she settled Joe in front of the television with the remote control. He flicked inquisitively through the channels for a few minutes, his eyes wide with a mixture of amazement and puzzlement at the things he saw, before alighting on a documentary about pollution. There were pictures of factory chimneys and power stations belching smoke out over a town full of grey streets, tailbacks of cars on motorways, underpasses and flyovers, cranes towering out of the smog in newly built Chinese cities, islands of plastic floating in oceans and airliners leaving white trails across clear blue skies. A doom-laden voiceover was giving a history of the industrialisation process of the twentieth century and the toll it was taking on the health of people, plants and animals.

"Why do you think no one's doing anything about sorting this stuff out?" he asked after watching for a few minutes. "Surely everyone knows about it by now."

"Everyone knows about it," Sophie said as she pushed things into the microwave, "but no one wants to give up their comfortable lives by getting rid of their car or cancelling their foreign holiday, and no one wants to stop earning money by closing factories or stopping drilling for oil and gas, and everyone wants their food to come conveniently packaged and unbruised. All the millions who still live in poverty look forward to the day when they too can drive a car or install an air-conditioning unit. Unless governments are forced to change the laws in order to make it illegal to pollute the air, land and water, then the clean up is going to happen too slowly to save the planet."

"Do you think these people are going to be able to help?" Joe pointed at the screen.

Sophie came over from the oven to look. "It's just a bunch of kids going on strike from school to protest about the number of species being forced into extinction by the things mankind is doing to the forests and the climate. They're just idealistic kids with no power. They come out onto the streets for a day or two and everyone says how terrible it is and agrees with all the things they are saying and then tells them to go back to school and things go back to how they were. The ones running the oil companies and the banks and ruling the world are older people who will not be around when the planet finally overheats and is too hot to grow food on, and when the water runs out and millions of people in the tropics and sub-tropics come north in search of some means of survival. The kids have the right ideas but no one is taking them seriously, or at least no one who is in a position to do anything about it. By the time they are old enough to take over the decision-making processes it will be too late."

"But man has had choices all through the last two millennia," Joe said. "They didn't have to do any of this. They could have followed a different path."

"Where have you been all your life?" Sophie was genuinely shocked, as well as charmed, by his apparent innocence. "Of course we had choices, but we chose greed and self preservation. We put ourselves and the human race above everything else. We wanted to increase our populations and live longer, be warmer in winter and cooler in summer, eat more food, be safer from predators and travel wherever and whenever we wanted, all of which meant destroying everything from tigers to potentially valuable bacteria. We did everything too fast and unbalanced all the natural systems. Now we are going to have to pay the price."

She topped both their cups of wine up as he went back to watching the screen, noticing that they were already more than halfway through the bottle, even though she had only had a couple of sips herself. She finished preparing the meal and carried the plates over to the sofa, sitting carefully down beside him. He was obviously hungry and had cleaned his plate by the time she was still only halfway through hers. She was stupidly flattered by this sign that he had enjoyed her cooking. She could feel the warmth of his thigh as it rested casually against hers and found it uncomfortably hard to concentrate on chewing and swallowing her food.

"I would offer you more," she said, getting up and going to the cupboard, "but there isn't any. I think there's a packet of biscuits, though, which will do for dessert."

"Sounds great," he said, taking the packet from her and eating his way through it, taking occasional gulps of wine and staring intently at the television screen, every so often firing a question at her.

It felt wonderful to Sophie to have someone so interested in her opinions and so keen to hear her voice them. Most people either raised their eyes to the ceiling when she started talking about the state of the planet, or they tried to convince her she was overreacting and being too dramatic. Her family were forever telling her to "lighten up" and have "more fun", which was one of the reasons she didn't bother to go home that often anymore. She knew that she made them all uncomfortable with her intense opinions and her apparent inability to find a partner she could bring home to meet them. But Joe didn't argue with anything she said. He simply listened, nodding to indicate that he had understood whatever point she was making, and then returning his attention to the screen. He was the best pupil she had ever had the pleasure of teaching and Sophie had never felt so comfortable sitting this close to a man before. The feeling confused her. Every part of her longed for him to touch her, but the fact that he didn't seem to have any intention of making a pass made him all the more attractive.

Once they had finished eating, she took the liberty of snuggling in close to him on the sofa without being invited. He put his arm around her shoulders in a brotherly way, as if it were the most natural thing in the world, giving her an affectionate squeeze. It was as casual and relaxed as if they had been living together all their lives.

"I had a dream about you the other day," she confessed after a few minutes of companionable silence.

"Oh, yes?" He didn't sound surprised.

"Before I even met you," she added, wanting him to understand how weird it was, "which is strange, don't you think?"

He cocked his head to the side so that he could see her face more clearly and she felt the softness of his beard brushing across her forehead, filling her head with the aroma of warm spices.

"So what happened in this dream?" he asked.

"You were just there," she said. "But I had another dream at around the same time, which was about some Bible scrolls being discovered during an archaeological dig in Jerusalem. It was a bit like an Indiana Jones movie or a Dan Brown story. Everyone was very excited because the scrolls were a source for the well-known gospels. There were all these old theologians who had been convinced that they existed, but now they actually had the evidence."

"Do you think that's likely?" he asked.

"I don't think I am the right person to be pontificating about theology," she laughed.

"But what are your beliefs?" he insisted. "Whatever they are, they are just as valid as any theologian's."

"I'm a fully fledged atheist," she said, hoping that was not going to prove to be a problem in their developing relationship. He didn't seem to have judged her about her veganism, so maybe it was safe to talk about more contentious things like her religious beliefs, or lack of them. She couldn't imagine him becoming upset about anything, which was one of the things that made it so pleasant to be curled up next to him.

"You don't believe in God or anything?" he asked.

"The whole thing is a bit far-fetched, don't you think?" she said, tucking herself in so close to him that she could feel his heart beating steadily against her shoulder.

"There have been a lot of pretty amazing stories told over time," he agreed. "I can understand that it is hard to know what to believe, how to sort the fact from the fiction."

"Especially now that we know everyone in power lies all the time."

"All of them? Do you think so?"

"It's beginning to seem that way." She gestured towards the television. "It's like one revelation after another and none of them show our leaders in a good light. Not just here, everywhere. In fact it is better here than in most places. Everyone is out for themselves."

"Well then, we definitely need to do something about that," he said, draining his wine and holding the cup out for a refill.

"Are you teasing me?" she asked as she topped him up.

"Would you mind if I was?"

"You're still doing that thing."

"What thing?"

"Answering every question with another question."

"There's a lot of things I'm trying to understand. I have a lot of questions that need answers."

They lay comfortably together for another hour, talking about whatever subject came to mind or popped up on the television screen as it flickered in front of them, until eventually Sophie felt her eyelids becoming too heavy to hold open any longer, no matter how much she wanted to keep talking. Resigning herself to the fact that Joe was not going to make a pass at her, she slid off the sofa and stood up.

"I'm off to bed," she said. "Make yourself comfortable, help yourself to a towel and anything else you need from the cupboard in the bathroom, there's a sleeping bag over there and I'll see you in the morning."

"Thank you," he said, showing no sign that he was going to try to stop her leaving the room.

Plucking up her courage she leaned down and kissed him gently on the lips. He tasted sweeter than she could ever have imagined. He responded but gave no indication that he expected to go any further. She straightened up, pretending that to her it was no more than a goodnight kiss and went through to her bedroom, hoping that she might have lit a spark of desire in him and that he might follow, having realised that he had to have her.

Despite her exhaustion, she found it hard to get to sleep once she was lying in bed, her mind spinning round and round, listening to the sounds of him moving about in the other room. He had told the children his name was Jesus, and he'd certainly made himself look like someone from the time of the Bible, but he hadn't tried to preach to her when she announced she was an atheist. He had also hinted that he had something to do with the blacking out of the sun, which seemed ridiculous, unless she accepted the fact that he actually was Jesus, and therefore the Son of God. But all her life she had believed that everything to do with religion was nonsense and that only science held the answers. So did that mean that she was as blinkered to other possible answers as she always thought religious fanatics were towards scientific facts? Was it actually possible that she had the Son of God in her apartment? Even thinking that made her want to laugh – it was laughable, after all. Wasn't it?

ELEVEN

When she woke, Sophie could hear loud banging and crashing noises coming from the other room and it took her a few moments to remember that for the first time since she joined the school she had a guest in her tiny home. The memory of the previous day flooded her with an unexpected feeling of joyousness, igniting her to jump out of bed with an unusual amount of enthusiasm. She also checked her appearance in the mirror before opening the bedroom door, something she never normally had any cause or any wish to do. She was pleasantly surprised by how good she looked considering she had just lifted her head from the pillows. For the first time ever she noted that her smile was wide and her eyes bright with excitement. Her short hair was sticking up at some odd angles but she didn't think Joe would be one to judge such things and, if she was absolutely honest, she thought it made her look kind of cute and rumpled.

Joe was kneeling on the floor, rummaging through the kitchen cupboard with a puzzled look on his face. He had examined virtually every cooking implement and grocery item that she possessed and was no nearer to finding anything that he could turn into breakfast.

"I wanted to make you breakfast," he said, looking up at her, "but I'm not sure where to start."

"Nice thought," she laughed, "thank you. But toast is probably the only option unless you want a protein drink."

"A protein drink sounds good."

"I'll make you one – and I'll do some toast."

"Okay," he said, raising his hands in mock surrender, "and then I will teach myself how to cook something better for you next time."

"Cool," she said, "you can watch cooking videos on the internet all day long, not that there is much here for you to work with."

She felt a flutter of excitement in her stomach at the easy way in which he suggested that there would be a "next time". Was he planning to move in permanently? Was he assuming that they were in a relationship already? She turned her face away from his gaze and towards the blender so that he couldn't see the grin she was unable to suppress. "No," she told herself firmly, "he said nothing about a relationship. He just wants to learn how to cook eggs! Get a grip, girl!"

Having whipped up a thick, greenish health drink from what was left in her vegetable rack along with some protein powders, and having produced a few slices of nearly burned toast, Sophie made coffee and they sat together on the sofa for breakfast. A knock on the door made Sophie jump but Joe kept on eating as if no interruption had occurred.

"This could be awkward," she said as she went over to open the door, expecting to be confronted by a furious headmaster or perhaps a couple of stone-faced security guards.

"Hugo?" she said. "How did you get in?"

"The door downstairs is open for the cleaners," he said. "Can I come in?"

Sophie was too surprised to do anything but stand back and let him past.

"Good morning, Hugo," Joe said, as if it was the most normal situation in the world. "Did you sleep well?"

"Not really," Hugo admitted. "I kept thinking about you."

"Oh," Joe grinned. "Would you like some toast?"

"Yes please."

Joe patted the seat beside him and passed the plate of toast over.

"Drink?" He held up his glass of green sludge for Hugo to see.

"No thank you."

"Why are you here, Hugo?" Sophie asked, quickly closing the door before any passing members of staff decided to poke their noses in.

"I spoke to my mum last night."

"What, after leaving here? You know you're not supposed to use your phones in the dormitories." Sophie tried to sound as if she actually believed that such petty rules should be enforced, but Hugo didn't seem convinced enough to bother to reply.

"She asked if you two would like to come home with me at the weekend, unless you have anything else that you need to do. It can be quite interesting at her house sometimes. She knows a lot of interesting people."

"I'm sure she does." Sophie sat down and tried to get her head around the invitation. "That's very kind of her. Isn't there anyone else you would rather ask?"

"Not really." Hugo wrinkled his nose up at the thought of introducing any of his classmates to his mother and her friends.

"Any reason why we can't accept?" Joe asked, apparently as unsurprised by the invitation as he was by Hugo's early-morning arrival. "I would like to meet Hugo's mum – and her interesting friends."

"No," Sophie said after a moment's thought, "no reason at all, I guess. That would be great, Hugo, thanks. Please thank your mother for us."

"Okay," Hugo said, standing up, still holding his piece of toast, "I will. She says can you ring her about the arrangements. This is her number." He passed her a piece of paper.

"Oh." Sophie felt unaccountably nervous at the thought of having to make such a call, but took the paper from him. "Okay. Thanks. I'll do that."

"See you later," Hugo said, letting himself out and taking another bite of toast.

"Oh my God, do you have any idea who his mother is?" Sophie asked once she could see from the window that Hugo was safely out of the building. "She and her husband are two of the richest, most politically high-profile and well-connected people in China. They made a fortune. They make the smartest machines in the world. Yung – Hugo's mum – is a world-class expert in AI and Information and Communications Technology. His dad, Liang, is a world-class expert in genetic engineering. Yung is one of the most brilliant women in the world. They have been outspoken in their opinions of their government and on the course that they believe China should be taking when it comes to human rights and freedom. I think they believed they were so rich they were untouchable. Anyway, the authorities decided to show them otherwise and imprisoned Liang, with no explanation. At least that is what everyone assumes has happened because he just disappeared one day on the way to work and no one has seen or heard of him since, which is the way the government over there works. They had already built this amazing house in New Zealand, so Yung fled here for her own safety, and for the safety of Hugo."

"I wonder why her government just let her do that."

"Who knows what their plans are for her? The point is she's a very important figure and it will be fantastic to be able to talk to her in her own home. She has shown huge courage in speaking out against powerful people and she has been politically active on a number of fronts on behalf of the planet.

"She is also a great champion of China as a country, which she believes is doing almost everything right, while at the same time campaigning for changes to the law which will make it impossible for the government to simply 'disappear' people like her husband, seemingly on no more than a whim of someone at the top. It will be awesome to get to spend some time with her."

"Awesome," Joe agreed.

"You don't seem that overwhelmed by the idea."

"No, really. It'll be interesting."

"Plus we get to hang out all weekend together."

"That will be interesting too," he grinned, and she got the distinct impression she was being teased so she concentrated on putting Yung's number into her phone.

"Hugo seems an unusual name for a Chinese child," Joe mused.

"Not really. A lot of the younger generation in China give their children English names as well as Chinese ones, especially if they are planning to send them overseas for education."

She dialled the number and to her astonishment Yung picked up after just two rings.

TWELVE

"The headmaster wants to see you in his office," his secretary announced from the door of the classroom, causing almost all the children in her class to simultaneously let out one of their favourite ironic "ooh" sounds.

"Be quiet, all of you," Sophie told them before turning to the smirking secretary. "Thank you. Please tell him I'll come as soon as class is over."

"He's asked to see you now," the secretary said, turning on her heel and walking smartly away before Sophie could say anything else, and at the same time removing the need for them to walk together to the office in an awkward silence.

"You better go, Miss," one of the more theatrical boys said, clutching at his heart and throwing his head back dramatically, "or the headmaster might die of unrequited love."

"Don't be so cheeky," she said as the others laughed noisily.

In fact in her current mood she rather liked the idea of herself as a femme fatale. What she didn't like was the thought of being in his office again having to explain why she had a strange man hidden in her room.

"Just get on with some work until I get back."

"Come in, Sophie," the headmaster said in a voice that sounded too friendly to be genuine. "Sit down."

"I'm okay here," she replied, saying nothing more, biding her time until she found out what was on his mind.

"I'm told that you have a man in your room," he said, averting his eyes from hers, "and that he spent the night there."

She said nothing, looking at him questioningly, as if waiting for him to get to the point.

"Is that true?" he asked.

"Yes it is."

"But did he get clearance? Have security been informed? We can't have people living on the premises without knowing anything about them."

"He's the most trustworthy person I think I have ever met," she said.

"That's not the point. We are in positions of responsibility here, particularly those of us who live on the premises—"

"I understand that," she interrupted, annoyed at being lectured again, "but I am happy to vouch for my guest's good behaviour."

"But who is he?"

"His name is Joe."

"Joe what?"

"Just Joe."

"You don't even know his full name?" Now the headmaster seemed genuinely shocked. "How long have you known him?"

"He turned up yesterday, during the darkness."

"Seriously? You just met him yesterday and you let him stay at your place, a guy as weird as that?"

"What makes you think he's weird?" Sophie felt herself blushing angrily at the insult to someone she already felt close to.

"I've seen the security footage, and the kids have been overheard talking about him…" Aware that he was starting to raise his voice he paused and took a deep breath.

"Listen, Sophie, you know how much I value you as a teacher and how much I like you as a person…"

She decided this was the moment to lay all her cards on the table. "He is staying with me until he sorts himself somewhere to live and we are going together this weekend to visit Hugo's mother."

"Yung Zhang? You are going to stay with Yung Zhang? That's ridiculous!"

"Why is it ridiculous?"

"She's a global political figure and…"

"And I'm just a humble teacher?"

"Don't put words in my mouth!" He slammed his palms back down on the desk, making Sophie jump back closer to the door. Seeing that he had scared her he took another deep breath and tried to speak in a level voice. "This is exactly what I have been warning you about, getting too close to the children. This is inappropriate. Not to mention the possible political implications of befriending someone like that."

"Someone like what?"

"Someone who is such a high-profile activist."

"Who I visit at a weekend is nothing to do with you. I am informing you as a courtesy; that is all. I am a great admirer of Yung Zhang and her husband and I think it is a measure of the sort of woman she is that she is happy to invite her son's teacher for the weekend. She is making me feel very welcome."

"You have already spoken to her?"

"Only to make the arrangements for a car to pick us up."

The headmaster fell silent for a few moments as if processing the information. This was not a situation he had ever had to deal with before and he wasn't sure how to proceed. If he were to be honest he was experiencing a twinge of jealousy. He too would have jumped at an invitation to get to know Yung Zhang and stay in her famous home.

"All right," he said eventually, "your friend can stay until he sorts himself out with somewhere more suitable to go, but he must remain in your apartment while he is here. He cannot be seen wandering around the school. If a picture got into the media we would start to look like some sort of religious cult."

"I will be taking him shopping to get some more normal clothes," she said, making a small concession in the negotiation.

"And maybe a haircut?"

"I will ask him. I can hardly order a grown man to cut his hair."

She had actually been planning to get Joe tidied up before the weekend anyway. It had never occurred to her that she would ever be invited to the home of such a wealthy person as Yung. Now that she had got used to the idea, however, she was extremely keen to make a good impression and not to feel out of place. She had also already realised that Joe's wild appearance would be inappropriate for visiting someone famed for her taste and elegance. She remembered briefly shaking Yung's hand at a recent parents' evening and feeling painfully dowdy by comparison.

"I am warning you, Sophie," the headmaster was saying, "you are getting way out of your depth."

Sophie thought it was entirely possible that he was right about that, and she found the prospect of embarking on such an adventure into the unknown thrilling.

THIRTEEN

"We're going late-night shopping," Sophie told Joe when she got back to the apartment from class that afternoon.

"Shopping?" he asked, putting down the autobiography of Nelson Mandela which he was already halfway through and standing up to give her a welcoming embrace, like they were an old married couple.

"We have got to make ourselves look at least slightly presentable if we are going to be staying in someone's house." Sophie breathed in his scent as he wrapped his arms around her, wanting the moment to last for ever.

"Do I not look presentable?" He spread his arms out wide, releasing her and looking down at his robe.

"You look amazing," she said before she could stop herself, "but a little too unusual. It's polite to fit in with other people a bit, especially if you are going to be in their homes."

She could hardly believe she was saying such things, having always prided herself on her individual and unorthodox style. Her parents had tried for years to persuade her to just occasionally trade her jeans and T-shirts for a dress or skirt and the more they had told her how pretty she would be if she "just made a little effort" the more determined she became to do no such thing. Now she was advocating doing exactly what they would have wanted her to do in the circumstances.

"You don't want to look like you are trying to draw attention to yourself," she added lamely. "I never normally spend any money on things like clothes, so it will be an interesting experience for both of us."

"I like interesting experiences," he said, squeezing her shoulders and kissing the top of her head like she was his little sister. "I am happy to be guided by you."

They made an unusual couple as they strode into the shopping mall. Sophie could see that people were going out of their way to avoid them and then staring at them from a safe distance, unsure what to expect, whispering to one another and some of them giggling. Some people were looking around for hidden cameras, assuming it was some sort of stunt for television and that this eccentric-looking man was going to start singing or talking to strangers and making them do stupid things. Being so exposed made Sophie feel a little nervous, but at the same time she liked the idea that they were both so unabashedly being themselves and she was determined to be unbothered by whatever other people might be thinking.

Joe's wide-eyed look of amazement took in everything going on around him in the busy shops and restaurants. He smiled broadly and anointed everyone who was brave enough to stare or respond to him with a friendly greeting. Sophie noticed that whenever he did that the other parties would not shy away. They would look him squarely in the eye and smile back or mirror his cheerful greetings. Some would even come forward to shake his hand or take a selfie with him as if he were a celebrity. First it was younger people and children who responded, but gradually others lost their reserve and allowed him to strike up conversations with them as he passed. She guessed that many of them had mistaken him for someone off the television.

His passage from one shop window to the next seemed to set up connections between other people, who either responded with smiles and returned greetings or exchanged amused or puzzled looks with other shoppers. People who would normally have been going about their business with their eyes on the ground or focused blankly on the shop windows, laughed and paused in order to comment to total strangers about the strangely dressed man who was sweeping through their midst, exclaiming in wonder like an excited child at everything he saw. Something changed in the atmosphere of the whole mall. It was as if a magnetic field had been reversed and instead of repelling people they started to attract them closer. One or two people seemed to be deliberately hanging around them, trying to catch Joe's eye and start a conversation. He didn't disappoint any of them.

"Let's go in here," Sophie said, feeling self-conscious at the number of people now staring at them and leading him into the relative privacy of one of the clothes shops. Several young sales assistants converged from different corners, apparently all eager to talk to Joe.

"Hi," Joe said. "I need some clothes."

"What sort of look are you after?" one young man asked.

"Smart casual?" another suggested.

"Linen would be a good look," added another.

"You guys know much more about this than us," Joe laughed. "We are happy to be guided by you."

"We have a budget," Sophie warned them, aware that she would be the one paying the bill, but they weren't listening to her. It was like she had ceased to exist as anything other than Joe's shadow.

Joe took her hand and squeezed it. "Don't worry about the money," he whispered, "they won't charge us."

"Are you kidding me?" she hissed. "Have you never been in a shop before?"

Joe said no more, just grinned and kept hold of her hand, which made her more than happy, until the assistants all brought things for him to try on and she had to release him. Other shoppers stopped what they were doing to watch, at first from afar and then drawing closer when they realised that Joe was happy to talk to all of them, asking their opinions of the different shirts and jackets as he tried them on. Some of them were pulling out their phones and taking pictures as Joe twirled in front of the mirror, laughing happily with the assistants who were struggling to hold his attention as more and more people came up to talk.

An hour later the shop was filled with people and Joe and Sophie were submerged at the centre of the crowd. More people were peering in through the windows, trying to make out what was going on. Joe was now dressed in a white linen suit, deck shoes and open-necked cotton shirt and his old robes had been spirited away. Assistants were packing other clothes into carrier bags and passing them to Sophie, who realised they thought she was some sort of servant or personal shopper. She asked about paying but no one seemed to be listening to her, it was like her voice had become inaudible because everyone was tuned in to Joe, laughing at everything he said, repeating his bon mots to one another so that they could enjoy them again, pulling out their phones to take pictures and videos.

When they were finally ushered towards the door Sophie realised he was right. Everyone wanted to watch him and talk to him and that although the assistants had removed all the security tags no one was going to ask him for any money.

"Haircut," she mimed to him, unable to make herself heard over the babble of voices surrounding them. She pointed towards a barbershop on the far side of the mall. He nodded his understanding, reached out to grip her hand again and made his way slowly through the crowd, touching people's shoulders and heads as they came close, shaking outstretched hands, bending down to better hear what they were trying to say, always smiling, somehow giving the impression of looking everyone directly in the eye but still not letting go of Sophie's free hand.

The barbers stopped what they were doing in order to watch their slow approach and were ready and waiting by the door when they finally got there. Other customers grinned from the chairs where they sat, swathed in pale blue sheets, apparently not bothered that their haircuts had been interrupted by the arrival of some sort of celebrity circus.

"What can you do for him?" Sophie asked the assembled barbers.

"A little bit late twentieth century perhaps?" one of them said, holding up Joe's long, dark curls for inspection.

"Please just make him look presentable," Sophie said, stacking the carrier bags in a corner. "I'll be back in an hour for him. I have to do some shopping for myself."

"No problem," the youngest of the barbers said, already steering Joe towards a basin. Joe let go of her hand and gave a little wave as the other barbers closed in between them, all of them wanting to feel the hair and make suggestions about shaping the beard.

Sophie backed out of the shop but no one noticed. She was relieved to get clear of the crowd and to be able to breathe on her own for a moment. She had no idea what sort of clothes she should buy for herself. She was well aware that Yung often made it onto lists in magazines of the best-dressed women in the world. There was no way she was going to be able to compete with that, but she was pretty sure that her beloved sandals, shapeless T-shirts and frayed jeans would not be appropriate. She also wanted to make herself attractive to Joe, which surprised her. He was the first man who had ever provoked that reaction in her.

Taking a deep breath she walked to a shop which did not

yet seem to be full of people staring in Joe's direction and asked one of the assistants for help. "I need a reasonably smart outfit to be someone's weekend house guest," she explained.

The woman smiled kindly and set to work. Nearly an hour later the job was done. The assistant had never had a customer who was so willing to take her advice and Sophie felt drained by the experience, but also buoyed by how attractive she looked in the changing-room mirrors. She had forgotten how good her figure could look when it wasn't disguised by baggy T-shirts and ended up buying more than she had intended. She was so pleased by the look of herself with a waist and exposed legs that she even decided to wear one of the new outfits out of the shop.

The bill was higher than anything she had ever spent on buying for herself in her life, and there was no doubt that this shop was not going to let her just walk out without paying as Joe had done, but money no longer seemed of any importance, even an amount which would have seemed obscene to her only a few days earlier.

Opposite was a small beauty shop and Sophie noticed that the girl behind the counter didn't have a customer. With her heart in her mouth she walked across and asked the girl if she could have a "make-over" – hardly able to believe that she was even using such words.

"Sure," the girl said, giving no indication as to whether she was remotely interested in doing it or not. She set to work with nimble fingers and an expressionless face, talking all the time in a robotic voice about a variety of products that Sophie had never heard of. Fifteen minutes later the girl offered her a mirror and Sophie was unable to stop herself from letting out a small gasp of amazement.

"My God," she said, "you've made me look beautiful!"

The girl seemed surprised by such spontaneous praise

for her handiwork. "You've got good bone structure and beautiful eyes," she said matter-of-factly, "and good skin. You should make more of yourself. Do you want to buy any of the products?"

"God, yes!" Sophie said. "All of them."

By the time she got back, the crowd outside the barbershop had grown and it was a few seconds before she realised that the man she could see standing at the centre of it was Joe. Shorn of most of the beard, and with his hair cut almost short but with a fashionably floppy fringe still falling over his forehead, he now looked more like an international film star than a hermit. For a few seconds Sophie forgot to breathe as she watched him apparently talking to everyone in the crowd both simultaneously and individually, seeing the absorption in the faces of all those close to him as they listened.

As she elbowed her way through, ignoring the protests of others who were attempting to do the same, she called out his name. He turned to look and she could see that it took him a few seconds to recognise her, too.

"Wow," he beamed at her approvingly. "You look beautiful."

"You too."

She knew she was blushing and was grateful to him when he put his arm around her shoulders and held on to her protectively as the crowd pressed closer. The barbers came out of the shop to give them their other bags. As they made their way slowly towards the exit, Sophie was excited to catch him several times staring at her with what she chose to believe was a twinkle of desire in his eyes.

"This is a strange place," he whispered to her. "Why is everyone buying so much stuff?"

"The same reason as us, I guess," she grinned. "It is kind of fun, I have to admit."

"But they already seem to have so many clothes and the shops are so full of things. Why does there need to be so much choice?"

"I have no idea," she laughed. "More to the point, why are they all crowding round you like this? Why are they all asking so many questions and wanting to touch you?"

"They can sense the presence of God," he said.

She laughed at what she thought was a joke but then realised that he was serious and couldn't think of anything witty to say in response. Joe wasn't listening anyway. He seemed determined to work out exactly what everyone was doing in the mall that evening.

"Why do you want to buy so much?" he asked a couple of well-dressed women who were loaded down with carrier bags.

"We just love shopping," one of them giggled. "And I married good."

"And she divorced even better," her friend chimed in.

"But do you need any of it?" Joe asked.

"You can't have too many clothes or too many shoes," they replied in unison.

"But the planet can't sustain all this overconsumption," Sophie interjected, remembering her own personal hobby horse and forgetting that she was also weighed down with parcels. She was aware that Joe was squeezing her tighter as a sign to keep quiet. No one was listening to her anyway.

"What about you?" Joe turned to an overweight man who was in the process of pushing a burger into his mouth. "Are you actually hungry? And you?" He added a woman sharing a box of doughnuts with her children to the conversation. "Are you and your children actually hungry?"

"Always," the man laughed, spraying half-chewed food in all directions, making those around him simultaneously laugh and exclaim in disgust.

"Keeps the little buggers quiet," the woman with the doughnuts replied.

"Is this place making you all happy?" Joe asked the crowd and a chorus of affirmative answers came back.

"Supposing," he continued, apparently unfazed by their reactions, "that instead of worrying about how many things we need to own or consume, we directed our energies into thinking about the things we might be able to do to help others and for the good of the world. Rather than buying another pair of shoes, for instance, we could maybe make a meal for an old person who is living alone, or spend time playing with our children or reading a book which teaches us something useful?"

The crowd pressed closer to hear his words, many of them continuing to eat and drink as they listened, despite the lack of elbow room.

"I believe there was an American president called Kennedy," Joe continued, "and he made a speech in which he said something like, 'Ask not what your country can do for you, but ask what you can do for your country.' If you followed that idea but substituted the words 'neighbour' or 'world' for 'country', might that make you all feel better about yourselves? Might that seem like the right thing to do?"

"Always so many questions," Sophie murmured as she listened.

The crowd now stretched right across the mall and the people at the back were only there because other people were passing the word around that something interesting was happening. None of them could actually see Joe, even though he was taller than most of the people around him. Sophie remembered how she had gone to sleep wondering if she actually had the Son of God in her apartment because just by being there he had made her question the things she had

86

believed unquestioningly all her life. As she looked around her, she could see that he had the same effect on everyone who came near to him.

In the control room of the mall the Head of Security was becoming increasingly alarmed at how the crowds were building and the unpredictable ways in which they were moving around. It seemed highly likely that someone was going to get injured if they didn't disperse soon. Usually at this time of day the mall was beginning to empty in preparation for closing, but no one seemed to want to leave and more people were turning up all the time, apparently hearing on social media that something unusual was going on and wanting to witness it for themselves. He was talking simultaneously into the earpieces of the operatives he had around the building, all of whom seemed as close to panicking as he was.

Joe, on the other hand, seemed entirely untroubled by the crush of bodies and was happy to spend as much time talking to everyone as they asked for. A young girl was pushed close to him in a wheelchair by her mother and Joe laid his hand gently on her head.

"What is your name?"

"Jane."

"Have you always relied on these wheels to get around?"

"All my life."

"She has never walked," her mother said.

"Just have faith," he smiled. "You will walk."

The authorities were ready to close the mall for the night and under the direction of their manager the guards started trying to herd the people towards the doors. It was impossible to hurry them and tempers were becoming frayed at the edges of the crowd. After they had managed to move a few metres forward Sophie glanced back and saw that the girl, Jane, had struggled out of the wheelchair and was standing up, taking some wobbly steps on her own. The astonished cries of her mother were attracting the attention of the onlookers, all of whom were getting their phones out and filming the apparent miracle. Many were talking to one another and pointing in Joe's direction as he and Sophie were finally swept out of the doors and into the late evening air.

"That was a miracle," Sophie said. "You actually performed a miracle."

"The child just needed to have faith," Joe replied.

"So you actually are Jesus," she said, more to herself than to him, "the Son of God. It wasn't a dream; it was a vision."

He smiled down at her, stooping to kiss her upturned forehead and she realised what the dreams meant. Out of seven and a half billion or more people in the world, she had been chosen to help him spread his messages.

A shiver ran through her as she remembered what happened to Jesus the last time he came to Earth.

"Come on," he said, "let's buy some food and I'll have a go at cooking a meal for you."

FOURTEEN

No one in the loosely knit network of international security services used real names. They didn't even bother to make up code names or aliases or any of the other staples of twentieth-century spy fiction. There was no longer time for anything like that and it was also no longer possible to discern when you were dealing with a real person and when it was no more than a bot created by somebody else's computer. Information travelled around at such speeds and in such quantities, constantly being exaggerated and contradicted as it went, that it was normally impossible to work out who was real and who was fake, who was talking, who was listening to whom at any given moment and who had any number of alternative agendas behind the things they were saying. It was pointless to believe anything they heard, but they still had to listen because to discover that you were ignorant of some vital piece of information would be even worse.

Fresh lines of both communication and miscommunication had opened between a number of state security services following the blackout of the sun, integrating into whatever arrangements and alliances already existed, growing them and transforming them at the same time. Some of the operatives had started cautiously sharing information over secured channels of communication they had never used before, putting out feelers in the hope that others knew more than they did and might accidentally drop hints that could be pieced together to make a pattern that they could understand, or perhaps even produce some predictions or answers as to what was going to happen next.

Rows and rows of nameless people in different government bunkers around the world stared at screens, their fingers flickering over keyboards, headphones covering their ears and shielding them from the real world around them as they searched for answers twenty-four hours a day, continually monitoring everything that was being written or said until interesting trends finally started to emerge from the online noise and confusion and turned into patterns which could actually be studied.

"What is it with Christchurch?" one American operative asked another at a neighbouring screen. "Where is it anyway?"

"New Zealand," came the reply. "It's where that guy shot up the mosque, remember?"

"They got that guy though, didn't they? Caught him the same day?"

"I think so."

"So why is there so much internet activity coming out from there now? And why are the Chinese paying it so much attention?"

"The Chinese are watching that activist woman, the one who's getting this group of high-profile thinkers together; the sort of people who get millions of kids to follow them. They are looking for answers to climate change and extinction and Christ knows what else. Potential rabble rousers and troublemakers, perhaps even terrorists."

The operative flicked a few more keys. "Do you mean Yung Zhang?"

"That's the one. The Chinese already have her husband in a cell and they are watching her. Apparently biding their time before pouncing."

"Why aren't we watching her? Should we be?"

"We're trying. She's some kind of technology genius; it's hard to get close."

"But the Chinese are close?"

"Yep. Apparently the Russians have someone inside her house too."

"Do we know who?"

"No idea."

"Jesus Christ. Do we know anything any more?"

His colleague shrugged her shoulders. "We know there is some other guy in the area drawing a lot of attention to himself. People are posting videos of him that are going instantly viral. He seems to be performing healing miracles. He's pretty hot too."

"Is that relevant?"

"I suppose not," she laughed. "I just happened to notice, that's all."

"What's he doing, apart from getting you hot and bothered?"

"He seems to be some sort of charismatic, drawing crowds and healing people, that sort of thing."

"Is that relevant to anything?"

"It just seems like a coincidence that he would be there at the same time as the Chinese are watching Yung Zhang and her followers. I mean, like you said, who had heard of Christchurch ten minutes ago?"

"What do we know about this guy's background?"

"Absolutely nothing."

"Let's find out more about him."

"Already onto it."

Others noticed that the Americans were trying to find background information on a man apparently performing miracles in Christchurch, pictures of which were seeping across the internet.

"Why are the Americans interested in this guy?" a young Russian agent asked at a department meeting a few hours later. "What do they know about him?"

"They aren't finding out anything," another assured him. "No one can. The Chinese are afraid he's connected to Yung Zhang so they're putting a lot of hours into researching him and drawing a complete blank. It's like he didn't exist until that moment when the sun went out."

"Well he exists now," their boss snapped. "We can see him in the videos, unless they're faked."

"I don't see how they can be," another chipped in. "They are coming up all the time from different cameras at different angles."

"Do we have anyone on the ground in New Zealand?"

"Stop asking questions," a senior voice overruled the meeting. "We don't know who is listening."

However much misinformation the different security forces were feeding to one another, they could all agree that the emergence of this unknown man at the same time as the freak weather conditions and just a few miles from where an infamous Chinese dissident was living could be nothing, but it still seemed like a strange coincidence to people who were suspicious by profession.

By the time Joe and Sophie got outside the shopping mall most of the world's security networks were watching the videos being uploaded in real time, as were the Christchurch police force.

Considering the number of people jostling to get close to Joe it was surprising that the young carer was able to get to the front with her charges, all of whom were even younger than her. It was obvious to all the people watching, either with their own eyes or via the internet, that the group had special needs and that the crush of the crowds was aggravating their conditions. There were three of them, all clinging tightly to one another, fearful that they would be torn apart by the crowd and would become lost. All of them appeared to be panicking but the carer was determined to keep pushing them forward towards Joe.

When she got to the front the carer threw herself at Joe's feet and begged him to help her three troubled charges. Joe opened his arms wide and enveloped the three teenagers. Slowly, in front of at least a hundred phones and surveillance cameras, their panic subsided. Screams and wild convulsions were replaced with calm smiles and the crowd around them started to applaud.

"Could be a set-up," the watching American operative suggested. "They could be actors."

"Do you think so?" his colleague asked. "Maybe he's some sort of exorcist."

"What, like the movie?"

"I don't know what to think any more," he admitted. "Could be the Chinese or the Russians winding us up."

Almost identical conversations were taking place in both Chinese and Russian security bunkers.

The applause was turning into cheers and dozens of voices were shouting out to Joe, asking him to talk to them, to smile at their cameras, to lay his hands on them.

Every national security body now believed there was a possibility that this man had been planted by one of their rivals to cause trouble or create a distraction from something else that might be going on, but none of them could work out who would do that or why they would do it or how they had managed to remove all other traces of the man from the records. They were all so used to lying to people who they perceived to be their enemies, and being lied to by those same people in return, they could no longer work out where the truth might really lie. Highly trained operatives who usually enjoyed the complexity of their work were starting to experience a tide of panic rising around them as they felt the possibilities for exercising any sort of control on proceedings slipping through their fingers.

FIFTEEN

The black Tesla had tinted windows and paintwork that shone like a slab of mirrored granite as it hummed quietly away from the school with Hugo and his two weekend guests in the back. The driver of the car looked more like a bodyguard than a chauffeur and, with the help of Ray-Bans and an earpiece, kept a respectful distance from his passengers. Once they were on the road he gave no indication that he was hearing anything they were saying.

"I wish you hadn't cut your hair and beard," Hugo said, staring quizzically at Joe's new image.

"Why?" Sophie asked. "I think he looks cool."

"He looks okay, but he was more interesting looking when he was dressed as a hermit."

They both laughed. "I think your mother will feel more comfortable with me looking like this around the house," Joe said.

"I don't know," Hugo sighed, "she has some really strange people to stay sometimes. I described you to her and she didn't seem bothered. I told her you were really weird, like some mad monk from Middle Earth."

"Thanks, mate," Joe winked, "appreciate it."

"Your mother is a remarkable woman," Sophie said. "You must be very proud of her."

Hugo thought for a moment. "I sometimes wonder," he said eventually, "if my dad would still be with us if my mother wasn't so remarkable. I don't think they like remarkable people in China very much."

Joe stretched round Sophie, the warmth of his arm making her catch her breath, and placed a comforting hand on the boy's shoulder. Hugo pushed a tear away from the corner of his eye with the tip of his finger.

"What's your dad like?" Sophie asked as she casually rested her head back onto Joe's outstretched arm.

"He's great," Hugo said, his eyes shining for a moment and then glistening again with more tears. "I miss him a lot. We used to talk all the time. Mum doesn't have so much time to talk, at least not with me."

"I'm sure she would like to," Sophie said, "if she could."

"So am I," Hugo agreed. "But she can't." He was silent for a moment, lost in his memories. "I saw him being taken away. My dad."

"You did?" Sophie was shocked that he had suddenly opened this door in his mind to them.

"It was very fast. No one else saw. I never told anyone, not even Mum. He was leaving the house to go to work and I was watching from the window. I always did that. He always turned and waved before he went round the corner. I would wait there to see him come home at night too. We had a normal house then in Beijing, not one surrounded by guards. We used to come here for holidays then. A car was parked outside. The door opened as Dad walked past and two men got out and pushed him into the back seat. We never saw him again. I have dreams sometimes and see him being tortured."

"Why have you never told anyone this before?" Sophie asked.

"Because if they knew that I saw them then they would take me away too, and my mum and maybe everyone else in the family. Dad wouldn't want that to happen. I know that. He would do anything to protect us."

"Your father will be home with you soon," Joe said, and Sophie put an arm round the boy's shoulders. Hugo snuggled into the soft material of her new shirt, getting out his phone and flicking through his social media apps as if to distract himself from his memories of that morning and his fears for the future.

"Is it true," he asked after a few minutes, "that you are the Son of God?"

"Who says that?" Joe laughed.

"Lots of people. It's because of the videos."

"What videos?"

Hugo held up his phone for Joe to watch pictures of himself healing the girl in the mall and then calming the troubled youths outside.

"Ah, I see," he said, as if that explained everything. "What do you think?"

"Joe always answers questions with more questions," Sophie said.

"I don't know," Hugo said. "We don't really have gods in China. I know a bit about Christianity and Jesus and all that, and I've read about Islam, and I know about the Greek myths…"

"My days, Hugo," Sophie sighed, "if only all my pupils knew as much as you."

"I get a lot of time on my own and I like reading and researching," Hugo said. "People said Jesus would come back, didn't they?"

"I believe they did," Sophie said, leaning into Joe on the other side. "So maybe that's who Joe is."

Hugo stared up at Joe, pushing his glasses back up his nose. "Well it would be very cool but it would blow Mum's mind, and her friends'."

"Why's that?" Sophie asked.

"Well, they are all scientists and things. They don't believe in God, apart from Haki, I think he's a Christian and maybe Doctor Amelia too. She's great, like the grandmother I never had."

"Tell me about Haki?" Joe said.

"He's a young Rwandan who survived the genocide as a child and works for peace and reconciliation now," Sophie told him. "He's written the most amazing book. People call him the new Mandela."

"He's fun," Hugo announced. "He plays football with me even though I'm rubbish at it. He's not nearly as old as some of the others. He lost all the members of his family, his mum, his dad, everyone; saw them being killed and everything, so he understands how I feel about Dad. He says he gets nightmares too."

Joe took Hugo's phone from him and examined the video more carefully.

"They've gone viral," Hugo said. "Do you even own a smartphone?"

"No," Joe said. "I don't own anything really, Hugo. And I think I've got enough on my mind as it is."

All three of them fell silent and thoughtful for a few minutes.

"So what does God look like?" Hugo piped up eventually.

"Is that what you've been thinking about?" Sophie asked.

"Yes."

"What do you think he looks like?" Joe asked.

Hugo thought for a moment, screwing up his nose. "A bit like Santa Claus, maybe. Very old with a long grey beard. That sort of thing."

"Do you think maybe he doesn't look like any sort of person you have ever met?" Joe suggested. "Is it possible that he is more like a stream of energy, a force of nature that is everywhere at once?"

"Maybe," Hugo said, trying to imagine such a thing. "You mean like radio waves or something?"

"Don't worry if you can't imagine that," Sophie said. "There are some things which are simply too difficult for us humans to comprehend yet. Imagine, for instance, trying to explain to an ant why men go to war with one another."

"I don't think the ant would get it," Hugo giggled, "because I don't get it either."

"Well, there you go then," Joe said. "We may have to accept that some things are beyond our understanding and be content with that. Just have faith that there is a God. Do you think that is possible?"

"I need to think about it," Hugo said, and went back to googling on his phone.

"If you are the Son of God," Sophie said, "why have you returned to Earth now?"

"It's nearly the end for mankind," Joe said matter-of-factly, "you know that. But it's still not too late to change things and avert disaster. Mankind could still create paradise on Earth. I want to try to guide them in that direction before it is too late. I want to help reduce suffering by creating a more peaceful, harmonious society, with everyone in the world working together instead of working against one another."

"What can we do to help?" Sophie asked, more than happy to go along with anything Joe wanted to do, regardless of whether or not she was totally convinced by the 'son-of-god' story. All she wanted at that moment was to be at his side wherever he went, listening to everything he said.

"What would you like to do?" Joe replied.

"You're right, Miss," Hugo said.

"About what?"

"He does always answer questions with more questions."

SIXTEEN

"There's a link," the Chinese agent informed her superior as she passed by. The girl was hardly able to suppress her excitement at having made a breakthrough where everyone else seemed to be failing.

"Please explain further," her superior replied, sitting beside the younger woman at her screen, polishing her glasses before replacing them and leaning in to look at the screen.

"The boy's phone…"

"Yung Zhang's son?"

"Yes, madam. These are the viral videos of the miracle worker, which the Americans and the Russians are so interested in – the boy is linked to this man. He is staying at the boy's school."

"This is the man who has no past?"

"That is correct. We have found nothing about him but we know from the boy's phone that the man is on his way to Yung Zhang's home with the teacher. It seems that Liang Zhang is a subject of interest to him."

"They have talked about him?"

"Yes, madam. The boy believes that he saw his father being arrested on his way to work."

"That is impossible," her superior said, staring at the screen without blinking. "Nothing is known about this man. He has simply disappeared."

"Of course," the young girl said quickly, worried she had spoken out of turn. "I am just reporting what the boy is saying."

"He is just a boy, so we must make allowances for imagination."

"I understand, madam."

"Anything else?"

"All the members of the group of twelve are also on their way to the same house, including the British lawyer who was recently asking questions in Beijing."

"So the man with no past is part of the same group of revolutionaries?"

"It is a possibility. Or perhaps they are planning to recruit him."

"Do we have any access into the house itself?"

"Very limited, madam. The only phones that are making it all the way inside the house belong to Yung Zhang herself and they are being swept for bugs every few hours, which limits what we can listen to."

* * * * *

The connection between Joe and the other high-profile people on their way to Yung's house was being made simultaneously in Washington and it was decided that it was time for the Director of National Intelligence to brief the President fully on what was happening.

"The President has already received briefings on the situation regarding Liang and Yung Zhang," he was informed, "but he does not know about this new connection."

"How do we know about it?"

"We overheard the Chinese talking about it."

"The Chinese knew about this before us?"

"Yes, sir."

"Goddammit! That will make him really angry."

"Perhaps it is a detail which is not relevant to the briefing," the agent suggested.

The Director nodded grimly and left for the White House. Inside the Oval Office the President was already puzzling over the report.

"Who are these damn people in New Zealand?" he demanded, before the Director had even made it all the way into the room.

"It is the group we mentioned to you before, sir. They are all highly regarded activists and experts in their various fields and they have formed a sort of think-tank…"

"Are these the climate change and meditation, re-forest the world and to hell with the economy bunch?"

"I think probably they are a little more than that, sir, but…"

"Don't you start trying to sell me all that bull about 'creating a better world'," the President barked. "We are doing a damn fine job with the one we've got. These guys are communists, liberals and anarchists, right?"

"It depends on your point of view, sir…"

"That is my point of view."

"Yes, sir."

"Is it a Chinese plot?" the President asked, slamming the report down on the desk. "Are they behind it? They sound like Chinese names to me."

"Yung Zhang is Chinese but she has had to flee the country. Her husband has 'disappeared'. The Chinese are just as concerned about what this group may be up to as we are."

"So we are concerned?" the President interrupted triumphantly. "We damn well should be. These people are trying to undermine international law and order and looking for ways to overthrow legitimate governments."

"Perhaps not exactly 'concerned', but we are aware of them and we know they all have big followings among the younger generations who are concerned with the way things are going. All they have done so far is meet and talk."

"We need to nip these socialist ideas in the bud, before the general public becomes any more infected by them. And this man who is doing all these healing tricks online; he's joining this group as well?"

"It's possible, sir."

"Tell the New Zealanders to close them down. They're potential terrorists. Lord knows what they are plotting down there. Didn't they have a shooting there in a mosque which hit the headlines?"

"Yes, sir."

"Well that's a good enough reason to close them down. Send in the troops. Do we have any troops down there?"

"I'm not aware of any in the area, sir."

"And you're head of our National Intelligence Service? My God, sort this mess out!"

The Director could see there was no point trying to explain anything in a logical fashion and withdrew to allow the President time to calm down and become distracted by something less vexing for him.

* * * * *

The Russian President was also being informed that Joe was on his way to Yung Zhang's house.

"We still have someone inside the house?" he asked, although it sounded from his tone as if he already knew that fact and was merely requiring confirmation.

"We do, sir."

"And they are well placed to inform us of anything that happens there?"

"They are, sir."

"Then let's wait and see what happens."

*****

The Chinese President listened carefully to the briefing from his nervous advisors.

"We need to understand much more about this group and their intentions," he said eventually. "Has Liang Zhang given us any information about what his wife and her co-conspirators are planning?"

"Nothing yet, Mr President."

"Then let's talk to him some more."

*****

Liang heard the sound of approaching footsteps and knew that they were coming for him. In a way he was grateful for a distraction from the endless hours of silence in the brightly lit cell, where he had nothing to do but sit on his chair and wait, all the time thinking about Yung and Hugo and wondering if they were safe or even still alive. But he still shivered and let out an involuntary whimper at the thought of the pain that the footsteps would inevitably bring with them.

It was the first time he had heard of a man called Joe. He was unable to answer any of the questions that his interrogator was putting to him and was therefore unable to stop the pain which was simultaneously being inflicted on bones that had been broken in previous interrogations. By the end of several hours of intense questioning he was able to ascertain that this man had a connection with his family. If the authorities were trying to find out more about that connection it suggested that Yung and Hugo were still out of their reach. Liang took considerable comfort from that thought once he had been dragged back to his cell and thrown onto the floor.

SEVENTEEN

Sophie and Joe noticed the armed guards even before they reached the tunnel and the gate inside the mountain. The uniformed figures were sitting at various vantage points along the mountain road, watching them through binoculars and apparently reporting on their approach into radios.

"Is there always this much security around your mother?" Sophie asked Hugo.

Looking up from his phone for a moment Hugo absorbed the scene and nodded, as if he took such matters for granted.

"Ever since Dad was arrested," he said. "Some of them have guns and everything. They are like mercenaries. It's quite cool, like a video game. I haven't seen them kill anyone yet, but I think they are trained to do it if they have to."

Sophie opened her mouth to say something but closed it again as Joe gave her hand a warning squeeze. He was right; this was not a good time to get into a philosophical discussion about the merits of violent video games. She would talk to Hugo later, once they were back at school.

As the car drove through the gates of Yung's house the increased levels of security were even more obvious now that more of the valuable guests were inside. The guards were still immaculately polite, but they insisted on searching both Joe and Sophie and their bags, and even Hugo had to relinquish his phone like all the others, although not without putting up a struggle. Once the security measures were complete and they were inside the mighty mountain structure, Sophie and Joe followed Hugo like sheep, with no idea where he was leading them.

The glass entrance hall contained a tropical garden, complete with full grown palm trees and groups of people strolling around or sitting amongst the foliage, talking and drinking coffee. It felt more like walking into a recess period during a conference in a very luxurious Middle Eastern hotel than being in someone's home.

"That's Haki," Hugo said, waving happily to an elegant young African man, who immediately broke off from the two earnest-looking women he had been talking to, and opened his arms to receive Hugo in a hug.

"Hugo, my man," he said, "how good to see you. Who are your friends?"

"This is my teacher, Miss Sophie."

"How do you do Miss Sophie." Haki shook her hand with a dazzling smile.

"Just 'Sophie' is fine," Sophie said. "This is my friend, Joe."

Haki shook hands with Joe, obviously assuming they were a couple, and returned his attention to Hugo.

"We are going to be spending some quality time together this weekend, my man," he said. "If your mother lets me out to play. I'll catch you later."

"That is Tanzeel Gemayel," Sophie whispered to Joe as they moved on past another group. "I've read all his books on the brain and meditation. He's a genius. And that is Dr Amelia Muloni who has created a chain of free healthcare centres all across Africa. I heard her speak once at a conference on world health. People say she is responsible for saving more lives than any other individual in history. She is awesome."

"She's the one Hugo looks on as an honorary grandmother?" Joe asked.

"That's her."

"These are all your heroes then?" Joe asked with a grin. "It looks like you are going to be having a wonderful weekend."

"It feels like a dream," Sophie replied.

Hugo ran across the room as his mother emerged from a door at the far end. Just as Sophie had imagined, Yung looked immaculate in the simplest but most expensive grey silk outfit she had ever seen. As her son skidded to a halt in front of her Yung bent elegantly from the waist, placing a beautifully manicured hand on his shoulder, and kissed him on both cheeks.

"This is Miss Sophie and Joe," he said as the others caught him up.

"Hello Sophie." Yung shook their hands. "We spoke, and I believe we met at the school. Hello Joe, welcome. It's a pleasure to see you both. Hugo has told me a lot about you. You seem to have made quite an impression."

She was obviously taken aback by how glamorous Joe was as she focused her attention on him. He was not at all how Hugo had described him but she could imagine how her son could be attracted to a man with such obvious charisma. It was more mysterious to her as to why such a man would want to spend the weekend at the home of a small boy he had just met, or why he would be with a simple schoolteacher, however nice she might be. She dismissed the thought from her head, having too many other, more urgent things to think about.

"I'm so sorry that I am not going to be able to spend much time with you this weekend," she said, "but I did warn Hugo that there would be a lot of people here. Hopefully you will find plenty of things to entertain you. Hugo will give you a tour and show you where the pool and the gym and the cinema are. There are also some fabulous mountain walks around here." She turned back to Hugo. "Introduce them to the kitchen staff, darling, so that they know who to ask if they feel they need anything." She turned back to Joe. "You are both very welcome to join us in here for meals but I would ask that you treat anything you might hear in the strictest confidence."

"Of course," Sophie replied, before Joe could say anything. "We completely understand."

"Settle them into the Blue Room, Hugo. They will enjoy the views from there."

Several people were standing a little way back now, waiting for a chance to speak to Yung. Sophie and Joe backed away, aware that their time with her was up.

"Your mother is so beautiful, Hugo," Sophie said as they left the hall.

"I know," Hugo said. "I take after her."

Sophie and Joe exchanged smiles above his head.

"You are indeed a beautiful soul, Hugo," Joe said as they walked down a seemingly endless corridor, the walls lined with carefully lit modern paintings.

The staff working in the quiet hum of the kitchen welcomed Hugo as fulsomely as Haki had done, despite the fact that they were obviously under pressure. Sophie guessed that he had probably spent more time with them over the years than with his preoccupied mother.

The recreation areas, including the swimming pool, were eerily deserted as Hugo continued the tour, ending in the deep blue bedroom that had been allocated to them, where the personal contents of their modest luggage had already been neatly laid out on the king-sized bed.

"This is one of the nicest rooms," Hugo announced, gesturing at the panoramic mountain views and then round the blue walls which were hung with North African paintings. "Mum says she saw this colour in Yves St Laurent's garden in Marrakech. Whoever that is."

"He was a famous fashion designer," Sophie said, absent-mindedly.

She felt herself blushing as she stared at the bed. Glancing at Joe she saw that he was watching her with an amused look. He winked, forcing her blush to darken still further and she walked quickly over to join Hugo who was gazing out at the mountains, her heart pounding in her chest.

"I didn't realise that your mother was friends with all these famous people," she said, eager to distract attention from the bed.

"Her 'group of twelve', do you mean?" Hugo replied, apparently not finding the subject particularly interesting. "That's what she calls them. Her 'group of twelve' or sometimes even 'The Twelve'. They often meet, but not usually all of them at one time. Mum says they are trying to work out ways to make the world a better place for everyone to live in, so it is important that I don't complain when she has long phone calls with them, or stays away for a meeting somewhere. Some of them are a bit boring but I like Haki."

"Do you mind her being so busy?" Sophie asked.

Hugo shrugged. "It would be nice to see more of her, but if they are going to make the world a better place then that is important too, isn't it, so sacrifices have to be made. That's what my dad would have told me."

"You are a wise young thing," Sophie said, putting her arm round his skinny shoulders and squeezing fondly.

"Shall we go for a swim?" Hugo asked, wriggling free and making for the door, unsure how to respond to physical shows of affection.

Half an hour later all three of them were in the pool, where they were joined by a slight man in his forties who dived straight in, causing barely a ripple, and swam ten fast lengths of immaculate crawl before surfacing, lifting his goggles and introducing himself.

"Hi," he said, with a dazzlingly white Californian smile. "My name is Lalit Wadia."

They talked for a while, exchanging admiring remarks about the house and the location and then Hugo became bored and persuaded Sophie to swim away with him in an underwater race.

"I'm told you are a very successful businessman," Joe said as the two men climbed into the Jacuzzi and laid back to enjoy the streams of warm bubbles.

"I have been very lucky," Lalit laughed. "So much of success is luck, don't you think?"

"It has a role to play," Joe replied doubtfully.

"I have a feeling you disagree. Are you humouring me, Joe?"

"Well, I would say you have to work hard too. The harder you work, the more likely you will come across opportunities which you might then classify as luck."

Joe lay back, closing his eyes and savouring the warmth of the water jets.

"So, what is it you do?" Lalit asked after a few moments.

"I try to help," Joe said without opening his eyes.

"Help who?"

"Whoever needs it."

"Help in what way?"

"Any way I can."

Sensing he wasn't going to get any more information than that, Lalit returned to the subject of himself, assuming that if Joe knew who he was, he might be feeling inadequate in his presence and was feigning ignorance to cover his discomfort.

"I am an investor, so I help people too. I help people who have good ideas to make them a reality."

"What sort of good ideas?"

"Alternative energy sources, energy conservation schemes,

anything that will assist us to clean up the air or the oceans, stop the degradation of forests, that sort of thing. There are a lot of people with very good ideas and in the past they have been crushed by the traditional investors who were too heavily in debt to the oil companies and other polluters. Electric cars, for instance, should have become the norm years ago, along with solar power and wind power. But we are beginning to turn the tide. Electric cars will be the norm soon, and solar panels and wind turbines are already playing a major role…"

"And you make a lot of money from these investments?"

"I do now because there is an appetite for clean products and sustainability, but it took a few years to convince people. We still have a long way to go. Too many companies pay lip service to sustainability but actually do whatever they have to do in order to keep growing their companies and paying their shareholders bigger dividends, regardless of the impact on the environment, or even the impact on their employees. It's pure greenwashing."

"Is that why you are here? To find ways to help more effectively?"

"Absolutely; and to exchange ideas with other people at the top of their fields. Yung is a powerhouse. It is her who has brought us all together."

"I was sorry to hear about her husband."

"That is what I admire most about her," Lalit said. "However hard it has been for her personally she has not allowed Liang's disappearance to deflect her from fighting for the causes she believes in. She is also a great believer in the potential of the Chinese way of doing things, once they have caught up with the rest of the world on the human rights issues." He was sitting forward now, warming to his theme. "You have to remember where the Chinese are coming from before you rush to judge them. Fifty to sixty years ago, when

111

everything was booming in the West with the 'swinging sixties' and all that, China was back in the Dark Ages with millions of people dying of starvation and maybe even resorting to cannibalism to survive. They have had to take some draconian steps to catch up, which makes them look very authoritarian to liberals in the West."

"People in the West know about the cannibalism?" Joe was obviously surprised.

"Not many people. The Chinese don't exactly go around shouting about it. They were bad times and when people are hungry enough they do desperate things. I have heard from reliable sources that they used to hang the bodies of people who had been found guilty of holding the wrong ideologies or beliefs on hooks outside the restaurants before butchering them and eating them inside."

"Every nation has times in its history that it would rather forget," Joe said. "What is it that they want to achieve ultimately, do you think?"

"The Chinese? They want harmony. That is what they have always believed in. That is the word they virtually worship. All that 'yin and yang' stuff. They want to create a harmonious society and they believe that the best way to do that is to make everyone think the same way and behave the same way. It's true, of course, that if an entire nation is pulling in the same direction – especially a nation as big as China – then you can create great things. But if you believe in the rights of the individual and the need for people to be free to follow their own paths in life, as Yung and Liang do, then it is not a comfortable place to live. What they have achieved in the last few decades is astonishing, but some of my colleagues here would say it has been at a terrible price for the environment and human rights..."

"You don't agree?"

"Well…" Lalit thought for a moment. "Most of the people in mainland China are happy to embrace their leaders, as often happens under dictatorial regimes. This is partly because of the very low levels of trust that the people have in their local leaders, who are often corrupt. This trust, however, will only last as long as the people continue to feel the benefits of strong economic growth – and that sort of growth always comes at a price."

His flow was interrupted by Hugo and Sophie joining them in the Jacuzzi.

"It was Joe who made the sun go out," Hugo announced once he was submerged up to his chin in bubbles. "And his videos have gone viral."

"Is that right?" Lalit raised a well-groomed eyebrow.

"Apparently so," Joe said. "Hugo is my adviser in such matters as the internet and smartphones."

"It is my belief that Hugo is going to grow up to change the world," Lalit said. "I will certainly be backing any ideas he has."

"Oh, I agree," Sophie said. Her encouraging smile was lost on Hugo who had taken his glasses off before throwing himself into the pool.

Dinner that evening was presented on a long buffet table covered in a variety of dishes. Small tables were set up around the main hall so that people could choose who they sat with. Sophie and Joe found themselves at a table with Lalit and Simon Dalton, the human rights lawyer who had just been in Beijing, trying to locate Liang's whereabouts, and Lalit's daughter, a student called Alice who happened to be travelling around New Zealand at the time the meeting was arranged and jumped at the chance to enjoy a few days of luxury, with the added hope of spending some time with her father.

Simon rose slightly from his chair as they joined the table, shaking them by the hand and nodding a greeting. He was not a man who indulged in unnecessary small talk and he was obviously wary of these two newcomers. The others had glasses of wine and plates filled with selections of delicacies in front of them but Simon was drinking from a tumbler of water and eating a large bowl of minestrone.

Hugo had lost interest in adult company and had found a young girl called Shani, the daughter of Salma, who also joined their table. Simon obviously had no interest in engaging in conversation with the children. However much he might adore his own grandchildren, the charms of other people's children entirely passed him by.

Lalit made the introductions as Salma sat down. "This is Sophie, who is Hugo's teacher and an educationalist like yourself, Salma. This is Joe, who performs miracles."

"Do you indeed, Joe?" Salma said, nodding a greeting to Sophie, who suddenly realised that she was sharing a table with a woman she had read a great deal about. Salma had made it her mission to educate every girl in the world to the same standard as the most educated boys. Being from Egypt she had met with great resistance in many of the more traditional Middle Eastern countries but had refused to be discouraged, even by death threats. So far she had set up schools in virtually every country where a proportion of the population was either too poor or too discriminated against to be able to get any other sort of education. Sophie had a feeling that she had read somewhere that Lalit was one of Salma's most generous financial backers.

"He does indeed," Lalit laughed, "according to Hugo. And if only we were allowed access to our phones we could watch the videos."

Salma took a mouthful of food and stared thoughtfully

at Joe as she chewed. "Ah," she said eventually, "you are that man. I believe I have been shown the videos. You healed some people in a shopping mall somewhere around here, am I right?"

"I helped them, yes," Joe said, raising an eyebrow at Lalit.

Lalit laughed. "That is what he told me his profession was, Salma, when I asked him. 'I help people', was all he said. The man is an enigma!"

"You are a healer?" Salma asked, ignoring Lalit.

Sophie was bursting to announce that Joe was claiming to be the Son of God, but even as she ran the thought through her mind she realised how foolish it would make her sound, so she remained quiet. No doubt they would find out soon enough, when Joe was ready to reveal himself. Under the table Joe pressed her hand, as if he knew how much she wanted to blurt out the full story. The warmth and strength of his palm encasing her small hand made her fearful for a moment that she might faint from a surge of pleasure the like of which she had never experienced before. All she could think of was that in a few hours they would be sharing a bed in the most beautiful room she had ever seen.

"Hugo also informed me that Joe was responsible for turning the sun out the other day," Lalit said. Sophie could tell that he didn't believe any of it and was subtly trying to expose Joe as some sort of charlatan. Her instinct was to speak up in Joe's defence but still she resisted the temptation, knowing that he was perfectly capable of looking after himself and unsure how much he wanted to share with this group of people.

"Is that right?" Simon finally joined the conversation, assuming Lalit was joking. "Well I wish you hadn't because it meant I was stuck at Hong Kong Airport for a couple of very uncomfortable hours while they decided whether it was safe to resume flying."

"My apologies," Joe grinned and there was no way for any

of them to tell if he was teasing them or not. "I did not fully think through the consequences."

Simon looked at him hard, as if trying to see inside his head and work out if he was a fraud of some sort, while several of the others laughed, assuming it was no more than dinnertable banter. Simon was beginning to think that he might like this young man, although it was too early for him to commit himself.

Once the evening was over and Sophie and Joe were back in the blue room, they opened the curtains so that they would be able to wake up the next morning to the spectacular view. Sophie followed Joe's lead and tried to make it seem like the most natural thing in the world that they should undress in front of one another and then climb into the same bed. He lay on his side and she could smell his sweet breath on her face. She wanted to kiss him but didn't know how to start without risking rejection or demonstrating that she had misunderstood whatever was going on between them. She had never before been in the position of being in bed with someone and wanting them so much it physically hurt. Joe let out a satisfied sigh, as if preparing himself for sleep, and put his arm around her, holding her close. She wished that her body would soften and she could just melt into him, but instead she felt herself become rigid with doubt and indecision, staring at the outline of the mountains against the starlit sky as she sensed him slipping into a deep, peaceful sleep beside her.

She remained tense throughout the night, which probably contributed to the overwhelming urge she felt in the morning to burst into tears. Joe appeared not to notice that anything was wrong as she climbed out of the bed and headed for the door.

"I'm going for a swim," she said, grabbing her costume on the way. "I'll meet you for breakfast."

He opened his mouth to say that he would like to swim too but she had already left the room, desperate to be out of his sight before he noticed her tears.

Simon Dalton was leaving the pool as Sophie came in and gave a curt nod of greeting.

"Good morning," he said.

"Good morning," she replied, unsure what to say next. "Are you going to breakfast?"

"I plan to take a short walk before breakfast," he informed her matter-of-factly. "The scenery out there really is spectacular and I fear we are going to be stuck inside a great deal in the coming days." He gave another nod and walked briskly on without a backward glance.

Sophie watched him for a moment and wondered how old he was. His manner suggested he might be over sixty but he was obviously in peak physical condition. She guessed that must have something to do with the fact that he swam and walked before breakfast and ate and drank only soup and water at dinner, even when presented with an unending choice of delicacies.

Dr Amelia Muloni was already doing lengths in the pool when Sophie got there. She was obviously a powerful swimmer. Sophie dived in quickly, hoping that the doctor had not had time to see the redness of her eyes, and ploughed up and down the lengths in another lane. A few minutes later they arrived at the shallow end of the pool at the same time and the doctor paused, lifting up her goggles.

"Are you all right, child?" she asked.

Sophie nodded silently, not trusting her voice to stay steady. Amelia was not fooled for a moment. Opening her arms wide she folded Sophie in against her and held her tightly until the sobbing had died away.

"You poor, sweet child," Amelia crooned. "Is it a man that

is causing you this grief? Is it that glorious-looking man you arrived with?"

"He is glorious looking, isn't he?" Sophie sniffled.

"He is indeed, my child, but so are you, and there is no glory to be gained from making a lovely young girl cry."

Sophie laughed, her store of tears temporarily spent and Amelia joined her with a deep, throaty chuckle.

"That's better, child," she said. "No man is worth your tears. Has he hurt you physically?"

"Oh no," Sophie said, shocked by the very thought. "He is the sweetest, gentlest creature that ever lived. This is not his fault. He has no idea how I feel about him. We are not in a relationship, we are just friends. I only just met him. It's difficult to explain."

"You don't have to explain anything, girl, not unless you want to. But you need to work on your self-esteem. Have you any idea how beautiful you are? Just look at yourself." Amelia gestured down at Sophie's figure. "Damn, I wish I looked like that in a swimming costume."

Sophie laughed again. "Thank you."

"I've done enough of this exercising for today," Amelia said, pulling herself out of the pool in one fluid movement. "I'm going to look for some breakfast. You up for that?"

"Yes, I believe I am," Sophie said, taking a towelling dressing gown from the doctor's outstretched hand. She could completely understand why Hugo was so fond of her.

Joe had reached the breakfast buffet while Sophie was still in the pool and was aware that he was receiving even more curious looks than had come his way the previous evening.

"Word has spread," Lalit said, joining him at the buffet table, "and everyone has had time to check out your miracles online." Joe glanced back at the room and saw that everyone was now staring at the two of them, as if trying to read their lips. "You seem to have caught everyone's imagination."

"I thought electronic devices weren't allowed in the house."

"Yung has hers because she gets them swept every few hours, the rest of us have to get ours from security and go outside, like secret cigarette smokers. You should have seen us all huddled against the side of the mountain late last night, watching you raising the dead."

"Not sure I went quite that far…"

"Well, whatever you did had much the same impact."

"I see." Joe chuckled at the image of these global intellectuals all staring at their phones, watching the goings-on in a shopping mall.

"Hugo is now telling everyone that you are claiming responsibility for turning the sun out, and that you initially told him and his friends that your name was Jesus."

"And how does everyone feel about that?"

"Well Haki nearly fainted in ecstasy, as you can imagine. The scientists don't want to believe it, obviously, because otherwise they are going to have to re-think everything that they have believed throughout their adult lives. Big brains don't always lead to the most open minds, you know. There were some very heated words exchanged last night after you had retired to bed."

"And you? What do you think?"

"Me?" Lalit took a bite of a croissant and chewed thoughtfully. "I'm not sure, but I look forward to seeing what you are going to do next."

EIGHTEEN

"We cannot remain locked inside this building for the whole week," Yung announced to the entire house party after breakfast, "so we have arranged for transport to take us for a late-night adventure to a very special place tonight. It is called the Church of the Good Shepherd on Lake Tekapo. Whatever our religious views might be, we will all benefit from a little spiritual time out. During the day the church has some of the most spectacular views on the planet, but it also becomes very crowded with tourists, so we have decided to wait until they have left. The sky is forecast to be clear tonight and so our view will take us beyond the immediate scenery and out to the stars."

At the mention of the words "religious views" everyone looked in Joe's direction again, but he appeared not to notice, sipping contentedly on his coffee while waiting for Hugo to make a move on the chessboard that stood between them.

The Twelve spent the day locked into their meeting in the room with the picture window, while Joe and Sophie and the other guests entertained themselves around the pool or strolled outside, under the watchful eyes of the guards. The extended group was already starting to bond as if they were the last people left on Earth. Several of them had noticed that when they were with Joe they were able to talk in their local native tongues without even thinking about it and he would be able to answer fluently. It was the first time Haki had ever met someone outside Rwanda who was able to speak Kinyarwanda and just hearing the language of his childhood so far from the jungle village made him weep with a mixture of pleasure and pain.

Changing languages to fit the ear of whoever was listening seemed so natural to Joe that some of the others didn't immediately notice that they had moved away from English when they were with him. Once they had realised, and had heard him doing the same in other languages with other members of the group, they began to feel even more strongly that this was not an ordinary man who was now moving amongst them. They could not, however, quite work out what he was or why he filled them with such illogical feelings of awe, way beyond any logical admiration for his skills with languages and his ability to heal.

During supper, an air of excitement built up as they prepared for their outing, like children being allowed out of school for a special treat. On the courtyard at the front of the house a fleet of electric limousines was lined up in the spotlights, ready to receive the party as they made their way obediently outside. Their progress was discreetly overseen by a number of people wearing earpieces and talking into radios. Each car had a driver who looked more like a soldier than a chauffeur and there were two Range Rovers which contained more security staff, one to ride at the front of the caravan of vehicles and one at the back.

"If going to church had always been this much of an adventure I might have gone a bit more often," Sophie whispered to Amelia as the two of them were ushered towards one of the cars with Joe and Amelia's elderly husband, Pius.

"Going to the house of the Lord is always an adventure," Pius said, having overheard the comment, and for the first time Sophie noticed he was wearing a clerical collar.

"This is my husband, Pius," Amelia chuckled. "He is a bishop back home in Uganda. He has been hiding himself away in our room today, resting after our journey here."

In deference to the Bishop's age Joe and Sophie stood back as he was ushered into the front seat beside the driver.

"Pius, dear," Amelia said once they were seated, "this is my young friend, Sophie. We swam together before breakfast. And this is her young man, Joe, who everyone has been talking about."

The Bishop twisted uncomfortably in his seat and shook both of them solemnly by the hand.

"I believe my wife has taken a shine to you, young lady," he told Sophie, before nodding curtly to Joe. "And I shall be interested to hear your views, young man, on the things that some of the people here are saying about you."

"I'm not sure I have any views on what other people say about me," Joe laughed, "but it will be an honour to hear what you think."

"What I am wondering," the Bishop said in the same sing-song voice he used for his sermons, "is whether you fully understand the meaning of words such as 'blasphemy' and 'sacrilege'?"

"Pius, dear," his wife admonished him and gave the back of his seat a sharp smack. "I trust you are not going to get on your high horse all the way to this lovely place."

"Your husband has nothing to worry about," Joe assured her. "I am fully conversant with all the words of the English language. Hopefully by the end of the day he will have found faith."

Despite the stiffness in his old neck, the Bishop turned again in his seat and stared hard at Joe. "By the end of the day?" he said, but Joe was already staring out of the window at the mountains silhouetted against the night sky.

"Men!" Amelia murmured under her breath, squeezing Sophie's hand reassuringly. "They just can't leave anything be, can they? Tell me more about your school, my dear. Yung tells me that you are a wonderful teacher and Salma was singing the praises of the school and your headmaster."

The Bishop and Joe fell silent as the women talked and the caravan of cars snaked through the mountains, eventually emerging beside the spectacular moonlit waters of Lake Tekapo, drawing up in an empty car park beside a small stone church that stood alone in the headlights of the cars. The security people in the Range Rovers fanned out around the site, scanning the silent black horizons in every direction.

"Oh, my Lord," Amelia said as they climbed out of the car, "that is a truly beautiful sight."

"God is bountiful indeed," her husband agreed, straightening up slowly and breathing the crystal-clear air deep into his lungs as he walked slowly and purposefully towards the door of the church.

"This is how the whole world once looked," Minenhle said to no one in particular as she walked over from the following car. "And one day maybe it will again. Hallelujah!"

"No doubt she will find evidence of climate change here somewhere," the professor's wife muttered to her husband.

"A bountiful sight indeed," Joe whispered in Sophie's ear, holding out his arm. As she looped her own arm over his elbow she felt herself glowing with a heat she had never experienced before.

"Please extinguish the lights," Yung called to the drivers. All the car engines fell silent and darkness settled over the landscape. As their eyes adapted to the moonlight they all looked up at the glittering blanket of stars that covered the sky above the tips of the surrounding mountains. A murmur of amazement at the beauty, majesty and enormity of the sight passed across the group as they stared upwards and for a few moments nobody spoke.

The warmth which had filled Sophie's body was intensifying, making her feel a little dizzy as she stared up into the never ending universe above. She wondered if she was going to faint and leaned more heavily on Joe's arm to stop herself from falling, closing her eyes to try to clear her brain and maintain her balance. The heat inside her grew more intense and she heard several people letting out exclamations of surprise. Opening her eyes and glancing around, she saw that everyone was now staring in their direction and she felt simultaneously embarrassed and inordinately proud.

"Oh my Lord, child," Amelia murmured, "just look at the two of you."

Looking down at herself, Sophie realised that her skin was actually glowing, sending out a radiance which all the others could see. It was even outshining the spectacular skies above. She knew it must be emanating from Joe because she could feel it passing through her and he was glowing too. She looked up into his face and saw that he was entirely at peace, unconcerned by the looks of amazement all around him.

"Pius," Amelia called out to her husband, who had just reached the door of the church, "what do you have to say to this in all your wisdom?"

The old man turned and stared towards the light shining from Joe and Sophie, which now bathed the entire party in its golden glow. He walked slowly back as everyone waited to hear his reply.

"Who are you, Son?" he asked as he drew close. "In God's name, who are you?"

"Let's go into my father's house," Joe replied, walking forward with Sophie still on his arm, placing a reassuring hand on the Bishop's shoulder as he passed.

As they entered through the door, Sophie could barely breathe. This, she thought, must be how brides feel on their wedding days.

The light stayed with them as they went inside, spreading to every corner of the modest building and turning the simple altar at the far end to pure gold. The rest of the party followed behind, many of them speechless, others whispering to one another in a mixture of puzzlement and amazement. Joe guided Sophie to a seat in the front row and then released her arm and stood by the altar, facing the door with his arms spread open in a gesture of welcome as the others all followed and found seats.

When the last member of the party was inside, Yung instructed the security men to close the doors and encircle the building. The expectant silence was total. One by one, Joe called out the names of the group of Twelve and asked them to come up and stand in a line in front of him. One by one they obeyed, with no idea why they felt so compelled to do so, some of them looking as if they had been hypnotised or dazzled by the light, none of them questioning his instructions.

"I have come back out of love for this planet and its inhabitants," he said once they were all assembled, "to tell you that I have chosen you to be my apostles, the twelve people who will lead mankind into the light under my guidance."

Haki crumpled to his knees and bowed his head in humility and Dr Amelia let out a murmured "Hallelujah" as the others watched in confusion, unable to work out how they were feeling or what they should be doing about it.

"The road will be long and difficult," Joe warned, "and you will have to make many sacrifices. You are flesh and blood and you have all succumbed to many of the temptations of that flesh. You must come out from behind the walls you have erected around your houses and from behind the security gates and move amongst all the people whom you are going to save."

None of them looked up but all of them knew what he meant. Yung's house wasn't the only one covered in cameras and alarms and surrounded by armed guards. Many of them had separated themselves off from the rest of the world since becoming rich and successful, claiming they were protecting their families when in fact they were really protecting themselves against imagined enemies they had never actually seen or heard.

"You will have to give up your private jets and yachts," Joe continued and Lalit let out an involuntary sigh, knowing that he was the worst offender when it came to indulging in expensive and climate-destructive toys.

Even the most sceptical atheists in the group were finding it hard to hold back the tears as they realised that everything they had ever believed to be true now had to be questioned. As they emerged from the church the Bishop lowered himself painfully to his arthritic knees and kissed Joe's hand as others gathered around. Sophie stepped back to allow them to get closer, watching from the sidelines.

"Wow," a voice next to her said.

She turned to find Lalit's daughter, Alice, staring at her with wide-eyed amazement.

"Can you believe that your boyfriend is actually the Son of God? I mean, can you actually believe that?"

Sophie laughed. "He's not really my boyfriend. I wish he was."

"Doesn't it scare you?"

"What?"

"Well the whole thing, but mainly becoming one of the most famous people in the world and having billions of people knowing everything about you. Just the thought of it totally blows my mind. I mean it's weird enough to think that my dad is one of the twelve apostles chosen to save mankind – but to actually be hanging out with the Son of God… I mean – Wow!"

"I hadn't quite thought of it like that," Sophie admitted. "But now you've said it…"

"He's so cool about the whole thing too. It's like he knew this whole scenario was going to happen. And my dad has been saying for years that we need someone to save us, some great spiritual leader to step forward, unite the world and show us the way out of the mess we have got ourselves into. And now he just appears out of nowhere in this amazing place."

"Do you have a boyfriend?" Sophie asked.

"I did until I told him I was going to go travelling for a year. It seems he had different plans."

"Well at least you know something about this whole relationship business. This is the first serious relationship of my life, and I'm not even sure it is a relationship yet. It feels more like I've got a crush on this unattainable figure."

"What, like I might have felt about Justin Bieber when I was twelve?" Alice grinned.

Sophie sighed. "It doesn't sound that great when you put it like that."

Alice laughed and linked her arm through Sophie's. "I reckon your chances are a lot better than mine ever were with the Bieb, even though my dad hired him to sing at my birthday party."

"Your father hired Justin Bieber for a children's party?"

"I know," Alice grimaced. "He is so going to have to rein himself in if he's going to do this gig."

As everyone returned slowly to the cars they had come in, all of them reluctant to admit that the golden moment by the lake was over, the Bishop held open the front door of their car, indicating that Joe should now take his seat.

"No," Joe said shaking his head and embraced the old man gently. "You must travel in the front. You have served God faithfully all your life, you have earned some privileges."

Too choked up to be able to speak clearly, the Bishop climbed into the front, pulling out a neatly folded linen handkerchief from his top pocket to wipe away the tears. Several of the scientists were huddled together; their heads close as they whispered to one another, trying to find a logical explanation for the scene they had just witnessed. Sophie noticed that they seemed to be splitting into different factions as they were ushered back into the cars.

NINETEEN

Back at the house the atmosphere had changed. A light meal had been prepared but it was a strangely subdued affair. Joe and Sophie sat with Yung and a sleepy but cheerful-looking Hugo, almost as if they were a family unit, while the others talked quietly at other tables, often casting glances in their direction. Now and then some of those who had not spoken to Joe before came over to introduce themselves and profess their admiration while others held back, unable to let go of their long-held scepticism.

"I think we should have a short meeting of the Twelve before we go to bed," Yung told him as they ate. "Would you like to join us?"

"Will you be okay on your own?" Joe asked Sophie.

"I don't think I will be on my own much any more," Sophie replied. "It seems like everyone would now like to be my friend."

"Most popular teacher in the school!" Joe laughed. "Enjoy it. You deserve it."

Once the Twelve and Joe were settled in the main drawing room with pots of coffee and tea, Yung took the floor, addressing Joe directly.

"I am not sure what to say," she said. "If you are the Son of God then you will already know everything that has happened and everything that we have been talking about in our meetings over the last few years. We have spent most of our time brainstorming and making plans for the steps mankind needs to take in order to avoid imminent extinction. Individually we have all been doing our best to disseminate the ideas that we have been discussing through talks, articles and academic papers.

"Although we have all been successful in our own fairly narrow fields during those years, we cannot claim that we have been able to catch the public imagination or the attention of the mass media when it comes to explaining the urgency of the problems facing mankind. We have all now had a chance to see the impact of your miracles on the internet. That is exactly the sort of viral coverage we have always been hoping for in order to get our messages out there and to provoke fast reactions from those in power, but of course we have never achieved it. Most of the world does not want to listen to the dry ramblings of a bunch of professionals and academics. Even with the social media skills of people like Lalit, we have not been able to ignite the imaginations of people in the numbers that we need. We know exactly what we want to achieve by way of changes and we have prepared plans to meet all the possible outcomes of the things that are going wrong. Simon, for instance, has prepared a detailed SWOT analysis which shows the essence of the actual situation of mankind on Earth."

"SWOT?" Joe raised a quizzical eyebrow. "Like swatting an annoying fly?"

"No," Simon smiled, "not quite. It's an acronym for analysing the 'Strengths, Weaknesses, Opportunities and Threats' that face any company, so that you can draw up a realistic plan. It occurred to me that there is no reason not to apply the same principles to the problems facing mankind."

"SWOT?" Joe tried the word out again.

"You analyze the internal organisation by identifying the

most essential strengths and weaknesses and you also look at the external environment, such as markets, where they are active in identifying the most important opportunities and threats. And then you check how the internal situation and the external environment are connected. It is a very useful tool as a starting point for setting up a long-term strategic plan. As always it is a precondition that the managers who participate in this process dare to be vulnerable because the interests of the organisation are higher than theirs.

"It doesn't just apply to businesses. I have developed the habit of rewriting my own funeral speech every ten years. So I imagine that I have died and I look back at myself. I started doing it when I was twenty. Only after I have written the new one do I remove the previous editions from my safe. Then I read them all and I see how my ideas, my strengths and talents, my weaknesses, my possibilities, my fears and my environment have developed. So I do a SWOT analysis of myself, which helps me to make a strong assessment of whether I have become a better person towards others or whether I am stuck in selfish and self-centred attitudes. It clearly illuminates the possibilities for the future. I realised that you could make such an analysis of mankind as a whole."

"When Simon joined this group," Yung interrupted, "the global SWOT analysis became the basis of our approach, as a means, of course, not as a goal. We wanted to set up this analysis and create a plan for the world, without limiting ourselves to existing frameworks and obstacles."

"In other words," Simon said, unable to control his enthusiasm for the idea, "we asked ourselves the question: What if we were indeed the boss of the world and had a licence to implement a coalition agreement, what would we do? And how? And with whom? And at what pace?"

"And what were the results of this SWOT analysis?" Joe asked.

"What did you consider to be the main strengths of mankind?"

"We, Homo sapiens, have always been very creative. It is incredible what we have achieved in the relatively short time that we have been here, from the pyramids to the music of Bach and Elvis, the paintings of Van Gogh, penicillin, photography, telephony, cars, aircraft, nuclear capacity, the theory of relativity, the DNA discovery, landing on the moon and on a comet, the PC, the microchip, the internet, MRI, the Channel Tunnel, robots…"

"Okay," Joe laughed, "I get the message."

"We also possess huge reserves of perseverance, dealing with so much suffering and injustice. We have endured famine, wars and terrible epidemics and we always carry on. Combine creativity and perseverance with an infinite curiosity and an unbreakable streak of optimism and you have identified our strongest points."

"And the weaknesses?"

"We have a lot, and we face a lot of threats as well. We have become materialistic and greedy. We are the most devastating mammals that have ever existed. We have eradicated countless other species and now we find our own survival threatened. The concept of 'survival of the fittest' has led to enormous inequality. One and a half billion people still live in extreme poverty; nearly a billion people are chronically undernourished. A child dies from starvation every six seconds. A significant percentage of the world's population has no access to clean drinking water, primary care, housing and education. The solidarity needed to solve these problems does not exist in the rich countries. We pretend that poverty is a natural phenomenon and that capitalism is a natural drive but it is not. It is man-made. We have chosen it. And the financial world just wants business as usual.

"There is also a lot of intolerance, which has led to

mankind creating an enormous arsenal of terrible weapons and raised the amount invested in defence every year to more than 1,800 billion US dollars. At the same time the battle against drugs seems to have been lost and we may face catastrophic terrorism with biological, chemical, nuclear and conventional bombs being launched by evil lunatics and fundamentalists. And soon autonomous offensive weapons, which cannot be killed, will be able to fight us without mercy."

"A really huge problem, of course, is the overpopulation on our planet," Yung said. "And by 2050 the global population will have increased by another thirty per cent."

"Then we have climate changes caused by human activities," Minenhle added. "Reducing global warming is an absolute necessity if we are to avoid weather which is too extreme for us to survive. Our continual thirst for growth is totally incompatible with the care our natural system needs and deserves."

"Raw materials are running out," Simon explained, "and soon there will be wars caused by water and food scarcity."

"To continue as we are is really not an option," Yung said. "A momentous blow is coming, but if we work together we may have just enough time to avert the collapse. If we don't, within a few generations mankind will become extinct, or will have to live on a hostile Mars, which is the only potential 'Planet B', and that will only be possible for those rich enough to afford the fare.

"To be able to implement an effective plan, humanity have to be united but we are enormously divided, Joe. The speed at which the current world leaders are developing a joint worldwide policy is far too slow. I'm afraid even in a global pandemic or after a devastating meteorite impact, they wouldn't work well together, but would all try to manage it on their own.

"And then we have the technological developments which

create opportunities but bring other dangers. We are investing trillions of dollars in fields we do not understand, like children playing with explosives. Only a few visionaries have seen where this could all lead. My husband is an expert in genetic engineering, searching for ways to fight hereditary diseases. Every day a new biological tool is added to modify genes, manipulate DNA and enable us to create variants on the norm.

"We can already equip people with non-organic body parts, soon we will be able to make brains and computers interact, adding knowledge and skills or burning away traumatic and undesired emotions or barriers. We will become less and less human. The rich will be able to buy degeneration-inhibiting treatments, staying young forever, increasing the population still further.

"We also need to watch the data-people carefully. In the age of dataism, unscrupulous people who can collect enough biometric data will be able to manipulate people, making all their decisions for them with far less heart.

"Deep learning on the internet will allow machines to become even more intelligent. An electron is a million times faster than a human neuron. I cannot guarantee that robots will not be able to create their own will, intuition and consciousness, which means eventually they will be able to create a strategy. What value would we be to them then? Will they need us once they are capable of reproducing themselves, causing an intelligence explosion? AI is alien intelligence and people will become less and less human if they do not stay in control of it.

"So do we continue to cherish freedom and democracy, or should we govern in a more autocratic way, admitting to ourselves that people have always proved bad with handling power? The big challenge for us is to get listened to on the global stage. Most of us can raise an audience in any university or on a platform at the United Nations or at Davos, but when it comes to talking to the other ninety per cent of the world's population...

"We have been saying for some time that what we desperately need is a charismatic figurehead who can unite the whole world. It seems that you truly are a gift from Heaven."

To her own surprise, Yung found her voice cracking with emotion. She had been working for so many years, chipping away at all the problems of the world, being knocked back every time she seemed to be making any progress that it was hard to believe they were finally on the cusp of making a breakthrough. It felt like all the fears and frustrations that she had been bottling up for years had suddenly been let free and she was being swept away on a wave of emotion. Joe stood up and hugged her tightly, aware of the tension trembling through every muscle in her spare frame as she sobbed into his chest.

"I'm here now," he said. "Allow me to serve you in any way I can. And for those of you who do not yet quite believe that this is true, I understand. I also know that one of you will betray me." He held up his hand to silence them as they all raised their heads and voices in protest. "The traitor already knows who they are and they need to know that I understand them as well and that when the time comes I will forgive them."

TWENTY

"It's like a snowball," Hugo explained to Sophie and Joe as they drove back to school the following afternoon. "When a video goes viral it starts by being shared by the people involved and their followers. If each of those people shares it with two or three more people and each of those people does the same – well" – he pushed up his glasses, which had slid down his nose as usual – "you can see it will just spread faster and faster."

"Like that ancient Indian story of doubling the number of grains of rice on each square of a chessboard," Sophie added. "If you keep doubling up then on the last square you end up with more than two hundred billion tons of rice."

"Plus," Hugo said, excited by his own understanding of the subject, "word of mouth makes other people start searching the video out and continuing to share it with their followers, including news organisations and influencers with thousands or even millions of followers of their own. That's how it comes out at billions of viewings within a few days."

"You make it sound so simple," Joe laughed.

"You should become a teacher, Hugo," Sophie said.

"It is simple," Hugo said. "Unless you're thick or something."

"Hugo!" Sophie laughed.

"He may be right," Joe said ruefully.

What Hugo did not anticipate in his explanation, was that because the videos of Joe had become hard news, the traditional media, renowned for their ruthlessness in pursuit of scandal and sensation of any sort and desperate to stay ahead of the digital news cycle, now wanted to follow the story up and were already digging around for other angles and more in-depth explanations than were available on platforms like YouTube and Twitter. They also wanted to do it faster and more eye-catchingly than any of their competitors and whatever they came up with would then be spread on the internet as well, increasing the noise but diluting the core messages, making Joe even more famous but confusing people as to who he actually was and what he was actually doing on Earth.

The scale of what had been happening over the weekend, while they had been locked inside Yung's mountain retreat, only fully dawned on them as their car drew close to the school premises and they found their way blocked by an ocean of bodies, many of whom had cameras and recording devices. The crowd had been further swelled by people who had seen the videos and wanted Joe to perform personal miracles for them, hundreds of them bringing their sick friends and relatives in the hope that he would be able to heal them in the same way as the miracles they had witnessed online.

"I am not going to be able to get through to the gates," the driver warned.

"Don't worry," Joe said, "drop us here and we'll walk."

"Are you sure, sir?" The driver obviously didn't think that was a good idea but did not feel it was his place to insist. Seeing that there was already a police presence on the edges of the crowd which would provide his charges with some protection, he reluctantly unlocked the doors and released them.

Joe stepped out, not noticing how scared Sophie and Hugo looked as they followed him into the crowd. For a few moments no one spotted he was there, those standing near to the car assuming it was just one more person trying to jostle their way closer to the school gates, but as he moved further into the dense mass of bodies people began to turn round and the exclamations of those who were closest to him spread outwards like ripples on the surface of a pond. The tide turned and the weight of struggling bodies surged in on them.

"Joe," a harsh man's voice with a Scottish accent cut through the noise, "do you really fancy yourself to be the Son of God?"

Joe was taken aback by the rudeness of the voice and simply smiled in the direction it had come from. Other voices now competed for his attention, photographers and cameramen wanting him to "turn this way", reporters pushing their phones under his chin and shouting questions at him like "How does it feel to be divine?" and "Can you walk on water, Joe?" and "Aren't you worried about being killed again?"

It was as if they were angry with him for daring to become so famous overnight, challenging him to justify his existence, to prove himself to be who he claimed he was. There were too many voices now for him to hope to make any sort of personal connection to any of them, but that didn't stop more from joining in, raising the noise level and increasing the pressure coming from the back of the mass of bodies that was now struggling to get closer, threatening to crush those at the front.

If the media seemed to want to expose him as a fraud and no more than another cult leader, the rest of the crowd were clamouring out to convey their adoration and to attract his attention, wanting to let him know how much they loved him and how much they needed his help and his blessing. Scuffles began to break out as the well-wishers attempted to break through the ranks of reporters and photographers who were blocking their way to him. A punch was thrown and a nose spurted blood. Temperatures rose and more punches were traded as tempers snapped after a long day of standing around, waiting in the hot sun for this moment, for this chance at the biggest story on the planet in two thousand years.

Joe heard Hugo calling out for help and turned to see that he had been knocked to the ground and was unable to get back on his feet. Leaning over, Joe lifted him up so their heads were level.

"Are you okay?" he asked.

"I think so," Hugo said, "but I've lost my glasses."

There was no chance of being able to find them beneath the trampling feet of the herd as it pressed ever tighter around them. Joe saw Sophie's head bobbing around as she was pushed from side to side. With his spare arm he reached out and pulled her to him. The police, dressed in riot gear, had seen the violence breaking out and decided it was now time to intervene. They charged, cutting a path through the bodies with their batons and encircling Joe, Sophie and Hugo, forcing back the crowd. Joe could see that there was a group of wheelchairs in the middle of the scrum, both the people sitting in them and those pushing them were looking desperate and were obviously frightened that they were about to be crushed between the police and the media.

"We'll escort you to the gates, sir," the closest policeman shouted.

"It's all right, officer," Joe said. "They will let us through. I trust them. Just let me get to the people who need me. You can trust them. Have faith."

"Sir!" the policeman shouted, but Joe was already moving out of earshot.

With Hugo in one arm and Sophie held close with the other he began to walk, one step at a time towards the wheelchairs and the sea slowly parted in front of him like a withdrawing tide. The reporters still shouted their questions as they drew back but allowed Joe a few feet of space on each side as if held back by an invisible cordon. The police lowered their batons and watched as he reached the wheelchairs and talked to the people, laying his hand on their heads and on the heads of those who were with them. Everyone he touched rejoiced and wept and embraced him.

The shouting seemed to grow quieter at the centre of the crowd, while those at the back still bickered and pushed to get closer. Everyone, both media professionals and visitors, watched as Joe moved amongst the sick and touched them and talked to them. As things calmed down he was able to put Hugo back on the ground and Sophie took a firm hold of the boy's hand as they stood watching with everyone else. Hugo did not protest, straining to see everything that was happening without the help of his glasses.

All the time more people were arriving at the site. As word spread through the internet that Joe was actually there and actually healing people, more media started to turn up and the sound and wind of helicopter blades above the heads of the crowd added to the dust and the buzz. The pressure from the outside of the crowd was increasing, despite the fact that the police were trying to hold people back, and new media people were managing to fight their way to the front. As Joe crouched down to talk to a pretty child in a wheelchair there was a sudden surge of photographers trying to get the perfect picture.

"Heal her Joe!" one shouted.

"Get her to walk!" shouted another.

"Look this way, love!"

The people behind the chair were knocked over and the chair tipped to the side. Sensing that a great news story was unfolding, the media pushed harder and the force of their numbers knocked the chair over, spilling the child beneath their feet. Now they had a real drama to report. A child was about to be trampled by a crowd, and in their enthusiasm they became that crowd, taking pictures and recording the frightened screams as they pushed and shouted and stamped on her flailing limbs.

Joe lunged forward and scooped the little girl up in his arms, holding firm with his feet spread wide as the hungry reporters jostled him and shouted more questions. The girl stopped crying and smiled up into his face.

"Who is she?" a voice shouted.

"What's wrong with her?"

"What's your name, love?"

"Can you perform a miracle on her, Joe?"

"Do you hold yourself responsible for this accident?"

The police had fought their way through to the front again and used their batons to push the crowd back, giving Joe some space and righting the wheelchair so that he could place the smiling child safely back down.

"Look into your hearts," Joe said, straightening up and talking directly to the cameras, "you people from the media. And ask yourselves some questions. Do you believe you are doing the right thing? Are you giving the world a true picture of what is happening here? Are you driven by a need to educate and inform or are you simply wanting to sell newspapers and advertising at any cost? Was this child lying in the dirt because of me or because of you with your aggression and your carelessness?"

The media drew back a little and the shouting grew less, some of them were apparently feeling pangs of shame but others could be seen simmering with resentment, believing they were being patronised by someone they were in the process of making into a global superstar.

Having gained some calm, Joe moved forward again towards a woman on crutches. He was showing obvious signs of fatigue, having been working through the crowd for over an hour, and he gratefully accepted a paper cup of water thrust towards him by an anonymous well-wisher. He drained it and handed the empty cup back to the same outstretched fingers, returning to the job of placing his hands on the heads of those around him.

The man who had passed him the drink was swallowed back into the crowd, immediately disappearing from view with the cup, so that no one noticed him slide it carefully into a plastic bag, like precious evidence from a crime scene.

TWENTY-ONE

The American President stared around the room. Some of the generals had taken the time to introduce themselves to him, others he had heard about by reputation. None of them looked happy. The President was holding a one-page briefing document in his hand and was trying to take in the key points while talking at the same time. As a result, the words babbling out of his mouth did not make complete sense. The generals waited with barely hidden impatience for him to ask a question which they could use their military experience to respond to.

"Mr President..." the Secretary of Defence took it upon himself to interrupt the President's flow, to everyone's relief. "We believe that we need to put the military on high alert. There is a restlessness in the world and we need to be ready to take control wherever and whenever it starts to threaten the status quo."

"I've seen them," the President said, "I've seen them on the television and on the internet. But they are not the majority. I have seen them marching and I have read their banners and I do not think that we need to see them as a threat. They are just small-time troublemakers. Losers in life. If you look at the crowds, and I have studied them closely, probably more closely than any of you, I can see that they are mostly women and children, communists and agitators."

"It is true, sir," one of the generals agreed, "that the demographic for most of these protesters is under thirty, and that there are marginally more women than men, but I think it would be a mistake to dismiss them for that reason. It is nearly always the young who take to the streets in any movement, but that does not mean that there is not something bigger happening in the background. We believe that there is likely to be civil unrest on the same scale as the civil rights movement, the worst race riots and the anti-war movement of the nineteen sixties, and this time it isn't just confined to America. It is happening all over the world. There are things happening in New Zealand which are causing us a great deal of concern."

"New Zealand is long way away, General," the President replied, having already checked that fact on Google.

"With respect sir, this is the twenty-first century and nowhere is a long way away from anywhere any more. You may be right and it may all come to nothing, but we believe for the time being we should cancel all leave and put the military on standby, just in case they are required for peace-keeping activities."

"You really think things are that bad?" The President looked a little rattled. He stared hard at the paper again as if willing the words to enter his head and make sense.

"We are monitoring the situation closely, sir," the general replied, "but we have every reason to think that there might be some sort of global revolutionary movement building up and we need to get on top of it quickly, before it becomes anything bigger."

"A revolution?" the President asked, his eyes widening with excitement at the thought of an impending battle. "Do we need to send troops to New Zealand? We could maybe send some warships. What about drones? Are we using drones?"

"At the moment, sir, we are using every sort of surveillance mechanism that we have. We feel that we need to know much more before deciding on a course of action. We would like to have the troops available to send in should things escalate. It seems possible that the Russians and the Chinese are up to something, but we can't work out what. We need to be ready."

"This guy performing these miracles, claiming he's the Son of God or something" – the President seemed almost to be talking to himself. "I saw him on the internet. He's just some kind of hippy healer, right?"

"At the moment we are having trouble finding out anything about him," the Director of Security admitted. "It's like he's appeared from nowhere."

"Everyone comes from somewhere," the President said, looking pleased with his own moment of wisdom. "If he's hiding his past then he must be some kind of crook, right? We need to know what he's done. Where's he been hiding all these years? What's he out to achieve? Where are the bodies buried? Find the smoking gun…" He seemed to run out of crime story clichés.

The Director of Security cleared his throat. "We do at least know where he has been for the last few days, sir. He appears to have been with Yung Zhang and a number of other prominent liberal thinkers."

"He's with the communists?"

"They're not exactly communists, sir. Lalit Wadia is one of them."

The President's colour was rising. "People say that guy is a potential future president of this country. That would make him the first Muslim president. These people are all a threat. Why are they meeting? Why aren't the New Zealand authorities clamping down? Find out more about this hippy healer guy. He must have come from somewhere. Do something, for God's sake!"

Slamming his fists on the desk he pulled himself from his seat and left the room, muttering angrily, still clutching the crumpled one-page briefing.

* * * * *

In a similar room in Moscow things were altogether quieter.

"What are the Americans doing?" the Russian President asked.

"The Americans are putting their forces on high alert," the Head of the Russian Foreign Intelligence and Security Service advised him.

"Are they?" the President smiled. "They must be feeling threatened."

"It seems so. They don't know who this man is that is getting all the attention online. They don't like not knowing things."

"No one likes not knowing things," the President purred. "Do we know anything about him?"

"We are looking into it," the Security Chief responded, avoiding the President's snake-like stare.

"And what are we hearing from inside the Chinese woman's house?"

"At the moment there is an information blackout. Our informant will not be able to report until after their meeting is over. They are locked inside this house for a week with limited access to their phones."

"And this healer is now in the house too?"

"He has left now, with the teacher and the boy. They have arrived back at the school but there are huge crowds there, blocking their progress."

"What is his connection to the Chinese woman?"

"We don't know yet, sir."

"It seems there are a lot of things we don't know." The purr had changed to a low growl, making the other men in the room shift uncomfortably in their seats.

"We are working on it, sir."

"What do the Chinese know?"

"The Chinese may know more because they still have Liang Zhang in custody, unless he is already dead."

"We should have more than one source inside that house," the President said after a few moments' thought. "I can't believe they are all so incorruptible. What about the security forces around the house; do we own any of them?"

"We are working on it, sir."

"We seem to be 'working' on rather a lot of things," he hissed. "I think we need to work a little harder, and I think we need to put the army on high alert." With that he left the room, making barely a sound.

*****

"The suspect sweeps her electronic equipment regularly," the Technical Chief informed the President of China, "which is interrupting our reception from time to time, but we are still able to hear most of what is happening inside the house."

"And what are we hearing?"

"Zhang's co-conspirators seem to be interested in the new man, the one with no past. Some of them appear to think that he is some sort of god in human form."

Something close to a smile flickered for a second across the President's face.

"This is a religious movement then?" he asked. "Zhang is leading a religious movement? That is very surprising. She is a woman of great intelligence."

"All the people in this group appear to be of great

intelligence," an advisor murmured, "but they also seem to believe that this man can perform miracles."

"That could be very dangerous," the President said. "How far is Christchurch from here?"

"About 10,000 kilometres, sir," a voice in the crowd of advisors replied.

"We do not want this contagion to spread. If the Americans are putting their military on high alert then we must do the same. Someone like this can build a following of millions very quickly on social media if he is not discredited. We don't want him to get inside the heads of our great people. We need to be ready to nip this in the bud."

"We believe the Russians are already drawing up a plan for that contingency, sir. Some senior Russian military figures have been making contact secretly with senior American military figures."

"Secretly?"

"Neither of their presidents seem to know that they are talking. They appear to be considering the need to raise private finance to help with the military reaction."

"Then we need to be raising our own military capabilities in line with them," the President said and the whole room rumbled with the sound of agreement. "We cannot have this man put on a pedestal and handed a power base which could cause discontent with the way things must develop in China."

* * * * *

The viral videos of Joe's healing abilities had rattled the financial markets just as they were rattling the politicians. Nothing worried the money men as much as uncertainty, and the fact that no one could work out what was happening in New Zealand was making them feel very uncertain. The recent anti-capitalist and climate-change marches and protests which had been taking place all over the world had already taken their toll on share prices; the bankers were willing to do anything to stop the rot from spreading any further or deeper. The idea that all the discontent simmering below the surface in different countries could be brought together by one charismatic leader was focusing their minds and making them nervous.

Having already had the confidence of the markets rocked by the unexplained extinguishing of the sun, the bankers had a lot of questions which they wanted the politicians and the consultants to answer. Was there about to be a worldwide eruption of protest and discontent which would alter the power structure for ever? Were all the world's governments going to have to clamp down on dissent, and if so how would that affect the markets? Was there any chance that the sun would be extinguished again, maybe even permanently? Were there opportunities for profit to be found amidst the impending changes? No one seemed able to give any convincing answers, no matter how highly paid they were for their advice.

The nervous reactions of the political leaders suggested that they believed there was something disruptive brewing and that meant that a lot of big financial players were already liquidising large swathes of their assets in order to be ready to take advantage of changes. All the senior bankers and fund managers were spending the weekend in emergency meetings with rolling news services flickering silently on television screens in the background. They were anxious to restore calm and encourage everyone to get on with their normal lives before global productivity became affected and too much value had been wiped off their balance sheets for a full recovery to be possible, but it felt like circumstances were now running way beyond their control. Several of them had made informal contact with senior military figures to discuss ways in which unrest on the streets could be kept to a minimum if too many of the world's governments failed to act decisively.

"What we will have to get used to is that the economy and the financial system can no longer continue as they have in the past," the leader of the International Monetary Fund had informed a select group of central and private bankers at an emergency meeting. "They are changing because increasing numbers of people want a different 'scoring system'. They want a 'better game'.

"The current feeling seems to be that our capitalist system encourages people to compete and to grow, which results in a larger part of the resources of the Earth being used and more waste products being left behind. In addition, the system creates injustice worldwide and that will only increase in the future if nothing changes. You always have winners and losers in a system that works on the basis of a market mechanism and maybe we have all been too hard on the losers, allowing the winners to take all.

"It is quite possible that the concept of nation states is now outdated because as the problems get bigger there is much more that binds us than separates us. Is it therefore reasonable to assume that we could become a 'one world community'?"

Her audience knew that the question was rhetorical and waited for her to continue. She was a highly respected figure in their world since the IMF's primary role was to maintain global financial stability, which they believed to be in everyone's interests. Many believed that there was a case to be made for using "justifiable force" to slow down or even suppress completely the changes she was talking about.

"I believe we can assume that there will soon be a much more powerful market master who will ensure that the interests of all parties involved, including the environment, are sufficiently reflected in the market. That means more far-reaching regulation and even more transparency and responsibility.

"Here at the IMF, however, we see a number of very significant risks if these major changes come about too soon or too fast. Chaos is always dangerous. The public's trust must remain intact. Not only are the global stock markets based on trust, our total financial system stands or falls with it. We have a money system in which the citizen, the public, has had remarkable confidence for a long time. That is why we can respond to threats of depression and often prevent it. The system gives us, as policymakers, quite a few degrees of freedom.

"Take the huge debt level that we have created together, for example. Did we do wrong? Are there too many debts in the world? If so, what should the cap on debts be? We really cannot determine this, because that too is purely based on trust. We do know that it is probably not wise to find out where that point is, because if you invent it, it will be too late.

"And if one world community were to emerge, could they not make a lot of new debts for their policies, as long as they enjoy the trust of the public? Does that not provide endless possibilities for creating a 'better game', as long as we could also eliminate many existing debts? In many countries, part of the government debt is on the central bank's balance sheet, which means it is government institutions that have claims on the governments themselves. So setting these debts and claims against one another is a perfectly viable option. It is like robbing Peter to pay Paul.

"This 'better game' that so many people now seem to want cannot be achieved without great sacrifices. And that will have many detrimental consequences for the dividends and bonuses that we receive, also for our incomes, our assets and our liberties because people will want to block the experts whom

151

they see as being responsible for the current financial system.

"I would say that in a worst-case scenario it is quite possible that all the currencies will collapse simultaneously. These people would see that as an opportunity to impose a single currency across the globe, ending the opportunities for currency speculation in the future. Do I have to continue?"

None of the people in the room, many of whom sat at the helm of the capitalist system, wanted to allow all that to happen. It now seemed likely that they were going to need the help of the military to keep people calm and to eradicate the troublemakers, but would the politicians have the will to take the necessary steps? Believing that they needed to take things into their own hands, a group of central bankers decided to reach out formally to the highest military leaders in several countries to explore the possibility of co-operation between former enemies. If enough finance could be raised could the armies be persuaded to act in unison to restore global order, regardless of what their political masters might tell them?

TWENTY-TWO

After several hours' working their way through the crowd outside the school, Joe finally noticed that Sophie and Hugo were exhausted.

"Come on," he said, "enough for today."

Taking them by the hand he walked slowly and steadily through the school gates, which the nervous-looking security guards inside opened for just long enough to let them in while the police held everyone else back. There was a lot of angry shouting from both sides, which Joe seemed not to hear.

"Wow," Hugo said once they were safely inside the slammed gates and heading for the buildings, "that was intense."

"Do you have a spare pair of glasses back in the dorm?" Sophie asked.

"Yes."

"You run along and find them."

As Hugo ran off, Sophie and Joe walked quickly towards her apartment, neither wanting to have to stop and talk to anyone else.

"I need a cup of tea and you will need a rest after that ordeal," Sophie said. "Our bags must still be with that poor driver. I guess he'll get them to us eventually."

As they climbed the stairs of the staff block they became aware of men's voices on the landing above them. The door to the apartment was open and several security men were inside, packing Sophie's belongings into bin-sacks.

"What's going on?" Sophie asked. "What the hell are you doing?"

"We are going to have to move both of you off school premises," the senior officer informed her.

"What do you mean?"

"It's for the safety of the children. We can't have that many people congregating outside the gates and it will only be a matter of time before they break through, especially the media. We've already had to evict several incomers. We need to move them all on but that will never happen as long as you two are here."

"I can go," Joe said. "You don't need to move Sophie. It is me they are here for."

"I disagree." The voice of the headmaster made them both turn. "Sophie is also now part of this ridiculous circus. You have made her so. She won't be able to carry out her duties as a teacher while the media are showing this much interest in her love life."

"No one is interested in my love life!" Sophie protested. "There is no love life." She blushed at having inadvertently blurted such an uncomfortable piece of personal information.

"Again, I disagree," the headmaster said, unable to stop a small smirk from tilting the corners of his mouth. "An extraordinary number of people seem to be interested in everything about you. I have been receiving a number of calls from concerned parents who are worried about the effect this level of publicity will have on their children's education, not to mention their safety. Personally, I am also worried about the effect it will have on the school's long-term reputation for discretion. I have worked very hard to make it a place where the children of high-profile people can be safe from the prying eyes of the public. I do not want it to forever be identified as the location for whatever this publicity stunt is all about."

"How am I going to teach effectively, and provide pastoral care, if I am living off campus?" Sophie protested.

"That will not be a problem. You are suspended from all your teaching and pastoral duties. I have already reallocated all your classes. I do not want you back on these premises until this entire fiasco is over."

"You can't do that!"

"It's already done, Sophie," he said. "You've totally brought this on yourself."

Joe put a restraining hand on her arm. "Don't worry about the past," he whispered in her ear, "think only of the future."

"Where am I supposed to go?" Sophie asked the room in general.

"It seems that you made some very useful friends over the weekend," the headmaster said turning to face Joe, cutting Sophie out of the conversation, "and arrangements have been made for accommodation to be booked for you at a hotel. Since it is your appearance here that has caused all this trouble, I am assuming that you will insist they look after Sophie as well as yourself. I'm hoping you won't just throw her to the wolves." He gestured towards the gates where the crowds could be heard chanting for Joe to come back out.

"Of course," Joe smiled benignly, refusing to allow the headmaster to anger him. "Sophie and I are a team, isn't that right?" He put his arm around her shoulders and gave her a reassuring hug.

"How are you going to get us out past the gates?" Sophie asked.

"We thought it would be an idea for you to go out the back entrance in the van that has been delivering the vegetables to the kitchen," the headmaster said. "A little undignified for the Son of God, no doubt, but probably a wise precaution."

Joe laughed. "I don't think our dignity is dependant on our

mode of transport. It is kind of you to make the arrangements, Headmaster, thank you."

Joe stepped forward towards the headmaster and opened his arms wide. The headmaster flinched but did not jump back quickly enough to avoid being enveloped in a bear hug.

"God bless you," Joe said, "and all the good work you do here."

The headmaster wriggled free and gave a curt nod. Joe returned to Sophie and gave her arm another warning squeeze as he saw her open her mouth to say something else in anger.

"It'll be an adventure," Joe said.

The headmaster strode away without looking back and the security men escorted Joe and Sophie through a back door and into the waiting van, throwing the bin sacks containing her life's possessions in after them.

"I should have stood up to him," Sophie said once the doors were shut and they could feel the van moving. "If I spoke out to the media about the way he just sacked me I could destroy his career."

"You could do that," Joe agreed, "but do you want to? What about the harm to the school and the children? He is obviously in love with you and he is evidently a weak man."

"In love?" She was startled by the suggestion. "I doubt it."

"You are much stronger than him," Joe said. "So should you destroy him or help him to do better?"

"That's an annoying argument," Sophie said. "I'm going to have to think about it and get back to you."

"Good plan," Joe said. "I wonder who organised this hotel. Do you suppose it was Yung?"

"I expect the Twelve have a war chest for this sort of thing," Sophie said as the van went over a bump, throwing them together, defusing the tension and making them both laugh. "Do you mind me tagging along on your coat-tails like this? You can tell me if you want me to go."

"No, no" – he was obviously genuinely horrified at the thought – "please don't go. I am going to need your help with what is to come."

"So it's okay for me to stay at this hotel with you?"

"Of course." He put his arm around her to steady her against the swaying of the van and she rested her head against his chest. For a moment, Sophie couldn't imagine how it would be possible to feel any more elated.

The van was able to drive right inside the service area of the hotel before helping hands opened the doors and released them. The manager was waiting for them with an elegantly attired bell boy in attendance to carry the bin bags.

"Fortunately we have been able to give you the whole of the top floor," the manager gushed as he led them to a service lift. "You will have complete privacy and the security people will be able to keep an eye on anyone coming and going through the main lobby."

"You realise we have no money?" Sophie said, aware that such a mundane issue would not even occur to Joe.

"That is not a problem, madam," he assured her. "It is being taken care of by well-wishers. And a driver delivered your luggage, which has been taken up to the suite."

When they reached the top floor, the manager triumphantly threw open the double doors to reveal a huge suite with views over the city and parkland. Every surface seemed covered with baskets of fruit and flowers.

"These just keep arriving," he said.

Sophie looked at the labels on the various gifts and saw that they were all from people they had met over the weekend. It seemed that the Twelve were now looking after them. The cases which had been in the boot of the car they had last seen in the crowd were standing by the door. The bin sacks containing her life's possessions were being brought up from the grocer's van and discreetly emptied into wardrobes.

"Please take them," Joe said, gesturing to the gifts, "and redistribute them among the staff. Just leave us with one fruit bowl. We couldn't possibly eat all this."

"Maybe leave one bunch of flowers too?" Sophie suggested.

"Whichever one you like the best," Joe laughed as Sophie pointed to the biggest vase of pink lilies she had ever seen.

Once the manager and his team had finally backed out of the room, still bowing despite their arms being full of flowers and fruit, Sophie and Joe collapsed onto one of the many sofas with the remaining fruit bowl between them.

"This is the sort of thing I thought I had warned them about," Joe said. "Conspicuous extravagance. There must be much cheaper hotels than this."

"I suspect it's the sort of place people like Yung and Lalit and Simon live in all the time," Sophie said. "They wouldn't know how to do it any differently."

"They too have a lot to learn," he said. "But we must be grateful for their kindness and it is nice to be away from the crowds for a few moments."

"I think that is exactly what these sorts of places are designed for," Sophie said, unzipping herself a banana. "While we are on our own, I have a favour to ask."

"Really?" Joe bit into a ripe fig.

"I've never been baptised. My parents were both atheists and they brought me up to be the same."

"Would you like to be baptised?"

"I never thought I would hear myself saying such a thing, but now that I have met you – yes I would."

"Where would you like to do it?"

"There is a cardboard cathedral in Christchurch, which was built to be a temporary replacement after an earthquake damaged the original cathedral. There were three earthquakes in just two years and the worst one, which damaged the original cathedral, killed 165 people. The memories are still painful for many people and the cardboard cathedral is like a symbol of remembrance."

"Cardboard?"

"It was designed by a Japanese architect. It was only supposed to be temporary but it has been there for seven years already. It is kind of a cool space and not too 'churchy', if you know what I mean."

"I know exactly what you mean. Since you are not joining any particular religious community I can perform the same ceremony as in the days when I wandered in the desert. Shall we see if the concierge can set it up for us? That would be an interesting challenge for them."

"Thank you," she said, unable to stop herself from leaning across and kissing him. His lips tasted of fig and to her joy he responded to her tongue, cupping her chin in his hand and gently tilting her head back. Without saying a word he lifted her effortlessly from the sofa and carried her to the bedroom, never taking his mouth from hers as he laid her gently down and made love to her.

Over the years, Sophie had managed to convince herself that sex was always going to be mildly disappointing, but with Joe she felt that she had truly made love with someone for the first time in her life. That evening she knew that she had experienced the sort of ecstasy that she had heard other women talk about but which, after numerous anticlimaxes in her past, she had come to assume was a myth.

Although Joe had been half-joking in his suggestion, the hotel's concierge actually was able to get permission for him to baptise Sophie in the cardboard cathedral late that night. They were smuggled out of the back entrance of the hotel to a waiting car and the lights inside the triangular structure glowed through the multicoloured stained glass windows as if to welcome them as they approached the huge cardboard cross at the front. The driver kept watch outside once they had gone in. A puzzled-looking young priest, who had obviously been roused from his bed with the instruction to open the cathedral but had been given no explanation as to why, welcomed them and asked if he could help in any way.

"Thank you for your trouble," Joe said, "but there is no need for you to stay."

The priest nodded, as if he understood who they were and what was going on, although he obviously didn't, and left them.

"Safe to say," Sophie whispered as he left, "that I don't think he spends much time watching the news or surfing the internet."

"A man perhaps who has decided to dedicate his life to higher matters," Joe smiled.

Silence fell with the disappearance of the priest's footsteps. The lights were low and there was just the two of them beside the font. As he cradled her in one strong arm, sprinkled water on her forehead and gently caressed her hair, she felt an electricity pass between them as if they had become one person, indivisible, but she had no way of knowing if he felt the same as he gazed down at her with his kind eyes. They stood silently at the font for several minutes, allowing the night-time atmosphere of the cathedral to seep into their souls.

Back at the hotel, she offered to sleep in a different bedroom in the suite but he simply placed a finger on her lips to stop her talking and led her back into the master bedroom where they had made love. Was he confirming that they were now a couple? She couldn't tell and she couldn't find the right words to ask.

The following morning they both woke from a deep sleep and made love again as if it were the most natural thing in the world. When Sophie finally ventured out of the bedroom she found that someone from room service had fanned out the day's newspapers on a table in the sitting room. Across all the front pages was the story of Joe's mass public healings outside the school, although the various editors seemed unsure whether to praise Joe as the Son of God or accuse him of being some sort of clever charlatan and rabble-rouser. There were dramatic pictures of him carrying Hugo through the crowd and of the girl from the wheelchair who had been trampled, which gave an accurate idea of how frightening it had been to be at the centre of the storm. Sophie carried the papers back to the bedroom and threw them onto the crumpled sheets, settling down, cross-legged, to read them.

"Don't waste your time reading other people's opinions of this," Joe said, kindly. "They will either flatter you or annoy you. You know what happened; you don't need to know what other people think about it."

She considered his words for a moment, part of her still wanting to read stories about herself written by other people, even if some of them did annoy her, but finally nodded her agreement.

"You're right," she said. "We wouldn't want to start believing our own press cuttings, would we?"

"Exactly!" he laughed. "Spoken like a true superstar."

They ordered breakfast and Sophie flicked idly through the inside pages of the papers as she ate, trying to show an interest in what else might have been happening in the world while she had been so engrossed in her own immediate adventures. Buried deep inside one of the more serious papers she spotted a headline about some ancient scrolls which had been discovered in al-Eizariya, formerly called Bethany, a village near Jerusalem on the south-eastern slopes of the Mount of Olives. As she read on she felt her heartbeat increasing dramatically, thumping like a drum in her temples. The scrolls had been found in jars in a niche in the rock under the tomb of Lazarus, which is connected to his house.

"This is exactly like my vision," she said, dropping the paper in front of Joe and searching through some of the others to see if they had the same story. Joe glanced at the article.

"Lazarus was my best friend," he said. "I often stayed in that house in Bethany with him and his sisters, Mary and Martha. It was my base when I was in Jerusalem. I have such fond memories of those times. It is the most wonderful city."

"I would like to go there one day," Sophie said.

"We can go together," he said, but she couldn't tell if he was teasing her.

"Really?"

"Of course. I would love to share it with you."

"Is that a promise?" Now she was half-teasing and half-hoping.

"Yes," he laughed. "I promise."

"So this is the same Lazarus that you raised from the dead in the Bible story, right?" She returned to the story.

"That is the same man, but it wasn't anything like how they wrote about it. Our friendship was extremely close and the Romans knew that, so they arrested Lazarus and tortured him in order to get him to tell them where I was. He refused to talk. I should have gone to help him earlier but I was afraid for my own life and delayed the journey by a few days. By the time I got there with the disciples it was too late and Lazarus had already died from his injuries. We buried him there in that tomb. I would not have been able to bring him back to life by then. I felt deeply sad and also guilty that I left it so long to go to him. I would dearly love to go back there and pay my respects now that I am back on Earth."

"So, how did the scrolls get to be there?" Sophie asked, trying to get a clear picture in her mind of what had happened all those years ago.

"We had the scrolls with us. They were written by a scribe called Amos, who was always with us, watching and listening to everything; seldom speaking but chronicling everything he witnessed or heard. We hid the scrolls deep inside the floor beneath Lazarus. I'm amazed they managed to find them. I guess there have been technological developments which have helped them in their excavations."

"But don't you think it's weird that I dreamed exactly this?"

"I said we were a team, didn't I?" he said over his shoulder as he made his way into the shower.

"Doesn't this change everything?" she asked, but he had already turned on the water and didn't hear.

Sophie woke up her computer and fed the information from the story into the search bar. By the time Joe had finished in the bathroom she had fired an email off to the professor who had been quoted in the article, explaining who she was and describing the dream which she had experienced before Joe's arrival. She asked if he would be good enough to keep her informed of any progress they might make with their research. She didn't really expect to receive a response but she felt better for having reached out.

TWENTY-THREE

The paper cup that Joe drank from in the crowd was being examined like no other cup before it. Clive, the newspaper reporter who had taken it, left the crowd immediately with his prize and drove directly to a nearby university campus where a distinguished, if sceptical, group of international forensic scientists and pharmacologists had been ensconced in secret for two days. These normally impatient experts were aware that their findings from the item they were about to analyse could make their reputations for life and they were therefore willing to wait. They had also been well paid for their time and were intrigued by the challenge they had been set.

The operation had been planned to the smallest detail. Once Clive had handed over the plastic bag containing the cup, he went to the university cafeteria to wait to be informed of the results. That was the deal. Whatever they found in their tests, he would be the first one outside their erudite circle to know about it. It would be his world exclusive – hopefully the greatest scoop of his career. After that the scientists, or their paymasters, would be free to use the findings in any way they saw fit. The adrenalin was making Clive feel physically sick as he tried to sit still and attract as little attention to himself as possible from the students coming and going around him. Their youth reminded him of just how long he had been waiting for a story this big. He wished, not for the first time, that he had not given up smoking.

His doctor had told him that he had no choice, but it had been as hard as he imagined giving up eating or sex would be. He had been getting through at least two packs a day since he was sixteen and first went to work in Fleet Street as a junior reporter. Initially he had taken it up to try to make himself look older and to make out he was as hard and cynical as all the world-weary senior reporters whom he admired so much and wanted to impress. He suspected now that in their eyes it had probably merely served to accentuate how young and green he was. He had loved the image of the dogged investigative reporter staying up all night drinking coffee and smoking cigarettes, maybe even taking occasional hits from a hip flask as he winkled stories out of people with secrets to hide; only finally sleeping once the first editions had hit the streets. He had learned to play the part so well it had eventually become who he actually was, but forty years later he could feel that the cigarettes were actively trying to kill him and he wasn't ready yet to give up the pleasures of chasing the hottest stories around the globe, particularly this one, which promised to lead to the whole world order being transformed almost overnight.

He was tired of having young people tell him that printed newspapers were dead and that old-fashioned investigative reporters had had their day. He wanted one more chance to prove them wrong. He hated the internet but he could also see its potential for spreading a story fast once it had appeared in print. If he was able to break this story first they would all be forced to follow and his piece would go global on a scale he would never have been able to dream about when he first became a journalist. All these thoughts and feelings churned through his mind as the time ticked by and every second he imagined how good it would feel to go outside and join the group of smokers he could see gathered outside the canteen windows.

It was several long hours before two of the scientists came to look for him. They had puzzled expressions and were still deep in debate when they found him imbibing his sixth shot of caffeine.

"Well?" Clive snapped, the coffee having exacerbated his already high levels of impatience. He couldn't believe the slowness with which members of other professions chose to impart information. "What did you find?"

"Very hard to say at this stage," one of them replied.

"It's undoubtedly very interesting," her colleague added.

"Just give me the top line," the reporter snapped, his phone already recording as he steered them across the room to a quiet area where he could be confident no one would be listening in.

"Whoever drank from this cup has different DNA."

"Different to who?"

"Different to human."

"Go on."

"Under the UV lamps, the DNA bands lit up in a way we have never seen before. The only possible explanation is that the subject has male mitochondrial DNA."

"In plain English?" Clive could barely contain his excitement. Had he actually found a real, genuine alien?

"Mitochondria are the power plants of a cell and although most of the human DNA is in the cell nucleus, the mitochondria also contain a part. The male mtDNA is always in the tail of the sperm cell and is normally lost when the sperm cell fuses with the egg cell. As a result, only the female mtDNA is retained in the offspring. The fact that the subject has male mtDNA is unusual."

"Unusual?"

"You could say miraculous," the second scientist added.

"So is this guy some kind of alien? Could he be the Son of God?"

"These findings endorse his potential divine identity and go some way to explaining his many special abilities."

"That's a 'yes' then?"

Neither of the scientists could quite bring themselves to agree that their findings proved that there was a God and that he was now back on Earth, but nor could they deny the evidence which they had seen with their own eyes. They handed a sheet of paper with the findings over to the reporter who was already calling his editor in London.

"The scientists say he is the Son of God," he shouted, "the DNA proves it."

He proceeded to read out the scientific details from the sheet as the two scientists exchanged worried looks and left the room to rejoin their colleagues, so that they could perform more tests and discuss the matter in greater depth. They had discharged their side of the deal with the media owner who had arranged for the cup to be brought to them, and now they were free to do what they loved more than anything: in-depth research into a phenomenon that none of their competitors yet had access to.

The printing presses in London were ready and waiting for the story and the newspapers were hitting the streets within a few hours. Minutes after the first editions were being read, Clive's story was out there, hurtling through cyberspace, shooting out tentacles in every direction, and his phone began to buzz with rival media wanting him to give them a quote. His name was appearing everywhere as the man who had scored the greatest scoop in history. For the moment at least, he had ownership of the hottest news story of the day and it felt good. As he read the first editions he celebrated with a cigarette, which he cadged off a passing fifteen-year-old, telling himself that he had earned it and promising himself that it would definitely be his last.

The entire scientific community, the vast majority of whom were lifelong atheists or agnostics, stopped whatever they were thinking about the moment they heard the news. They looked up from their screens and microscopes and opened their minds to the shocking possibility that there might be elements of truth to be found in the holy scriptures of the various religions which they had been dismissing as fairy tales for so long.

Within a few hours, senior figures within the pharmaceutical industry were also instigating conversations on the subject of divinity and considering the marketing ramifications of what they were hearing.

"If this guy actually is divine," one chief executive was saying to a trusted colleague, "then we could learn a great deal from studying him."

"You mean we might be able to work out exactly how immortality works? Develop a pill, maybe – Viagra for the soul? That would certainly be a product that would fly off the shelves."

"You joke, but there must be some explanation behind these findings. Imagine if we could work out the formula for divinity and bottle it."

"We can't be the only ones thinking this. There must be conversations like this happening inside the offices of every one of our competitors."

"So we need to make sure we stay ahead of the pack."

"I don't think it would be good to use hunting analogies outside this room."

"Hey, we're just shooting the breeze here. But supposing we could get this Joe guy to co-operate with us. Supposing he let us do some tests, let us have samples of body fluids and tissues; suppose he let the researchers spend some time with him on an exclusive basis… that could put us years ahead of the competition. Imagine what we could do if we had a sample of his semen. Imagine the market value of something like that. If people could breed from divine DNA the entire human race could eventually be up-graded."

"Does he seem like the kind of guy who would be willing to spend time being poked and prodded by a bunch of people in white coats?"

"Everyone has their price."

"I don't think money is of any interest to him. He's the Son of God for God's sake."

"So then we would need to find another way to persuade him."

"What do you mean, torture him?"

"We're just shooting the breeze here."

"Yeah, you said."

"When I was a kid I used to catch butterflies. I had this net and I would chase them around the fields and collect as many different species as possible. It was fun."

"Not so many butterflies around these days," his colleague reminded him. "They got pretty much wiped out."

"Yeah, but there have been other compensatory factors like better pesticides, better crop yields…"

"So are you suggesting we net this Joe guy and pin him to a specimen board?"

"I'm just…"

"…shooting the breeze. Right. But we could put out some feelers, yeah?"

"Let's do it."

Now that the revelation about Joe's DNA was out there, there were only two ways for the rest of the media to handle the story. They could either go all out for celebrating the fact that the Son of God had returned to Earth and might be able to save mankind, and then rely on the fact that millions if not billions of people would be hungry to read more about him and what he was going to do for the world, or they had to take the opposite tack and look for ways to "expose" what some believed must be an elaborate con trick or practical joke. Either this was the greatest story ever, or it was the greatest fake ever – which came to almost the same thing.

They divided pretty much in half when it came to making that decision, with some of the more ruthless ones following both lines simultaneously. The result was a complete eclipse of all other news for several days. What was the point of journalists writing about anything else when there was only one thing that everyone wanted to read about and talk about? The story consequently attained something that media people had been dreaming about ever since the invention of the printing press: one hundred per cent media saturation.

Joe and Sophie stayed in the hotel suite, most of the time camped out on the giant bed, watching the story unfold online and fielding any phone calls and visitors who managed to make it past the growing army of security guards and public relations handlers that was building up around them, regardless of Joe's protestations that he did not need guarding from his own flock.

"It seems the medical establishment wants to study you in more depth," Sophie said as she flicked through the messages on her phone while snuggled into a pile of pillows beside Joe. "And they seem to think that I might be a way of getting to you."

"Studied how? Like a laboratory rat?" Joe laughed at the idea.

"I think that would be their ideal scenario, yes," she replied with a straight face. "Don't underestimate how ruthless these people are, Joe. I have been involved in a few protests against big pharma over the years, fighting against vivisection and for animal rights and stuff, and I know how powerful they are and how low they are willing to stoop in order to get what they want. I've heard stories from activists in some parts of the world about kidnappings and even executions."

"The pharmaceutical industry?" Joe was obviously shocked. "Really? I thought they were the good guys. I thought medicines were supposed to help people."

"Well, you'd think, yeah. But it's the same in any industry where there are billions of dollars to be made. Greed always wins the day because greedy people are willing to use force. It's bound to be that way if you think about it."

"I had not realised quite how bad things had become."

"I know," she said, curling up close to him, "that's why you need me to look after you."

"Indeed I do," he said, making her spirits soar. But then he laughed good-naturedly, as if he was only joking, which made her feel more disappointed than she would ever have imagined possible. She had never before fully appreciated what people meant when they talked about being on an "emotional rollercoaster".

TWENTY-FOUR

"The President wants to talk to you direct," the official said.

"Which president?" the Russian President asked innocently.

"The President of America, sir."

"Oh. What does he want?"

"He is concerned that there is a groundswell of support for this Son of God impostor and that it could lead to a great deal of political unrest."

"Unrest here, in Russia?" The President chuckled at the suggestion.

"I think he believes it will spread everywhere. He would like to present a unified front to the people of the world, West and East. The representatives of the 'status quo' against the 'chaos' of upheaval; the reassuring, known and trusted elements versus the unknown and feared ones."

"Do the Americans know we already have someone placed inside the movement?"

"We do not think so, sir. They seem to know very little."

The President let out another chuckle, which sounded like something between a laugh and a cough. "Perhaps so, but never underestimate their ability for treachery and deceit. We have been caught out by them before."

"I understand, sir. We will continue to monitor the situation. Can we arrange a time for you to speak directly to him?"

"Let him wait a few hours. Tell them that I am taking a walk in the woods to clear my thoughts."

The message was relayed to the office of the President of America.

"No need to share that last detail with the President," an advisor said. "The Russians are just trying to annoy him. They are playing mind games. Let's try to keep him calm until after the call."

A few hours later, the Americans were informed that the President of Russia had returned safely from his walk in the woods. He felt suitably refreshed and would be happy to receive the call.

"This guy is beginning to give me the creeps," the American President said as an opening gambit once the line was established.

"Which man is it we are discussing?" the Russian President asked.

"This guy that everyone says is Jesus come back to sort everything out. I mean, come on. Can you believe the nerve of the guy?"

"I'm told that he already has many followers."

"Sure he does, because he's selling something that everyone wants to buy – and he photographs better than you and me…"

The Russian let out another throaty chuckle which suggested that he didn't entirely agree with the last statement but that he was willing to accept it contained some humour.

"Maybe the media will expose him as a fraud and it will all be over in a few days or a few weeks," the Russian President suggested.

"But what if it's not? He could become a catalyst for every dissident in the world. Not everyone thinks we are doing such a great job of running things, you know. If this guy suggests that there might be a different way of doing things… Well, you know."

"He has no power base," the Russian President replied, already tired of the conversation. "He is not a threat. You can stop worrying. Just be patient and everything will work out."

"I think we need to work together on this, though."

"Sure."

"While you're on the line," the American continued as if he had only just thought of something else he wanted to talk about, "I've heard rumours that some of my generals are talking to some of your generals. Do you know anything about that?"

The line clicked dead.

"Did he just hang up on me?" the American President asked all those who were listening in to the call.

"No, Mr President, I'm sure not. The line must have been cut off."

"What is this, the nineteen fifties? The 'line was cut off'? Give me a break. The son of a bitch hung up on me. What does he know? Does he know what the military are plotting?"

A few hours later the Director of National Security was summoned to the Oval Office. The President had decided to make it look like he had instructed his generals to reach out to their former enemies, so that all the governments could demonstrate a united front.

"We need to work more closely with the Russians and the Chinese and the rest of them on this," he informed the Director. "Whether they want to or not. If we don't stick together this guy could be sitting in any one of our offices by the end of the year and we could all be left holding our dicks, and looking for new jobs."

"It might be a mistake to trust the Russians too much, Mr President," the Director warned.

"We can trust them," the President blustered. "It's as much in their interests to get rid of this guy as it is in ours. I mean they do not have a great record when it comes to being nice to church-going folk. Am I right? And the Chinese – do the Chinese even have a religion? I don't think they do. I think they put people in prison for that sort of thing. Come to think of it, maybe they know a thing or two that we could learn from."

"International theology really isn't my subject, Mr President." The Director seemed to be backing away across the carpet. "But if you would like me to find some experts on the subject…"

"Damn right we should bring some experts in on this thing. Fight fire with fire, that's what we need to do."

* * * * *

The Chinese President was informed that there was a growing international movement asking for Liang Zhang and other political prisoners to be released.

"What do we know from inside the house of his wife?" he asked the messengers.

"It seems that everyone in that group is now tightly linked to the man who is dominating the news and the internet. They are turning him into the figurehead for their movement."

"This healer man with no past?"

"That is correct, sir."

"He cannot be allowed to dominate the media that are seen by our people. We are able to stop that, yes?"

"We can stop that, sir," they told him, even though every one of them knew that it was too late because virtually every citizen in China had already heard or read the story. Everyone in the room knew that there was absolutely no point in burning books after virtually the whole population had already read them. "But it might be more important for us to show a united front with the Americans and Russians. Their military leaders have reached out to ours…"

"Have they indeed?" the President seemed lost in thought. "Do they believe they need our help?"

"I think they are hoping to show international solidarity. If all our armies are working together against a common enemy then they will be more effective."

"Do you think the Russians or the Americans are clever enough to work that out?" The President sounded doubtful.

TWENTY-FIVE

"It's like a perfect storm," the media guru was explaining to the host on a late-night chat show. "People all over the world are aware that all the political systems are broken. For years there has been this great hunger for transparency but whenever it actually happens people are inevitably disappointed by what they see, because they had imagined that the things that were hidden from them were much better and cleverer than any of the things they already knew."

"Like when Toto pulls back the curtain and exposes the Wizard of Oz," the interviewer suggested, "revealing just a small, insignificant man working all the levers?"

"Quite."

"Are you saying that knowing a lot about the people who govern us is a bad thing?"

"I am saying that people want to have something to believe in, something that they believe is better and stronger than they are. They want to believe that there is someone out there looking after them. In previous centuries that role was taken by the religions with their stories of God, and in many parts of the world it still is, but in increasingly large areas since the Enlightenment, increasingly secular societies have removed the hope that there is a god looking after our interests and replaced that with a succession of human heroes like politicians, revolutionaries and 'stars' of all sorts, all of whom have been shown to have feet of clay when the spotlight was trained on them too intensely. They were expected to step into the shoes of the gods that came before and there was never any chance of them being able to do that. So people are disillusioned. People have always needed ecstasy. They might find it in religion, sports, drugs, music or spirituality, but it is basically the same thing.

"The idea that the Son of God has come back and will take over the reins of power is very attractive to everyone, apart from the people who currently hold those reins, of course. It is tapping in to the religious and spiritual ecstasy that we all crave, whether we choose to admit it or not. So it is not surprising that so many people are heading to New Zealand in the hope of being part of something this big."

Sophie and Joe were lying on the bed, half-watching the television as they prepared to drift into sleep.

"Tell me about your mother and father; Mary and Joseph, I mean," Sophie said. "What were they like?"

"They were good people," Joe replied after a few moments' reflection. "My mother, Maria, cut hair for other women and she used to let me sweep up the customers' hair from the street. She used to cut all our hair in the family."

"How many of you were there?"

"I was the eldest of seven. I had four brothers and two sisters."

"And you were all born in Bethlehem?"

"No," he laughed, "none of us was born in Bethlehem. We were all born in Nazareth. Joseph happened to be in Bethlehem the night I was born because of the census that was underway. My mother could not go with him because it was 130 kilometres and much too arduous a journey for a woman who was about to give birth. People invented the whole 'stable in Bethlehem' story later."

"Wow! All those school nativity plays I sat through. Who'd have thought?"

"Well, it is a good story."

"Did you get on with Joseph?"

"Oh yes. He was a great man. He was a carpenter and metal worker and I helped him as I grew older, but I was never as good as him. I had other interests. I also used to spend a lot of time with my mother's parents, Anna and Joachim. My grandmother used to make the most amazing fruit tarts, I remember, and Joachim taught me to read and write. He used to tell me stories about Abraham, Moses, David and Elijah, too. I loved listening to him. It's how I first learned about the power of storytelling."

"So how did you find out that Joseph wasn't your real father?"

"He told me himself, when I was about twelve. We were walking back from working in Sepphoris, which was about an hour's walk, and he explained to me that I was the Son of God and because of that life would not be easy for me."

"That must have been a shock."

"He told me that he would always think of me as his son and always love me like all the other children, and he was as good as his word. I never felt I was any different to the others in his eyes. When he died I was thirty-two and I realised that I had never really been cut out to be a carpenter and I became disillusioned by my working life. The contractors were earning huge amounts, but the workers were usually exploited. I didn't think this was good for anyone. When Joseph died in an accident at work my brothers wanted to continue the business but I decided to become a teacher. I gave my possessions away to people whom I believed would use them well and I was baptised by John. Baptism brought me a deep awareness of the fact that I was the Son of God. It was a tipping point in my life.

"I went off into the desert to sort out in my head what I really wanted to do with my life. John's idea of baptism was very different to mine. He saw it as a way for people to avoid the 'Day of Revenge'. I didn't believe in all that. I saw it as a moment when you start living differently, because that was how it was for me. I soon had my own students, or disciples, and we started to travel around baptising people ourselves."

"Had you been to school at all?"

"Oh yes. When I was six I attended some classes, but the other children and the teacher all laughed at me because I said I thought the world was round, like the sun and the moon. I remember the teacher becoming very angry because he couldn't convince me otherwise."

"How old are you now?"

"Well, I was thirty-five when I left the Earth last time, so I guess I still am. There really isn't any concept of time where I have been for the last two thousand Earth years."

"So, what happened once you were out there baptising people?"

"We decided to baptise people ourselves, but for different reasons to John. I did not believe that God wanted human sacrifices.

"For us, baptism represented the moment when you decided to start living differently, taking more responsibility for the weak in society. I wanted a world in which the goodness of people would rise to the surface rather than the selfishness and hardness that was so common. I called such a world the 'Kingdom of God', a kingdom of wisdom and not a kingdom as an end-time.

"As more and more people were baptised, the Romans became alarmed, claiming we were causing unrest. My friend John was arrested and killed and we had to be very alert. We withdrew for a while into the desert while I transformed from overseer to prophet.

"We went to Capernaum, a town near the mountains where

my friend and disciple Peter owned a nice house. It became our base. I liked to go to the synagogue there, on the Sabbath. But we wanted to reach more people, so we travelled through Galilee and Judea. We came to villages, in the countryside, going to people's homes and telling them about our vision of a future in which people live together harmoniously, without self-enrichment, without hypocrisy and with compassion for others who are less healthy or less fortunate.

"We were also critical of the Jewish authorities, who were complacent and only interested in their own position and prosperity and not opposing the Romans, who were very cruel and greedy.

"We got more and more followers. Some embraced our mission, others longed for a strong political leader, or for a king like before, a new David or Solomon. I was generally called 'rabbi', a master, and I thought that was fine.

"I have the divine gift to heal people, a privilege for which I am very grateful. That allowed me to give many a better life. I was a child of that time, a contemporary man, albeit with divine gifts. I was convinced that I was casting out the devil on mentally ill or epileptic people. Now, with the knowledge of today, I am able to think about it in a much more nuanced way.

"Not everyone was happy with me. There were people who were deeply disappointed when I indicated that I had no ambitions to become king of Israel and that I believed this would only lead to a bloody defeat. They did not want to hear it; they wanted a decisive leader who would initiate liberation from the Romans. As a result, we narrowly escaped being stoned a few times.

"I often differed with Jewish scribes. I challenged the religious thinking at the time and did not avoid confrontation. We had different opinions about many things; about the

Sabbath, about fasting, about unclean food, about attitudes to family, about dealing with criminals, lepers and prostitutes. They were more concerned about appearances than about inner cleanliness. And they struggled to forgive people their mistakes. They were very strict. And then there were the Romans, who feared that I did indeed want to claim the kingship. Herod Antipas had a network of spies throughout the country who reported on our gatherings.

"During a stay in the temple in Jerusalem we got into a conflict with the temple police. We became very angry that the temple had become like a market instead of a holy place of prayer, reflection and help. There was trading in sacrificial animals and other products, at very high prices; money was exchanged, money was borrowed, bets were made. To be honest we created a lot of chaos there.

"We heard that an arrest warrant had been issued by the Sanhedrin against me for temple violation, an act that was punishable by death, so we fled. We continued to travel but stayed for shorter times at each location. In between we went back to Capernaum. Not only to rest, but also to avoid the growing crowd that followed us. The assemblies were catching the attention of those in power too often.

"The tension increased and one day we received the message that Lazarus had been arrested and tortured and killed. After we buried him I decided to go to the Pesach celebration in Jerusalem, the final goal of my tour. I had not been in town for very long when I was arrested by soldiers of the high priest at the Mount of Olives. From that moment on I was treated like a criminal and I clearly acknowledged that I was the Son of God. I also confirmed that I had a vision about the destruction of the temple in Jerusalem if they did not change their ways, something that actually happened about forty years later. They came to a judgment very quickly, because unrest in the city during Pesach had to be prevented. Pontius Pilate, the Roman governor, was asked to put me to death. I had become too dangerous for those in power. I was crucified, which was the most dishonourable method to end someone's life. I wanted a better world and had to pay for it.

"My body died, but the divine spirit within me always survives, so I actually rose from the dead. My disciples, who subsequently became apostles, promised to continue our work, even in areas where our message was not yet spread. My Father called to me, so I went there and now I am here again."

Sophie would happily have stayed inside the hotel suite watching television and talking with Joe for the rest of her life, but he was becoming increasingly stir crazy. Several times a day he would cause alarm amongst the police and security forces surrounding the hotel as he stepped outside without warning to talk to the crowds of people and media who were willing to wait day and night for the chance of even a glimpse of him at a window.

It was apparent to him that people were travelling to Christchurch from all over the world because of the range of different languages in which the crowds called out to him, begging for a word or a touch. It wasn't long before the media noticed that he was able to talk to all these people in their own languages, even dialects from the remotest parts of India, China and Africa, where no more than a few hundred thousand people spoke the same language. One or two of the editors put him to the test by infiltrating people into the crowd who could speak an obscure language and springing them on him unannounced. Never once did he hesitate in responding to them in their native tongues.

Every time he stepped outside the hotel he fed the world's endless appetite for more stories. Every miracle of healing or speaking in tongues that he performed was immediately recorded on a hundred different phones and shared with millions of others within hours.

Each time he stepped from the elevator the police and security representatives would rush across the foyer and try to dissuade him from walking out into the crowd unprotected, warning him of possible assassination attempts, begging him to wear a bulletproof vest, or to remain inside the foyer and allow them to bring people to him in an orderly fashion, searching them for weapons before allowing them close enough to strike. Each time he would smile sweetly, thank them for their concern, promise them that he would be safe and walk straight past them.

The increasing numbers who wanted to believe that he was the Son of God put forward the evidence of the unique DNA, the healings and speaking in tongues – the shrinking numbers of those who resolutely refused to believe it, led by the American President, who continued to shout "fraud" to anyone who was still listening, claimed that it was either a very clever hoax or simply a normal man with some freak abilities to learn and speak languages and perform faith healings.

His message of hope was irresistible to anyone who had previously felt that life was hopeless. People who had been struggling with poverty for generations now believed that Joe would be able to bring an end to the inequality that had blighted their existences, that he would be able to make the changes necessary for their children and grandchildren to live long, decent lives, free of hunger, poverty and disease, with equal opportunities for health and happiness. It was a compelling message and anyone in authority who agreed with the President and attempted to say it was all a trick succeeded only in appearing mean-spirited and pessimistic. Words like "faith" and "hope" trended heavily in online chatter.

The Pope, watching events unfold from Rome, was the

first of the leaders of the biggest religions to ask his advisors to begin contacting other religious leaders through diplomatic channels.

"Let's gather together twelve leaders as well," he suggested. "The religious world has been too fragmented for too long."

"His Holiness would very much like to discuss what these developments are likely to mean to all our followers," the diplomats told others, leaving unsaid the subtext that, just like the political and military leaders, they also wanted to discuss the possible effects on their own power bases of a new leader who might unite all the previously separated factions.

Initially, just like the politicians and generals, the religious leaders chose to believe that Joe was a confidence trickster and a potential troublemaker, but as the evidence of his divinity continued to build they began to understand that he might be speaking to mankind on behalf of all their gods. Some were more willing and open to accept this possibility than others. Some shared the American President's view that if things were allowed to continue along the same path, they might soon find that their own positions, which had been carefully, and in some cases ruthlessly, built up over many hundreds of years, had dissolved away to nothing like sand beneath their feet.

There were many who held positions of unimaginable power who whispered to one another behind closed doors that "something" might have to be done to remove such a potential threat to their positions.

TWENTY-SIX

"We would very much like it if you could join us at the house for some face-to-face time," Yung was talking over Skype. "This is such an insecure way to communicate."

"I have no secrets," Joe laughed. "I am an open book for all to read."

"I understand," she said, "but overheard conversations can be misunderstood and twisted out of context if they fall into the wrong hands."

"It would be nice to see you all again," Joe said, "and nice for Sophie and me to get out of this hotel suite for a while."

"Oh," Yung said, obviously taken aback, "is Sophie still with you? I hadn't realised."

"I have been suspended from my duties at the school," Sophie chipped in, leaning across the bed in order to come into the camera's range. "Didn't Hugo tell you?"

"Ah, yes, of course, I had forgotten. It would be great to see you too, Sophie."

It seemed obvious to Sophie that Yung, having ascertained from the school authorities that her son was safe after his experience of being trampled in the crowd, had not found time to talk to him since they had left the house on the Sunday evening. It had always amazed her how quickly the parents of boarders managed to forget their children as they pursued their own busy lives. Being 'out of sight' most definitely led to being 'out of mind'.

It was arranged for one of Yung's drivers to pick them

up from the service area of the hotel, in the hope that none of the people waiting outside would realise that Joe had left the premises, but someone in the media must have bribed a member of staff to keep them informed of his movements and, as soon as one journalist peeled off from the pack at the front of the hotel and jumped into her car, others realised that there was something going on and followed suit. Within ten minutes of Joe and Sophie leaving the grounds of the hotel there was a convoy of cars and television trucks on their tail. Ten minutes later, a police helicopter appeared above them, soon followed by several more unmarked ones.

"Are they all from the press, do you suppose?" Sophie asked, peering up into the skies.

"Some will be media, ma'am," the driver replied, "but Miss Yung warned that there might also now be military and security surveillance teams on your case."

"Military and security surveillance?" Sophie tried to get her head around the idea. "Why would they be interested in where Joe goes?"

"The Chinese government is interested in anything to do with Miss Yung," the driver replied, "and other governments are interested in anything the Chinese are interested in. Many of the big corporations are also worried and are reaching out to the military, offering financial backing. They are all beginning to fear the possibilities of widespread civil unrest. We have been instructed to stay on high alert at all times."

"They think there is going to be some sort of revolution?" Sophie was amazed. "In New Zealand?"

"They are afraid it is going to kick off everywhere, ma'am, starting with here."

"Seems you have become the global Che Guevara of the cyber age," Sophie said, sinking back into her seat and taking hold of Joe's hand.

"You think they'll be putting my face on T-shirts?" Joe laughed. "That would be cool."

"He was executed on the orders of the President of Bolivia," Sophie reminded him, and they both contemplated that thought for a few moments.

"I suppose what I am suggesting mankind should do is a sort of revolution," Joe said eventually, "but hopefully a peaceful one."

"Maybe we should design some T-shirts anyway," Sophie joked, wanting to shake off thoughts of death and crucifixion.

"If they are bringing in the military," Joe said, "I guess they are expecting it to be anything but peaceful."

Sophie leaned forward to the driver again. "Would any of those helicopters be armed?"

"I would imagine so, ma'am," he said, "for your protection."

"Or our annihilation," she muttered, sitting back and holding herself close to Joe, feeling suddenly vulnerable and hunted.

"You worry too much," he said, gently stroking her hair. "Have faith."

"That's easy for you to say, but you don't understand just how much of a hornets' nest you have stirred up here," she said. "When people in power feel threatened they always lash out viciously. Now we have politicians, big business and the military wanting to shut you down."

He smiled and kissed the top of her head and repeated, "Just have faith."

"Yeah, right," she replied, making them both laugh.

"What's happening there?" Joe asked the driver after they had been driving for twenty minutes, pointing at a sea of tents and camper vans which seemed to stretch from the side of the road all the way to the horizon. "That was all wide open space last time we came this way."

"That's one of the tented villages," the driver replied. "The city has overflowed. There are areas like that all round it. It started with the army setting up camps to house anyone who was unable to find a hotel room or a homeowner willing to put them up. Then people started arriving with their own equipment. It has mushroomed from there. Were you not aware?"

"We have been avoiding the news the last few days," Sophie said, staring out in awe. "It looks like some gigantic music festival."

"It is kind of a religious festival," the driver said. "With every religious nutcase – begging your pardon, sir – setting up their stall and shouting out their message to anyone who will listen."

"Why have they come here to do this?" Joe asked.

"They want to be close to you, sir. They believe that wherever you are is going to be where things will start to happen."

"Stop the car," Joe said. "Let's talk to them."

"Are you sure that's a good idea?" Sophie asked. "There are so many people, you could get mobbed. And the media are right behind us."

"She's right, sir," the driver agreed, "things could get out of hand."

"They are believers," Joe said. "Many of them must have travelled a long way to be here. I trust them to look after me. Stop the car, please."

The driver pulled over to the side of the road and unlocked the doors, allowing Joe to climb out. Sophie scrambled across the seat, determined to stay close to him. There was a screeching of tyres and brakes as the media caravan realised they were stopping. Car doors slammed and there was a flurry of running figures shouting instructions to one another and then questions to Joe. He beamed back at them but said nothing as he strode in amongst the tents.

Police men and women who had been surreptitiously patrolling amongst the campers were startled into action by the sudden burst of noise and activity. Their radios crackled into life, the voices soon drowned out by the roar of the helicopters as they came in lower for their aerial shots. Sophie couldn't work out which were police cameras and which were the media. She strained her eyes against the sun, trying to see if there were any guns showing but couldn't be sure. She had been on enough protests over the years to know that despite the carnival atmosphere in this camp the situation was charged with potential danger.

Passions were inevitably running high since everyone was there because they cared about the future of the world and wanted things to change. These were people who felt strongly enough to travel across the world and to live in considerable discomfort in order to make things happen. Some of them would undoubtedly be willing to go to extreme lengths to achieve whatever their personal goals for mankind might be. That had to open up possibilities for clashes between different ideologies and different agendas. There were simply too many people in this camp, which stretched as far as the eye could see, for the numbers of police and soldiers in evidence to be able to keep control if people started to fight. The driver was still in the car, talking on his phone, no doubt reporting this alarming change of plan to Yung and the Twelve.

Apparently oblivious to everyone else's anxieties, Joe was walking forward with his arms outstretched, shaking hands with anyone who came up, his smile demonstrating how welcome everyone was to come to him and embrace him. Word ripped through the camp like a forest fire in a gale and people came running from every direction, shouting out the news of his arrival in their midst. Some of the police tried to move on the increasing numbers of cars which were now stopping wherever they could on the road, while at the same time attempting to form a ring of protection around Joe as the crowd grew. Their voices were drowned by the helicopter engines, the wind from the blades roaring through the camps and making the tents flap and the dust clouds rise as if they were all trapped in a desert storm.

Joe did not attempt to compete with the noise but simply waded deeper and deeper into the sea of people, placing his hands on their heads, submitting to their physical requests for handshakes and kisses. Sophie felt a rising panic as she watched his head bobbing ever further away from her, unsure how she would ever get him back into the car and onto the road. It felt like watching a man deliberately choosing to swim in an ocean of hope and adoration, blissfully unaware of the dangerous undercurrents swirling beneath the surface, threatening to pull him under.

A call must have gone out for more assistance and within half an hour a battalion of riot police had been delivered in buses with cages across the windows. Sophie, having given up trying to stay close to Joe, had returned to the road to stand with the driver at the car, apparently invisible to all the eyes which were focused on one person only. She watched as the police sliced into the crowd with their batons, forming a black ribbon of body armour around Joe and providing a path back out towards them. The cordon of police bodies held firm despite the hundreds of arms and beseeching fingers that forced their way through in the hope of touching Joe as he strolled back, smiling and nodding from side to side, mouthing the words "thank you" to everyone who was there for him.

After what seemed like an age they persuaded him back into the car. As they pulled out they were now surrounded by vehicles, many of them seeming to want to push them off the road as they swerved close enough to get a good picture of the couple together. Some of the journalists continued to shout questions at them from moving cars, their words carried away on the wind as their granite-faced driver pressed the accelerator to the floor as hard as he dared.

"It's okay," Joe assured him, "stay slow and steady. We are not trying to escape anything. We are not afraid of anyone here."

Sophie was about to suggest that perhaps he would be wise to be a little more aware of the dangers in his surroundings, but when she saw the gentle smile of pleasure on his face as he looked out at the waving crowds, she changed her mind and told herself to breathe as deeply and slowly as Joe, waiting for her heart rate to settle down.

"Is it my imagination," Joe said as they drew closer to Yung's house, "or are there fewer guards in evidence?"

Sophie peered past him and scanned the mountains around them. "Well, you did tell them they needed to get out of their ivory towers and be less distrustful of the outside world."

"Well, that's a step in the right direction then."

As they reached the tunnel and gates the following cars dropped back, aware that they were in danger of trespassing on private land. As they waited for the gates to open, a few of the more intrepid reporters ran from their vehicles and shouted a few final questions through the car window. Joe smiled and waved cheerfully to the cameras and then the gates swallowed up the car, leaving the noise of the rest of the world outside.

There might have been fewer guards surrounding the property, but the terrace was crammed with people in suits talking into radios. It was as if Yung had pulled her forces back inside the fortress walls in order to protect her stronghold more tightly. The doors of the car were opened for them the moment it drew to a stop as if their guardians wanted them undercover in the house as quickly as possible.

"That's the Prime Minister's official car," Sophie said as they were hurried towards the door and into the main reception area. "Why would she be here?"

TWENTY-SEVEN

The Prime Minister rose from the table where she was taking coffee with Yung and Simon and extended her hand.

"It's a pleasure to meet you, Joe," she said with genuine warmth, showing no irritation at how long she might have had to wait for him to arrive, "and you Sophie. I have been hearing so much good stuff about both of you. I hope you don't mind me barging into your meeting like this."

"This is the Prime Minister," Yung prompted him.

"Of course," Joe beamed, "I've heard a lot of good stuff about you too, Prime Minister. Thank you for being so understanding about taking me in without any papers."

"Have you heard of manaakitanga, Joe?" the Prime Minister asked. "It is a traditional value of Maori culture, all about being hospitable, looking after visitors and caring how others are treated, no matter what their standing in society. It has had a positive influence on Kiwi hospitality down the generations."

"It is a lovely concept," Joe replied as other members of the Twelve and their families came over to say hello.

"It seems you have disrupted all our lives, Joe," the professor's wife said as he bent down to kiss her cheek like an old friend.

"I'm sorry about that," he laughed. "What is it they say about having to break some eggs in order to make an omelette?"

"It seems we are all going to be living here for the foreseeable future while you and the rest of them change the future of mankind." May held onto his hand a little longer than was strictly necessary for a handshake.

"We will do whatever we can to make your time here comfortable, May," Yung assured her.

"I have no complaints about the facilities," May sniffed. "It would just be nice to know how long we are likely to be here. Some of us have busy lives of our own to lead."

Joe squeezed May's hand with genuine affection. "It will all be worth it, May," he said. "I promise."

"If you don't end up getting the lot of us murdered in our beds," May giggled girlishly as her husband led her gently away.

"I'm so glad to get this chance to chat," the Prime Minster said as May and the professor rejoined another group. "You have done a great deal for my popularity around the world."

"I have?"

"You have indeed. A few weeks ago it was hard to get any other world leaders to answer my phone calls, now they are lining up to talk to me. It seems I have the trump card in my hand." She smiled with a genuine sweetness.

"You have?" Joe was unsure what she was talking about.

"You, Joe," she laughed. "You are the trump card in the pack at the moment. Everyone now wants to know exactly what is going on in little old New Zealand. No longer are we just famous for being the location for *The Lord of the Rings*. There is, however, a downside to our new-found popularity in the world – or rather your popularity."

"I'm sorry to hear that," Joe said.

"When all is said and done we are only a bunch of smallish islands in the middle of the ocean with less than five million people living on them. That's less than a third of the combined populations of New York and London. At the moment we have nearly double that number of people here, and there are many more heading this way as we speak."

"So I have heard."

"A number of cruise lines have commissioned ships to carry people here from Australia because every flight is booked up for weeks to come and there are literally millions of people wanting to get here because you are here, and because they believe you are going to solve all their problems from climate change and world peace to unexplained headaches and nasty little rashes."

"I don't think I am going to be able to do all that," Joe admitted with a chuckle, "and I really don't think I will have time to talk to all of them individually."

"Quite," the Prime Minister laughed, "but people are willing to take a chance. I suppose it is the same thinking that makes millions of people buy lottery tickets every week, even though they know the odds of winning are millions to one. The point is, they are coming, for whatever reason, and we don't have the infrastructure to handle this many people. There are already tented cities rising up all round Christchurch. People are actually willing to give up their comfortable homes and live like refugees just to be near you."

"Yes," he nodded, his face now serious as he thought through what she was telling him. "We stopped at one on the way here."

"Then you saw the problem. We are having trouble even getting enough drinking water and toilets to these places. There is a limit to the numbers we can handle, and yet we pride ourselves on being an open and welcoming country. Do you see my problem? We do not want to have to close our borders to visitors, but we also don't want to run out of food to give them, not to mention healthcare and everything else they are likely to need while they are here. We need your help, Joe, to stem the tide before it overwhelms us."

TWENTY-EIGHT

"The Prime Minister is meeting with him? Is she kicking him out of her country?" The President of America appeared confused. It was nearly midnight and he wanted to go to bed. "She must be kicking him out, right? I mean he's a troublemaker and he has no papers to be there in the first place, does he?"

"As far as we can tell he has no papers at all, sir. It is a little hard to ascertain what he does have," the Director of National Intelligence replied. He was trying to limit as much as possible the information he shared with his leader at this stage. He was under pressure from the diplomats to keep things calm on the international stage. The financial markets were already reacting badly to what looked like was turning into some sort of global revolution and he was finding it increasingly hard to get the generals to talk to him at all. If the President started sounding off with ill-informed sound bites, ill feeling between a number of nations, where mutual suspicion was already an established norm, could escalate dangerously fast.

"I'll tell you what he has; he has a hell of a nerve." The President was sounding like an exasperated parent discussing an unruly child. "The guy is a hippy and now he's turning the whole of her country into some sort of festival of peace and love. It's a beautiful country, New Zealand. I've heard that it is. Have you seen *The Lord of the Rings*?"

"I haven't, sir. I did read the books as a child."

"Dumb film, full of pixies and elves and God knows what

else, but beautiful scenery. That's New Zealand. It's a beautiful country. God's own country and she's letting this guy and his followers mess the whole thing up with their tented cities or whatever. Have you seen the piles of garbage and the queues for the bathrooms on the news? People are living like rats, like cockroaches. Why do so many people want to put themselves through that just to be in the same country as him?"

"Might it be an idea to invite him here?" the Director suggested tentatively. "Better to have him inside the tent pissing out rather than…"

"He's not coming near my country!" The President slammed his fist on the top of the desk, making the phone jump. "But we can offer help to the government down there to deal with him. Find out what they need. Get her on the phone."

"The Prime Minister is out of reach at the moment…" the Director started to say.

"Okay, I get it!" The President stood up, not wanting to hear that his calls were not being accepted. "I'm going to bed. I'll talk to her tomorrow."

With that he was gone and the Director felt his whole body relax. He pulled out his phone and punched a button as he followed his leader out of the Oval Office. "The President has retired for the night," he informed his next in command. "Keep trying to get hold of this woman so he can talk to her tomorrow."

*****

The President of Russia was just waking up and already talking on his phone as he climbed out of bed, pulling on a T-shirt.

"The Prime Minister is meeting him personally?"

"Yes, sir."

"At the Chinese woman's house?"

"Yes, sir."

"Is our informant still in place?"

"Yes, sir, but they are unable to communicate. The group of Twelve have all cancelled their plans to leave at the end of the week. It looks like they are going to use New Zealand as their headquarters for whatever they plan to do next."

"They are all staying in the house together, with their families?"

"It's a big house, sir."

"I know it's a big house. I've seen the pictures!" he snapped. "And we can make no contact with our informant?"

"Not until they are away from the house. The American President is trying to reach the Prime Minister personally. We think he favours the idea of removing this healer permanently."

"Permanently?"

"Yes, sir."

"He's an idiot," the President grumbled, "but he may prove useful to us in this. We don't want it to appear that we feel threatened by this man and his followers, but it would be better if he was gone. It would also be better if the Americans were to take the blame for removing him. Let's explore some of the possibilities for making that happen."

* * * * *

The Chinese President was having an early lunch as he took the briefing from his security adviser.

"The Prime Minister is now inside the house with Yung Zhang and the man with no past. Both the Americans and the Russians are worried at the levels of support that are building up for him. They think this could lead to large scale unrest and eventual instability everywhere."

"Do we know what they are talking about inside the house?"

"Not at the moment, sir. The technical departments are working on that."

"Do the Americans or the Russians know more than we do?"

"The Russians still have their informant in place but they have had no information from them."

"Would they be willing to share information with us, or anyone else, when they have it?"

"They might say that they would be willing, but I don't know if we could trust the information they chose to share. They have lied to us before."

The President nodded his understanding as he chewed thoughtfully.

"Does Liang Zhang know anything about the man with no past? Does he know why his wife is so interested in him?"

"We are pretty certain that he knows nothing about this man, sir. We have been very persistent with our questions and he has been very consistent with his answers."

The President nodded his understanding again and closed his eyes to concentrate on his food and to let his security advisor know that the conversation was at an end for the moment. The security advisor bowed his way out of the room backwards, even though he knew his leader could not see him through lowered lids, fearful that they might spring open to catch him unawares.

TWENTY-NINE

The Prime Minister was standing beside Joe, looking out at the view from Yung's picture window. The Twelve were all sitting behind them, listening intently to their quiet words.

"I wouldn't want to tell anyone that they can't come to see me," Joe said.

"I understand, but the laws of physics are working against us," the Prime Minister pointed out. "Unless you can come up with a particularly clever miracle I don't see how you can be seen in the flesh by five million people, plus however many million more are already setting out from their homelands as we speak in order to get here. Correct me if I have misunderstood the nature of your appearance amongst us, but you currently seem to be only one man, with the same limitations of time and space as the rest of us."

Joe returned her smile and nodded. "No," he sighed, "you have not misunderstood, Prime Minister."

"Perhaps we could make use of the man-made miracle of modern communications," Simon suggested and they both turned to look at him as he continued. "Would it be an idea to set up a live global television interview, beaming it out simultaneously all over the world, allowing people in every country to ask whatever questions they want without having to make the trip to New Zealand?"

"How would you choose the questioners out of all the millions who would rush forward for such an opportunity?" Haki asked.

"I would imagine there are a limited number of important questions that everyone would want to ask." Simon was thinking it through as he talked. "We would need to ask people to put their questions in advance, via text maybe, and algorithms would then be able to work out which are the most popular questions and an interviewer would be able to ask them on behalf of all the people who sent them in. Would that be technically possible?"

"Yes," Lalit and Yung said simultaneously.

For the next hour they passed ideas back and forth until they had outlined a rough idea of how the broadcast would be organised and Simon was tasked with the job of setting it up. The Prime Minister, grateful to at least have something positive to go back to her government colleagues with, glanced at her watch.

"I have taken up far too much of your valuable time," she said, heading for the door, shaking the hands of each of the Twelve as she went and bowing low to kiss Joe's hand. "Please let me know if there is anything I can do to help with the setting up of the interview."

Once she was gone, Yung invited Joe to sit down next to her.

"I'm sorry about that," she said. "That was not why we asked you back today. We did not realise she was going to make a surprise visit like that. I did not feel that we could turn her away since we are relying so much on the hospitality of her country."

"I don't think we should turn anyone away," Joe agreed.

"Well," Yung laughed, "as she pointed out, that may now prove a little difficult in practice…"

"So, why did you ask me back?"

"Now that you are here on Earth to lead us in spreading the message of how imminent the extinction of mankind has become and how we can avoid it, we feel we should waste no time in deciding exactly what that message should be and what solutions we are offering. There are plenty of people pontificating out there about what is wrong with the world, very few are offering well thought-through solutions. The whole world is now listening to what you have to say and we can't afford to let that opportunity slip past. We want to check with you that you agree with us on the changes that need to be made to human behaviour if mankind is going to survive the coming years. We also feel that we need to create a new set of guidelines for everyone to live by and we want to show that to you."

"You are thinking of replacing the Ten Commandments of Moses?" Joe asked.

"Not just that. Every religion has its own version of those basic rules, with a few variations, but all of them were drawn up thousands of years ago. We believe we need to make them totally relevant to people today if we are hoping to persuade them to agree to abide by them. We also need them to be acceptable to every religious denomination."

"Rather than calling them 'rules' or 'commandments'," Lalit added, "we prefer to think of them as 'guidelines'. They will be chosen for their ability to help people think about their behaviour and the behaviour they would want to see in others, and to agree on what is most important in life."

"Have you made a start on the list?" Joe asked and Yung handed him a wooden disc about two centimetres thick and more than forty centimetres in diameter.

"This wood is from a monkey puzzle tree," she said. "I have lasered the text of the twelve guidelines onto it. It seemed symbolic somehow."

Joe took it from her and read the first line. "Be kind."

"The Dalai Llama, Tenzin Gyatso, says 'my religion is

kindness'," Yung explained. "Doesn't it start there? Just to be kind. It costs nothing."

Joe nodded his agreement and read the next line. "Be honest."

"It may be a cliché," Yung said, "but if you tell the truth you do not have to remember anything. Maybe you cannot always tell everything but what you do tell must be correct."

"What do you mean by 'Know yourself'?"

"The words are attributed, among others, to Socrates and stood on the pediment of the Temple of Apollo in Delphi; 'Know Yourself'. Knowing others is intelligence, but knowing yourself is wisdom. We believe being honest towards yourself about your strengths, your weaknesses, your desires, your fears and your thoughts is the start for all personal growth. Self-knowledge is difficult but it is a great investment if you can train and coach others in how to achieve it."

"Do as you promise," he read.

"We should always think before we promise something because when you promise something you should do it. It is a good agreement between people to do so. If it really isn't possible then tell the other person in time so that they can take it into account. Trust is fertile soil for further growth."

"'Be modest' is the next one," Joe said.

"People are all too often too demanding and assertive. Each person needs to consider how important they are in relation to the whole."

"Next we have 'Work hard'."

"If you are lucky enough to be healthy and fit, you are also lucky enough to work hard to build a world, a society with others. It is also good to try to do what you enjoy and what you are good at, because then you are at your most productive, whether that is running a bank or bringing up children, farming the land or creating works of art."

Joe nodded and read out the next guideline. "Be tolerant."

"If every person at least tries to be open-minded and not to judge too quickly, the world will soon become much better. Just try to accept others as they are; we all have the same right to live on this planet, haven't we?"

"I agree," Joe said. "The next one is 'Try to forgive and say sorry'."

"There are so many conflicts where people think only in black or white, when we know that most of the time the truth lies in the grey areas. We need to be brave enough to be vulnerable and ask ourselves if we might not always be perfect and then to look the other person in the eye and say, 'Sorry, I was wrong'. But if the other person is clearly in the wrong, can we forgive them? Releasing negativity sets you free. So we counsel people to try not to let the sun go down over their anger."

"Okay. How about 'Help and share where possible'?"

"We should all consider whether we can do more for other people, especially when we have a good life ourselves. It is almost a definition of love, don't you think?"

"I do indeed," Joe smiled. "Treat nature like you treat the people you love."

"Most people are happy to do good for those they love. They want to take care of them. This guideline asks you to treat nature like you treat the people you love."

"Do not do to others, what you do not want them to do to you."

"When we tried to summarise the essence of most successful religions and philosophies of life in one rule, we came to the words that you used last time you were here; 'Do not do to others, what you do not want them to do to you.' It is the most eternal of truths."

"The next one is 'Enjoy and be grateful'."

"This will never apply to everyone all the time, but we should all laugh, sing, dance, love, eat, drink, experience, learn, travel, discover, exercise, make jokes when we can. Yes, you are allowed to enjoy life. Just don't hurt other people while doing so. And be happy and grateful."

He sat in silence for a moment, lost in thought, and then read the text to himself again. None of the Twelve interrupted him. Eventually he looked up at them and smiled.

"I knew I was choosing the right people for this job," he said. "They look perfect to me. Thank you, Yung. If all people could adopt these good intentions as the starting point for their behaviour, the field will be ripe for harvesting. And it would indeed help enormously if these guidelines were introduced in all education programmes whether they are based on secular, religious or spiritual principles."

"So," Lalit spoke up, "from that we moved on. Based on the SWOT analysis we told you about, we had almost decided that it would be impossible to find a way to save mankind. But now that we have you on board we believe it can happen. We are pretty sure that most people will try to follow the twelve guidelines when you ask them to. That will greatly help us to introduce an ambitious, social and just plan for a better world because the thoughts behind our plan will obviously be in line with the essence of the guidelines. If well-intentioned people do not make any decisions, then people with less good intentions will. The history of mankind has demonstrated that that is how it works.

"So we asked ourselves: What would we do if we were in charge of the planet? Could we all agree on a master plan for mankind to live by? Is there a higher priority for mankind and its survival on Earth than to create a good, liveable world for all children, grandchildren, great-grandchildren and their future descendents?

"We believe the installation of a world government with a strong mandate would be effective, cost-saving and economically better than the protectionist nationalism that has evolved, as long as it is transparent and has no double agendas. In order to be effective, the essence of the plàn should not be negotiable, but direct democracy via the internet can be organised so that all other matters can be decided in a democratic way with the press of a button on people's phones."

"We would insist on the surrender of all weapons apart from a small residual supply which would remain in the hands of the UN," Yung said.

"And there would need to be a reform of the financial and monetary system," Simon added, "limiting the amount of wealth individuals can stockpile. We would provide everyone with a basic income and they would need to accept the moral responsibility to work in exchange for that if they are able, with a cap on the highest salaries. We do not believe everyone should have the same income since we all need stimuli and money is an important one, but there has to be a radical levelling, plus the expropriation of crucial sectors and companies where necessary, such as genetic engineering, AI and the largest data companies in order to protect us."

"We wanted to keep the plan as simple as possible so everyone could understand it," Lalit said, taking back the explanation. "We decided to use the number twelve again and we defined twelve agreements for mankind to live by, which pretty much reflect the seventeen Sustainable Development Goals for 2030 from the United Nations. We want to start with the eradication of poverty. It sounds ridiculously altruistic and unrealistic, but it isn't."

"It's become such a political cliché," Tanzeel said, "and to a degree it is when politicians pay lip service to it when they are running for election, but then do nothing once they are in power. But mankind has already managed to raise billions of people from abject poverty over the last hundred years; we believe there is no reason not to bring everyone else up to the same standards. Look what they have achieved in China in just a few decades."

"And this includes eradicating hunger," Sofia, a botanist from South America who had made a global reputation through studying ways in which plants could be developed to sustain a growing population. She and Sophie had already bonded over the possibilities of eradicating the use of meat by humans in the food chain. "There is no reason why anyone in the world should be hungry."

"Good health is another area where we have to reach an agreement," Amelia spoke up. "Obviously I would say that, since I have dedicated my life to it. But if everyone was to agree on the steps that are needed to prevent the basic illnesses that soak up the majority of the time and the funds of the medical profession, we would then be free to concentrate on helping those with conditions that are not yet preventable. To a degree it is all about education."

"And that is where I have the most to say," Salma took over. "I made my name fighting for equal educational opportunities for women, but that doesn't mean I don't want the same for men. We need everyone to agree on the importance of education before we can hope to achieve any of the other goals. Up till now it has been the educated elite making all the decisions for the uneducated masses. People who are trapped in ignorance can't hope to move forward. With all the developments in communications technology there is now no reason why every child – and every adult for that matter – can't receive a good education."

"Salma's work in education is also linked to the need for an agreement on gender equality in all things," Yung said, "not just education. There is no faster remedy for overpopulation than ensuring that every woman receives a good education and suitable work."

"We also think that contraceptives should be free of charge, by the way," Amelia said.

"The provision of clean water and sanitation to every individual on Earth is something else that we think everyone can agree on," a Canadian voice that Joe was familiar with cut in. Tom Butcher was a primatologist and Sophie had played Joe several of Tom's television documentaries, in which he was studying polar bears as they struggled to survive on shrinking ice caps.

"You and I have already talked about the need to find affordable and clean energy sources," Lalit reminded Joe, "with safe nuclear energy plants and thorium reactors as part of one strategy for the whole planet. We also want to link that with the provision of decent work for all those who are able to, with the aim of continuing economic growth, as long as it is not gained at the expense of any of our other goals. We do not believe in growth simply for its own sake; that is wasteful of everyone's energies."

"But at the same time," Haki interrupted, "we need to do something about the widening inequality between the haves and the have-nots."

"Isn't that the same as eradicating poverty?" Joe asked.

"Eradicating poverty is only half of the solution," Haki explained. "We also have to find a way to curb the excesses of the rich, without disincentivising them too much. We need to make them want to contribute to the communal pot rather than always looking for ways to siphon off money which they don't even need. We need to show why it is better to pay your fair share of taxes than buy a bigger yacht. Even if we manage to get rid of poverty, people will still be unhappy if they see that some people earn and consume way more than their fair share, which obviously includes a number of the people in this room."

"Not you and me, though Haki, eh?" Joe joked and the others laughed uneasily. "¡Viva la revolución!"

"Okay," Yung interrupted, showing no sign that she might be enjoying the joke. "We get it."

"We need also to have a plan for building a great many sustainable cities and communities" – Austin spoke quickly in an attempt to cover the moment of awkwardness – "which fits in with the idea of promoting responsible consumption and production."

"None of this means anything" – Minenhle sounded angry, her loud and sudden interruption making the others jump – "unless we fix the climate. If the world becomes too hot, the water will disappear and mankind, along with every other life form, will have disappeared off the planet before we have been able to implement any of these grand plans. Climate action is by far the most urgent priority."

"Even if we manage to halt climate change," Ahmya, the oceanologist added, "we are still going to have to put in a great deal of work developing the possibilities for life both on and below water. If the oceans are rising and land is becoming scarcer and more crowded we will need to build some of Austin's sustainable cities under water, or float them on the surface. We need to work out how to inhabit and farm the ocean beds effectively and sustainably."

"We also need to draw up a global legal structure," Simon joined in, "building strong institutions which cannot be undermined by any rogue leaders, creating a partnership of shared goals that every single person on the planet can buy into and vote for through their phones and computers.

"We have a plan which is now ready to be activated,

but there are still many vested interests amongst the existing leaderships in maintaining the status quo. That is why Yung's husband is still in a cell somewhere in China and world leaders of every political persuasion are trying to discredit us, making out that we are just a bunch of idealists with no practical plan, now led by a 'hippy healer', as the President of America likes to refer to you, Joe. We have to show them that there is no option to these changes if the world is going to survive. If they don't support us it will create tensions that will soon escalate into violence, or even full-scale war, between those who believe in the changes and those who want to resist them. They have to accept that this is a revolution that they can't afford to ignore."

"I don't think they are ignoring us any more," Yung said quietly, "but there is still a very real danger they will try to silence us and buy themselves a little more time in power. It would seem that some of them would rather see the whole world destroyed than lose even a small fraction of the power and wealth they have managed to accrue. We need to continue protecting ourselves, Joe. It is very nice to think that we will one day be living in a world where we can trust everyone, where we do not need to lock and guard our gates, but that time has not yet come. The supporters of the status quo will be willing to use violence to silence us if they have a chance. That is for sure."

They all sat for a moment, contemplating the possible consequences of having the majority of the world's most powerful people wanting to silence them as quickly as possible.

"However many guards you surround yourselves with," Joe said eventually, "they will find a way to destroy us if they want to. They have weapons that they will be willing to use, but we would not want to use weapons against them. So we have to have faith that they will not decide to do that. We have no choice. We are vulnerable in every way and must remain so, even to one another. I've told you before, one of you in this room will betray me…"

They all protested at once but he held up his hand to calm them.

"That person already knows who they are, and they should also know that I will forgive them, as I have said before. It doesn't matter how many armed guards you put on your gates, Yung. No one can ever be safe because that is not nature's way. Trying to achieve some mythical level of security from all risks is one of the causes of mankind's current predicaments. Unless a person accepts that they are mortal and vulnerable, they will never be happy."

The ripple of protests had died away and they all looked around at one another in horror as they took in the full impact of what he was telling them, each of them trying to work out who the traitor could possibly be amongst this small, self-selected group of people.

THIRTY

The hotel reception staff were under strict instructions not to put through every call to Joe's room because they were pouring in in such numbers, so it was a shock for Sophie to be woken by the persistent ringing of the bedside phone. Joe appeared to be sleeping peacefully beside her as she rolled over and fumbled for the receiver, more to silence it than anything else.

"Yes?" she said when she finally got it to her ear the right way round.

"I'm sorry to disturb you, Miss Adams" – it sounded odd to be addressed by her surname – "but we have a Professor Martin on the phone from Oxford."

"Oxford?" She tried to focus on this information. "The university?"

"I believe so, madam. I told him that you don't accept unscheduled calls in the room but he insisted that you would want to take this one. He said to tell you it is about the scrolls."

"Oh." Things began to come back to her as she struggled to bring herself to a state of wakefulness. She had heard that the scrolls had been flown from Jerusalem to Oxford to be authenticated and had sent another email to the relevant department at Oxford to tell them of her interest, but this was the first response she had received. "Okay, put him through."

"Miss Adams?" The voice sounded elderly and a long way away.

"Yes."

"My apologies for disturbing you. My colleagues and I have been examining the scrolls that were recently unearthed in Jerusalem. I believe you have expressed an interest in being kept up to date on the subject. I have been following the story of your friend in New Zealand…"

"Joe."

"Quite. There was a lot of scepticism in academic circles about his claims to be the reincarnation of Jesus Christ, as I am sure you can imagine, but I thought you would like to know that things are changing, partly because of these scrolls."

Sophie was fully awake now and pulled herself up on the pillows, concentrating hard on what was being said. Joe was beginning to stir beside her but she wanted to find out what the professor had to say for himself.

"We have found four rolls in stone jars. All rolls consist of twenty-four parchment sheets of lamb's leather skin." The professor was talking as if delivering a lecture and she wished she had some means of recording his words so that she could play them back to Joe after the call. "The skin was first stripped of hair, fat and meat in different baths, scraped again and then stretched very tightly to dry. Once dry it was rubbed with salt. We are very lucky here that a unique mix of salts has been used, giving the rolls an unusual light colour and a very smooth surface. This considerably increases the contrast with the letters of the text, important for legibility, of course. These specific salts also have a lowered tendency to absorb water, so there is less effect of moisture, which has benefited the preservation process, despite Jerusalem being naturally higher than the dry environment of the Dead Sea, where many rolls have been found in the past.

"With a scanner and an advanced computer algorithm we investigated the rolls on material and ink, redrawn in 3D and were able to partially decipher the text. The quality is, of

214

course, not great any more and we will still need quite a lot of time to be able to read everything that has been written, but it is good enough to be able to make a number of statements.

"We were also able to determine the age based on the usual Carbon-14 dating method in combination with an analysis of writing material, style and other artefacts in the first half of the first century. The text is written in Galilean Aramaic, which is the language that Jesus and his disciples would have spoken. A detailed description is made of which people belonged to the permanent group around Jesus and what their roles were and it confirms that the writer was a scribe called Amos. In addition, the texts contain various counselling and statements, comparable to those in the apocryphal gospel of Thomas. For example, one statement from Jesus that we were able to decipher was: 'The Kingdom of God is a Kingdom of wisdom, not a Kingdom to rule and not a Kingdom of the end'.

"We have read parts of reports of a number of important events that took place in the years that Jesus and his disciples roamed, reports of events that we also know from the gospels of Mark, Matthew and Luke. Exegetes will enjoy a number of deviations in these found texts compared to those three gospels. This feels so incredibly authentic, the texts must absolutely have been written down by someone close to Jesus, such as Amos.

"The theological world has always been fascinated by the relationship between the gospels of Mark, Matthew and Luke. It is certain that the gospel of Mark was written as the oldest gospel around AD 65-70. The Gospels of Matthew and Luke are probably around 10–20 years younger. The gospel of John is 10–20 years younger than that of Matthew and Luke. Mark has been a clear source for Matthew and Luke. Another important theory, however, is that the gospels of Matthew and Luke were also based on an older common source Q (after the German word 'Quelle').

"We cannot yet jump to conclusions, but we have already established, for example, that the sequence in the story of Jesus' famous Sermon on the Mount exactly matches the rolls and the gospels of Matthew and Luke. And we have also been able to conclude that the version of Our Father's prayer in the scrolls is almost identical to that in Matthew, while the prayer in Mark's gospel does not occur in its entirety. We see this as a clear indication that these scrolls have at least served as a source for the later gospel writers, Matthew and Luke, and we are hopeful that we have now found the Q source.

"So what we have clearly been able to read is the prophecy recorded by Jesus himself that he will die on the cross, will rise from the dead after three days and will go back to his Father. And we have been able to ascertain without any doubt that he planned to return to another place on Earth at a time when all humanity is at a turning point and needs his guidance the most.

"There is no doubt that these scrolls are authentic. We will be making an official announcement in due course, but I thought you would like to know."

"That's very kind of you, Professor," she said, "very kind of you indeed."

"Not at all," he replied politely. "We would also be very interested in receiving an exact account of your vision, for the record."

"It was just a dream really," she said, "and it's hard to remember now. So much has happened since."

"Indeed," the professor agreed. "These are enormously exciting times we are living in, Miss Adams. If there's anything that you feel you could tell us we would be extremely grateful. Obviously we would keep your words confidential until you gave permission for them to be shared. If at any stage you felt able to make the trip to Oxford you could be assured a very warm welcome."

"Let me think about it, Professor."

"Of course. Thank you. We are going to be watching your friend's progress with enormous interest."

Once the professor had hung up she lay for a few minutes watching Joe as he slowly came to the surface on the pillow beside her and thinking about the professor's news. Her heart was racing and thumping loudly in her ears. Real life was turning out exactly as predicted in her dream and she felt like she was sitting at the centre of the entire universe. If she genuinely was some sort of divine prophet, it confirmed that she had a central role to play in whatever was about to happen in the world. Her name was going to be written about and talked about for generations. Scholars would be studying her life in thousands of years' time, like they now studied John the Baptist. Maybe she would even be made a saint. More important than all that, it meant that she and Joe were bound to be together for as long as...

Her heart gave a lurch as she considered the possibility that Joe might be taken from her as abruptly as Jesus was taken from his followers the last time he was on Earth. The thought of being separated from him was too painful to bear and she was unable to stop a sob from escaping her throat and tears springing to her eyes as Joe lifted his head from the pillow and looked at her.

"Are you okay? What's wrong?"

He put his arms around her and held her close until the sobbing had subsided for long enough to get out the words, "The scrolls have been authenticated. They all believe you now."

"Who do?"

"The theologians. The scholars in places like Oxford University. They all believe that you are the Son of God."

"And this is making you cry?"

"What is making me cry is the thought of what they might do to you – as they did last time. It's the thought of losing you. I can't bear it."

"Don't be frightened," he whispered, "God will be with you always. We will always be together."

She found her sobs turning to laughter.

"Did I say something funny?" he asked, pulling back to see her more clearly.

"No. I was just thinking how corny and ridiculous those words would have seemed to me a few months ago, but now they actually sound true."

"Does that count as another miracle, do you think?" he grinned.

"They want you dead, Joe," she said, refusing to allow him to lighten the mood. "The most powerful people in the world want you dead."

Unable to deny that she was right, he held her tightly as she cried.

THIRTY-ONE

The American President had finally managed to get through to his Russian counterpart.

"This healer guy is causing a lot more trouble," the American waded straight in, never knowing how long it would be before the Russian grew bored and hung up. "The media don't seem to be able to discredit him, however hard they try. People actually seem to believe his bullshit."

"Have you talked to the Chinese?" the Russian asked.

"Have you tried talking to the Chinese?" the American spluttered, "it's like drowning in riddles. I can't get a straight answer about anything."

"Did they talk about Yung Zhang?"

"What do you think? It's like they never heard of her. I don't even know if her husband, this Liang guy, is still alive. They're sticking to the line that they know nothing about his disappearance, which is obviously a crock of shit. And you'd think they would want to neutralise the guy's wife because she's a troublemaker, but they just pretend they don't understand what I'm talking about."

"It would be hard for them to take her out now," the Russian suggested, "with the whole world watching New Zealand."

"You think they care about that sort of thing? They're playing some sort of long game and they don't intend to let us know what it is. I asked them what they think of this Son of

God crap and they just start talking about Confucius. A lot of other world leaders have been calling me. They are all looking to me to do something about it. They all think the healer guy should be stopped."

"The British and the Europeans think that?"

"They don't know what they think. A lot of the tough guys in Africa and the Middle East, they can see he's a danger to them. There are a lot of people in Africa who swear by all the Jesus stuff and a lot of them don't have a pot to piss in; they could easily be stirred up to start making demands and asking for changes. And the Israelis certainly don't want him stirring up all this religious stuff again. There's a lot of people who would like to see him disappear. Do you know what I mean?"

There was a significant pause and then a throaty chuckle from the Moscow end of the line. "Of course I know what you mean. But do any of them want to go down in history as the ones who killed the Messiah for the second time?"

"He's hung up again!" The American President threw the phone down, too furious to even bother putting it back on its cradle.

"I think he understood what you were saying, sir," the Director of National Security said, trying to calm his boss. "I think you'll find he will set the wheels in motion."

"I hope so because I really don't want to have to bomb the hell out of New Zealand!"

Everyone in the Oval Office laughed nervously, aware that their president wasn't even smiling.

THIRTY-TWO

The Pope leaned in closer to catch the words of the professor who had been sent to Rome from Oxford to explain the findings of the theologians. Overawed by the surroundings and by being in the presence of the man who was possibly the most famous and revered figure on the planet, at least until recently, the professor was virtually whispering.

"We believe this manuscript must have been a key source for the later gospels," he was saying, his head bent reverentially low, covering his mouth and making it even harder for the pontiff to make out his words.

The findings of the scholars had been sent to the twelve leaders of the major religions on the Pope's list but it had been decided that personal visits would also be in order. The news that the scrolls had come to light at the same time that someone believed by many to be the Son of God had returned to Earth, meant that it was not hard for the scholars to get audiences with the men who were normally impossible for mere mortals to reach.

"We are praying hard for guidance on how to advise our followers," the Pope said. "It seems that we have been presented with an opportunity to heal the many historical divisions that have existed between the different religions. This man in New Zealand seems to have the potential to be a unifying force. He has raised the consciousness of people everywhere."

"Not just Christians, either." The professor became

suddenly enthusiastic, forgetting for a moment that he was in the presence of the pontiff. "There is nothing to say that he is the son only of the Christian God. This is a chance for all the religions to promote the gods that they have always believed in. His teachings are entirely non-denominational."

The Pope sat back in his chair and nodded thoughtfully. Many of his advisers had been warning him against recognising that Joe might be who he claimed he was, but he was beginning to think that would not be a wise course to follow. Just because he spent the majority of his time holed-up in Vatican City did not mean that he was cut off from everything that was happening in the outside world. He had seen the news programmes showing the millions of people all over the world marching upon their capital cities, carrying banners with slogans praising Joe and demanding that he be recognised and listened to by those in power. It was obvious that the energy for most of the marches was coming from young people and the Pope, along with other religious leaders, was aware that he was being classed alongside politicians and even dictators as one of the older generation who had caused the many problems that mankind now faced, and who were clinging to power regardless of whether it was in the best interests of the world. The slogans on the banners, which demanded that the elite changed their greedy, egotistical and short-termist ways, seemed to be aimed at the religious leaders as much as the politicians, business tycoons, generals and hated oligarchs.

For the next few hours, His Holiness appeared to be absorbed in the theological details that the professor was laying out for him, but at the back of his mind he was already planning how he might get to meet and talk to Joe without seeming to be pushing to the front of the queue. The last thing he wanted was for other religious leaders to feel that the Catholic Church were trying to claim some sort of exclusivity over the returned Messiah, but at the same time he was aware that a large proportion of his 1.3 billion followers would very much like to see him take the lead.

There had been an announcement of a televised broadcast being planned, which would reach every citizen in the world, and the Pope wanted to be able to talk to Joe to find out what he would be saying before it went out, perhaps even offering some advice on areas that were likely to prove sensitive. Not for the first time he felt like he was walking a tightrope and that whichever way he might fall he was likely to suffer and inflict considerable damage.

*****

Over the following weeks, religious leaders who had never spoken to one another sent their diplomats and representatives out to make contact and to explore the possibility that they would all send a request for Joe to meet them before he made his television broadcast to the whole world. Many of their highest officials were wary, unsure where such communications could lead, fearful of insulting their own leaders or those of other religions. Some suggested that they might invite Joe to Rome for the meeting, but it was soon seen that this would look far too partisan. After innumerable letters back and forth it was decided that it would be far more appropriate for them all to go to meet Joe in New Zealand.

Initially the diary planners of the church leaders threw up their hands in horror at the thought of organising something so enormous at such short notice. Most of their leaders had their days mapped out for years in advance, but as it gradually became clear that this was the will of their leaders, and since none of them wanted to be the only major religion not represented at the meetings, diaries were adjusted and a request was put in to the Prime Minister of New Zealand.

"Holy shit!" was the Prime Minister's exact reaction when told of the request from the twelve most powerful religious leaders in the world. "These men represent close to five billion people. If they all come here at once for a meeting that historic the whole world is going to want to be here to see them. We'll sink under the weight. Apart from anything else, how will we look after that many representatives of God at the same time? We're having enough trouble catering for the followers of one of the buggers."

"I don't know how well they will take being rebuffed," the Minister for Home Affairs warned her. "People don't say 'no' to these guys very often."

"Perhaps," the Minister of Foreign Affairs suggested, "we could tell them that we would love to welcome them but we fear we would not be able to guarantee their safety. It's the truth, after all. I mean how would we keep that many VIPs safe when the whole place is swamped with visitors? Our police are already stretched beyond anything they have ever experienced before."

"Okay." The Prime Minister made a decision. "Tell them we are sorry but it's not possible. Word it any way you like."

Messages of regret were conveyed back to the offices of all the leaders, couched in diplomatic language, and it was agreed that they needed to find a more private place for the meeting. Someone suggested that they hire a cruise liner and position it somewhere a long way from land, flying all the various leaders to it in helicopters. Enquiries were made but no suitable ships could be found. Then someone suggested that they look into the possibility of hiring a private island somewhere in the South Pacific.

Research soon made it clear that the only island big enough to take all twelve leaders and their entourages, and private enough to ensure that no one who was not specifically invited could get there, was an atoll called Tetiti. It was owned by a Hollywood film star who needed so much money to maintain her penchant for buying beautiful pieces of international real estate that she was always working and never able to take advantage of any of them. As a result it was fully staffed and available for hire as a private resort, usually for discreet corporate functions where senior executives were eager for their shareholders not to see how they spent their profits.

"Tetiti? Wow!" Sophie said when she heard. "Can I come?"

"Of course you can come," Joe grinned. "You can be my 'entourage'."

"There's no chance they are luring you into a trap, is there?" she asked after a few moments' thought.

"You need to have more faith, Sophie," he said.

"I wish you would stop saying that."

THIRTY-THREE

"Is this healer man with no past carrying a phone yet?" the Cyber Security Director in Beijing enquired.

"Apparently not. He is very clever," the researcher replied.

"No electronic devices at all?" the Director shook his head in disbelief. "We have no way of tracking him or listening to him?"

"Nothing on him personally. Many of the other people who are attending this island meeting will be carrying phones and tablets and laptops, but they will almost certainly be made to hand them in before any important meetings."

The Director was famed throughout his department for his cool head and it was the first time that his staff had ever seen anything close to a look of panic flickering across his impassive face. The thought of having to report to his superiors that there might be a corner of the Earth that they could not listen in to, filled him with trepidation. He took great pride in the job he had done for them in recent years but first Yung's house and now this island in the middle of the Pacific had taught him that he wasn't yet invincible. He picked up a phone and dialled.

"We need to guarantee satellite coverage of an atoll in the Pacific," he instructed the person who answered, without bothering with any of the usual courtesies. "It's called Tetiti. We need to be able to see and hear everything that is happening there."

* * * * *

"The Chinese are moving their satellites so that they can spy on Tetiti," a young technician deep inside America's Military Intelligence Department informed his immediate superior.

"We'll need to do the same. How long have we got?"

"The meeting is taking place in a week."

"A week? Dammit. Can we get set up in that time?"

"If permission is given now we might."

Several layers of bureaucracy held up the message for two days before it reached someone with the authority to act, by which time it was too late to be sure they could catch the Chinese up.

"Can we rent satellite space off one of the media people?" a general asked at an emergency meeting. "They cover most areas don't they?"

"We cannot channel top secret military information through a media-owned satellite," another pointed out. "You might as well print the whole thing directly onto the front page of every newspaper in the world."

"We can tie them down with official secrets contracts. We can appeal to their patriotic pride."

"No one respects official secrets any more and none of the media owners have any patriotic pride. Most of them aren't even American any more."

* * * * *

"Who is going to be on this island from New Zealand, then?" the Head of Security in Moscow enquired. "Will our informant be among them?"

"The healer is going alone," the operative informed him, "just with his girlfriend."

227

"Have we tried to reach out to this girlfriend?"

"We have tried but she is out of reach now, always surrounded by security. We don't yet know exactly who will be escorting the other delegates. Hopefully one of them will be someone we have already reached."

"Hopefully?" the Head of Security's voice had gained an edge of fear. "You think I can take a word like that to the President? Find out who is on this trip from each denomination and see who we can reach. We have to know what they are talking about before the Chinese or the Americans. If the church leaders are planning on coming together to assist in toppling the current political systems we need to be prepared. We need to have plans ready. We need to take action!" He pounded the table with a clenched fist to drive home the importance of each announcement.

"Is it possible that they are meeting him there in order to remove him?" the operative suggested.

"Do you think so?" The Head of Security was momentarily quietened.

"Perhaps we could just wait and see what happens."

The Head of Security nodded his agreement. "That is what I will suggest to the President."

THIRTY-FOUR

The Ukrainian was sitting on the balcony of his apartment in Double Bay, overlooking the glittering waters of Sydney Harbour and the silhouette of the city beyond. The sounds of the birds and insects in the trees, whose densely knitted branches and leaves kept off the worst of the heat, were the only things he could hear. He had several mobile phones laid out on the table beside his coffee, all of them on silent. Occasionally one of them would flicker with a message and he would glance at the screen, but nothing was exciting his interest enough to take his eyes away from the view for long.

He had been up for several hours already, working out in the gym before the heat built up and then shaving himself with an obsessive precision. Shaving was a ritual he often indulged in several times a day. If he didn't then his thick dark hair would give him a sinister appearance, which was something to be avoided at all costs. He took pride in his clean-cut appearance, like most young men, but he was also anxious not to stand out. It was an advantage in his trade if no one remembered seeing him passing by in the street. He liked to think he was good looking, but not good looking enough to turn heads.

The dense foliage all around the house meant that he was not overlooked by any of his neighbours and he made a point of never walking around the surrounding streets. If he left the house it was behind the tinted glass of his Mercedes or on a bicycle with helmet and goggles, which made him anonymous and unrecognisable to the casual glance. Some people in his line of work liked to live in isolated places, miles from the nearest neighbour, but he preferred to live in plain sight, in an area where everyone minded their own business.

Recently he had pared his professional life down to the bare minimum, only accepting one or two commissions a year. All he had to do the rest of the time was keep track of the various phones, and replace them on a regular basis. They were all cheap and disposable and although he knew that didn't mean that the sort of people who employed him would never be able to track him or listen in to his calls, it made it much harder for them. He would rather have operated without any electronic devices at all, but that would be impractical with the way the world now functioned. People who wanted to hire him had to be able to make contact somehow.

He was a little uneasy by the number of calls he had been getting that morning. Like the rest of the world, he had been following the stories coming out of New Zealand about the healer who could perform miracles. He had not been entirely surprised when his contacts told him that there were people who would like the man silenced. Anyone who became that popular that quickly was bound to be seen as a threat by vested interests. He was pretty certain that the request which had filtered through to him most strongly was originally from the Russian government, but he would never know for sure. The Americans were just as capable of coming up with a similar plan. Not that he cared who was behind it. As long as the money arrived in his bank account as promised it didn't matter who was sending it.

What had surprised him with this job was the other calls that had followed. News must have leaked out that he had been approached about the possibility of removing this man and others had made enquiries about whether they could have the body, if he was going to be killed. As far as the Ukrainian could make out it was the pharmaceutical companies who were interested in studying the chemistry and biology of a man who was claiming to be divine. One contractor, who had a strong Far Eastern accent, had suggested that rather than killing Joe, it might be more sensible to kidnap him so that the scientists could study him and carry out their experiments while he was still breathing and the blood was still pumping through his veins. He had not replied to that suggestion. Experience had taught him that the dead were the only people you could trust not to give you away.

Even after twenty years as a professional mercenary and assassin, the Ukrainian had to admit that he had been shocked by the level of interest being shown in this one target. His contacts had made it clear that he would be able to make enough money from this one job to retire for ever, which was an attractive prospect on such a beautiful sunny morning, but he was still wary of the thought of executing, or even kidnapping, someone who was being followed and watched by so many pairs of eyes every minute of the day.

Usually his targets were people who lived hidden and secretive lives, which made it easier to catch them alone at some point of the day or night. Not many of them courted publicity and drew crowds on the scale that this man was doing. On the other hand, large crowds could provide good cover, as long as he positioned himself so that he could make a clean getaway once the job was completed.

Having been trained originally as a soldier, he was more comfortable with the idea of a quick kill than the thought of any man being tortured. He had a picture in his brain of Joe pinned down on a laboratory table somewhere, while scientists stuck needles into him to study everything from his brain to his secretions. Maybe he was letting his imagination run away with him. Maybe he had watched too many old horror films late at night. But still it seemed that a sniper's bullet to the head, or a knife slid straight into the heart would be more honourable ways to remove the problem, and more achievable goals for him.

"There is a contact on the inside of his inner circle," he was told in one of the calls. "They have been feeding information out when they can, which isn't often. This person has been informed that things have changed and that they must support you if or when you make contact."

"Were they happy with that?"

"Their happiness is not your concern," the voice replied, which suggested to him that the plant could not be totally relied upon. As usual he would be relying almost totally on his own skills and experience.

That was all he had been told about the set-up so far, and after the call he had dissolved the phone in a container of acid which he kept solely for that purpose. Now he was waiting for the instruction to go to New Zealand.

THIRTY-FIVE

"You realise this has blown my carbon footprint for the rest of my life, right?" Sophie shouted over the engine noise as she gazed out of the window of the small plane which was carrying them from Fiji's airport to a small platform floating in the sea off Tetiti.

As they dropped lower over the atoll they could make out the boat coming towards the platform to meet them and ferry them the final half mile to the beach. The atoll itself looked like a CGI recreation of the perfect holiday destination. Pristine white beaches were fringed with palm trees where plantation style villas nestled in the shade beside the turquoise water. Several of the tiny islands were linked by bridges and it was possible to make out members of staff gliding around in snow white uniforms, ensuring that everything was ready for the arrival of possibly the most important guests they would ever have the privilege of serving.

Another small plane was just taking off from the platform, having already deposited its cargo of elderly, sweating clerics who were now being helped onto another rocking boat by kind, strong young hands.

"It actually does look like paradise," Sophie said, unable to wipe the smile off her face.

"Seriously?" Joe laughed. "You think this is what paradise looks like?"

"Please," she retorted, "give me a break. I don't get to

go to places like this, except in my dreams. Don't prick my bubble."

"Okay," he said and held up his hands in mock surrender, as the plane circled round and took its place gently on the water beside the platform. "Welcome to paradise!"

"When I die," Sophie burbled on as she looked across at the island, "I want to come back as a rich movie star."

"Sure you do," Joe teased her; "we'll have to see what we can do."

The island's staff members were so polite and discreet it was almost like they weren't there as they escorted them from the boat to the gardens which surrounded their villa, guaranteeing privacy on the other side of the sand.

"It feels like we're on honeymoon or something," she whispered as they made their way through the flowering bushes, sending clouds of brightly coloured butterflies and hummingbirds up into the air as they went.

Joe put his arm around her shoulders and pulled her to him, kissing her playfully on the nose, but saying nothing. The honeymoon feel continued once they reached their villa and a staff member showed them where everything was, poured them cool drinks and left them to settle in. They sat together on the veranda, staring through the gardens to the sea, sipping their drinks in silent thought. Sophie could see that Joe was lost in his plans for what he would say to the religious leaders and didn't interrupt him. After half an hour both of them had fallen asleep to the buzz of insects and the lapping of waves on the beach a few yards away.

Sophie must have slept for an hour before she woke to find Joe watching her from the other chair.

"Fancy a walk on the beach?" he asked when he saw her eyes flutter open.

"Sure," she said, sleepily pulling herself from the chair.

They were both in swimsuits as they emerged from the trees onto the hot sand. There was no one in sight in either direction. They ran to the cool of the water, allowing it to lap over their feet as they strolled along the edge of the island with their arms entwined, looking for all the world like young lovers. As they passed the various villas they could hear muffled voices talking in a variety of languages. Some of them sounded angry.

"They have a lot of issues to work out between themselves before it will be worth talking to them about a way forward," Joe said when Sophie looked up at him enquiringly.

"You can hear what they are saying?"

He gave a little shrug, as if the answer to that question was obvious but he was too discreet to say it out loud.

"We can't expect them to end centuries of rivalries overnight just because I ask them to," he said. "They're only human, after all."

Sophie laughed. "Is there any chance that they will see the light in time to help you to change things, do you think?"

"Oh yes." He gave her a reassuring squeeze. "They will see the light, I'm sure of it. They are all good people, after all, even if they have been a little misguided from time to time."

They both chuckled contentedly as they walked on past the arguing voices. The heat was beginning to drop out of the day and the sky was tinged with orange by the time they completed their circuit of the island and came back to their own villa. A little further up the beach they could see the dark shapes of the Sunni Grand Imam and his entourage praying to Mecca on mats which had been carefully laid out for them. Joe put his finger to his lips and steered Sophie back into the trees.

"Let's leave them alone with Allah for a little longer. We can talk to them tomorrow."

The following morning, they rose with the sun and walked back down to the beach.

"Now that," Sophie said, "is a sight I never imagined I would see."

The Pope, the Grand Imam of the Sunnis and the representative Imam of the Shiites, all in their dignified, flowing robes, one in white the others in black, were walking on the sand, deep in conversation with the Archbishop of Canterbury, who was wearing baggy khaki shorts and what looked like a farmer's checked shirt. The Archbishop also had a rather shapeless fishing hat on his head, but it was obviously an afterthought since his face already looked like it had caught a little too much sun. Around them buzzed coteries of followers, whispering amongst themselves and translating where they could between their leaders.

Joe waited, the sand not yet too hot to stand on in bare feet, watching their earnest approach. It was a few seconds before one of the assistants spotted him and realised who he was. The others immediately sensed their colleague's excitement and looked up, shading their eyes against the low sun to try to discern who the figure was that seemed to shimmer in front of them in the morning haze.

Everyone in the group stopped talking but they continued to walk towards him, slowly because the sand hampered their movements and many of them had an elderly shuffle. As they came close the Pope extended his hand and Joe lowered his head, allowing his lips to brush against the old man's skin. He then turned to the Imams of the Sunnis and the Shiites and repeated the gesture of respect with each in turn. The Archbishop, apparently flustered by the heat and the many different protocols which were coming together in one unique moment, lunged in for a handshake. Joe took his hand but turned it over and showed the Englishman the same respect as the others. He noticed that the Archbishop's pulse was rising and he seemed to be having some difficulty catching his breath. Joe placed a calming hand on the old man's shoulder for a few moments before continuing to move through the whole group with the same gesture of generosity and modesty, causing considerable flutterings of awkwardness amongst those who felt it should be them kissing his hand, not the other way round.

"I'm so pleased that you all took the time to come here," he said and Sophie could see that all of them could understand him as if he were speaking simultaneously in all their native tongues. She noticed that some of the followers were making phone calls and sending texts and a few minutes later other figures emerged from the undergrowth, summoned by their phones.

"Do you have a copy of the guidelines?" Joe whispered to Sophie.

"In the room," she said, "I'll go get them."

"Shall we sit?" Joe suggested, pointing to an area where the shade from the palm trees had been supplemented with some thoughtfully placed umbrellas by invisible staff. There were a number of chairs but Joe sat cross-legged on the ground as the others gathered around him. Some of the more elderly members of the group perched on the chairs, while others joined him on the ground, not wanting to appear to be putting themselves above him.

"I imagine many of you are unsettled by my unannounced arrival amongst you here on Earth," he said, with a warm smile. A few of them gave almost imperceptible nods of agreement but most remained silent and impassive, waiting to hear what he would say before they voiced their private worries and questions. "But I am here to ask for your help."

There was a slight stirring in the group as Sophie returned and slipped Joe the circular piece of wood. He smiled his thanks and indicated that she should sit beside him.

"The great religions and all the people who have worked for them down the centuries have done a wonderful job of steering mankind towards a better and higher life." He spoke quietly and some of them had to lean in close to hear him, all of them still able to understand his words in their own languages. "But now it is time to change course because there are still so many divisions. There are not only the divisions between the different religions but also the different nationalities, different races, different generations, different classes, even different genders. Those rivalries, coupled with the greed and selfishness which are instinctive to most men and women, have led mankind to the brink of extinction. If we do not bring everyone together with one common set of goals and beliefs then catastrophe will soon be upon us. We need one set of guidelines which every individual in the world is signed up to, then one set of goals that every individual can work towards."

"Is this not what the current Chinese government believes and is working towards already?" the New Celestial Master of Taoism asked.

"In many ways, yes," Joe agreed, "but it must be global and must also take account of human rights and freedom. Here" – he passed over the wooden plaque that Sophie had fetched for him – "these are the guidelines I suggest, the new 'commandments' if you like."

He paused for a moment as they passed it around, turning it in order to follow the spiralling words, reading over one another's shoulders, exchanging whispers as some translated for their colleagues. Waiters appeared with trays of cold drinks and the Archbishop of Canterbury drained his in one go.

"So you are saying these will be the new 'commandments'?" the Pope said eventually, "replacing the ones that we have all been living by for thousands of years."

"Well, not exactly," Joe corrected him. "I prefer the word 'guidelines'."

"Indeed" – the Pope nodded his understanding of the

subtle difference – "but still… I notice there is now no mention of instructions such as not killing, not stealing, not committing adultery…"

"The world now has international and national laws which cover such issues as stealing and killing. I think everyone knows that they are not acceptable and that they are crimes which will be punishable by secular law. Also, if all the other guidelines are absorbed and followed, such as 'honesty', 'kindness' and 'do not do to others what you do not want them to do to you', that covers all violent or dishonest behaviour. If you are obeying those guidelines you will automatically 'honour your father and mother' and you automatically avoid 'covetousness' and you will not 'bear false witness' because you have agreed to be honest in all things."

"What about the advice to avoid lewdness?" the Sunni Grand Imam asked. "There is nothing here at all about sexual morality."

"For many thousands of years people in authority have tried to control people's sexual desires," Joe said, "and it has only led to bitterness and unhappiness and cruelty. Again, such things should be guided by kindness, tolerance and treating others as you would like to be treated. Who are we to decide who other people should love or choose to be with, as long as they don't hurt other people?"

The Grand Imam's advisers leaned in, muttering in his ear and Joe waited to hear what else they would bring up.

"To many of our followers," the Pope said quietly and apparently on behalf of all of them, "we are all seen as God's representatives on Earth. If you are the Son of God, as you claim, then there is no need for us any more…"

He left his words hanging as they all looked towards Joe. Sophie felt her heartbeat quicken. Was this some sort of veiled threat? Was this the moment when an assassin would appear from the bushes?

"You have all served God well," he said eventually, "and he is grateful to you for dedicating your lives to him. But you are still divided. He asks that you now work together to spread his word."

"These words?" A Chief Rabbi held up the piece of wood.

"These words and many more," Joe said. "These are really just the headlines, if you like. There are many more detailed agreements which need to be accepted by everyone. If you all tell your followers that these are the words of God and that they should now follow them, imagine how much more powerful that united voice will be. Together you will be talking to almost every individual on Earth. Together you will be representing God on Earth far more effectively than you have been able to do separately.

"I am only visiting. Once I am gone again you will still be my designated representatives on Earth, working alongside the Twelve who I have chosen to lead mankind on its secular path into the future."

"What do you suppose would happen if any of us didn't agree to these guidelines, or didn't wish to amalgamate with every other religion?" the Archbishop of Canterbury asked, lifting his hat to dab the sweat from his brow which was now a deep red.

"If everyone does not work together in this way, then the world, as mankind has known it, will soon end. Then you will be the leaders of nothing, representing no one and God will know that you had an opportunity to save the Earth but declined to accept it."

There was a sharp intake of breath amongst the group, their automatic response to the feeling that it was now they who were being threatened in some way. Joe seemed unperturbed by the possibility that he had offended them.

"It is not going to be easy," he continued. "I understand

that. Some people will have to re-think many of the prejudices that have been passed down to them over the millennia. The Catholics, for instance, will have to reconsider their position on matters such as the celibacy of priests, the ordaining of women priests and the encouragement of contraception, but I understand there have already been movements in the right direction."

A number of heads were nodding cautiously among the Pope's followers.

"If you could all agree on these guidelines as a start, it will unite almost everyone on the planet and provide a basis for a future global education programme, with the aim of persuading every individual to agree to the same guidelines. When the guidelines lead to a better world for all who could possibly be against them?"

The Sunni Grand Imam stood up with surprising speed for a man of his age.

"You are asking too much – whoever you are."

Without another word he swept away towards the restaurant area, followed by his entourage, some of whom were obviously nervous about showing disrespect to Joe, feeling torn in their loyalties. One by one the other leaders followed his example.

"That went well," Sophie said with a wry smile once they were alone.

"He's right. I am asking a lot," Joe smiled. "But they will come round. Have faith, Sophie. Shall we go for breakfast?"

"I love your optimism," she said, shaking her head as she got up to follow him.

"Faith, optimism; maybe they are the same thing…" Joe paused and held his arm out to her. "I need to give that some thought."

THIRTY-SIX

Never before had so much satellite time been concentrated on one small speck in the Pacific Ocean.

"He wants what?" The American President wasn't sure that he had heard correctly.

"He wants all the leaders of the major religions and philosophies to agree with one another on one set of behavioural guidelines which will unite all their followers," the Director of Security said again.

The President fell silent for a few minutes, trying to get his head around such a radical concept.

"He wants the Sunnis and Shiites, the Catholics and the Pentecostals, the Orthodox Jews and the Liberal Jews, the Hindus and the Buddhists, and all the rest of them to get together and form one giant religion?"

"Not exactly, but he does want them all to work together to get mankind back on the right track."

"What right track? We're on the right track, aren't we? Are we talking wind turbines and solar panels and climate change bullshit here? Is that what we're talking about?"

"I believe changes in energy policy are part of the secular plan, but I think it is a bigger and broader canvas than that."

"This is just mischief-making, right? This guy is just trying to stir up trouble, trying to get control of everything. Who's paying him? What's their angle?"

"His followers would say he is trying to bring people

together in a common cause," the Director pointed out. "They would say that it's the world's politicians and business people who are the mischief-makers, trying to cause divisions and spread suspicion and hate, trying to extract profit from every human transaction. So far we have not been able to trace any money coming to him from anywhere. Yung Zhang and her friends are paying his living expenses, but that seems to be the extent of it. He doesn't even have a bank account or a credit card – nothing."

"Communists!" the President slammed his fist on the desk, making everyone in the office jump as it always did. "The same damn communists as before coming back in through the back door! Can we just bomb the damn island while they're all on it?"

"I think that would be a war crime, sir," the Director fidgeted nervously, aware that the President was not joking.

"We're not at war with them!" The President was obviously pleased to score a debating point for once. "So how can it be a war crime?"

"Just a common or garden crime then, sir."

"We could blame the Israelis."

"A Chief Rabbi is on the island, so I don't think anyone would believe that."

"Dammit!"

* * * * *

"He wants to unite everyone?" the Russian President was equally perturbed by the same information, but quieter in his responses. "All the religions?"

"It would seem so, sir," his Security Chief replied.

"Are they agreeing to that?"

"Not yet, sir."

"Do we have any influence over anyone on this island?"

"Not at the moment, sir."

"It would not be to our advantage for all of them to be united; you do understand that, right?"

"Yes, sir."

"It is harder to persuade people to do what we want if they are all united," he spat the final word out like it was poison. "If they are all talking to each other it will make our job much more difficult. Do we know what the Chinese think?"

"The Chinese are very much in favour of uniting their people, sir. They like the idea of harmony. Their system has been praised on the island."

"He's praising the Chinese?" The President's eyebrows shot up.

"With some reservations, sir."

"The Americans? What are they thinking?"

"Apparently the President favours bombing the island." The Security Chief gave a small smile, which his president returned.

"He has gone public with that?"

"No, sir, we heard it from a source at the White House."

"That would certainly cause some divisions. Perhaps we should provide some encouragement for the idea."

"I believe he has been talked out of it, sir, at least for the moment."

"Shame," the President laughed with apparently genuine amusement. "Keep me informed."

THIRTY-SEVEN

"You have to understand, Joe," the Archbishop of Canterbury, who seemed to be having increasing trouble catching his breath, spoke slowly. He had an avuncular tone to his voice which made Joe smile. "You have done tremendously well to persuade so many of us to come all this way for a meeting of this sort, but you are talking to people who are steeped in holy scriptures and texts which are thousands of years old and which they are expressly forbidden to reinterpret. Those teachings have proven their worth over those centuries, despite being attacked and questioned from many sides. You are asking us to throw all that away and start again?"

"I think the point is exactly that; they were all written thousands of years ago," Joe said. His voice was calm and reasonable. He was aware that if he was too confrontational he would get nowhere. He had to allow time for the intelligence of these great men to take in the message that he was giving them and to see the sense in what he was suggesting.

At least they had all returned to the beach after breakfast to hear more, which seemed encouraging to him, even if their manner was frosty and distracted in some cases.

"Much of what is written in the holy books is now known not to be literally true, and much of it is now actually harmful to mankind and the planet."

There was another hiss of shock and several of the more junior members of the party actually moved forward as if about to make the discussion physical. The seniors all put out restraining hands to indicate that they did not need to be protected from Joe's opinions.

"You are all on the same side," Joe continued evenly. "You are all on God's side. You just have different words for things and you have had different traditions and rules made up and handed down over the years; all of them are differences that are too trivial for God to even consider. But you all want people to live in peace. You all want people to be kind to one another. You all want people to look after the planet and one another. All of you believe that personal greed and selfishness is harmful at every level. There is nothing on that list of guidelines that any of you would fundamentally dispute."

He paused for a second and nobody else took the opportunity to speak up.

"God is asking for your assistance, gentlemen, and he understands how much he is asking of you. He wants you now to realise that you are all on the same side and that all the historical differences between you, most of which are trivial in his eyes – have to end if mankind is to survive. He is asking you to work together, under the guidance of my twelve wise apostles, to save all your flocks from imminent extinction."

"How does God feel about having his name taken in vain?" one of the cardinals asked.

"And being depicted in graven images," an Imam added.

"God is not without a sense of humour," Joe assured them. "He gets the jokes. Really, he does."

"So what are you hoping to achieve with your twelve apostles?" the Chief Rabbi enquired.

"It's not what we hope to achieve," Joe corrected him. "It is what we have to achieve. We have to achieve many of the things that religious leaders have been trying to achieve for thousands of years, but which the secular world has been slow to accept. We need to eradicate war and poverty, which means doing away with all the armies and ending the expensive arms races immediately. Then we need to create true stability by forming one global government and doing away with all the squabbling and competing between nations. We also need to ensure there is equality for women and homosexuals in all things."

There were more low mutterings of disapproval amongst those seated furthest from Joe.

"I am asking some of you to adjust your thinking in order to be effective in a world which has changed greatly since the majority of the holy texts were written, and to remember that they were written by people and not by Our Father."

"And if hundreds of religious leaders have not been able to achieve these goals in thousands of years" – the Pope verbalised what many of them were thinking – "how are you and just twelve apostles going to do it now?"

"With your help," Joe grinned, "and by using all the tools of modern communication which we now have at our disposal. We no longer have to wander through deserts converting people one at a time, as I did two thousand years ago. Now I can talk to every person on the planet simultaneously."

"We have been shown your miracles online," the Archbishop wheezed, "they are very impressive."

"But people want more than that," Joe said. "They want to ask me questions. They want me to suggest what they should do to save mankind and to live better lives. They are coming to New Zealand by their millions..." Several of the religious leaders exchanged glances, envious despite themselves at the idea of being able to attract millions of people to hear their words, "but it is not practical for New Zealand to accommodate them all. So that is why a television broadcast is being planned. It will go out worldwide and I am grateful for the opportunity to talk to all of you before I talk to your followers."

"Not all of our followers have access to televisions," the Archbishop pointed out irritably.

"I guess it will be online as well," Joe said, "and people will be able to watch it on their phones, or on someone else's phone. I still don't fully understand how all this technology works."

His audience all mumbled their agreement at the difficulty of mastering the intricacies of the modern electronic world, relieved to find an area where Joe shared their ignorance.

"So exactly what is it that you want us to do?" the Pope asked. "Do you just want us all to make announcements that we back what you are doing?"

"That would certainly be great," Joe said. "But we would also be grateful for your help in reaching the world leaders. The political leaders of the secular world seem to feel threatened by the idea of changing the way that the world is run. Understandably, they want to cling to the old ways of doing things because that way they maintain their power bases. But there is no room for factions and divisions if the world is going to be saved. Nation competing against nation, man against man, that has all helped to develop the world and to reach the point where mankind is today, but the future needs to be different and they need to understand that. They need to support the necessary changes, even if it is against their personal, short-term, national interests.

"If you go to them as a united force then they will have to listen to you. You represent too many of their followers and citizens for them to be able to ignore you. If you tell them that you accept and will advocate the twelve guidelines and that you endorse the overall plan to create a better world together now, then they will have no choice but to do the same. However many millions of people might follow me on the internet or come to New Zealand in the hope of meeting me, I am still just one man to them. The American President calls me a 'hippy healer', and the others feel pretty much the same, even if they are too diplomatic to say it. They can't say that about you if you are united."

"None of the national politicians are going to be willing to surrender their power to a global government without a fight," the Grand Imam warned. "If you are asking for all the armies to be disbanded and all the weapons removed then many of the generals and other military leaders will be eager to support the status quo against you. They might be forced to listen to us if we stand together, but that doesn't mean they won't fight back against all these changes that you are asking for. They are the ones who have the bombs and the guns. We only have words."

"Have you considered your own personal safety?" the Chief Rabbi asked. "Once you have made all your plans known to the world your life will be in danger, if it isn't already. There isn't a political leader in the world who isn't capable of ordering an assassination, particularly if the armies are on their sides. Do you have protection, or is this it?" He gestured towards Sophie, who looked a little startled by the suggestion that she was there as Joe's minder.

"Sophie is all the protection I need," Joe laughed, "Sophie and my Father in Heaven."

A loud cry of surprise from one of the cardinals made them all turn in his direction. He was bending over the Archbishop of Canterbury who had slumped sideways in his seat, his eyes staring fixedly at the sand. The reactions of the group were a mixture of shock and panic, calls for medical assistance mingling with the sound of prayers being offered up. There were disagreements amongst those closest as to what to do for the best but those who said he should be laid down on the sand won the argument. The Chief Rabbi took charge of trying to restart the dead man's heart while the others offered more advice and more prayers from the sidelines.

Sophie, who had been trained in what to do in such circumstances, stood up to help but Joe caught her hand and gestured for her to sit back down beside him. She was about to protest but he held up his hand to quieten her and, for some reason she couldn't explain, she knew she should do as he told her. The two of them sat for several minutes and watched as everyone else tried in vain to revive the Archbishop. The manager of the island appeared from the building with a portable defibrillator, having been summoned by a panic-stricken waiter.

Ten minutes later the panic subsided and only the sounds of praying remained as the group accepted that the Archbishop had gone and the Chief Rabbi gently closed his lids. Several pairs of eyes were now turned onto Joe and Sophie as they sat watching impassively.

"It was all too much strain for him," an angry voice spoke from the crowd. "He should never have been made to travel all this way and come out in this heat. None of us should."

Several other voices murmured their agreement. After a few moments, Joe got to his feet and walked over to the Archbishop's body, kneeling beside him. He looked slowly round the crowd, staring each one of them in the eye and holding their gaze until they blinked or looked away, then bent his head and closed his eyes, pressing the palms of his hands over the old man's still heart. The others continued to offer up their prayers behind him, only falling silent when they saw the Archbishop's eyelids flicker. As soon as he felt the beat of the heart restart, Joe lifted his hands and signalled Sophie to take the old man's other arm. Together they helped him to his feet and he took several long, deep breaths, his body grateful for the oxygen and a smile returning to his puzzled face.

The whole group fell silent for so long that Sophie wondered if they were ever going to speak again, then they started to debate quietly amongst themselves, sitting back down in the shade, many of them apparently overcome by shock and relief and by a sense of wonder at what they had just witnessed. The Archbishop listened in amazement as his assistant described to him what had occurred while he was unconscious. Sophie and Joe sat back down again on the sand and waited to see what would happen next.

The Pope was deep in whispered conversation with his cardinals. After what seemed like an eternity, he pulled himself back to his feet. He seemed suddenly exhausted from all the deliberating. He shuffled a few steps towards Joe and his entourage stood respectfully behind him, all looking puzzled and unsure what their pontiff was going to do next. Joe watched the old man approaching with calm eyes and Sophie stopped breathing for a moment. With some difficulty, the Pope got down onto his knees in the sand and bowed his head so low his brow was touching Joe's bare feet.

"You have convinced me of your divinity," he said, "and I am humbled by your modesty. On behalf of all Catholics I accept that you are the Son of God and will advise everyone to follow the twelve guidelines as you request and to endorse your overall plan in the interest of all mankind."

Joe placed his hand on the Pope's head. The Sunni Grand Imam watched through hooded eyes, the snap of the prayer beads as they rolled back and forth through his fingers the only sound apart from the insects in the trees and the waves on the sand.

"Bless you, my beloved son and trusted servant," Joe said.

The cardinals followed their master's lead and fell to their knees, bowing their heads low and then standing in order to assist the Pope back onto his feet. As he was helped to his seat, the Chief Rabbi knelt before Joe and bowed his head.

"So," he chuckled, as Joe gestured for him to stand, "we've been wrong about the Messiah all these years."

"Not wrong," Joe grinned, "just mistaken."

The Rabbi gave a wry shrug of his shoulders and stepped back.

Next came a Hindu high priest and then a Pentecostal Minister, both followed by their entourages, all of them kneeling in the sand and kissing Joe's feet. In the background, the Sunni Grand Imam's prayer beads continued to click like angry cicadas. Once the Archbishop and his Anglican party had shown their allegiance and their acceptance that Joe was indeed the Son of God, all eyes turned to the Grand Imam, apart from his followers, who kept their gaze firmly on the ground, hardly daring to breathe as they waited for him to show them the way.

As if emerging from a trance, the Grand Imam leaned close to the representative Imam of the Shiites and the two men whispered for several minutes as they continued to play aggressively with their beads. Eventually the Grand Imam flexed his shoulders and stood up in one fluid movement, the beads now hanging silent in his hand. He embraced the Shiite Imam before taking two steps forward and looking down at Joe. The two men stared into each other's eyes for what seemed like an eternity, Joe smiling and the Grand Imam stern. The Grand Imam took a long intake of breath, as if preparing for the deepest of dives, and then descended elegantly into the sand, bowing his head low and allowing his lips to linger on Joe's feet.

"Allah be praised," he said when he finally lifted his head. "He has sent his servant to save us and show us the way into the future."

"We both serve him as faithfully as we are able," Joe murmured gently.

The representative Imam was the last to bow down and accept that Joe was who he claimed to be.

"God help you, Joe, in the face of the fury to come," the Chief Rabbi said, and the others murmured prayers of agreement.

THIRTY-EIGHT

Virtually all the customs and security employees in New Zealand were working double shifts, and still the authorities were struggling to keep the crowds moving through the air and seaports. Anyone who was able to show a diplomatic passport would be rushed through with even more haste than in normal times; anything to get people through quickly and to speed all the processes up.

The Ukrainian's diplomatic documents were entirely convincing. He had used them before, but not for several years. He liked to rotate his different identities and had arrived with a thick beard and small, wire-framed glasses, wearing a nondescript brown suit and knitted tie.

Just as if he were a genuine diplomat, a sleek black car was waiting with a uniformed driver to take him into the city centre, where an unassuming studio apartment had been rented for him. It was on the ground floor of a modern block. The walled courtyard at the back had a door to a street which could be locked, giving him another means of coming and going without bumping into any neighbours who might show an interest in who he was and what his business might be in Christchurch.

An elegantly dressed woman was waiting in the apartment when he arrived. He noted with approval that she was startlingly beautiful as he had been promised. She stood up sharply when he came in and for a moment it looked as if she might salute.

"Are you my lunch date?" he asked.

"Yes, sir."

"Don't call me 'sir' again," he instructed. "You are supposed to be my date not my junior."

"Yes…" she said, unable for a moment to think of an appropriate alternative, "… darling."

The Ukrainian gave a rare smile. "Better, but not terribly convincing. Try to relax. What time is the reservation?"

"In two hours."

"Good. I will sleep. Wake me when it is time to go."

They were an impressive-looking couple when they reached the hotel but it was the woman that everyone was looking at, not the man escorting her. If anyone had been asked to describe them later, they would only have been able to give the very vaguest of descriptions of the Ukrainian. They might have remembered that he wore nondescript glasses, but he intended to throw those into the first bin he saw once the meal was over. The beard, which had grown in just over a week, would also be going as soon as they returned to the apartment and he did not intend to wear the brown suit again.

Whoever had made the lunch reservation had done a good job at convincing the staff that they were people of importance who needed to be treated with discretion. There had been plenty of journalists trying to get tables in the restaurant in the hope of being able to find out some interesting titbit of gossip about the most famous couple in the world who were living upstairs in the royal suite. Because Joe and Sophie were away on the atoll, security was a little more relaxed than usual, so no one paid any attention to the distinguished couple beyond the staff who took them to their table and helped them to order.

The woman made a great fuss about ordering, asking a lot of questions as if she were a gourmet. The Ukrainian was impressed by her performance. She obviously convinced them that she was genuinely interested in food because when she asked if she could meet the chef and see the kitchens at the end of the meal, in order to thank him and ask him more questions, the maitre d' was delighted to arrange it, personally escorting the woman and her quiet, unremarkable partner down to the kitchens.

As the star-struck staff showed the glamorous woman around their kingdom, basking in her oft repeated amazement and admiration for all she was shown, her partner wandered quietly around the outskirts, apparently less interested in what was being talked about and in reality checking out the security and the layout of the kitchen and service entrances and exits, making a note of the names of various staff members, knowing that it was going to be hard to get back into the premises through the front reception area when Joe was back in residence upstairs.

Once back at the apartment, after the woman had been paid and disappeared and the beard had been removed, the Ukrainian brought some floor plans of the hotel up on the computer and studied them for an hour, like he was planning a military operation. He had to admit that the whole place had been well designed to provide security for the residents. While it was one possible location at which he could reach his target, it might not be the safest or the easiest. He was going to have to spend time familiarising himself with the target's habits and come up with some alternative plans before deciding when and where to strike. He ignored the phone, which flashed repeatedly on the table beside him. He was a professional and as such he did not respond to pressure, whoever the client might be.

THIRTY-NINE

The entire world knew about the plans for the television broadcast because everyone had been asked if they had any questions for Joe and had been told that he would be answering the most popular ones. There had never before been an event which virtually every human on the planet knew about and which they were all talking about with such intensity. In every coffee shop and on every street corner from Manhattan, Moscow and Beijing to the smallest village in Africa or India, people were comparing notes on what they wanted to ask.

To begin with, the New Zealand authorities tried to keep the location of the broadcast a secret but it grew obvious that that would be impossible. Too many people were involved in the planning, staging and distribution of the event for the information not to leak out. Plans had to evolve constantly, adapting to the ever-changing circumstances. No one had ever staged such a complex broadcast before; they were all learning on the job.

The first idea had been to film it in a location with just Joe and the interviewer who would be asking the questions, but it soon became clear that would not work technically. They needed a fully staffed studio if it was to be broadcast simultaneously to the entire world and, once it was known that the Twelve wanted to be there for the recording, other people started to ask to be included on the guest list as well. It was hard to say "no" to people like the Prime Minister, who had been so helpful and hospitable and had even persuaded her cabinet to agree to underwrite the costs of staging the event with the promise of access for all of them and their families. Then other names started to appear on the list as everyone involved had pressure put on them by their friends and relatives.

As the numbers continued to grow, the organisers needed to hire more people to handle the logistics and those people also found ways to invite their friends and loved ones. It was decided to scrap the idea of a closed studio and put up a stage at a venue where more people would be able to watch live. That increased the security needs and the number of people involved swelled exponentially. It was soon evident that tens of thousands of people, many of them already living in the campsites and townships which had sprung up to accommodate them, were planning to simply turn up in the hope of getting into the venue at the last minute or, failing that, of catching a glimpse of Joe. That meant that more police and private security firms had to be involved in order to get Joe and the invited guests in and out of the premises safely.

Within a few days of the announcement being made, the event had taken on the proportions of a major rock concert. Twenty-foot fences had to be erected around the venue, catering caravans were rolled in, lighting rigs went up and competing production companies staked their claims to be the official film crew.

Instead of having a quiet conversation with an interviewer in a room, Joe was now to be displayed on a high stage, with a film crew projecting the conversation up onto giant screens around the venue. Because the numbers of people who would be able to get into the venue had increased, a VIP area had to be roped off at the front and another team of organisers was hired to make sure that happened smoothly.

Security systems had to be set up to ensure that the stage area did not become swamped with people wanting to get close to Joe. Security passes became a valuable currency in their own right.

The Ukrainian read everything he could find about the plans for the venue and, five days before the event, while it was still a building site, he casually strolled in wearing a hard hat, a donkey jacket and work boots, carrying a tool box. No one challenged him as he walked purposefully around, taking in every detail, occasionally stopping, getting out a tool and pretending to adjust it in order to give himself time to study a particular entrance or exit more closely.

This, he decided, would be an easier venue for him to move around in unnoticed, but he would need to have a pass hanging around his neck on the day if he didn't want to risk being stopped and questioned. Late that night he rang a number he had been given and told them what he needed.

"It will be hard to get," he was told.

"You have someone on the inside. Get them to arrange it."

"They are becoming reluctant to expose themselves any further."

"Then you will need to apply the correct amount of pressure."

The Ukrainian hung up and a few days later a messenger arrived at the apartment where he was staying with a parcel containing a lanyard with an "All-Areas" security pass attached, bearing a doctored version of his photograph. All he had to do now was make sure that he looked like the photo on the day.

It was going to take time to get the crowds in and out and so musicians were approached to entertain from the stage for a couple of hours before and after Joe's interview. Everyone who was approached wanted to perform, even if it meant interrupting touring obligations in other countries and being flown into New Zealand specially. In the heat of the excitement, any voices that questioned the environmental costs of such extravagance were drowned out. Another team was set up to handle the booking and the care of the acts. Within weeks it had become the most well-publicised concert ever, with Joe's conversation topping the bill.

FORTY

Joe was allocated a trailer to get ready in before the show, but he had nothing that he needed to prepare, so he was happy when Sophie knocked on the door and asked if he needed company. They could hear the first musical act playing on stage a hundred yards away and the rumble of the crowd both inside the venue and outside the fences.

"Are you actually going to be answering these questions then?" she asked once she had settled into one of the sofas and had helped herself from his fruit bowl. "Or are you going to fall back on your usual trick of answering every question with another question?"

"What do you think?"

"Oh, ha ha!" She threw a cushion at him. "It's chaos out there. Everyone is trying to get into the VIP area and getting really angry that they are being turned away, and everyone who is actually inside the velvet rope wants to get in here."

"They can come if they want," Joe shrugged.

"Security won't let them through. Quite right too. This place couldn't hold them and the ones who couldn't get in would feel left out."

"Just you and me then."

"Yeah," she grinned happily and passed him the fruit bowl. "So have you seen the questions in advance?"

"They showed me the most popular ones."

"And do you know what you are going to say?"

"The truth." He bit into an apple and winked at her, making her heart give a familiar skip.

There was a knock on the door and a well-groomed woman in way too much make-up poked her head in, letting the noise of the concert in with her for a moment. Sophie recognised her as a television newscaster and interviewer.

"Hi," she said, "I'm Gilly and I'm going to be asking you the questions that the people have sent in."

Joe shook her hand and she showed none of the signs of deference that Sophie had grown used to seeing in everyone who met him. This woman, it seemed, had true self-confidence and was determined to keep her journalistic distance.

"Is there anything you want to run through before we go on?" Gilly asked.

"I think it will be fine," Joe smiled disarmingly, and Sophie was alarmed to feel a pinprick of jealousy.

A young woman wearing headphones appeared in the doorway.

"Time to go," she said, ushering Joe and Gilly towards the steps at the back of the stage.

The Ukrainian, dressed as an anonymous technician, with a clipboard, an earpiece and radio that he could talk into if he wanted to avoid anyone starting a conversation with him, walked a few paces behind, apparently going about his own business. None of them felt the need to turn and look at him.

Since she was now being completely ignored, Sophie made her way back to the VIP area and found Lalit's daughter Alice, who had managed to smuggle several friends past security with the sort of rich-girl self confidence that Sophie half envied and half resented.

The crowd was already high from the music and a roar of approval went up as Joe's face appeared on the screens, magnified and glowing down onto the crowds below in a golden light. More screens had been erected outside the fences so that the thousands who were unable to get in could still feel involved. With an explosion of music, an introductory video beamed out across the crowd, showing digitally enhanced versions of his miracles and clips of him speaking in a multitude of languages, followed by spectacular aerial shots of the giant crowds and campsites that had grown all round the city. A booming voiceover announced the findings by the scientists of evidence of divinity. Finally the cameras cut to live aerial pictures taken from drones that swooped over the heads of the crowds at the event and an even greater roar of anticipation rose up as people realised the moment had come.

Gilly stepped out first into the spotlight and for a second the ecstasy seemed to calm.

"Ladies and gentlemen," she announced, "now is the moment you have all been waiting for. Has Jesus Christ returned to walk amongst us once more? Please make plenty of noise for Joe; the man who many believe will be our Saviour!"

As Joe stepped out onto the stage the cameras followed his progress and beamed it out through the screens so that no one would be left out. He and Gilly took their seats to the crash of drums and applause and waited for the noise to die down.

After several minutes, the crowd noise had finally subsided and Gilly was able to make her introduction with a précis of Joe's achievements since his return. The Ukrainian slid into a position at the side of the stage where he was able to see Joe and Gilly and could also watch most of the guests in the VIP area at the same time.

"So," Gilly said, turning to him with a broad smile, "are you, Joe, the same person as Jesus, the Son of God and Mary, who was born over two thousand years ago in Bethlehem?"

"Yes," Joe smiled modestly, "I am the Son of God and I have returned as Joe, but I was born in Nazareth, not Bethlehem."

"With God as your father and Mary as your mother, are you a human being or are you divine?"

"I have the privilege of being both."

The crowd received this confirmation with ecstatic rapture.

"Is it different this time?" Gilly asked.

"It is different," he replied after a few moments of thought. "And I am also different from then. When I think back, I was perhaps a little naïve. My knowledge and experience are now richer, but even now I will still bear the shortcomings of this age on Earth. I still recognise myself, yes."

"Now that you are so open, and thank you for that, can I ask, was there a 'companion', a woman, in your life back then?"

"Ah, you are looking for a love story, Gilly!" He laughed and for a moment Sophie thought he was going to evade the question. She held her breath, not sure if she wanted to hear whatever he might say next, wanting to believe that she was the only woman for him in this life or any other, but knowing in her heart that was unlikely. "I knew women during my life here, but it never led to a marriage. I needed all my energy for the work. But if you are asking whether I know how love feels, then yes, I have experienced it."

Sophie felt tears prickling up behind her eyes. Could she dare to hope that he was thinking about her when he said that?

"Can you tell us a little more about your father, about God?" Gilly asked.

"Gladly. People used to picture God the way they wanted him to be. They liked to create a familiar image of an old wise man with a beard. That is the way they used to look at gods. Many things happened in nature that people did not understand, so they wanted a God who was not only almighty but also performed miracles, read thoughts, punished sins, answered prayers. They even wanted him to be vengeful because that was how they were themselves. Over time their interpretation and insights of God have changed. But God himself has not changed.

"Now you need to try to see God in the non-figurative sense. You cannot see God as a man of flesh and blood, so let go of that image. God, my father, is also your father; he is the father of everything and everyone. He is an energy that is everywhere. You find God everywhere in the cosmos, in nature on Earth, and sometimes in yourself. This picture is sufficient."

A ripple of applause as he paused grew in volume as it spread through the crowd.

"Why does God need a trinity: the Father, the Son and the Holy Spirit?" Gilly asked once the applause had settled down.

"The trinity is unknown to me," Joe replied. "The Christian church invented it because it fitted into their reasoning. God is God, God is the Holy Spirit, who is not a separate entity, and God is also his Son, whom he has now sent to this planet for the second time."

"So has God actually created everything, quantum mechanics, the Big Bang, the universe, the laws of nature?"

"They are all the work of God. Also this universe, as you know it, and the laws of nature. God is the embodiment of the laws of nature, not as a human being, but as a force of energy."

"You say 'this universe'. Does that mean there are multiple universes?"

"They come and go. You may be able to prove that they exist but you will never be able to explore other universes. Just accept that they are there."

"A huge number of people have come to understand the theory of evolution. I confess to being one of them. So if that theory is true, how can the whole 'creation by God' theory be true?"

"Is it possible that evolution is a gift to the world from God, do you think?" Joe asked.

"You mean like giving us free will? Like, he gave us the freedom to evolve?"

Joe spread his hands wide, as if offering her the idea without insisting she believed it.

"As with most things," he continued, "it does not have to be one or the other. Yes, God makes big bangs take place, creating universes. And this beautiful planet is part of this overwhelming universe. You have determined that the Earth is about 4.5 billion years old and that the first single-celled organism came into existence quite soon afterwards. That statement may be correct. If so, then this first living, single-celled organism is the creation of God."

"By far the most asked question, Joe," Gilly announced, "is 'Why are we here?' Everyone wants to know that. I know I certainly do."

The crowd bellowed their agreement and their approval of the question, hungry for enlightenment.

"Perhaps it is simpler than we think," Joe replied. Instantly the venue was silent and everyone was listening intently. "Do you think it is a question that bothers any other species? Does the lion worry about why he is here when he is dozing in the shade with a full stomach? Does the butterfly wonder as he settles on a flower? We are here to look after one another and love one another, to grow strong and to procreate and then to fade away. We are here to create beautiful art and music, to start companies and invent helpful things. We are here to form networks and learn new skills. Or perhaps we are here simply to wonder what our purpose is. Confucius said that compassion is the only universal answer to everything. So perhaps compassion is the reason we are here."

"Different religions have different names for their gods," Gilly went to the next question. "What is his correct name?"

Joe laughed. "There can be as many names as there are

languages. He is happy with all of them, but he is more than just a name, more than just a hundred names. He is also nature and the spiritual source of everything. It doesn't matter what you choose to call him, as long as you remember that he is there."

"So God is the same as Allah, Jahwe and Brahma?"

"Absolutely, yes."

"Can you prove that God exists?" Gilly asked and the crowd gave a low murmur as if they now disapproved of such an impolite public challenge to someone they had already chosen to believe in.

"Why do I need to prove it?" Joe asked, genuinely puzzled. "Just look around you at the world and all its wonders. He proves his existence every day by making the sun rise and set, by making the water flow and the natural world reproduce. I am also proof, sitting here in front of you. Do you really need more? And what is proof anyway? Can you show me proof that lying is morally reprehensible? Of course not, but it is still true."

"How can someone have a personal relationship with God?" Gilly asked once the bellow of approval from the crowd had died away.

"It's easy," Joe said, "just do good and show love to everyone around you."

"The next most asked question," Gilly returned to her script, "is why God allows so much suffering in the world when it must be within his power to stop it?"

The crowd fell silent once more, thousands of people craning forward as one to hear the answer to a question that had occurred to all of them at some time or another.

The Ukrainian busied himself consulting his clipboard as he noticed an armed security man watching him from the other side of the stage with a puzzled expression. Pretending to receive a message through his earpiece, he said, "On my way," into his radio and moved quickly out of the security man's eye line, circling round to the VIP area.

"Suffering is part of life," Joe said after a few moments' pause. To Sophie it almost seemed like he was leaving dramatic pauses on purpose to increase the impact and theatricality of his own words. "It is part of nature. We don't question it when we see a cat jump upon a mouse or a lion upon a zebra or when a tree's roots rot in the jungle and it is toppled by the wind. What we question is why suffering happens to us, and why it appears to be so unevenly distributed. Why do some people seem to have to suffer so much more than others? Why are some born painfully disabled and others lose their children in terrible circumstances? But that is Nature's way, God's way. We are no different to those animals."

"But surely mankind is a higher species than mice or zebras, or trees..." Gilly had gone off script.

"Well I would like to think so," Joe smiled, "but then I have a human mother, so I may be biased."

There was laughter from the crowd and Sophie could see that Joe was enjoying himself, like a rock star soaking up the love of his fans. She felt simultaneously proud to think that she was his closest friend on Earth and jealous of the thousands of other people around her who were at that moment sharing his love. She didn't want to share him with anyone, but she knew it was going to be impossible to keep him to herself and that thought brought on a physical pain.

"Imagine you are a devoted grandmother," Joe continued, "but your relationships with your husband and your children have grown unhappy, and that unhappiness is affecting everyone in the whole family. Then your beloved grandson dies in a terrible accident. You think your heart will break but you find comfort in sharing your grief with your husband and children, growing closer to them in the process. Will the loss of your grandson become a little more bearable as a result? Will your improved relationships with the rest of the family trigger other positive changes, making the bereavement a little more relative?"

"What will the Afterlife be like?" Gilly asked, aware that the minutes were ticking past.

"Well, you aren't going to be seated on a throne next to God, Gilly," Joe said, "and no one is going to be rewarded for their activities on Earth with seventy-two obliging virgins..." there was a moment of shocked silence before the crowd laughed. "But by the same token there are no lakes of fire awaiting those who have disobeyed the rules laid down by the priests and their holy books. Remember that all these pictures of the Afterlife were painted for us by men who had not been there, and many of them were thought up many thousands of years ago as ways of keeping less educated people in line, offering potential punishments and rewards on the other side of the grave in order to control their behaviour on Earth."

"So what will it be like?" Gilly asked again. "People want to know. Death is a frightening concept for many of us."

The Ukrainian walked into the VIP crowd with all the authority of a man with an all-areas pass, making eye contact with no one as he moved close to where Sophie and Alice were standing. Everyone's eyes were on the stage anyway, no one would have been able to identify him in a line-up if they had ever been called to do so.

"Do you remember what it was like before you were born, Gilly?" Joe asked.

"Of course not."

"So it does not frighten you to look back to that time when your consciousness did not occupy a physical body?"

"No."

"Then there is no need to fear what is coming, because it will be the same. You will return to being part of nothing and part of everything."

"Will there be no reward for those who have done good and great things?"

"If you do good and great things, Gilly, you will feel good now because it is what you are supposed to do. That will be your reward. There will be no special prize-giving at the end."

"Why did you have to be crucified for the sins of other people?"

The Ukrainian was so close to Sophie he could breathe in her perfume. He absorbed every detail of her appearance, watching the way her eyes were glued to Joe on the stage, soaking up every bit of information, storing it in his memory without yet knowing how he would use it.

"I died because the people who had the power were afraid I was going to take it away from them," Joe replied, "much like the powerful people today. But I only wanted to open people's eyes to the truth so that they got along better, much as I am still trying to do today. I did not expect to 'take on the sins of humanity'. That was a concept invented by someone else much later. To be honest, I don't really understand what they mean."

Gilly returned to her clipboard. "Are Homo sapiens the last link in the evolutionary chain?"

"That, my friends," Joe said, looking straight out into the crowd, "is up to all of you. There may be further developments possible, but they always bring risks, just like every previous development, from the discovery of fire, which can create terrible destruction as well as enormous good, to the wheel, which can lead to millions of road deaths. You guys will have to decide which risks are worth taking."

"Of all the world's religions," Gilly said, "which do you think is the best?"

The crowd laughed nervously and Joe grinned. "Are you determined to get me into trouble, Gilly?"

"No, no, of course not." Gilly seemed flustered for a moment.

"It's all right," he assured her, "I'm just teasing. I'm here for all people, no matter what books they have read, what churches they have been worshipping in or what their parents and their priests taught them when they were children. I do not like teachings which exclude other people and I don't think that any interpretation of scriptures should incite contempt, hatred or violence against others. All religions should be forces for good and not divisive, but given that proviso I have no objection to any of them. Great acts and great crimes have been committed by people who purport to follow all religions."

"What is your opinion of the Prophet Mohammed?"

"He brought many new insights and his intentions were good. Times were different then too. He was brave, just, giving and averse to hatred."

"Do you think mankind has been a force for good on the planet or bad?"

"We have done a lot of harm, eradicated many other species for example, but we have achieved great things too, in the arts, in medicine."

The Ukrainian had moved to stand behind the group of Twelve, who were all together at the front of the roped-off area, all watching the stage, none of them aware of how closely they were being scrutinised from behind.

"What is your opinion of the Bible?" Gilly asked.

Joe sighed and rubbed his eyes, giving himself time to think before answering. "It was written by men, not by God and it is full of beautiful stories which have been passed down through the generations. Many of those stories taught useful lessons but many of them got their facts wrong when it came to telling my story. I never met Matthew, Mark, Luke or John. Mark wrote his gospel forty years after my death, John wrote his sixty years after, but the messages of living for others not yourself are good. I don't remember ever walking on water" – he paused to allow the crowd to laugh – "and Judas did not betray me. I think they blamed him later because he left the Christian church soon after I went. And I am pretty sure my dear mother was not an eternal virgin since I had a number of brothers and sisters."

"What about the Old Testament?"

"Wonderful, exciting stories, but I don't recognise God in them at all. He is not evil, imperialist, destructive, jealous or vainglorious. He certainly didn't persecute the Egyptians. So on balance I would say, cherish the stories and the psalms you find in the holy books, but do not base your truth on them."

"Bringing us back to the problems of today," Gilly said, changing the subject, "a lot of people have asked: How do you feel about capitalism?"

"I'm not an economist, but I do know that it has brought prosperity to many people. There will always be a need for financial mediation because there will always be people with ideas and no money and people who have money to invest but no ideas. I also know that it is much too hard on those who do not win the game. The system itself is not immoral, it is amoral. It is individual people's gluttony and fear of losing what they have which causes the problems. The rich must share the rewards they receive much more generously, and not just with their own children. Too big a gap between those at the top of the pile and those at the bottom should never be allowed to happen."

"And do you believe in equality for women?"

"Of course!" he laughed. "I'm surprised you even have to ask, Gilly!"

There was a roar of approval from the crowd and Gilly pointed to her clipboard in defence. "Just following the script," she said.

"Gender is entirely irrelevant. People are people. It makes no difference to me if they are male or female. I understand that in many parts of the world men still believe they are superior to women. They are not. Nor are they inferior. It is time to change that. Everyone must be equal and we must remember that most religious scriptures were written by men in times when they put themselves above women."

"How do you feel about celibacy in the church?"

"I don't think celibacy is ever good – unless it is what you want with all your heart. Having a partner enriches everyone's lives. It is something that the church leaders are going to have to think about."

"You mean change the Papal rule?"

"It is perfectly possible. Petrus, the first Pope, was my friend and he was married."

"And lust?"

"I don't think lust is a problem as long as no one is hurt by it. Sexuality is too great a gift to be used only for the purposes of reproduction, just as eating good food is about more than simply fuelling the body to survive. Disapproval of sexuality expressed by religious leaders has too often become linked to contempt for all things feminine, and sexuality has become confused with sin. But at the same time mankind also needs to combat population growth and stem the spread of diseases so people need to be helped with the provision of effective contraceptives."

"And what about homosexuality?"

"People's sexuality is of no more interest to me than their gender. People are people and they should all be free to find and give love wherever they choose."

The crowd erupted with another explosion of approval.

"And abortion?" Gilly continued as soon as she could be heard. The crowd fell silent, eager to hear his answer.

"Women should be the ones to decide what they do with their own bodies, but both men and women should try hard not to create pregnancies unless they really want the responsibility of bringing up a child. Every child needs happy parents. I wish I could give one wise answer that would cover every situation but sometimes it is not possible to find easy solutions to difficult questions."

"And euthanasia?" Gilly continued in the silence.

"I think that it can be right to offer people a gentler way out, just like offering them medication for pain. But careful and compassionate policies need to be worked out first."

"A lot of people have asked what you feel about genetic modification and mankind making changes to the bodies and faces that God gave them."

"It's fine, as long as it is done for the right medical reasons and it is a free choice," Joe grinned. "People can be works of art too. But if the goal is simply human improvement, I doubt that is possible to achieve."

"How should we deal with dangerous radicalisation?"

"If all of mankind has shared, collective goals and wants world peace, then there will be no place for the radicals to go with their arguments. They will find no support anywhere. There will be no one left for them to hate."

"Do you believe that mankind can ever be truly free, or do we always have to have rules to follow?"

"We will always need some supervision, guidance and control because tolerance has limits and although no baby is born bad, mental illness and wickedness do exist and can't be allowed to prosper and hurt other people. But that supervision must come in a form that is acceptable to all. It cannot be forced on a majority by a minority."

"And so there should be punishments for those who break the rules?"

"Yes, but all the penalties should be designed to educate the recipient so that they can live better lives as a result."

"Here's another popular question, if a little left of field." Gilly wanted to get the crowd cheering again. "Is there life on any other planets?"

Joe spread his hands wide. "Do you think this is all I do? Once every two thousand years?"

There was a puzzled silence for a few seconds before the eruption of cheers. Feeling that she had the crowd back on side, Gilly stepped back into dangerous territory.

"What is your view of the Israel–Palestine conflict?"

"I think it is unlikely that God promised the land to any one race or tribe or people. But everyone has a right to live in peace, don't you think? Parties should realise that they are all sons and daughters of Ibrahim, or Abraham if you prefer. The Israelis and the Arabs are brothers and sisters. It is a family conflict; a battle between tribes just as might happen in Africa. It is a very deep conflict, a cocktail of territorial, economic, political, cultural and religious causes. Everyone must learn to forgive and allow divine beauty to shine."

"So, why have you returned?" Gilly asked, putting the clipboard down as if she were now making the questions up herself.

"I want to help reduce suffering by creating a more peaceful, harmonious society. I want to make it possible for everyone to work together. I want to help every individual to find self-knowledge and to learn to forgive. I also want to ask each and every one of you to make an individual effort to help save the planet." He turned to the camera that was on him. "There are twelve people among you who have devised a master plan for the whole world to live together in peace and harmony. I am here to help them to put that plan into practice, providing guidelines for every living soul to be able to live happily with themselves and with every other citizen on the planet. There are things which all of you can do today. Stop eating meat, for instance. Only use planes and cars when strictly necessary and choose to have one less child. If everyone took these pledges it would make an enormous difference."

"I believe these guidelines will be appearing on the screens once the interview is over," Gilly said.

"They will also be circulating widely through social media," Joe said. "They will not be hard to find and we hope they will help everyone to see the right ways forward."

"And why have you chosen New Zealand for your return?" Gilly asked. "Why not return to Jerusalem with all the symbolism that would entail?"

"I have the strongest feelings for Jerusalem and will be returning there," he assured her, "but this is a new start."

"But still," Gilly persisted, "why New Zealand?"

"Your Prime Minister explained 'manaakitanga' to me recently," he said, and for a few seconds the cameras swung onto the Prime Minister's beaming face in the VIP area of the crowd. "The people of New Zealand are exceptionally hospitable, friendly and helpful. Combine that with the fantastic landscapes and anyone can see why you call your country 'God's own'." He turned back to Gilly. "Can I take a moment here to thank someone who has helped me more than anyone?"

"Of course," Gilly said, glancing nervously at the clock on the camera to see if she had time for this.

"I want the world to know what a huge part my friend, Sophie, has played in helping me to reach out to all of you."

Sophie heard her name booming from the speakers but it didn't seem real. It was as if Joe was talking about someone else. She felt suddenly afraid at such exposure, at the same time as feeling excitement at the thought he had actually acknowledged her in such a public way.

"She is the only visionary who foresaw my coming, and she is as saintly a person as it is possible to be. We should all seek to emulate her."

As the initial frisson of fear wore off, Sophie found herself simultaneously thrilled and embarrassed to be picked out so conspicuously. People close to her, who knew her, were turning to face her as they raised their hands to applaud and nodded their approval of this praise. Social media lit up with her name as the whole world tried to find out more about her and within seconds the haters had started to target her.

"You have talked elsewhere about forming one government for the whole world, guided by twelve people of your choosing," Gilly said. "Are you truly suggesting that the whole world should be a single totalitarian state, run by a bunch of your own cronies?"

"Absolutely not," Joe said quietly as the crowd waited silently, surprised by Gilly's forthright use of language but at the same time wanting to hear his answer. "Democracy must be protected at all costs. You have seen the rise of totalitarian leaders all over the free world in recent years, men and women driven insane by their lust for power and riches, and choosing to create hatred and divisions. That can never be right. All I am suggesting is that all people should work together for the good of others. That means everyone. No one should be excluded; not you, Gilly, not the poorest villager in Central Africa or the richest capitalist on Wall Street. We are all God's creatures and in our hearts we all know right from wrong. We all know when we are doing the right things and when we are doing the wrong things because God gave us consciences. We just need to agree on the right way to go forward."

Behind the scenes the organisers had assembled a mighty gospel choir and an orchestra, which were now preparing to provide the lead into the final part of the show. Everyone was concentrating on the part they had been allotted to play, none of them noticing the Ukrainian, who had returned backstage from the VIP area, talking into his radio as if he had been summoned to do a particular job. He just looked like one more technician as he moved amongst them, watching everyone, memorising every detail of what he saw.

"And will you be staying on Earth this time?" Gilly asked Joe.

"God only knows," he shrugged and the conductor raised his baton. The scenery parted to allow the celestial music and voices to wash out over the heads of the delirious crowd. Gilly rose from her chair and knelt respectfully at Joe's feet, the showman in her soul sensing that it was what the crowd wanted to see.

The Ukrainian took a deep breath and moved to the side of the stage where Joe would be exiting.

FORTY-ONE

The power of the singers' voices carried the spirits of the crowd even higher as they cheered and clapped and whooped their encouragement towards Gilly and Joe who were now taking discreet bows and moving off towards the side of the stage. Joe was fiddling with the microphone which had been fitted to the lapel of his jacket and the Ukrainian was suddenly beside him, as if ready to help with its removal, his fingers gripping the handle of the knife secreted inside his jacket.

"You were fantastic," Sophie said, accidentally elbowing the Ukrainian aside in her eagerness to throw her arms around Joe's neck and congratulate him. "Sorry," she said to the man she assumed was a technician, aware that she must have winded him in her eagerness, but he was already hurrying away.

"The crowd loved every word of it," she whispered into Joe's ear. "And thank you for what you said at the end."

"It was fun." Joe returned her hug. He was on a high from the experience. The energy from the audience and the adrenalin from performing in such an unfamiliar setting combined to make his head buzz with pleasure.

The opportunity having passed, the Ukrainian vanished back through the crowd, which was now swarming around Joe, heaping praise on his performance, everyone wanting to catch his eye and perhaps even to touch him.

The moment Joe released Sophie from the hug she found herself being pulled backwards by eager hands and within seconds there was a sea of people between them; nearly all of them, she noticed, seemed to be attractive young women. Gilly was at the front. Sophie glanced around for the man she had elbowed aside, wanting to apologise properly, but he was nowhere in sight.

"There's an after-show party at a local nightclub," Gilly was telling Joe. "Everyone would love it if you came."

"Sure," Joe shrugged his agreement. He was enjoying the attention and the excitement of the show was still tingling through his veins and making his head feel light.

Sophie had to struggle to keep up with the group of people who now seemed to be sweeping him towards a line of limousines waiting just inside the heavily guarded perimeter gates to whisk them away, and she only managed to get into the last car by physically fighting her way through the crowd. Joe was in the front car and it felt like she was being left behind, even though she was still part of the entourage.

The Ukrainian had managed to slide into one of the cars in between them, concentrating on texting on his phone to avoid having to make eye contact or conversation with anyone else who had been crammed into the same car.

He had been on jobs before where all the planning had gone out of the window at the last moment and he was forced to go with the flow of events, alert for all possibilities. Part of him enjoyed the feeling of unpredictability, like a hunter crawling through the undergrowth towards his prey, unsure which way it would jump or whether it would catch his scent and run.

FORTY-TWO

The club's own full-time security staff had been swamped with newcomers, all of them with different agendas and different people to protect, all of them with different uniforms and all-areas passes to flash at one another when challenged. As Joe and Sophie were both swept into the dark interior in different groups, the Ukrainian was able to walk in between the stern-faced guard of honour lining the red carpet, simply raising his security pass to anyone who looked like they might challenge his right to be there. He strode straight to the bar and picked up one of the already poured glasses of champagne and moved into the darkest, most deserted corner he could see, from where he would be able to watch almost the entire room. He raised the glass to his lips to look like he was just another celebrating guest but did not sip. He wanted to keep his head as clear as possible for whatever opportunities might present themselves.

It was many years since Sophie had been inside a nightclub and the atmosphere made her feel uneasy. She had never been comfortable in places where there was too much noise and where people were too drunk to hold proper conversations. Plenty of people were coming up to shake her hand, kiss her cheek as if they knew her, and tell her how wonderful she was and how much they admired her, but she couldn't think of anything to say to any of them. She was sure she could sense their disappointment. She was already aware of the trolling she was receiving online after Joe singled her out for special thanks and she couldn't help wondering if any of the trolls were in the room with her. The lights were so low it was hard to orientate herself and feel safe. She felt deeply vulnerable and wished she had Joe's protective arm around her.

Joe was now wedged into a booth by a group of young women, all of whom were working hard to anticipate his every need, gazing at him adoringly and laughing loudly at everything and nothing. She couldn't get into the same booth but found one directly opposite where other people happily shuffled along to make room for her without trying to talk to her.

From there she was able to see that one of the girls at Joe's table had surreptitiously lit a joint and was passing it around. When it came to Joe's turn she saw the girls showing him how to take small puffs to avoid feeling faint and to hold the smoke in his lungs for the best effect. He sank back into the cushions with a comfortable look on his face as the smoke curled slowly back out of his nostrils. She looked quickly round the room to see if she could see anyone using a camera. Even in the dark she could see there were at least twenty phones taking pictures and most of them were pointing in the direction of Joe's booth.

She knew for sure that the internet would already be circulating images of the Son of God inhaling drugs in the middle of a group of excited-looking young women but there was no way she was going to be able to get close enough to warn him. It was probably too late anyway and she didn't want to appear like a jealous, possessive girlfriend, although she actually felt nauseous with a mixture of jealousy and a terrible fear that she was about to lose him. If she tried to interfere in whatever was happening at his table she would only draw more attention to it and give the media yet another trivial story to blow out of proportion. She was aware that the fewer personal stories there were out there, the more space there would be for the serious messages that Joe and the Twelve wanted to circulate.

She remembered what he had said on stage about sex being too good to be reserved only for reproduction and felt the claws of fear dig even deeper into her gut. Being beside him in the previous weeks had been an otherworldly experience, but she now realised with a jolt that, no matter how affectionate he had been towards her, at no stage had he ever told her that he loved her and at no stage had he suggested that they were in any sort of exclusive relationship. The subject had simply not come up and she certainly would never have had the nerve to ask him how he felt about her. It would have seemed like the most enormous presumption on her part to even suggest such a thing, but at the same time she had allowed herself to presume that he felt the same way about her that she did about him. She suddenly felt foolish and wanted to cry. She downed her drink in one swallow and snatched another one from a passing waitress.

The Ukrainian was able to watch both Joe and Sophie from his vantage point in the shadows and could see exactly what was happening. His drink remained untouched and he simply ignored everyone who tried to catch his eye or make conversation. Once everyone else had had a few drinks, or taken a tablet, or smoked a joint, they became absorbed in their own bleary-eyed worlds, dancing or laughing, and he knew that he had become as good as invisible to them. Soon he would be able to move amongst them like a ghost, entirely unnoticed.

After an hour, he saw Sophie clamber her way out of her booth and make for the exit. He guessed it was because she was unable to bear to watch the girls pawing Joe on the other side of the room for a moment longer. Crossing the room to Joe's booth, she waved to catch his attention and signal that she was going, hoping that he would want to come with her. Instead he beamed happily at her, his eyes glazed with pleasure, and waved back. As she headed for the door, fighting back the tears, Sophie noticed a man in the shadows watching her with an unusual amount of interest. She recognised him as the sound technician she remembered she had pushed rudely aside backstage. She now realised that he was a good-looking man and she thought for a second about going over to him to apologise properly for her earlier rudeness, thinking that perhaps Joe might feel jealous if he saw her talking to another man.

The Ukrainian averted his eyes as soon as he realised that Sophie had noticed him, which made him look furtive and disinterested at the same time. She considered challenging him to look her in the eye and connect with her but decided that she wasn't going to stoop to playing such immature games. She was too confused and too angry to be able to make flirty conversation with a shifty-looking stranger who obviously wasn't interested, so she walked on to the exit, emerging out into the fresh night air, still boiling with a mixture of jealous rage and fear.

Being high was a new experience for Joe and he was enjoying it. Being on the stage in front of so many people, not to mention the billions more who would have been watching the broadcast on their televisions or their phones, had made him feel incredibly good and he didn't want that feeling to end. The smoke and the alcohol had made his brain pleasantly unfocused and the attention from the girls in the booth was simultaneously soothing and exciting. The sensual pleasures of simply being alive in a physical body were overwhelming and he allowed his tired, happy mind to surrender to them.

One of the girls pressed on his leg as she leaned in and whispered in his ear. He caught her scent in the air and felt her body warm and firm against his. When he touched her bare arm the skin was soft and inviting. She was asking if he would like her and her friend to give him a massage to help him unwind from all the tension of the evening. Her friend was sitting beside her, smiling equally invitingly and Joe smiled back as his good judgement drifted away on a cloud of champagne bubbles and fragrant smoke.

The Ukrainian watched as the two girls helped Joe out of the booth and guided him to a door at the back of the club. Everyone else in the group seemed to be having much too good a time to take any notice of what the guest of honour was up to. He guessed the door led to some private rooms. If he had known they were coming to this venue he would have found a way to check it out before arriving and would have been able to weigh up the risks he would run if he followed. He didn't like being unable to visualise what the layout might be beyond the door, where the exits might be and where they would lead him to if he required them. At the same time it made the adrenalin pump through his veins as he considered the risks of plunging himself into the unknown.

A couple of security men had seen the trio disappear and were moving discreetly in the same direction. He waited a few moments and then moved out of the corner he had been sheltering in and followed them through into whatever world might lie on the other side, just like any other punter.

FORTY-THREE

Joe closed his eyes and lay back on the cushions, allowing the pleasant fog to drift across his brain, relaxing his limbs and arousing him at the same time. The two girls seemed to be experienced with their hands and he permitted them to do whatever they wished. Although it was known as a "private room", and a security guard lurked discreetly outside the door in case of trouble, there were other people coming and going around them. Some of them seemed to be sleeping or tripping in various chairs and couches while it was obvious from the noises they were emitting that others were making love. There were oriental screens dotted about the room and the lights were low enough for the space that they were inhabiting to feel private even though it wasn't.

He was drifting into a trance-like state, which was close to sleep, as the girls unbuttoned his shirt and trousers. Their fingers felt pleasant against his hot skin, cooled by the iced champagne glasses they had been drinking from.

The Ukrainian slipped some money into the security man's hand without making eye contact and let himself into the room as the man nodded his permission and looked the other way. He waited for a few seconds until his eyes had accustomed to the gloom. He could now make out which of the couches Joe and the girls were lying on. The girls were so engrossed with their work that they did not notice as he circled round them, like a wolf in the night, patrolling the perimeter of a lambing pen. One of his hands was in his pocket, holding the handle of his stiletto knife.

As he came round the end of the couch, he had a clear view of Joe's stripped body and the girls' pale fingers working their magic across the darkness of his naked skin. None of them could see him in the shadows and the security man was still outside the door. No one else cared if there was a voyeur in the room. Everyone was entitled to get their kicks wherever they could.

After just a split second's thought he saw an opportunity to provide an extra, possibly even more valuable, service to his employers. If there was visual evidence of the situation in which Joe met his end it would carry all the more symbolism. Rather than dying a glorious death on a cross, this time he would be assassinated in the seedy backroom of a nightclub for the whole world to see. He let go of the knife and pulled out his phone instead. With experienced fingers he set the video going and casually pointed it at the action on the couch. Despite the gloom it was easy to see Joe's face and to make out exactly what the girls were doing with their fingers and lips.

It was less than a minute before their skills paid off and the Ukrainian was surprised to see one of them produce a small specimen jar from her bag in time to catch a sample of Joe's semen. The specimen jar then vanished into the palm of her hand as Joe let out a gentle chuckle of pleasure before falling into what looked like a deep, satisfied sleep. The Ukrainian slid his phone into his pocket and gripped the handle of the knife again.

Their job done, the girls exchanged a few brief words and then left the room, neither of them thinking to check if they were being followed, which struck the Ukrainian as a sign of amateurism. Something about the haste with which the girls left the room caught the eye of the security guard. Signalling to one of his colleagues to take over from him on the door he went into the darkened room and towards the couch where Joe lay. Seeing his only escape route blocked, the Ukrainian released the knife and walked casually out, leaving Joe to sleep.

He stayed a few metres behind the girls as they walked briskly from the club into the darkness outside, turning in opposite directions without saying a word to one another. The one who had taken the specimen jar was talking on her phone as she went. She was mumbling and covering her mouth with her hand, as if deliberately avoiding being overheard, and those words that he did catch sounded like a code. He guessed she was reporting a completed mission to whoever had employed her and decided she was the one to follow. She led him down several streets, past darkened buildings. He was careful to keep his distance and not alert her to his presence. She reached a building where lights were blazing in windows as if someone was waiting for her arrival. She had a code to enter by the front door. Staying tightly in the shadows the Ukrainian moved to the back of the building and found an unlit window which was sufficiently loosely latched for him to be able to prise it open with his knife.

Once inside the building, he slid from the room into a corridor, moving quickly and silently from one door to the next, pressing his ear to each in turn. Finally he detected voices and peered through a slit of a window into a room that was kitted out as a laboratory. The girl was talking to several scientists in white coats who appeared to be freezing the sperm in straws and storing them in liquid nitrogen containers. She seemed to be haggling angrily with someone on the phone at the same time as talking to them. The Ukrainian watched as the scientists obviously decided they had heard enough and all turned their backs on the girl in order to concentrate on their work. As a result, only he saw her lift one of the freeze boxes as she turned away and headed for the door.

The Ukrainian ran silently back to the window he had entered through and slid out. He then stood in the shadows and watched the door as the girl hurried out a few seconds later, glancing nervously over her shoulder. She was still clutching the bulky freeze box close to her chest. He had to admire her decisiveness, obviously deciding to steal some of the semen and acting on that decision within a few split seconds. He followed her to a parked car and watched her drive away, confident that he would be able to find her again as soon as she tried to sell her stolen goods.

Once he was back at the apartment, the Ukrainian forwarded the film of the sex act from his phone to his employers, where experts edited it carefully in order to make it appear as pornographic as possible, removed the part where the semen was collected and released it onto the internet a few hours later. They congratulated him on his decision to use a camera rather than a knife. They all knew there would be plenty more opportunities for him to use the knife later. He suggested the adjustment that he now wanted to his fee and nobody quibbled. The money was transferred within hours.

FORTY-FOUR

At four in the morning, when everyone but the cleaning staff had fallen out of the club premises and stumbled home, the individuals charged with Joe's personal security, relieved to have found him alive after a nervous half hour's search, woke him from a deep and peaceful sleep where the girls had left him in the private room, and ushered him out to a car that had been waiting for several hours. Refreshed from his sleep, and the effects of the joint having worked their way gently out of his system, he felt relatively pleased with the way the night had gone and he made no protest about being smuggled back into the hotel through the back entrance to avoid the twenty-four-hour media camp out the front. He was looking forward to going back to sleep as soon as he reached the bed.

He was genuinely shocked by the level of Sophie's fury that struck him as he entered the suite. She had been sitting on the sofa, staring at the door ever since she got back, trying to work out how she felt and what she should do about it. The moment she saw him come in she realised how she felt, which was furiously angry and bruised to the depths of her soul.

She flew across the room, thumping her fists against his chest and knocking him backwards into the wall. Recovering his equilibrium he encircled her with his arms and held her tightly, as you might hold a child in the throes of an uncontrollable tantrum, waiting for it to subside while trying to make sense of what was going on.

"How could you do that?" she demanded. "How could you behave like that with those women, flaunting it in front of me like it didn't matter?"

"Flaunting what?" He wanted to understand what she was talking about so that he could help her. "How could I do what?"

"Going off with those women! Letting them climb all over you!"

"Oh." He continued to hug her close to him, even though she was now wriggling to be free so that she could look him in the eye and confront him properly. He held on tight, needing time to work out what had happened and how he had unwittingly caused it.

"I'm sorry," he said after a moment, "it was just a party and I was relaxing."

"Where did you think I was? Did you give me a moment's thought?"

"I assumed you were having fun somewhere else in the room. Was I meant to be looking after you? Is that what you expected of me? Were you in danger? Did something bad happen to you?"

She realised they were genuine questions as she finally managed to pull back from his arms and look into his puzzled face.

"No," she spat, her anger still white hot, "you were not supposed to be 'looking after me' and nothing 'bad' happened to me apart from having my heart ripped out of my chest by you, but you weren't supposed to be carrying on with other women right in front of me!"

"Carrying on? I was just relaxing and enjoying myself for a few hours."

"I could see that," she said. "They were all over you in that booth."

The fact that he so obviously didn't know what he had done wrong had thrown her off balance. It wasn't the reaction she had been expecting. Why didn't he realise that he had behaved badly? Did he actually think that she wouldn't care if he went off with another woman – or women? Was she being unreasonable, acting like a jealous wife?

"How would you have felt if it had been me?" She immediately regretted asking the question.

"I would like it if you were having fun. You are my friend, why would I mind?"

It was like he had slapped her round the face and forced all the air out of her anger. She sank back into the sofa as if defeated.

"I see," she said in a small voice, "I'm sorry. I have completely misunderstood. I should have known. God knows I have been in this situation often enough before."

He sat beside her and put his arm around her shoulder, but she didn't move or soften the tension in her back, resisting his attempt to pull her close to him.

"Maybe it's me who has completely misunderstood," he said gently. "You are my best friend on Earth. You have been chosen by God for the role you are playing."

"Have you any idea how corny that all sounds?" she asked, managing a small smile through the tears.

He laughed. "I suppose it does. But it's true. I should not have caused you any pain."

"I shouldn't have fallen in love with you. It's a stupid thing to do. How could I possibly expect to be able to apply the usual relationship rules to the Son of God?"

"Well, when you put it like that you make me feel like a real heel. Was it my mistake to allow our relationship to become physical? Is that where the misunderstanding came about?"

She pulled a tissue from a box displayed on the ornate table at the end of the sofa and blew her nose violently.

"I guess," she said.

"But I didn't force you or anything, did I? You did want to, didn't you? I didn't misunderstand that, did I?"

"Of course I wanted to!" She was still feeling angry. "I'm madly in love with you! Why would I not want to go to bed with you?"

"And if you love someone you have to possess them completely?" He had reverted to his question-asking mode.

"No, obviously not! But I can't help it if I feel betrayed and jealous if I see you with someone else."

"But love should not be exclusive. I love all of mankind."

"Oh don't give me that!" Her anger had boiled up again. "What was going on with those women was nothing to do with you loving every living creature! Do you think I'm that stupid?"

"I was just having some fun," he said.

"I could see that!"

"I had no idea I was causing you pain."

As they talked, going round and round in circles, over and over the same ground, she was aware that messages were continually arriving on her phone. The light was beginning to make its way through the cracks in the curtains when she finally picked it up and opened one. It was a few seconds before she realised that what she was looking at was a film of Joe in a darkened room with the two girls.

She watched for a few agonising moments and realised that the pain of being with him now was going to be too great for her to bear. Without saying a word she left the suite.

"Where are you going?" he asked as she paused in the door, looking back at him.

"Alice has rented a place to be near her dad while he's

down here. I'm going there while I get my head together."

He nodded, surprised by how sad he felt at what was happening.

"I wish you would stay," he said, "but I understand if you feel you can't."

"I have to go," she said, "because my heart is breaking."

FORTY-FIVE

Without Sophie there to keep him informed, it was several hours before Joe found out that a film of him receiving a relief massage from two young women had arrived on the internet. Not surprisingly it had already gone viral by then, along with pictures of him enjoying the joint in the club. The media immediately pounced on the story of his betrayal of Sophie just hours after praising her to the world and elevated Joe to the status of "love rat". Then came accusations of a faked video having been made on the orders of Joe's enemies, which cast an element of doubt over the whole story but made it all the more intriguing to the watching world.

In some parts of society there was loud disapproval of Joe's failure to set a good example for young people regarding the use of soft drugs, followed by more thoughtful reactions which asked if his sins were really so terrible compared to those of most mortal men. His millions of followers soon started to come to his defence, liking the idea that he was able to relax and enjoy himself without doing anyone any harm (few of them had realised that he and Sophie were romantically involved and assumed the media was making it up). As far as many people were concerned it was a moment which should have been allowed to stay private (although they all still wanted to take a peek at the video and be told every last detail). Many expressed disappointment and even shock, but within a few hours the most widespread reaction from people was that they were tired of the media's endless appetite for negative stories of sleaze and the countless attempts to create confrontation and scandal where there was none and that they were also saddened by politicians and other public figures trying to bring down their rivals by leaking such stuff.

Joe's only regret was that he now understood how much the film was going to hurt Sophie and he was angry with himself for not anticipating that and being more careful with her heart. He knew that the joint and the champagne might explain his lapse of judgement, but they did not excuse it. He wanted to make things better for her but despite all his miraculous powers he was not sure how to go about mending a broken heart.

*****

The Ukrainian was surprised by the developing public reaction to his film. He had assumed that it would prove to be a powerful propaganda weapon in the hands of his employers, but on balance it seemed to be increasing Joe's popularity even further. He wished now he had stuck to his original plan and simply killed Joe in that backroom of the club while he had the chance. It was going to be hard to ask for more money for a while because the sort of people who employed him only paid for results and the film had definitely not achieved the desired result.

He watched movements on the Dark Web, waiting for clues as to who had stolen Joe's semen and what they were planning to do with it. Even though his film had not shown the girls stealing the sample, people were already speculating. If "divine semen" came up for sale people thought the interest might likely come from someone in the scientific community but it might equally come from someone who would like the idea of being impregnated, or having their partner impregnated, by the Son of God. The Ukrainian took in everything he read but bided his time before coming to any conclusions himself.

Then a seller appeared, and he knew it must be the same girl that he had followed. Again her approach seemed amateurish to him. It was not surprising. She was too young to have the necessary experience for such a job and it looked to him like she was trying to double-cross whoever her employers were. She was already talking to far too many people for her own safety. Her search for the best customer was not nearly as focused as he knew it needed to be. He was not surprised when he received a call a couple of days later from the Far Eastern voice from the pharmaceutical industry which had first talked to him about the possibility of kidnapping Joe.

"One of the girls in your film is trying to sell something that belongs to us," he was informed by the voice, which did not give away whether they were angry.

"I know."

"They are asking for ridiculous money but it seems there are some fools who are willing to pay. We need you to retrieve it for us. Then end things for the girl. We do not want to be blackmailed later."

"Understood," he replied, vowing to himself, not for the first time, that once this job was over he would retire from the business once and for all.

FORTY-SIX

"Is it wise for us to associate with such a man?" the elderly Cardinal was controlling himself because he was in the presence of the Pope. He had not seen the video personally but he had been told about it by a shocked acolyte and the mere fact that it existed was enough for him to know that it was something he did not want to think about for a second longer than he had to.

"My dear Carlo." The Pope placed a calming hand on his old friend's shoulder, aware that he was shaking with pent-up indignation. "I think we must maintain a sense of perspective. I believe this man is the Son of God and I have told the world of that belief. He has returned on a mission to save mankind. Such a tiny incident, which two thousand years ago would have remained entirely private, can hardly compare to such a mission."

The Pope hoped that he was succeeding in masking his own doubts and fears. While on the island, watching Joe raising the Archbishop from the dead, he had been entirely convinced that he had made the right decision in pledging his allegiance. There was now so much scientific evidence to confirm that Joe was who he claimed to be, but still it was an enormous effort to cast aside so much of what he had believed all his life to be true. He couldn't afford to let anyone see the doubts that tortured him in his darker moments. He had to have faith that he had made the right choice, otherwise he would never be able to inspire his followers to believe.

"But Your Holiness, he is consorting with prostitutes."

"That is a harsh judgement, Carlo. We don't know anything about these young ladies and I doubt very much if our friend was expected to pay for their services. I'm told that in the film they appear to be enjoying themselves. Besides which, if they are prostitutes then I suspect that Jesus would have wanted us to look upon them with compassion and forgiveness."

"I doubt he would have encouraged us to sleep with them, Your Holiness!"

"Well you may have a point there," the Pope smiled, obviously wanting to end the conversation but not to offend his friend's sensibilities any further. He found even thinking about the things which Joe was reported to have done with the women brought him physical pain.

"They were all drunk and there is evidence they were taking drugs..."

"Carlo," the Pope spoke more firmly, "can I remind you again that we are talking about the Son of God, who has returned to save mankind from extinction. These hardly seem important matters by comparison."

"I doubt if the Muslims will feel the same way..." Carlo pouted a little at what he took to be a remonstration from his beloved leader.

"I have already heard from the Grand Imam on the subject," the Pope assured him, "and he feels as I do. It is regrettable that these pictures are out there, but that is the world we live in. The acts themselves were not great sins."

"I disagree, Your Holiness, and there are many who will agree with me. Things are going too far, changing too fast."

"They have already changed, Carlo. It is us who are going to have to adjust our thinking now, not the rest of the world. That was explained to us on the island. We have fallen behind the times and this is an opportunity for us to regain our authority by guiding people wisely and realistically through the dilemmas and choices of today, not simply by repeating mantras that were concocted thousands of years ago and are no longer relevant in any of our followers' lives."

"With respect, Your Holiness, no good will come of it."

A knock on the door and an announcement that the President of America was now available to speak on the phone to the Pope put an end to Carlo's audience and he withdrew with a sour expression on his wrinkled features.

"Good morning, Your Holiness," the President's voice boomed down the line. "Did you enjoy your little holiday in the South Pacific?"

The Pope sighed but kept his voice level. "It was a deeply informative visit, thank you for asking, Mr President."

"And what did you make of our healer friend? Who I see has now got himself in a bit of trouble with the ladies." The President let out a chuckle, which he believed sounded manly and conspiratorial.

"I think it would be a good idea for you and the other great leaders of the secular world to meet him," the Pope said, aware that a little flattery would help to convince the President of the rightness of the idea. "He seems to represent the will of the people."

"You don't think he's a charlatan then?" The President sounded surprised. "You think he's the real deal?"

"I believe he is the Son of God and that he has returned with a mission to save mankind."

There was a long silence as the President absorbed the full impact of these words.

"I can't believe I'm hearing this," he said eventually. "You are telling me you are swallowing the line that this guy actually is Jesus and he's come back from the dead again, after two thousand years?"

"If you study your Bible, Mr President, you will see that this is not an entirely new idea."

"Yeah, right, but that's just religious hokum, isn't it? That's the stuff you tell the masses to keep them quiet."

"I think our views may be different there, Mr President."

"It's not exactly the return that John described in his Book of Revelation, though, is it?"

Someone in the Oval Office must have reminded the President who he was talking to and that he was not in a men's locker room because he seemed to take a breath before moderating his tone.

"You really think we should meet with him then?"

"I do."

"What about the Muslims and the Jews and all the others? Do they think the same?"

"I believe they do, Mr President."

"Okay, listen, you have a good day. Good to talk to you. We'll talk again soon."

He hung up with a face like thunder.

"Get me the President of Russia on the line."

An hour later the two men were talking.

"I was talking to the Pope this morning," the American President said, somehow making it sound like he was name-dropping. "He thinks we should meet this guy and talk to him."

"I'm busy running my country," the Russian replied.

"You're right. We're busy men. We don't have time for this crap. I understand that. I agree with you. On the other hand, the Pope and the others went to meet him and it made them look like they were in touch with what the people are thinking. I don't like being seen as a dinosaur."

"Someone is comparing you to a dinosaur?" The Russian had to struggle not to laugh.

"Of course not. Not just me. All of us. You too, my friend. We could easily look like we are out of touch with what people want. That's bad politics."

"People say I'm a dinosaur? I don't think so."

"I'm not saying we should go running to him, at his beck and call like the damn priests, but maybe a video conference of some sort. He did a television broadcast the other night..."

"I saw it."

"It was very successful," the American conceded. "He drew a big audience. Great viewing figures. He let himself down afterwards, of course..."

"We are all men," the Russian chuckled, "we all have needs. You know that, Mr President."

"Sure. I know. It's normal. But it doesn't look good on the news bulletins."

"You worry too much about how things look in the media, but if you want to put on some show for the public then I am willing to help."

"That's great. In an open argument I'm going to be able to make mincemeat of this guy. We have to confront him and expose him for the weakling he is. The guy has no idea what being in power actually involves, no idea at all. He's punching way above his weight."

* * * * *

In the following days both presidents made a number of calls to other leaders and at the same time requested meetings with the bankers who handled their personal finances. If there was an increased chance that they were about to be removed from power they wanted to be sure that they had ring-fenced as much of their personal fortunes as possible. If there was any chance there was going to be civil unrest and a change in global leadership they needed to be prepared to look after themselves and their families. It was those fundamental survival instincts which had allowed both of them, and all the other leaders they were now in regular contact with, to get to the top in the first place.

While the caretakers of the world's capital were looking for safe havens to store their money in case of sudden leadership changes, the generals and security forces in every country were working out where they needed to build up their military presence. Which areas of the world were likely to prove vulnerable if the world's populations turned against their leaders and demanded wholesale changes to the power structures and the way that the world was being run? At the same time, however, they were becoming increasingly aware of the very real possibility that their political masters might at any time instruct them to stand down and disband their armies.

When they were first informed that Joe was suggesting all global spending on armies and armaments should be halted with immediate effect it had seemed laughable, no more than a Utopian dream which could never become a practical reality. Over the previous few weeks, however, they had been aware of the changing mood both amongst the world's populations and even in the offices of their employers. As a result, they were coming to the conclusion that they needed to take steps to protect themselves because no one else could be relied upon any more. If the politicians were not going to support them, then they might have to look to the bankers and the business community for their future funding. Lines of communication were opened up and preliminary discussions were held in secret.

"Sounds to me like this guy is preaching some new form of communism," the American President confided to the British

Prime Minister. "My people are worried that he plans to grab power and then he'll misuse it just like Stalin and Mao did."

"Surely not!" The Prime Minister was shocked at the suggestion. "We tend to think he's more of a throwback to the nineteen sixties. A bit of a hippy dreamer, preaching 'peace and love' to the world with no practical experience in running anything. Confronted with the realities of power he will expose himself for the innocent he is."

"We'll do the broadcast with him and show the guy up for the flake he is," the President concluded.

As he hung up, he looked around the Oval Office for approval of this announcement, but everyone seemed to be avoiding making eye contact with him.

FORTY-SEVEN

The Ukrainian had retrieved a phone number for the girl who was hoping to sell the stolen semen via the Dark Web. When he dialled the number from a new phone she answered after only two rings.

"I hear you have a product and you are looking for a buyer."

"I'm looking for a million dollars." He was struck by how young she sounded.

"New Zealand dollars?"

There was a moment's hesitation, which suggested to him yet again that he was not dealing with a professional. She was making things up as she went along.

"American dollars," she said. "Cash."

"Not a problem."

"And we have to meet in a public place."

"Sure. Where do you want to meet?"

She named a coffee shop in a mall and he agreed a time to meet the following day. He promised to bring the money in cash.

"I will be wearing a green shirt and green-framed glasses," he told her. "When we meet, act as if we are old friends."

"Okay."

From the eagerness with which she accepted his offer he suspected that the other buyers she had been talking to had been far less co-operative. They had probably quibbled about the money and they had probably wanted to know how she could prove that the product was what she said it was. If she had more experience she would have realised that he was agreeing to the deal far too easily to be true.

That evening he visited the coffee shop, dressed in black and without glasses, to make sure he knew where all the entrances and exits were. He bought a coffee and watched the way the staff worked. He went to the toilet and checked out the windows and the security cameras both inside the premises and surrounding it. He did not want to repeat the experience of being in the club with no idea of the layout.

The following morning he stuffed a sports bag with newspapers to make it look like it was full of money, dressed himself as he had described to her on the phone, and drove to the mall. He went into a shop opposite the coffee bar and waited until he had seen her go in, buy a coffee and sit down, then he walked purposefully across, zig-zagging to avoid the security cameras.

Once inside he walked straight over to her.

"Hi," he said sitting down beside her and pecking her on the cheek as if they were old friends, or perhaps even lovers.

"Hi," she replied. "Lovely to see you."

He was impressed; she obviously knew how to act.

"Do you have the product?" he asked.

"Do you have the cash?"

"In the bag."

She glanced at the sports bag and then lifted a large holdall onto the seat between them. He glanced in and saw what looked like a freezer box.

"I brought your bag," he said in a normal conversational voice for the benefit of people at the neighbouring tables.

He placed the bag on her lap so that no one else could see that he had slid a knife up inside her rib cage. Even she didn't realise for a few seconds. She looked down and the blood was bubbling out behind the bag. By the time she looked back up he was already leaving the premises with the holdall and she was dead before she was able to cry out for help. It was several minutes before someone noticed that the girl slumped in the corner was not responding when asked if the seat next to her was taken. Then several people noticed the blood pooling on the floor around her feet and they started to scream. By that time the Ukrainian was driving away from the mall, wearing a white T-shirt and dark glasses with gold rims. The green shirt and glasses went into a bin several miles from the mall and were never found by anyone.

Once safely back in his apartment, he unwrapped a new phone and made a number of calls to let people know what he had to sell.

FORTY-EIGHT

Virtually every senior figure in the American and Russian armies had accepted the invitation from a consortium of banks, corporations and bodies representing industry sectors such as pharmaceuticals, guns, oil, real estate, cars and mining. The Chinese generals had also been approached and had cautiously agreed to send a few senior representatives. The invitation was for a long weekend at a Las Vegas hotel, which had been turned over entirely to hosting the event. If big business was going to be asked to provide funding for the armed forces in the future, its leaders wanted a chance to get to know the people they would be dealing with.

The hosts had shipped all the hotel's other guests out, finding them alternative accommodation along the strip, and had surrounded the premises with their own security staff. The media were not informed of the meeting and to any casual passers-by it would have looked like a large conference of business people, interspersed with soldiers who might well have been enjoying their leave.

None of the participants' presidents was officially informed of the event, although the Russian President had found out from one of his most trusted generals. The Chinese President had also been informed unofficially and was assured that his staff was listening in at any number of different points in the hotel, just in case they found themselves excluded from any of the discussions. The Chinese President was not averse to the idea of keeping a dignified distance from the other countries for as long as possible. He suspected that it would play better with his own population if he was seen not to be considering military options for maintaining his power base. From what he had heard it seemed that public feelings were more sympathetic towards the quiet approach of his regime than they were to the sabre-rattling proclamations coming out of the Oval Office. He wanted to maintain that advantage for as long as possible.

The trigger for the meeting might have been the rumours that Joe and his twelve followers were planning to call a halt to the financing of armies and the procurement of armaments, but the fact that their forces had been put on permanent stand-by to deal with whatever unrest might result from Joe's pronouncements to the world seemed to all of the delegates at the Las Vegas venue to confirm that they were still needed to maintain law and order and protect the status quo in a world that was teetering on the edge of revolution. None of them believed that it was either practical or right that they should suddenly be disbanded and told that their services were no longer required, their "guns to be turned back into ploughshares" as one of the Russian generals put it.

"Human nature doesn't change overnight," one of the American generals had been widely quoted in the media as saying. "If you suddenly do away with all the armed forces there will be nothing to stop rogue aggressors from invading unprotected countries. There will be nothing to stop the more unsavoury elements of society from rising up and taking control. Do people really want a world run by drug barons and religious fanatics?"

Many commentators had pointed out that throughout history it had often been society's most unsavoury elements who had controlled the most powerful and destructive armies, that many of the most respected "gamekeepers" had started their careers as "poachers".

When Joe's messages about creating a global government had first started to circulate in both the mainstream and social media, the general consensus in military circles was that each of their political leaders would want to protect their positions and that their budgets would therefore be safe and might even be increased to match the increased risk of insurrection. As the numbers following and liking the messages that Joe was putting out increased exponentially, some of the more politically acute military experts had sensed that their political leaders and supporters were beginning to waver in their determination to protect their military budgets.

When the weight of public opinion on the internet and other media started to talk seriously about the possibility of disbanding armies completely and directing the funds to places where they could do more good, such as healthcare and education, the political leaders did not immediately leap to their defence. The generals began to feel that they could no longer rely on the backing of their leaders. If giving up their armies was the only way that the politicians could cling onto their power, the generals were beginning to envisage their own powerbases being pulled out from under them. That was why they had decided it was time to make plans for their own survival.

The idea of unleashing hundreds of thousands of trained soldiers into the civilian world overnight, having stripped them of their jobs and their status, was alarming to anyone who understood well the average soldier's capacity for anger and destruction when not kept under control. Some predicted that it would lead to a rise in mercenary armies, with criminal organisations recruiting the soldiers for their own nefarious purposes. Others predicted epidemics of alcohol and drug abuse among a population of predominantly young people, suddenly feeling that they had been thrown on the scrapheap after being promised a lifetime's employment.

"It's obviously a naïve and short-sighted approach," one high-ranking American general announced to a conference hall full of his peers, "and entirely impractical to implement at such short notice. We have been told that they are claiming that trillions of dollars are currently being spent on armies, armaments and space surveys and that all that money should overnight be redirected towards raising people out of poverty, providing a universal basic income, providing free healthcare and feeding the hungry. All very altruistic no doubt, but wholly impractical.

"How are they going to be able to get food to those who need it in the middle of Africa without soldiers to guard the convoys? How are they going to stop the bullies who run the dictatorships around the world from simply marching across internationally established borders and plundering whatever they want? Who will stop the millions of dispossessed who are being affected by political turmoil and drought in the southern hemisphere from simply marching north and taking what they want from those who currently own it?

"The politicians blow with the wind. They see this crackpot and his young hippy followers as potential voters and they don't believe they can stand up to them. While they have us behind them they can still hold on to their positions, but if they agree to these demands they will have given away all hope of clinging to power. We need to be strong and take the decisions on their behalf if we are to save the entire global system from collapse."

There was a vigorous round of applause as a conference room full of strong men and women pounded their palms together and slapped the table tops in a show of international solidarity. Russians and Americans were united by what they saw as a mutual foe, a new enemy that they could only defeat if they worked together and forgot past differences. The few Chinese generals sitting at the back of the room applauded politely but their expressions gave away nothing of what they were actually thinking.

Entertainment had been laid on for the guests in the hotel theatre and dining rooms as well as in the casino. After a long day of meetings, the American general who had earlier been speaking had eaten a large meal and was digesting it with a brandy when he was informed that a Russian of equivalent rank to himself wished to have a private meeting, just the two of them with their translators.

"By all means," the general boomed, "bring him in."

Both men were aware of one another's distinguished military records and there was a cordial atmosphere of mutual respect as the Russian and his translator sat down and the heavy doors to the private room were pulled shut by hotel staff. An American and a Russian guard took up positions outside the doors to ensure there was no interruption.

"I believe we have both spent time in Afghanistan," the Russian said, as if merely trying to find some common ground upon which to build a relationship.

"A godforsaken country if ever there was one," the American replied.

"A lot of snakes," the Russian continued after a few moments of thought. "Dangerous ones."

"Indeed. My soldiers used to go out hunting them at night," the American agreed.

"The best way to deal with a snake," the Russian went on after a significant pause, "is to cut off the head, fast and clean. Don't play games with it. Don't wait to see what will happen next, just take off the head."

The American realised that they were no longer actually talking about snakes or Afghanistan.

"It was the same in Russia in 1918," the Russian continued.

"The revolution?"

"The Tsar and his family. Executed quickly and cleanly. Then the revolution could proceed successfully."

"An execution?" The American mulled the word over thoughtfully, his eyes boring into the Russian's impassive face. "Interesting suggestion."

They talked on for a while until interrupted by a knock on the doors. One of the guards stepped smartly in once his general had barked his permission.

"Apologies for the interruption, sir."

"What?"

"Reports are coming in of crowds of protestors forming all over the city and marching towards the hotel."

The two generals exchanged tight-lipped looks.

"Where is the Chinese contingent?" the American general asked.

"I believe they are in the casino, sir."

"Find the best vantage point to see the streets and take us there," the American commanded.

Three minutes later he and the Russian were standing side by side in a bedroom on the twentieth floor of the hotel looking down through binoculars at the streets below, which were already thronged with crowds waving banners and burning torches, shouting slogans up at the hotel windows.

"We stand for the Earth we stand on!"

It was possible to see more coming from surrounding streets, bringing traffic to a halt in every direction. The translators stood between the two generals.

"How in God's name did they manage to raise so many people so quickly?" the American wondered.

"Activists working on the internet," the Russian replied. "They have great power now. More than we ever had. They put out a call to micro-influencers and millions hear it and respond. This is the new warfare."

"Micro-influencers?"

"People with more than five thousand authentic followers," the Russian explained.

"You knew this was going to happen?" The American's tone had hardened. "Did the information leak to these micro-influencers come from your people in St Petersburg?"

The Russian ignored the question. "We are guests in your country, General." His voice was low and threatening. "I trust you are going to be able to ensure our safety."

"They're just pacifists," the American replied after scanning the crowd once more, "making their point. They won't hurt anyone. We will leave it to the police to deal with. I assure you, General, you and your colleagues are perfectly safe."

"Those are big crowds," the Russian mused, "and this is just one city. It will be hard for you to control them all. If we do not cut the head off the snake soon it will only grow larger, until it is big enough to swallow us all."

"I entirely understand what you are saying, General. You have succeeded in making your point," the American said, turning smartly on his heel and leaving the room.

FORTY-NINE

The Ukrainian was working in front of the mirror. He had padded his cheeks from the inside and fitted a set of different teeth over this own, transforming the appearance of his face. He then shaved his head with meticulous care and altered the shape of his eyebrows. He had not shaved for a few days and was able to carve the resultant growth into a fashionable style, the sort of style which would be popular with someone who worked in a television studio but different to the look he had affected at Joe's televised interview.

It was now more important than ever that he was successful in his mission. The previous night a phone which had not rung for many years had brought him a message from a source deep inside the CIA. It appeared that the Americans also wanted to hire his services, and they wanted him to target the same man as his other employers. He was fairly confident that neither side knew that the other had contacted him and he wanted to finish the business quickly, before they found out. This one killing would now result in several fees and make him rich enough never to have to work again.

He intended to perform the assassination at the television studio where Joe was going to be talking to the political leaders. That way the whole world, including all his various employers, could witness that he had completed his assignment successfully. He was aware that there would be a number of people at the studio who were also backstage at the previous broadcast. He didn't want any of them to see anything familiar about his face. He also knew that however careful he might have been before, he was bound to have been recorded on security cameras and he did not want to trigger any facial recognition algorithms.

Happy that he had done enough, he put on a fashionable pair of thick-rimmed, round glasses which would be the most distinctive feature people would mention when they were later asked to describe him. He opened a new phone and inserted a SIM card. Once it was working he held it up and took a picture of his new face. He then punched in a number and waited for the ringing to stop.

"I need another all-areas studio pass for the video meeting," he said without introducing himself. "I'm sending a photo with the relevant details."

"It can't be done," the voice at the other end replied. "I have already done enough. I owe your bosses nothing. There is nothing else I can do."

"This is the last request," he said quietly. "You do not have a choice unless you are ready to be exposed for what you have already done for us. Once this is done it will all be over."

"I'm serious," the voice protested, "I can't do any more. I think people suspect."

"I'm sending the picture and details now," he said, as if the other person had not spoken. "Finish the job and then you will be free."

He sent the picture and the details, then dropped the phone into the acid. The all-areas studio pass was delivered to a safe address the following day and the same woman who had accompanied him to lunch in the hotel restaurant picked it up and brought it to him.

FIFTY

The broadcast was due to take place at midnight in New Zealand. Screens had been set up in the studio for Joe to talk simultaneously to the twelve most powerful world leaders. He had insisted that the broadcast went out live to the whole world so that there would be minimal opportunities for misinformation to filter out before everyone had had a chance to listen, watch and judge for themselves. The advisors to many of the leaders were nervous as to how their bosses were going to come across in comparison to both Joe and rival leaders.

"I'm great at talking on my feet," the American President assured all those who warned him to be careful about losing his temper or sounding out of touch with the mood of the world's population. "This is where I excel. I've done it before, so many times! We are going to make this guy look so stupid!"

When he had first heard that the broadcast would be happening at eight in the morning in Washington he had been momentarily unsettled. Early mornings were not his best time. His staff suggested that he arrange to be woken at six so that he would have a couple more hours to prepare his arguments, but he brushed the idea aside.

"No need," he said. "I know all the arguments backwards."

In Moscow, the broadcast would be happening in the middle of the afternoon and in the early evening in Beijing. The presidents in both countries had set aside the whole day to ensure that they were fully briefed on all the topics that Joe was likely to bring up. The very best translators were lined up to sit with them, although Joe had assured the organisers that he would be able to understand everyone in their native languages. The broadcasters were arranging for simultaneous text translations to appear at the bottom of the live pictures, with voice translations available as an extra option for those who required it.

News of the broadcast had spread worldwide and virtually no one was asleep apart from the very young and the very old. The excitement which had built up for the first question-and-answer broadcast had grown even more intense with the additional attraction of seeing how their leaders justified themselves and how they reacted to Joe and to his plans.

Every citizen in every country felt that they were now involved in the search for solutions to all the most pressing global issues. They now believed they would be able to make a contribution to creating a better world for their children and their grandchildren and many as yet unborn generations in the future, whether that involved planting trees or cleaning rivers, building better housing or helping other people to lead healthier and happier lives. Even the smaller countries, whose leaders were not part of the event, felt that they were now directly implicated in whatever the outcomes of this broadcast might be.

Joe, conscious that it would be easy to cause offence to the other participants in the discussion, made sure that he was the first to arrive at the studio. He did not want to give them any reason to believe that he considered that he was the star of the show – even if the viewing public might see it that way. The technicians were still setting up and he went round all of them, shaking their hands, introducing himself to each of them in turn and exchanging a few words of gratitude for their help. Many of them fell to their knees or bent low to kiss the hem of his coat, his hands or his feet.

When he came to a bearded man with a shaved head and thick-rimmed, round glasses, Joe held onto his hand for a little longer than the others.

"I am very grateful for everything you will be doing here tonight," he said, still holding the man's hand and staring directly into his eyes. "It is important that you know that."

"You are very welcome," the Ukrainian smiled, making no attempt to avert his gaze or release his grip on Joe's hand, aware that although there was no way he could have known he was Ukrainian, Joe was talking to him in his own language. He did not incline his head or show the slightest sign of either reverence or shame. He had a job to do and he knew that he could not afford to allow a scintilla of doubt into his mind.

"There is a good chance that together we can make a big difference with whatever we choose to do and say today," Joe continued, still not releasing the Ukrainian from his grip.

"I hope so," the Ukrainian replied. "Everyone has their part to play."

"Indeed they do," Joe said, finally letting go.

One by one the screens on the walls around the studio were crackling into life as the various leaders arrived at the other ends of the broadcast. Live outside broadcast cameras had been allowed into the White House, the Kremlin and every other leader's designated place of work.

"Can anyone hear me?" the Prime Minister of India enquired. "I can't hear anything."

"I can hear you, sir," Joe replied in Meitei, the local language of the Manipur region of India.

"Is this going to take long?" the Australian Prime Minister enquired.

"How long can you spare to save mankind, Prime Minister?" the German Chancellor asked. "Do you have somewhere else to go?"

"My bed," the Australian growled.

The American President's advisers held him back from the camera for as long as possible, wanting him to be the last to arrive, but eventually his impatience overwhelmed their abilities to control him and he sat down behind his desk, grinning into the camera.

"This won't take long," he assured all those listening.

Once he knew that everyone else was there, the Russian President counted to ten and then stepped in front of his camera. His expression was unreadable and a rustle of discomfort seemed to run through all the other contributors, as if a cat had just stalked up to a bird feeder.

"So, young man..." The American President had been granted the honour of opening the discussion by the others as soon as the 'on' button was pressed, all of whom understood that he would be flattered by such a gesture of respect. "You think you know better how to run things than all of us put together?"

Joe looked around the screens at the array of angry faces staring back at him. "I would certainly like to help if I can," he said.

"We were all democratically elected!" The American slapped his palm on the desk, making everyone jump. "We are the choice of the people. Who the hell are you?"

"I am the Son of God," Joe said simply. "Sent to show you the way. It will be up to you to choose whether or not to follow."

"Damn right it will be up to us." The American ignored the warning waves coming from his aides behind the camera, advising him to keep calm, and not set out on a rant.

"I don't think it will help us to become aggressive," the Canadian Prime Minister interrupted. "This is too serious a matter for theatrical displays."

"Don't patronise me!" the American warned. "I am warning you. I will not tolerate it."

"Enough!" The Russian President's voice was not raised but it still silenced the American. "The things you are suggesting, Joe, are ridiculous. Do you not think with all our years of experience in power we have not tried all of them? Do you not think we would have implemented them years ago if they were possible? Do you imagine that any of us are reluctant to eradicate poverty or improve education and healthcare for the people we love and serve?"

"I think you may have been distracted by other more immediate priorities," Joe replied diplomatically. "You all had personal ambitions to fulfil, personal debts to repay – and I don't just mean financial – you all had elections to win. You have not had the ability to stand back and look at the state of the whole of mankind and work out what the best way forward might be for the entire world. If you had then you would never threaten one another with nuclear weapons, or invade one another or be so slow to send help during times of famine or natural catastrophe. You would not have continued destroying forests and raping the Earth of its mineral resources.

"None of you have looked beyond your own terms in office and your own legacies in order to see what is best for the long-term future of mankind and the planet. You have not listened to the wise advice of those who have…"

"Are you talking about your mafia of Twelve?" the Australian enquired. "Are they the ones with the 'wise advice' we are supposed to have been listening to?"

"Mafia?" Joe smiled. "That is an interesting word for you to use, Prime Minister, because there are a lot of people who see many of you in the same light."

"Joe, Joe," the Canadian interrupted, "that is not helpful language to use."

The Chinese President had been silent up till that moment, but the word "Mafia" cracked his glassy façade like a bullet.

"Listen!" he snapped. "Why are you all even willing to talk with this man? We are the leaders of the world and he is nobody. There is no dignity to be had from talking to such a person. He is deliberately trying to ferment unrest amongst people who are striving for peaceful lives."

"I think you are right, Mr President," the Indian Prime Minister agreed. "This is a confidence trickster who has managed to fool many people. We must not allow him to pull the wool over our eyes any longer."

"Gentlemen please," the German Chancellor said, attempting to calm things.

"You want us to change everything that we are doing and hand over power to you and your band of bogus professors?" the Russian President hissed.

"You need to rethink all your long-term plans for mankind and for the planet, yes," Joe confirmed. "And you need an international government that unites everyone, removing all nationalistic bickering from the equation."

All over the world the population watched in horror as they saw many of the people who were meant to be leading them lose their tempers and shout abuse and mockery at Joe, like a bunch of school bullies ganging up on a new boy in the playground. Several of them started to talk over one another, all of them shouting at Joe, accusing him of being a fraud, telling him that he might think he was fooling the world, but all the time assuring him that he did not fool any of them in their infinite wisdom. The voices of reason could no longer make themselves heard over the din. The more they shouted the more most of them sounded like old men who had lost touch with the real world, like drunks in a bar at closing time, railing against a world that no longer seemed to be going in the direction they expected or the direction that benefited them. Their failing powers, growing paranoia and obvious inability

322

to understand what was happening became crystal clear to the billions of people watching.

"Quiet!" Joe held his arms up high and to their own surprise they all fell silent simultaneously.

"If the one thing that is stopping you from doing the right things for the world is your lack of faith in me, perhaps I need to remind you just what your God is capable of. Have you already forgotten what it was like the day the sun went out?"

"And you're claiming that was something to do with you?" The American President could hardly contain his glee. "Okay then, let's see what you can do. If you are the Son of God, turn out the sun. Show us all your best tricks, Sonny!"

"Very well," Joe said. "It is done."

There was a few seconds of silence and then the assembled heads on the video screens all started to laugh and taunt him. "You see," they cried, "nothing! It is all a bluff. Now the whole world can see that you are a fraud!"

"What do you say now?" the Russian President asked.

"I say it will take eight minutes for the darkness to reach Earth," Joe replied calmly. "It is a simple matter of physics."

"I'm not wasting any more time on this man," the American roared, standing up as if about to storm out of the room.

"We will wait." The Chinese President had regained his usual level of calm. "What is eight minutes when balanced against the fate of the world?"

"Wise words, sir," Joe gave a small bow of respect towards the Chinese screen.

"But after eight minutes," the Russian joined in, "when we have proved that you are a fraud, we will need you to confess to your followers that you have duped them."

"I can't believe you all are indulging him," the American yelled, throwing himself back down into his chair, having been made aware by the frantic sign language of his advisors from behind the camera that he could not be seen to be the only one to walk away from the broadcast and that no one else looked as if they were planning to go anywhere.

For the following eight minutes the twelve leaders continued to bicker and shout abuse, with their translators struggling to keep up at the same time, increasing the number of voices that the bewildered world population had to try to disentangle. Advisors behind all twelve of the outside broadcast cameras desperately tried to calm their charges down in order to make them seem like the grown-ups at what was increasingly sounding like an unruly children's party.

When eight minutes was finally up darkness fell on the whole world and a stunned silence descended on the studio. Joe took a deep breath and sat down on the floor, waving away the assistants who rushed forward with chairs for him.

The satellite pictures flickered as the power sources around the world surged. The Ukrainian took advantage of the darkness to move a few steps closer to Joe, his eyes focused like lasers on his target, refusing to be distracted by anything else that was happening around him. Everyone was too spellbound by what was happening to look in his direction.

The Russian President's eyes had lit up, like a lizard disturbed by danger while basking in the sun. "It is possible," he said to the other leaders, "that he knew this was going to happen and timed his threat to the minute."

"Did any of our scientists predict this?" the Indian Prime Minister asked. "Were any of you warned this might happen again?"

They all muttered that they knew nothing and the voices of advisors could be heard shouting from the background on every screen.

"So what exactly is it that you want us to do?" the Chinese President asked quietly.

"Today, Mr President," Joe said, "you could make the first move by releasing all your political prisoners, starting with Liang Zhang."

"We can do that," the President replied without even taking the time to look in his advisors' direction.

"You're not going to give in to this blatant blackmail, are you?" the American shouted.

"Are you going to explain to your people how you are willing to end the world just to hold on to power, Mr President?" the Chinese President asked. "Are you willing to leave them dwelling in the darkness for ever?"

"We need to work together on this," the British Prime Minister chipped in. "It could be the start of something great." But no one was listening to him.

The leaders gradually disappeared from their screens as they conferred with their military leaders and the world was not able to see their rising levels of panic. In every country the military leaders were having to point out that none of them were in a position to be able to re-ignite the sun, however generous their armaments budgets might have been in recent years. It did not take long for some of the political leaders to realise that they had no bargaining tools with which to counter Joe's ultimatum, or for the military to realise that against a force powerful enough to extinguish the sun it did not matter how much money they could raise from other sources, they would still be an impotent force.

As the minutes ticked by in total darkness, Joe sat quietly on the floor with his eyes closed. It looked as if he was meditating, which brought a smile of approval from Tanzeel, as he sat quietly in a corner of the studio which had been reserved for observers. The watching religious leaders whom Joe had met on the island all knelt to pray to their Gods that all the political leaders would now fully accept that they were helpless to do anything when actually faced with the power of God and that they would choose to release mankind from the threat of permanent darkness.

One by one the political leaders reappeared on the screens. It was as if someone had let the air out of their egos. They suddenly looked ancient and tired as they begged for mercy and for Joe to show more understanding of their "difficult" positions.

The Ukrainian moved forward, sliding a knife from inside his sleeve into the palm of his hand. Years of caution and self-discipline told him that it was unwise to make such a bold move in front of so many witnesses and cameras, but he had slipped up and delayed too many times on this mission. He had to carry out the assignment now, regardless of the extra risks, or he would lose all credibility in the eyes of his employers.

FIFTY-ONE

The two friends had talked almost incessantly for nearly twelve hours after Sophie turned up on Alice's doorstep in the middle of the night in a state of shock. They had analysed Sophie's feelings for Joe and speculated about Joe's feelings for her from every angle possible. They had gone from deciding that Sophie should have no more to do with him all the way round to deciding that Sophie should go back to work beside him, regardless of any personal feelings of hurt or betrayal that she might be feeling.

"This is about the future of mankind," she had said at one moment, after they had consumed several bottles of wine, "my hurt feelings are hardly relevant."

"Maybe now that you have opened his eyes to how you feel," Alice had suggested, "he will behave differently towards you. Maybe you should just go back and see what he says. I mean, he's the Son of God, it's never going to be like a normal relationship."

They both slept through the next day and continued talking, and drinking wine, for several nights after that. After going round in the same circles of indecision many times, they decided that if Sophie were to simply turn up at the studio for the leaders' discussion, as if it was still her job to be at his side, rather than coming as Joe's partner, it would give him a chance to make amends for whatever hurt he had caused her. Since no one else knew what had transpired between them she was able to get access to the venue as the best-known member of Joe's inner circle, her all-areas pass getting her automatically waved through by the security staff.

On the day of the broadcast, she deliberately arrived just as it was about to start, knowing that Joe would be too busy watching the faces on the screens to notice her lurking in the shadows, and within a few minutes she became as transfixed by the paranoid rantings of the various leaders, and the struggles of their desperate translators, as everyone else. As she watched Joe first standing and then sitting serenely at the centre of the studio as the storm raged around him, she felt an overwhelming love for him. It was like a wave lifting her up, washing away all the petty feelings of hurt pride and jealousy that she had experienced after witnessing the scene in the nightclub, and carrying her towards the safety of the shore.

When he finally lost his temper and extinguished the sun she felt a rush of excitement, aware that she now had a privileged ringside seat at a spectacle that was being arranged by God himself. She felt the same warm glow as the one that swept through her when Joe first revealed his true purpose to the Twelve at the chapel by the lake, but this time it was tinged with a terrible fear at the realisation that the squabbling of the old men on the screens could actually lead to the extinguishing of all life on Earth. She hardly dared breathe as she watched their faces crumbling in panic as Joe remained still and quiet at the centre of the storm. Looking round the studio, she recognised a number of people she had grown close to over the previous weeks, all of them staring at Joe and the screens, none of them paying her any attention.

A man with a shaved head, beard and thick-framed round glasses stepped forward from the shadows behind her. For a second she thought she didn't recognise him but something about the way he was moving seemed familiar. It reminded her of the moments backstage, immediately after the broadcast question-and-answer event finished. She tried to work out who he was and had a vague memory of him trying to get close to Joe at the end of the show. He now seemed to be staring at Joe with a particular intensity, as if taking aim, cutting out everything else going on all around, refusing to be distracted by the hysteria of the leaders as they flailed about, trying to cling to at least some of their previous airs of authority. Then she remembered the same stare emanating from the man standing in the shadows in the nightclub. Joe certainly did attract a lot of very obsessive-looking people. She wondered if she was one of them.

Without thinking why, she followed the man as he moved towards Joe, keeping her eyes on him as she went. He was doing something with his sleeve and then she saw the flash of a knife blade reflecting in the studio lights. Acting purely on instinct she threw herself across the space between them, putting her body between Joe and the knife just as the Ukrainian made his deadly final move. She felt the full force of the blade as it entered her heart.

There was a few seconds' delay before anyone else realised that something more immediate than the switching off of the sun or the televised meltdown of the world's leaders was happening in front of their eyes. The cameras swivelled away from Joe and onto Sophie as she sank first to her knees and then sprawled onto the floor, blood pumping out into a lake around her.

Realising that he had missed his target, the Ukrainian knew he had no choice other than to abandon the mission and he attempted to vanish into the crowd. Many hands reached out to grab him and pulled him down towards the floor. His foot slipped out from under him and he landed in the pool of blood as the fists and feet of the crowd punched and kicked his prone body, all calmness and reason lost in anger. More people piled into the crowd from behind, all wanting to strike a blow, to show their defiance for anyone who would try to end their moment of hope with violence. The mob, filled with years of pent-up resentment and frustration, didn't care who he was or why he was doing what he was doing, they just wanted to tear the assassin to pieces.

"Stop!" Joe commanded as he pushed his way into the crowd and knelt beside the Ukrainian, placing his hand on the man's blood-soaked hair.

"Stand up, my son," he said, helping him to his feet.

Several of the world leaders were shouting questions out of their screens, wanting to know what was happening, some of them grateful that the world's attention had been drawn away from them, others resentful of losing the spotlight. The screen from Moscow appeared to have gone blank.

"I forgive you," Joe told the Ukrainian, ensuring that the crowd all heard his words.

Joe went down on his knees in the blood to where Sophie's body lay. The crowd pulled back out of respect and security men handcuffed the Ukrainian who stared silently at the floor, awaiting an opportunity to dodge his fate.

Joe cradled Sophie in his arms. Everyone could see that she was already dead as her head rolled loosely against his shoulder, her face as white as an alabaster statue.

Across the world, people sat in the darkness and stared at whatever screens they had, unable to take in the shock of witnessing a murder taking place. Billions felt as if they knew Sophie personally, as if she were a personal friend. They had seen her next to Joe whenever there were cameras around, almost as if she were their representative in Heaven, an ordinary woman raised up to dwell amongst the gods. Through her obvious adoration of him they had been able to channel their own feelings and now her life had been ended, their most human bond with Joe had been cruelly severed.

Joe said nothing, merely placing his hand across the wound in her chest and pressing gently. After a few seconds, the blood stopped bubbling through his fingers and the crowd watched in silent awe as a delicate pinkness began to flow back into Sophie's cheeks.

The rest of the world watched via the cameras as her lips parted and she took in several gasps of air, her body trembled, and her heart restarted. Joe kissed her gently on the mouth and slowly straightened up with her in his arms, his clothes drenched in her blood. He placed her on her feet, steadying her for a few seconds as she found her balance. Her eyes opened and a small, shy smile flickered across her face.

As she stood in the middle of the room, holding Joe's hand and shivering with shock, everyone in the room fell to their knees, the security men pulling the Ukrainian down with them, forcing him to bow his head and give thanks to God. Sophie draped her arms around Joe's neck, partly to show her gratitude and her forgiveness for the hurt he had caused her, partly to ask for forgiveness for her own self-centred behaviour and partly to support her trembling legs.

Having demonstrated his abilities to end the world, Joe allowed the sun to shine once more on the other side of the globe and the leaders' screens went dark, one by one. None of them could think of anything else they could say that would ever discredit Joe in the eyes of a world which they had, over the years, come to believe was their own personal fiefdom.

FIFTY-TWO

The Ukrainian had always known that the day would eventually come when he would slip up on a job and his career would be over. He knew he had enjoyed more than his fair share of luck over the years and he was more than ready to deal with that eventuality when it arose. He knew exactly the value of the information he held in his memory and he knew who would be the highest potential payers. Now, however, the price he would be haggling over would not just be financial, it would include his life and his freedom.

He knew all the people who had hired him over the years for a variety of jobs, including for the assassination of Joe, and he was more than happy to exchange that information for a package which included money, freedom and a new identity. Since he had obviously failed to carry out the final mission successfully and would not be paid all that he had been promised, he was going to have to drive a hard bargain. He needed to be sure that he would be able to live as he wanted for the rest of his life.

Within a few days he had disappeared from sight as far as the public and the media were concerned, and the CIA had all the proof they needed that he had been hired by the Russians for this and many other jobs. They ensured that there was no record that he had also been paid by them for the same job, nor did his contact with the pharmaceutical companies leak out into the public domain. Everyone agreed that it was best if the

Russians shouldered all the blame. It was a far more credible story, given their history of arranging political assassinations.

The Russian President said nothing on the subject. He was not entirely averse to the idea of letting the world believe that he was a dangerous enemy who was willing to do anything to protect the interests of his people, even to the extent of committing murder.

While the Ukrainian was having his appearance changed by a plastic surgeon, the CIA released their version of the assassination story onto the internet. By the time they had leaked enough of the details for the public to get the picture, the media was already halfway to confirming the whole story through their own sources. While the Russians were seen as the ones who pulled the trigger, it was clear to those who read a little further on the subject that all the leaders had been aware that the plan was being hatched and were happy to turn a blind eye to the ethics of ordering a political assassination of the Son of God.

The story went global instantly and the security forces in every country realised that the leaders they had sworn to serve could no longer hope to hold on to power and that it was time to switch their allegiances to other places. They too started to leak details of other plans which had been laid to dispose of Joe. They talked of attempts that were made to bribe kitchen staff at the hotel to poison his food and payments to drivers to arrange road accidents. Some of the plans were so ludicrous they simply brought more derision down on the heads of the politicians who ordered them and their security services who went along with them, confirming in the minds of the public that they were being ruled over by an incompetent bunch of old men.

The Prime Minister of New Zealand, one of the few leaders to escape with her reputation intact, found herself bombarded with calls from other leaders hoping to shore up their crumbling images and wanting to fly to New Zealand in order to be seen with her and with Joe. Most of the approaches went unanswered, while some were refused directly and without explanation. Old world diplomacy no longer held any value when everything was about to change and no one knew who would still be in power in a few hours' time.

"Our leaders have been behaving like gangsters," the anchor man on CNN was saying, "and we have been allowing them to get away with it for years. They have been building up personal fortunes, doing favours for one another, ordering executions, stealing and misusing information, torturing and bombing anyone who disagreed with them, using the armed forces and the central banks to carry out their dirty work for them."

His words were being amplified and echoed in a billion tweets and messages.

"We believe our way is a better way to run the world," Joe told every journalist who was able to get close enough to ask questions, "but it needs to be a democratic choice. The people of the whole world have to demand that it happens."

"What can people do?" he was asked, over and over again.

"In this digital age it is perfectly possible to arrange a global referendum," he would reply each time, "with every person voting as to whether they want to continue living as they have done for centuries, or whether they would prefer to follow the new path that I and my apostles have laid out for them."

"And where will this path lead us?" the journalists would ask.

"Towards the creation of a paradise for mankind on Earth. A place where everyone is equal and no one starves or is allowed to live in poverty, a place where there is no more threat of self-inflicted extinction."

"And what will happen with all the armies?"

"Every soldier and sailor must look deep into their own heart," Joe said, "and decide what they can do that will be most beneficial to the common good. They must put aside their fears, just as they have been trained to do in battle, and do what is right for everyone, not just for the people who pay their wages – be they governments or big corporations."

FIFTY-THREE

Joe informed the Twelve that he would like to meet them again at Yung's house. The atmosphere was subdued when he arrived, as if it was just dawning on them that soon it would be confirmed that for the rest of their lives they were going to be responsible for running the world. Dreams and plans and intellectual exercises, which they had been hatching and polishing for years, were actually going to become realities and would be tested in the heat of the real world. They were going to have to oversee the building of new cities, the creation of new legal and financial structures in order to avoid chaos, the re-routing of rivers, the re-stocking of the oceans and the replanting of forests. Above all else, they were going to have to communicate openly and transparently with every citizen on every subject because openness and trust would be paramount. All the necessary social media platforms were already in place for this to happen.

"My work is done now," Joe said once they were all gathered in front of Yung's picture window. "It is now time for you to move forward with all your plans. I believe the world is now ready to pay attention to our agreement based on your SWOT analysis, Simon."

Simon nodded his understanding but said nothing.

"Hugo tells me that there are a lot of rumours online about someone on the inside of this group working with the Ukrainian," Yung said. "Is that true? Is that the betrayal that you predicted?"

Silence descended on the room and everyone turned to look at Joe, each of them avoiding everyone else's eyes.

"I told you," Joe said, "I forgive them. No more needs to be said on the subject."

"So one of us was leaking information all the time that we were meeting and drawing up plans?" Simon asked. "I think it would be helpful if we knew who it was. It is important that we all trust one another a hundred per cent going forward."

"Perhaps the traitor had a good reason for the choices they made," Joe suggested. "Perhaps they were tricked into it and believed they were making the right choice at the time and then were unable to stop events from unfolding. Perhaps they had no idea what they were actually being asked to do. Perhaps they were caught up in the corruption of the old system and now that things are changing they too will be changing. There are a lot of possibilities which would make it reasonable to forgive them and move on."

"I agree with Simon," Lalit joined in. "We need to know, otherwise there will be a cloud of suspicion hanging over everything we do. How can we all talk openly and honestly with each other if we don't know that we can trust one another?"

"But if Joe is willing to forgive them," Yung said, "perhaps we could too."

"How do you forgive someone if you don't know who they are?" Tanzeel asked.

"Could we perhaps take collective responsibility for the act?" Minenhle suggested. "After all, that is pretty much what we are advocating for the rest of the world to do."

"Is there something you want to confess, Minenhle?" Sofia, the botanist from South America, asked.

"What do you mean?" Minenhle seemed to rise in her seat, like a cobra about to strike.

"I'm just saying that I don't feel inclined to share responsibility for an act of betrayal." She turned to Joe. "Was it really one of us that allowed the assassin to get that close to you?"

"When I first started building clinics in Africa" – Amelia spoke so quietly that it was a few moments before some of them realised the importance of her words – "I went to every international organisation that exists, begging for funds. I went to every government in Africa and every former colonial power. All of them told me I was doing great work and that I had their full support. They all wished me luck but none of them offered me any actual assistance, not a single cent.

"When the Russians offered me as much money and as much help as I wanted I was in no position to turn them down. In all honesty, I didn't want to turn them down. Why would I look such a gift horse in the mouth? I assumed they were doing it for public relations reasons, so that the whole world would be able to see that they were a benevolent state and that was fine by me, but they never publicised their involvement. They made me sign non-disclosure agreements with strict penalty clauses. So it seemed like they genuinely wanted to help without any payback."

The room was entirely silent apart from her low, husky voice.

"It was naïve of me to think that. I see that clearly now. But the work went so well. They never quibbled about the costs of anything I asked for. The clinics we built were incredibly successful. God alone knows how many lives we have managed to save through them with the help of the many doctors who came to work with us.

"It was only once the clinics were established and they knew the idea of closing them would be unthinkable for me that the Russian government started to ask for a return on their investment. They wanted access to the senior politicians and to the business communities in all the African countries where we were operating. They were aware that the Chinese were gaining influence and buying up land all over the continent and they were anxious to compete at every level. If I hadn't co-operated they would have withdrawn their funding overnight and all that work would have come to nothing, all the clinics would have disappeared within weeks, all those communities would have been thrown back on relying on good luck as their only form of healthcare. So I helped them wherever I could, introducing them to a prime minister here and a president there, assisting with the dissemination of propaganda at elections. It seemed a small price to pay for all the good that we were able to do with the money that they continued to give us.

"Then you did me the honour of asking me to join your group. I don't think they realised just what that invitation would lead to. I certainly didn't. Maybe none of us did. It didn't seem necessary for me to break my non-disclosure contract with them and tell you of the backing they had given me, so I said nothing."

"We were all friends," Yung said, "excited by our ideas, so we didn't feel the need to screen one another. There was a natural trust between us."

"I thought I was a good person and trustworthy," Amelia said quietly. "I didn't realise how completely they owned my soul until it was too late for me to be able to buy it back."

She stopped talking and everyone remained silent as they took in the enormity of the confession coming from a woman that they all trusted and respected. Joe walked over to where she was sitting with her head bowed.

"Stand up Amelia," he said and she slowly unwound from the chair, allowing him to wrap his arms around her but not feeling worthy to respond, allowing the tears to flow freely and her arms to hang lifelessly by her side. "All that was part of the old system," he said to the room. "If you organise the future better then there will be no opportunities for this sort of manipulation and corruption. The whole population will be behind great projects like Amelia's clinics and no one will have the power to use patronage for blackmail."

Amelia didn't raise her eyes from the floor as all the others came over, one by one, to embrace her. Some, like the professor, were obviously uncomfortable with the physical contact, but all could see that they needed to show solidarity. Who among them hadn't done something in the past that they now regretted? They had all accepted grants from corporations they did not wholly approve of and contracts and prizes from regimes that were known to have bad records for human rights. It was easy for them all to stay on the ethical high road now that they were wealthy, respected and successful; it had not been so easy when they were on their way up. None of them wanted to see Amelia exposed and excluded from the team just as they finally started to gain the ability to put into action the many ideas and dreams they had been talking about for so long.

"I have a favour to ask, Yung," Joe said once they were all sitting again and the atmosphere had settled.

"Of course," Yung said, "anything."

"I am going to be moving on now. Would it be possible to have a last supper here for all of us and our families?"

FIFTY-FOUR

The supper was arranged for two days later, which gave each of the Twelve time to make contact with their families and arrange for those who had moved on with their lives to return to the house.

"It feels a bit like being invited to a presidential inauguration," Alice told Sophie as the two of them met to catch up and talk about everything that had happened since Sophie returned to Joe's side. "It's like an official celebration of the handing over of power from the old regime to the new."

"I don't think it is going to be quite that smooth," Sophie said. "I think it's more like a retirement dinner for Joe."

"The Son of God is retiring?" Alice laughed. "That doesn't sound quite right."

"I think he plans to say goodbye and move on," Sophie said, and Alice saw the tears rising up in her friend's eyes.

"Oh," she said and put her arm around her shoulders, "I'm so sorry. I didn't mean to be flippant. This must all be so hard for you."

"It's pretty confusing, yes," Sophie smiled through the tears. "I'm not sure how I am going to live without him."

"I guess you are going to be kept pretty busy," Alice said. "I mean he has made you just about the second most famous person in the world, bringing you back from the dead in front of absolutely everyone and everything. In a way you are the luckiest of all of us. I mean, how many people have experienced love as completely and deeply as you have in the last few months?"

"Sometimes I wish he had let me die that day," Sophie spoke quietly.

"Well no one else does," Alice said, squeezing her friend's shoulders. "So stick around, babe."

They both laughed and deliberately talked about other things as Sophie struggled to ignore the lead weight which seemed to be pressing down on her heart.

Joe had arrived at the house early and was swimming before the last supper when Hugo burst through the doors to the pool, having just been delivered home from school by a driver. He was already in his trunks and hurled himself into the water with a yell of pure joy at being reunited with Joe.

"Is Miss Sophie going to be here?" he asked as soon as he bobbed out of the water into Joe's arms.

"I hope so," Joe said, "she has certainly been invited."

"Are you two going to get married?"

"I thought I was supposed to be the one who always asked questions."

"Well, are you?"

"No, Hugo. I'm not the marrying kind. I'm going to be moving on."

"Oh." Hugo took the news in, squinting in order to bring Joe's face more into focus above him. "Well I think that's a shame but I understand. I don't think I am going to be the marrying kind either. I would have liked it if you two ended up together, though."

"We can't have everything we want." Joe gave him a hug before releasing his squirming body into the water like returning a fish to its natural state.

"Even you? Everyone knows you really are the Son of God now. Doesn't that mean you can have whatever you want?"

"I'll race you to the end and back," Joe said, setting off before Hugo had time to ask any more questions.

The dinner was more sumptuous than Joe would strictly have wanted, but he did not want to mar the atmosphere by delivering another reprimand to the Twelve on their extravagant ways. He knew that they still had a great deal to learn about how most of the world lived. He couldn't expect them to instantly give up all the comforts they had grown used to. Throughout the meal, he moved from one seat to another, engaging with different people as he went.

"You will need to oversee the restructuring of the global financial system," he told Lalit, "so that inequality is erased once and for all with a revolutionary and far-reaching levelling of incomes. A few individuals cannot be allowed to horde vast piles of capital any more, money must be kept moving through the system so that everyone can purchase the things they need for a decent life, no matter what sort of work they do. A mother bringing up a child at home and a man cleaning out the sewers must be able to live as comfortably and securely as someone who buys and sells shares or manages to monopolise a part of the marketplace, but there can still be reasonable income differences in order to provide the necessary stimuli to people to work and to achieve beneficial results."

"We have been thinking for some time about how to finance all our plans," Lalit assured him. "We propose to ask for contributions from every UN member state, and there will also be a taxation system which ensures the very rich pay their share." He smiled ruefully, aware that this category included himself. "We can also make better use of the existing funds being spent on defence, space research, genetic engineering and other undesirable projects. Unreasonable profits and overly abundant assets will be appropriated from companies and we expect that once people are aware of how much better their lives could be there will be voluntary donations. There will also need to be some new debts from the IMF, based on public trust, which we don't think will be a problem once a majority of the world's population have voted in favour of the plans."

Joe patted Lalit on the back approvingly and turned to Simon, who was sitting on his other side. "It will mean that the whole world will need to have a fair constitution based on the Twelve Agreements and a global set of public and private laws that everyone can agree to."

"I understand," Simon said. "I already have people working on draft laws. It will take time."

"Enough time to get it right," Joe agreed, "but not so much time that it never gets completed."

"I understand," Simon said.

"You must take charge of all the armed forces too," Joe went on. "They could help play valuable policing roles but their war-like services must not be allowed to fall into the hands of the wrong people."

"Do you mean dictators and criminals?" Simon asked. "Or the big corporations?"

"I mean anyone who does not have the best interests of all their fellow citizens as their primary motivation."

When Amelia started once more to apologise for betraying him to the Ukrainian, Joe put a finger on her lips to quieten her, and her husband, the Bishop, held her hand tightly from the other side.

"The service you are going to do for mankind will outweigh any mistakes you have ever made," Joe assured her. "Concentrate on getting clean drinking water to every individual on Earth, and effective sewage systems, working with the professor on his cities of the future. You will save more lives than any doctor has ever done in the world before, and you will earn your place in Heaven."

"Amen," the Bishop murmured, dabbing a tear from the corner of his eye.

"What should my task be, Lord?" Haki asked when it came to his turn.

"You must continue to work to heal the wounds left by so many centuries of wars and ethnic struggles," Joe said.

"All of you," he told the engineers, botanists and conservationists, "must find new ways to clean and restock the land and the oceans, while also building sustainable new housing for everyone."

Feeling that they no longer had anything to fear from the authorities, Yung had allowed everyone to keep their phones with them in the house. All the time Joe was moving around the table, relatives of the Twelve were filming the proceedings. Joe had no objection, knowing that it meant his wishes would continue to be shared many billions of times online once he was gone. Everyone in the world would be able to refer back to them on apps like YouTube if they felt that those in authority were straying too far from the original vision, ensuring total transparency.

While he was sitting with Hugo, discussing the possibilities of Hugo's ideas for a video game in which the sun goes out and players have to fight one another to survive, Yung came over and whispered something close to her son's ear.

"Okay," Hugo said, turning back to Joe. "I'm just going outside with Mummy for a moment. She says she has a surprise for me."

"That's cool," Joe said.

"Do you want Joe to come too?" Yung asked Hugo.

"Sure," Hugo shrugged. "What's the surprise?"

"It wouldn't be a surprise if I told you," Yung said, taking hold of her son's hand and extending her other hand to Joe.

Security staff muttered into their radios as the three of them walked outside and Joe sighed to himself. It was going to take a while for people like Yung to trust the rest of the world and allow people to come and go through their gates unchallenged. He could hear the approaching thrum of helicopter blades and then lights swept round the side of the mountain and the noise and wind enveloped them. Hugo put his hands over his ears and watched as the helicopter descended onto the helipad and Joe exchanged a look with Yung, who was smiling, her face alight with a joy he had never seen her display before.

Even before the rotors had stopped turning, the door of the helicopter opened. A figure slid out and limped towards them, dragging a leg behind him. Hugo stared for a moment, then looked up at his mother for confirmation, not daring to believe that his prayers had actually been answered.

Before Liang had managed to reach them Hugo had run to his father and leaped into his arms. It was obvious that holding his son was physically painful for him, but he did not put him down, continuing on the long walk across to where his wife was waiting for him. The three of them embraced and Joe waited quietly until they remembered he was there.

"I believe that I have you to thank for my life and for my safe return to my family," Liang said, bowing his head low and kissing Joe's hand.

"Your wife and your son always had faith that you would return," Joe replied. "This is their reward from God."

FIFTY-FIVE

"I need your help," Joe told the Prime Minister of New Zealand.

"Of course," she said. "What can I do for you?"

"I need to get to Jerusalem with Sophie but I have no passport or identification papers and I would not want anyone else to know that I am going there."

"Jerusalem?" She was obviously surprised. "Can I ask why?"

"Perhaps I am just being sentimental, wanting to revisit my earthly roots, but I have many memories from before. I was only twelve when I first went to the temple and it made an impact which has stayed with me. And of course it was the last place on Earth that I saw."

"Of course," the Prime Minister blushed a little, "I'm sorry. I didn't mean to stir painful memories."

"No, you haven't. The memories of the smells and sounds of the streets are much more vivid to me than the memories of those last few difficult days and I would like to experience them again. If they are still the same, which I guess they can't be entirely."

"I think you will find much there that is timeless. There is still no other city in the world that speaks to the religious and spiritual imagination in quite the same way."

"And I would like another chance to say goodbye to Lazarus. He was my best friend and I let him down. I would be grateful if you could help."

"Does Sophie know about this trip?" the Prime Minister asked.

"In her heart I think she does," Joe replied, and the Prime Minister decided not to pry any further.

"I'm sure we can sort that out," she said. "Will you be coming back to us afterwards?"

"No," he smiled, knowing that she had already guessed that would be his answer. His work was done and mankind must now take responsibility for its own destiny. "Sophie will want to return but it's a one-way trip for me."

"I'm very sorry to hear that."

"But perhaps a little relieved at the same time?" he grinned.

"Perhaps a little," she laughed. "Life will be very dull without you."

"Whatever happens next," he said, "I don't think it will be dull. Everything is going to change and I'm sure that the Twelve will find a global role for you. You have more than proved your worth as a leader."

"Thank you," she said and held out her hand to him. "Whatever happens, I will do my best not to let you down."

While the Prime Minister made the arrangements for Joe's disappearance to Jerusalem, he went to find Sophie at Alice's flat. He had become as skilful at disguising his appearance when he didn't want to draw crowds as the Ukrainian had been and was able to pass along busy streets without anyone noticing when he wished to.

"May I come in?" he asked as she opened the door.

"Of course," she replied, feeling her heart leap at the sight of him but forcing herself not to allow her hopes to rise too far or to show in her expression.

"It was lovely to see you at the dinner," he said as they sat awkwardly together. "But we didn't really have a chance to talk."

"No," she agreed. "We didn't."

"Do you remember my promise?" he asked after a few moments.

"Which one?"

"To take you to Jerusalem."

"Yes, of course. I was really looking forward to it."

"Me too," he said. "I still am. Would you be willing to do me the honour of accompanying me there, even after I have treated you so badly?"

She paused for a second, trying to straighten out her thoughts before answering, then just blurted out the words, "Oh, yes please."

She didn't ask any more questions, wanting to enjoy the moment and frightened about what he might say if she tried to find out what the future held for them. He was grateful to her because he did not know how he would answer her without his own heart breaking.

*****

Later that night, Joe and Sophie were on the long flight from Auckland to Tel Aviv. He was wearing dark glasses and an Arab headdress and she had her face modestly covered in a black scarf. They stopped over at Sydney and Hong Kong but at no stage did anyone on the planes or in the airports recognise them. The anonymity suited them because they were both enjoying being in one another's company while also holding tightly to the pain in their hearts. They would have found it hard to strike up conversations with anyone else. The following day, Joe hired a taxi to drive them from Tel Aviv to Jerusalem.

The driver dropped them a couple of streets away from the archaeological site and Joe paused to breathe in the evening air. He squeezed Sophie's hand and smiled at her. She could see that he was content to be back in the city he had such fond memories of. They strolled round the corner, hand in hand, stopping at a bakery on the way. Apart from the addition of exhaust fumes and engine noise, the smells and sounds of the streets were very much how Joe remembered them from two thousand years earlier and how Sophie had imagined they would be: a heady mixture of cooking and spices and multiple languages.

The last of the day's tourists and academics were leaving the premises at Lazarus's house, their departure overseen by the stooped figure of the night watchman, who held the gate as they passed and pretended to be counting them out.

Joe waited until the last of the visitors had gone and sauntered up to the entrance.

"Excuse me," he called out to the old man as he shuffled away towards his shed. "Is this the place where the scrolls were found?"

"We're closed," the old man shouted back without turning. "Come back tomorrow."

"I would like to talk to you," Joe said. "Perhaps we could have a cup of tea together."

The old man paused and turned slowly. "You want to talk to me?" he said, obviously finding it hard to believe. "I'm just the night watchman. I don't know anything."

"I would still be interested to hear your views. I have brought some rugelach." He held up a bag of sticky chocolate pastries that he had purchased from the bakery.

"Rugelach?" The old man was interested now and shuffled back to the gate with a jangling of keys.

Inside his shed there was an old mattress, which he gestured to Joe to sit on. Sophie did the same, even though the old man had ignored her entirely. She kept the scarf across her face and her head lowered, playing the part of an invisible, dutiful wife, unsure what else Joe expected of her. The only other furniture in the shed was a small table supporting a battered electric kettle and a small television. The old man busied himself with making some tea before sitting beside Joe on the mattress and accepting a pastry in return for a steaming cup. He did not feel it necessary to offer the quiet woman anything and looked surprised when Joe offered Sophie his cup to sip from.

"So, what do you make of these scrolls?" Joe asked.

"I am not a scholar," the old man shrugged, obviously more interested in the pastry than the history. "If you want scholarly talk you need to come back tomorrow."

"I am not a scholar either," Joe said and laughed.

The old man seemed to recognise the sound of the laugh and peered at him more closely. "You are him," he said.

"Am I?" Joe laughed again.

"You are him. I have seen you…" He gestured to the television and then, overcome with confusion as to what the right etiquette should be for entertaining the Son of God in a shed, he placed his cup on the floor, pushed the rest of the pastry into his mouth and prostrated himself at Joe's feet.

"There is no need for that," Joe said, helping him back into a sitting position. "I am just a man like you."

"I don't think so," the old man said. "Why are you here?"

"In Jerusalem? There is no city in the world that is closer to God."

"I wouldn't know. I have not been to any other cities."

"You don't need to. This is the one," Joe assured him and the old man nodded proudly at the thought that his city was so important. "I wanted to come back and see it one more time and to say a final goodbye to my best friend."

Sophie felt a stab of pain her heart. Was he referring to Lazarus or to her?

"So much has changed," the old man sighed.

"Of course, as it has everywhere," Joe agreed. "But there is no need to give up hope."

Tears welled up in the old man's eyes and he rolled forward again, bringing his lips to hover above Joe's feet.

"Thank you for the tea," Joe said as he stood up and walked to the door. "Do you mind if we just walk outside for a moment?"

The old man sat back on his mattress and gestured for Joe to go ahead, jiggling his prayer beads in his calloused hands as Joe stepped out into the night, tightly holding Sophie's hand.

"You've brought me here to say goodbye, haven't you?" Sophie said as they walked through the moonlit ruins to the spot where Joe remembered last seeing the body of Lazarus.

"Still the visionary?" he laughed.

"I don't think it will be easy for me to go on without you," she said, her voice choking on the words. "My heart is still broken and the pain is so bad."

"I will be watching over you," Joe promised. Seeing the hurt in her eyes made tears come to his, as they had the last time he had stood by the grave of Lazarus. It felt like he was stabbing her to death just as the Ukrainian had done, letting her down as surely as he had let Lazarus down. "I have no choice but to go where my father wants me to go. God moves in mysterious ways and he knows that you must help the Twelve to fulfil their destiny. I have other flocks to tend to. You are a great teacher; don't let those talents go to waste. We will be together in Heaven."

They talked beside Lazarus's grave for an hour and then Sophie held onto him for as long as she could, neither of them able to stem the sobbing that seemed to rise up from their souls and convulse their entire bodies. Eventually they were both drained, with no more tears to shed, and Sophie had no option but to release her grip and allow him to go. It felt like her soul was being torn physically from her chest.

As the old man in the shed sat alone on the mattress, he tried to focus on what had just happened. If it hadn't been for Joe's empty cup and the crumbs left from the pastry, he would have been willing to believe that he had dreamed the whole encounter.

Through the small window of the shed, he saw a flash of light outside and pulled himself to his feet as quickly as he could manage. Opening the door, he had to shade his eyes against the dazzling brightness of the sky. He could hear shouts coming from all around as people tried to work out what had happened. Had the sun spun round to the other side of the world? Had someone ignited a bomb which had lit up the whole night sky? Was this the end of the world?

The old man looked around for Joe but there was no one there apart from the woman holding the scarf tightly around her face as if to hide her tears. Joe had vanished into the light. A few moments later, the darkness of the night returned.

SIGN UP TO THE JOE PROJECT

Humanity will have to radically change its way of life in order to survive all challenges that are emerging.

We need world leaders we can trust and who draw up, communicate and execute common and transparent plans for our future.

We need worldwide solidarity among governments, corporations, scientists, the media and every individual citizen.

We must start now with a global plan from co-operative and reliable leaders.

The Joe Project challenges them to take the necessary steps and has started the thinking process with the novel *Call Me Joe*.

To stay informed about The Joe Project sign up for updates via www.thejoeproject.eu

ABOUT THE AUTHORS

Martin van Es wants our children and grandchildren to be able to enjoy our planet as much as he does. But that means something radical must be done. What, he wondered, would happen if Jesus returned to put everything right? He spoke with a wide range of experts including scientists, economists, politicians and religious leaders and the result is *Call Me Joe*. It will encourage every reader to consider what they would do to save humanity if they had the necessary power.

Andrew Crofts is one of the world's best-selling ghost writers having published more than a hundred books.

Find out more about RedDoor Press and sign up to our newsletter to hear about our **latest releases, author events,** exciting **competitions** and more at

reddoorpress.co.uk

YOU CAN ALSO FOLLOW US:

 @RedDoorBooks

 Facebook.com/RedDoorPress

 @RedDoorBooks